BOREALIS

Worldmaker™

By Andri E. Elia

Book 2, First Edition,
The Chronicles of Phe'lak Trilogy

Fleeing the aftermath of brutal intergalactic warfare, Queen Asimia brings a small group of colonists on a trek across galaxies to find a promised land. Their trail is fraught with danger. Hundreds of years in the future, a world teeters on the brink of extinction… a boy loses his one and only love. What he must do to bring her back…

Worldmaker™

The Worldmaker of Yand Trilogy

Book 1. Yildun
Book 2. Polaris
Book 3. Eltanin

Book 4. Worldmaker Stories

The Chronicles of Phe'lak Trilogy

Book 5. Queen of Highwings
Book 6. Borealis

Follow the Author on Amazon.com: search Andri E. Elia in Books
    And please leave a review
Visit the Author's website at: Worldmakeruniverse.com
And follow her on X (ex-Twitter) @WorldmakerVerse
        Facebook, search Worldmaker by Andri Elia
        LinkedIn, search Andri Elia

Dedication

To my beautiful sister *Eleni Elia Derke.* Thank you for everything, my darling.

Acknowledgment

A special thanks to *Lily Dormishev* for the amazing cover and illustrations.

Chapters

Past Time: On Yand in the Yildar system, the year after the end of the Yandar-K'tul wars. *Active thinking in italics.* *"Mindspeak in italics within quotes."* See Appendices A and B for locations and people, including species descriptions. Asimia's POV.

1. Inception

*T*wo months after her harrowing ordeal with the K'tul, Asimia visited her grandad Ophiran-Blaze, the dragon, at his lair, to lunch with him and her uncle Yildiz. The lair was an elaborate cave system, like so many that studded the extensive mountain ranges of their homeworld of Yand, under the pale young star Yildun. Only this one smelled of dragon.

Yand's capital city, Dragonslair, sprawled below Grandad's mountains, straddling many foothills and spilling from spectacular heights into the ocean at its east side. Asimia's residence was only a mountain away from Grandad, so she sometimes flew to the lair—whenever she wanted to stretch her wings.

Today she chose to teleport. Her cat, Alex, hitched a ride in her pocket as was his wont. They found Uncle waiting by the caves' entrance with a huge smile for them. Alex leaped into his arms, then went limp and purred loudly. The two had become very fond of each other the past few weeks.

Today was Uncle's turn to bring a basket, and a humongous one rested by his feet.

"What, no dragon?" Asimia teased.

"Sleeping inside. Did you expect something different?"

"Grandad!" Asimia mindcalled from the first cave.

"Mmm," came his sleepy, disembodied voice.

"It's us, Asimia and Yildiz."

The dragon's tail appeared before his head—walking backward. *"Who else would it be, my darling? The rest of the world fears me."*

Uncle Yildiz put Alex down, and the rascal cat jumped onto the dragon's back. *"Alex!"* the dragon exclaimed. *"Is that you?"*

"It's me!" Alex purred. *"Who fears you?"*

Asimia giggled. *"Turn around, Grandad. Let's go outside."*

"Let me gaze upon you first, my sweet dear."

Of late, Grandad could morph into his Yandar man incarnation on his own, but only briefly. He still needed Asimia's help to stabilize him. So she hugged a reptilian neck and kissed an armor-scaled forehead but found herself in the man's arms.

"That's good, Grands!" she praised him.

"Ooh, you brought a basket!" –they always brought one. "Hello, Yildiz, my boy."

Yildiz, his *boy,* had more than five hundred years. But a son was always a boy to his dad. "Shall we catch some sunshine, Dad?" Uncle replied. "Do you not tire of this darkness?"

"The dragon likes it," Grandad replied mock-defensively.

Lunching with Grandad had become a daily routine for Asimia and her uncle in the weeks since their rescue. Two months earlier, a K'tul mage, K'nista, kidnapped Asimia for his admiral's evil purposes. The K'tul *Grand* Admiral, His Excellency Wolf, coveted Asimia's power. The power of a celestial wizard.

Asimia was a worldmaker, like her mom, Yanara, the storied Worldmaker of Yand. She had many wizardly skills, but those were nothing but ordinary to Wolf and his mages. Her celestial power was a different story. Asimia had the strength to bend heavenly bodies. Not that she wanted to, but she could upend worlds and destroy planets and moons. Once, under extreme need at the end of the war, her mother even bent their sun.

Wolf craved that power. He had attempted to abduct Yanara many times in the past, but she proved too powerful for him. So the monster resorted to napping children—although Asimia was an adult now, having turned eighteen earlier that year.

Her abduction was a violent affair. K'nista blasted her home and napped her despite desperate efforts by her family to stop him. He brought her to the K'tul spaceship, Hellbound, and from there to a stasis facility on the planet Turunc in the Polaran system. It was the same place where another K'tul mage, S'veksa, had imprisoned her uncle Yildiz!

Their family won their freedom in a high-value prisoner exchange. Not that Wolf would have yielded such a prize as Asimia. But he was more than a little dead at the time.

Since their rescue, lunch with the dragon-and-sometimes-Yandar-man became a ritual for Asimia and her uncle. It was a much-needed respite from nightmares that plagued them both. They came nearly every day, and she missed it dearly when they skipped.

They walked outside, Alex riding on Grandad Blaze's shoulder, licking his ear. Asimia spread their blanket under the huge dragontree that marked the lair's entrance. Uncle Yildiz produced the bottle of blueberry wine from their basket and poured a generous goblet for Grandad. He repeated for himself and Asimia.

"Are you a bit early today?" asked Grandad.

"Uncle Yildiz has something to ask you," Asimia replied with an encouraging look at her uncle.

"Hmm..." Uncle murmured and buried his lips into his goblet. But as Asimia's stare continued, he obliged them.

"Dad, in your travels with Mom, did you visit Draco?" He meant the constellation of Draco, galaxies away from their own Little Bear.

"We did. But you ought to know that."

"Ah! And how should I know it?"

"Did I not put a marker beside the dragon's head? Check your maps."

The dragon had deposited copious star maps in Asimia and her uncle's minds. She delved into hers, scrutinizing the space about Draco, especially the squarish celestial head. There, she found a squiggle beside one of the two stars that served as the dragon's eyes. It was either Eltanin or Rastaban.

"Is that what that meant?" she asked. "I wondered. It looks more like an arrow than a checkmark. I thought you marked the worlds you visited with checks. And which one is this? Elt or Ras?"

"This one was special. And it's Elt. Can't you tell?"

No. She couldn't tell. If not for the arrow mark, the two stars looked indistinguishable on this particular map, although Asimia knew they were dissimilar. One was an orange giant (Eltanin, Gamma-Draconis, K5 III), and the other a yellow supergiant with a dwarf companion (Rastaban, Beta-Draconis A, G2Ib-IIa).

Rastaban should appear huge, but Eltanin was nearly as bright. The two were the second and third brightest stars in Draco, most befitting the *eyes of the celestial dragon*. Asimia should be able to tell them apart from Draco's orientation, but she couldn't remember which way was up.

"Special, how?" asked Uncle Yildiz.

"Yira and I loved it so much that we planned to return to it eventually, maybe settle there. A native people, the Phe'lakir, welcomed us and..." he let that hang and fell quiet as if surrendering to memories.

"What?" Asimia prompted, eager to hear more.

"And... what?" added Uncle Yildiz.

"Well, to be sure, Yira liked that planet better than I did. There were few women there and many men. And they were big. I mean, biiig men. She could have all the husbands she wanted."

Asimia and Uncle glanced at each other, not expecting to hear anything of the sort. Uncle Yildiz smiled, and as if that opened a dam, Asimia took to giggles. Uncle joined her.

But what '*big*' men? Bigger than Granda? He was the tallest Yandar man Asimia knew, more than her dad, who had the height but not the girth.

"You were always so possessive of my ma," Uncle Yildiz cut in her thoughts with a twinkle in his eye.

"It's not funny!" Grandad objected. But he relaxed and smiled. "Oh, I guess it is, after so many years."

"And how many years would that be, Granda?" asked Asimia, her curiosity piqued. From what she knew of her uncle's life history, it had to be more than three hundred. Uncle spent three centuries in that K'tul stasis chamber.

Uncle's story was more tormented than her own. The K'tul mage who imprisoned him tortured him periodically to extract Yand's coordinates. But Uncle had hidden his heart in the Cave of Stars on Turunc's moon, Tuncay. A man without a heart could not divulge the vital secrets, no matter how the K'tul brutalized him.

Mom Yanara returned Uncle Yildiz's heart to him after the rescue. Asimia and her uncle returned to Yand to recover. Her trauma was more emotional than physical, but Uncle had hideous wounds, a few on his face and hands that clothing could not conceal. Asimia had to lend her worldmaking power to the doctors who treated him. Some of his afflictions only magic could mend.

The two bonded over their shared experiences and trials of healing. Their bond, vital to a species of empaths, connected them psychically, allowing them to share emotions and thoughts and mindspeak each other. It was a blessing to Asimia, who missed her parents dearly.

She had to live apart from them since she first unlocked her powers at sixteen, causing a worldmaker null between her mom Yanara and herself. That was at the end of the Yandar-K'tul war. Since that fated moment, she and her mom needed celestial space between them. The null not only caused them to lose their powers, but it would eventually kill the weaker—Asimia.

So her mom fled her beloved homeworld of Yand and migrated to Tuncay, under another sun, Polaris B, the companion to the supergiant Polaris A. Asimia's dad and second mom went with her. Asimia's four brothers, even her twin, Hawk, and her beloved Snowfox, followed them. Fox stayed on Tuncay until their betrothal. Hawk was still there now. Her fifth brother, Sunstorm, was born on that moon a few months ago, and Asimia had barely seen him.

After her rescue, her younger brothers Drace and Wolfpack, with their betrotheds and fellow Dragoons Squirl and Mouse, returned to Yand to guard her against a repeat. But Asimia didn't feel the same with them as with her uncle. Their Dragoon prodigies isolated them into their own hard-to-break-in little circle.

And her beloved Snowfox… it had become different with him. His absence over many months, plus their betrothal, changed things between them. They had been inseparable as sibs but were now strained as a couple.

"I don't know, my dear," Grandad replied. "Yildiz was a youngling then. Five hundred?"

"Oh!" Uncle Yildiz exclaimed. "Was it when I was first engaged to my wife?"

"Yes, about that time. But she'd already dumped you."

Uncle winced. He had a very complicated history with his wife. But Asimia was eager to hear Grandad's tale. "So, what happened, Granda? Did you visit a planet in Draco and meet the Phe'lakir people? Which planet? What star?"

Grandad began to phase. This was as much as he could do on his own. "Should I stabilize you?" she asked him. "Or is it too much?" As a way of an answer, he inclined his head, and she kissed his forehead gently, holding him to his Yandar form.

"Here it is then," he said. "But first, what made you think to ask, Yildiz? Did you have a dream?" Grandad was bonded to his son for many centuries, so he felt that Uncle had this dream.

"Yes," Uncle replied.

Asimia served their lunch, passing the best tidbits to Grandad. Uncle told his story among bites of fruit and sips of the fragrant wine.

"I see a dragon with a long, curvy tail and a squarish head. His eyes shine so bright, red or sometimes orange, suspended on his dark face."

"Why is my face dark?" asked Grandad.

"I don't know," replied Uncle Yildiz. "Is that important?"

"Could be," Grandad mused. "Is that the darkness of my face or the darkness of space? But go on."

"K'tul spaceships surround the dragon and sometimes blast it with fires like they did us so many times."

"Wait!" Asimia interrupted. She hadn't heard this part of the story before. "Uncle, what do you mean '*us*' and '*so many times?*'"

Did he mean the Yandar-K'tul wars? The K'tul first invaded Yand more than half a century ago with many attacks that could pass for separate wars. The Final War ended last year with Yandar victory, but only just. Some of the K'tul lingered after that, with a single remaining spaceship, Hellbound. One of those lingering K'tul was the devil K'nista, the mage who abducted her.

Was that what Uncle meant when he said, '*...blast it with fires...?*' The K'tul wars—with celestial cannons blasting from spaceships, burning and decimating Yand?

But Uncle had been in stasis during that time and for more than two centuries before that. The K'tul took him before their first Yandar invasion. A few times, Asimia wondered how that came to be. But her uncle was a wormhole master and had traveled far from Yand... maybe the K'tul captured him in another world.

"Weren't you in stasis during that timeframe?" she asked.

"He means other wars, I think, my darling," Grandad Blaze opined, with an expectant look toward his son.

Uncle inclined his head slightly. What? Yes? The K'tul-Yandar wars Asimia knew? Or other? But Uncle continued before she got to ask more questions.

"And sometimes they pry the dragon's eye from its head. One wicked twisted creature, S't.., I think, S'ti—"

"Ooh, that name!" Grandad exclaimed. "I know it! K'nista!"

No! Asimia thought. *Surely not K'nista!*

"No," Uncle Yildiz disagreed. "It starts with *S't, not K'n.* Maybe *S'ti.* I never hear it clearly."

"S'tilar?" Grandad asked.

"No—"

"S'tindar?"

"No! No, Dad—"

"S'tihsera?"

"Ah! No, but more like this last, like S'tih—"

"Never mind, Uncle," Asimia interrupted them. Grandad knew so many K'tul(!) whose names started with S't… This could take all day. Grandad had already begun to phase, stressed. "It'll come to you later—"

"But did you say they pry my eye out?!" Grandad insisted.

"No! It's not **your** eye, Granda!" Asimia reassured him.

"What other dragon is there, my sweet?"

"Lavender," Asimia replied, referring to her brother Drace's young dragon companion. But the little dragon was safe. Asimia saw her many times every day since the Dragoons came to stay with her. The dragonet was now at the residence with Drace and his merry gang. No one had attempted to plug her eye out.

"But Lav is safe at the residence, as are you here, Granda," Asimia continued. "The K'tul aren't back! Mom got rid of them for good after rescuing Uncle and me. She banished Hellbound from our constellation entirely. There has to be another explanation."

"Constellation? Ooh, I know!" Grandad exclaimed. "How about this? The dragon is Draco, the constellation. You think so too, right? That's why you asked me if I had been there."

Asimia glanced at her uncle. He inclined his head. But Grandad fell quiet.

"What is it?" Asimia prompted him.

"The K'tul homeworld is very far from Draco. It would take them millennia to get there. Where did Yanara banish them to?"

"Ketal. Their homeworld in Apus," Asimia replied, "although Mom said *to hell.*"

"And how is that different, my darling? Is their homeworld not hell?" Grandad replied.

"Huh!" Uncle exclaimed. "Apus, hell—regardless. That constellation is far away, even by worldmaker measures. How did Yanara manage? But millennia?! Isn't that a bit much?"

"Well, certainly centuries. They couldn't get to Draco at only lightspeed in this little time. They can't master wormhole travel like you two," he pointed at Asimia and her uncle, "or Yanara and my Yira. And now my wolf boy, your brother."

Asimia giggled. "Wolf Boy is the Pathfinder, Granda," she told him. "Stronger than me."

"Yes," he agreed. "But only in some ways. Didn't he learn to wormhole only just? And didn't his mom have to unlock him?"

"He did, but you should have seen him at our rescue. He led the entire Ops. Mom was as nulled as I until K'nista put me in that stasis pod." Asimia shuddered to mention that pod. And to think her uncle spent three centuries in one such.

"Wolfpack has clearly evolved from our beloved fifteen-year-old awkward kid," she continued. "He's like a god now. More powerful than the Dragoons." The Dragoons were Asimia's brother Drace, his betrothed, Squirl, and Squirl's sister, Mouse. The three were the most powerful mages in all memory. Sometimes Asimia included Wolfpack in that tight group, but he wasn't a Dragoon in truth. He was the Pathfinder.

"But why do I have this dream," Uncle asked abruptly, bringing the subject back, "if not for the K'tul attacking that world in Draco?"

"I don't know, my boy," Grandad replied. "Maybe because you want to go there?"

Bombshell! Grandad's words hit Asimia hard: Did Uncle Yildiz's subconscious wish to take him from Yand—and Ursa Minor altogether? To bring him to a new constellation to start anew with his wife, far away from the reminders of his bloody ordeal? And he worried that the K'tul would follow him?

But what if those reminders included herself? And what if the K'tul indeed followed him to Draco, be it now or in some distant future, to plug the celestial dragon's eye out? Momentary panic tightened her throat. The look she gave her uncle reflected her fear. A moment passed with Asimia unable to speak. Then another…

"Uncle—" she began,

"My darling—" her uncle said simultaneously.

"Asimia?" that was Wolfpack. Always so near.

"I'm fine, hon," she told her brother.

12

"You don't feel so fine to me." He popped out of wormhole beside them, his betrothed Mouse in tow. His colorful but quiet signature was nuanced to include her hue—amazing! But usually Mouse teleported them. Wolfpack had evolved, indeed. To Asimia's bonded senses, he felt larger, grander, no longer timid.

His wolves also materialized and jumped around them merrily. Alex hissed and growled at them, spreading his fur.

"Is it time to go?" she asked her brother.

"No, I just worried. You felt distressed," he replied. "We can return to the residence if you wish." He meant himself and Mouse.

"Is Fox back from the pasture?" Asimia asked.

The pasture was their new project for the preservation of unicorns. The K'tul wars had decimated the herds on Yenda, Yand's inhabited moon. Two foals with their dams arrived as gifts to Yand, the mares to breed with Asimia and Snowfox's unicorn stallions, Snowwind and Lightning.

Their grandmother, Queen Stardust—Uncle Yildiz's wife— gifted them the large pasture outside the city proper to accommodate the growing herd. Asimia and her sibs and betrotheds spend much time there amid the unis.

"Yes. And Luc," Wolfpack replied.

"Stardust must be wondering about me by now," Uncle said aloud. *"Don't breathe a word of all this,"* he put in Asimia's head in guarded mindspeak, *"until we have time to digest it. And no, I would never leave you behind. Might you wish to accompany me on such an adventure?"*

"Ok," she replied laconically, amazing herself. Did she just agree to follow her uncle to the stars? She needed time to process it. *"I'll have to dig deep, and talk to Fox and Luc."*

"Not to Luc yet, but do consult with Snowfox."

"Will do."

"What's 'all this?'" Wolfpack asked in her mind, also in guarded mindspeak. *"What to tell Fox but not Luc?"* Right. Like they could keep anything from a pathfinder.

"Later," she replied. She kissed her grandad and uncle and teleported Wolfpack, his betrothed Mouse, the wolves, the cat, and herself back to the residence.

13

She found Snowfox at the telescope tower in the South Wing of their home, scoping the heavens. "What do you see?" she asked, making him jump. He turned to her and flashed that double-dimpled smile that so reminded Asimia of their dad. His turquoise blues, a color so rare on silverbloods, sparkled like stars.

"Simi!" he exclaimed, "come see."

He made space for her at the giant telescope. The few astro staffers about him made themselves scarce once they saw her, giving them privacy. She trained her eye where Snowfox pointed, and lo! If it wasn't Draco and the star Eltanin! There was no mistaking it for Rastaban. It was not a binary and clearly smaller—and more orange than the supergiant. And bright enough to blind you.

"Wo, what a beauty!" Asimia exclaimed. "What made you look, Fox!?"

"You!" he replied. "Weren't you thinking of it? Or was it Rastaban? Let me…" He took the controls from her and manipulated the settings. "There!" he pointed. "That's Ras."

Wow! So beautiful! Both of these two stars!

"Where's Luc?" she asked while gazing at Rastaban.

"Don't know. We hit the showers when returning from the pastures. I came here. He's probably talking to the boys. They're thinking of returning to Tuncay on the morrow."

Boys always meant their brother Dragonlord—Drace—and his betrothed Squirrel. Drace was only one year younger than herself and two less than Snowfox, but that was plenty to doom him forever to the fate of younger brother. Despite being a Dragoon.

"I'm here, Simi," came a voice behind her. It was Lucent. But wow! Was he bright! Asimia forgot how bright a goldenblood could be. Of the three Yandar races, they were the brightest. Uncle and Grandad, also golden, had toned it down for her. But Luc…

"Come see, Luc," she beckoned her second betrothed, all too aware that Snowfox had tensed. The two seemed not to mind each other's company in Asimia's absence. One would think chummy, almost. But when she was present… it was a different story.

"What's this?" Lucent asked. Snowfox made room for him beside Asimia and kept on going.

14

"Snowfox!" she called to his back. "Where are you going? Can we have a conversation? I have something to ask you."

"Later," he replied, descending the stairs two at a time.

She had to deal with this behavior every day since their betrothal. She and Snowfox grew up together as siblings in this storied family: he was the adopted firstborn, and she, the Worldmaker's biological daughter. They bonded the moment she opened her eyes on her birthing bed and saw his smiling baby face gazing at her, welcoming her into the world.

Their bond only grew from there. Snowfox was her soulmate from the beginnings of her memory. His physical absence from her side hurt. The few months he spent on Tuncay with their folks before their betrothal had been unbearable. It was when she first realized she could sense him from another star system. Their bond was that strong.

She wasn't sure when it evolved beyond the familial into the partner-for-life realm. But it did and made things awkward. And this jealousy over Lucent was the worst manifestation.

Asimia had not chosen Luc. She would dissolve their betrothal to ease Snowfox's heart, but she didn't dare. Her grandmother, Queen Stardust, had accepted the match to seal a political alliance between the Crown and the powerful Principality of Orange.

Mom Yanara also accepted the young Prince's proposal. The forced separation the null imposed on them had left Mom anxious and fearful for Asimia's safety. She hoped a second husband would afford her daughter an additional measure of protection that she, her mother, could not. And Lucent was an exceptional swordsman who had distinguished himself in the war.

But what would a spare blade do against K'tul mages? They had witnessed that plainly during her abduction. Mom should have found her daughter an exceptional mage, a dragoon[*].

At first Asimia accepted the match only because she felt inhibited with Snowfox from growing up together as sibs. Plus she knew Luc from college, and he had been eager to fill the void of Snowfox's absence during the months Fox spent on Tuncay.

---

[*] A lowercase dragoon means a very powerful mage, on par with the three Dragoons.

And there was another reason. A secret that Asimia kept tightly hidden in her heart: a third man, dashing and smart, and different. He was the single scientist among the military men who surrounded her. She swooned in his presence. She went to ridiculous lengths just to catch a glimpse of him. But it was a match that couldn't be. She was the High Princess of Yand, and he completely untitled. Not that Asimia cared, but the Queen would never accept it.

Asimia sought to suppress this "infatuation" and erroneously thought Luc would fill that void in her heart. He didn't, and she got stuck with a second husband, longing for a third. Although... Asimia had become fond of Luc. They drew closer. It left Snowfox with jealousy and a sense of betrayal.

"Looking at Ras?" asked Luc. "It's so bright tonight."

"Eltanin," she replied. "Come, I need to speak to Drace."

"Wait, darling, I have news of the foals. The little colt is growing his horn!"

"Already?" They discussed the unicorns as they descended the stairs to the courtyard. They ran into Dragonlord.

"Simi," he called, "we're popping to the pasture. Join us?"

Lucent begged for a teleport to Orange to check on his folks, whom he hadn't seen for a few days. Asimia didn't wish to visit Orange or the pasture. So they all disappeared and left her behind.

She went to the kitchen to grab a drink. She found Fox at the counter with a bottle of the good brandy. His foxes lay curled up on the counter and snored softly. He had a good start on the bottle.

"Have you checked on Aunt Shadow today?" she asked him.

Their aunt Shadow was injured during Asimia's abduction. When K'nista attacked their home, Auntie leaped before her niece to protect her, taking the blast squarely onto herself. It was a miracle she survived. The explosion broke every bone in her body and mangled her wings. The mage fire burned her. It took all the medical skill and worldmaking magic their world possessed to bring her back from the brink. She still struggled.

Snowfox guzzled his drink instead of replying. It annoyed Asimia. But when he turned to look at her, the scars on his face that matched those on his hands reminded her that it was not only her aunt who'd rallied against her abductor.

"So why did you do it?" he asked.

"Which 'it' do you mean? The eye of the dragon?"

"No, the second husband."

"Should I divorce him?"

"You haven't married him yet. Just tear the papers."

"Is it so simple?"

"Yes."

"No, it's not! Your grandma wants an alliance with Orange."

"*My* grandma? And why sell *you* for it?" Sparks flew from his eyes. He refilled his glass. "Should I kill him, Simi? That'd get you nicely out. Not even have to tear the precious papers."

He was drunk. Asimia got up to leave, but he grabbed her wrist. "You're drunk," she yelled.

"Not so much."

"Let go, Snowfox, before we say things we can't take back."

"What? Don't tell me you're afraid I won't marry you."

That knocked the anger from her. He couldn't be serious. He was the one man she wanted above all. What was the point of marrying another if she couldn't have her Snowfox? "Fine," she whispered as tears welled in her eyes. "I'll tear the papers. I'll amend ours to say exclusive barring all others."

He bent to her ear and whispered, "Don't bother." He got up slowly, as if to steady himself, and walked out of the room with his foxes bounding from the counter and running ahead. Alex gave their retreating backs a few loud hisses.

Asimia passed the rest of the afternoon in misery. The Dragoons returned from the pastures, Lucent from Orange, they ate dinner with everyone loudly recounting their stories of the unicorn foals and the oranges at Orange. Snowfox was absent, but no one remarked about it. Lucent directed meaningful glances at her, but she ignored him.

She retired to her bed early. She had kept her room in the North Wing, which used to be the old Kids' Wing. They had rebuilt the part that collapsed in the war, grander, but Asimia kept her room simple as before. It was adjacent to the boys' rooms—to Snowfox's.

She brought a book to bed and tried to read it while not thinking about Snowfox, or listening for noises from Snowfox's room, or reaching out to Snowfox with her mind. Aghh! Alex had difficulty settling and fussed, making mittens on her stomach—pure excruciating misery.

Suddenly, a timid rap on the door. "Fox?"

"Can I come in?"

"Come." She got up to open the door. He stepped inside.

"I'm sorry, love—" It was the first time he called her love.

"No, *I'm* sorry. I'll tear the papers—"

"No, don't do that. There has to be a reason Luc happened to us. Give me a moment to get used to it. I can't live without you…"

He trailed off, staring at her, wounded, his misery exuding from the depths of his heart. She reached trembling fingers to his face to trace his scars. He gently grasped her hand, kissed it, brought it back to his face, closed his eyes, and let the tears flow.

"I better go before I break our vows." He spoke of the clause of chastity they had included in their marriage contract because Asimia should not have children. A worldmaker girl would kill her. They grew wings in the womb and flew out at their birth. Or, if the baby was born unlocked like their mom Yanara, she might instantly null Asimia as Mom had done to Yira, eventually killing her.

Asimia and her betrotheds understood—and accepted—the restriction. But it was one thing to understand and another to feel.

"How can you break vows we haven't yet taken?"

"We signed the papers."

"They are not yet vows until we speak them to each other at our wedding."

"Can I stay with you?"

"Please."

Asimia woke up in his arms in the morning. "Shall we go to the stars, my love?" she asked him. "Leave this world to Mom? She has the better claim to it."

"Eltanin or Rastaban?" came his sleepy reply.

"Eltanin."

"Yes."

They spent the next hour in bed talking about the stars and the celestial dragon, dreaming about their bright future navigating the heavens and exploring what wonders awaited them ahead. And their plans included Lucent! Snowfox seemed to have accepted the second husband.

Was this it then? Were they ready to fade into the celestial sunset and live happily ever after? But what of Asimia's wondering heart? Was the newfound intimacy with Snowfox enough to extinguish that errant longing?

Asimia and Yildiz with the Dragon at his Lair

Future Time: Two hundred years later. On Phe'lak in the Eltanar system, the year of Karia's fall. See Appendices A and B for locations and people, including military ranks. Willie's POV.

2. Willie

Willie took a shift at the cooking hearth that night. They had crowned their new queen in the morning, but Willie had a difficult time not to still think of her as Hrysa. Not that she knew The First High Princess of Highwings, Hrysa, well. She had been Gramma's Warleader back when Gramma still lived and had a city to defend. They had lost both Willie's gramma and the war.

It was over a month since their King led this pitiful few Karian survivors out of their failing city to safety. They sought refuge here, at the Crags, the extensive cave system chiseled into the Bladed Hills, the mountainous region on the Parian coastline.

Three weeks after that, Karia fell. King Snowfox brought another group of refugees out of the conquered palace—the royal family of Highwings: his wife, Queen Asimia, and baby daughter, Second High Princess Silvia, who was a worldmaker like her mom. The Yendal Lords Triex and Fatie and Phe'laki General George helped with that rescue.

It was a harrowing escape, the stories went. Queen Asimia had been incapacitated by an arrow wound and Princess Silvia's null, and they had to carry her. They crept through the palace underpass with minions of K'tul on their heels. Greyk'tul and K'jen witches cornered them many times. Countless times King Snowfox's bow sang together with the Yendal Lords' slings.

The flames of their swords burned their likeness into the walls, the legend said. All the while, Princess Hrysanthia, with the remaining few defenders, held the palace walls against the enemy, buying her family time to escape.

Eventually the fugitives joined them at the Crags, but with K'tul pursuit tight on their tail. And another disaster followed the next day. Willie's gramma, Ritchie, had been among the last defenders who held the walls with Hrysa, one of three Yandar archers among a dozen surviving Phe'laki warriors. The enemy took them alive! The top K'jen witch executed Gramma most cruelly.

Those bonded to her heard her screams all the way to the Crags when the demon took her wings. Willie wiped her eyes. It was all too fresh, only two days ago—or was it three now?

King Snowfox feared the K'tul witch had gleaned images of the Crags in the captives' minds and would come after them. Not wanting to expose the refugees, he took his wife and daughter and fled. The Yendal Lords and Phe'laki General went with him.

The K'tul caught them at an inn on the way to Paria, Karia's port city, where they had sheltered for the night. They captured Silvia, and the Queen succumbed to her wounds! The King vanished after that. The rumors said he chased after his daughter's abductors.

The Yendal Lords and General George returned alone. Princess Hrysa escaped her capture at the palace and found her way to the Crags. She was now their new queen. They coronated her that morning and held this feast tonight in her honor.

Willie took a shift at serving, too, although she didn't have to since she helped the cooks. But it passed the time. And to be truthful, she hoped to run into her friend, Sunny, while she served the food. Only she didn't. He was nowhere. She hadn't seen him for two whole days since he left the Crags on an errand.

Not that Sunny stayed put in one place for long. He came and went as he pleased, so she didn't think much of his absence at first. It was more of an annoyance. But when he missed the coronation that morning and now dinner… Willie started to worry.

His errand had him flying in all haste to the Keys, the fishing villages on the way to Paria. Did he make it there? Maybe he already returned and avoided her—he did often tell her that she annoyed him. But surely he'd turn up for dinner! Him miss a meal?

His errand seemed important. But why did they send a boy so small? *She* should have gone. She was the better flyer. And a year older! Now the K'tul probably took him like Silvia. She warned him to be careful. But even the uttermost care… flying made them targets… a small boy alone… Would the K'tul take his wings first, like Gramma's? Or kill him and eat him outright?

A commotion from the gathered folks distracted Willie from her worries about Sunny. Someone toasted their new queen. It was Professor Pietro, the leader of the scientists. Of the entire assembly, now. King Snowfox appointed him so in his absence, and he had been right. Everyone followed the professor's bidding.

The entire refugee camp had gathered in the giant common cavern for this event. It was a fitting conclusion to a day they spent in celebration, something they all needed amidst so much misery and loss. If not for the missing Sunny, Willie would have found it a pleasant day.

They had cakes! They baked them from *real* flour and eggs that Parian folks brought from their cordon. Willie helped with the baking. Mmm... they tasted divine. She saved a generous slice for Sunny. She wrapped it in a leaf and stashed it in her pocket.

"Willie, Have you seen your brother?" Ma's mindvoice interrupted Willie's musings. She sounded concerned.

"Tommy's with the orphans, Ma. He's eating good," Willie replied. She had just seen him at the kids' table eating his dessert.

A mental chuckle from her ma. *"He would. He'll pass you soon the way he eats."*

"We all eat like starving wolves," Willie told her mama, returning the phrase Ma used to tease the kids. Ma and every other adult here loved to watch the kids eat. They had starved for two years during the siege. The remaining adults always fed them first of what provisions remained in the palace's stores, but it wasn't enough. The Crags now provided more than shelter. They offered the ocean's bounty, Yandar food.

The ocean flowed endless on the Crag's east side beyond the entrance cave they called the Mouth. Inside the Mouth meandered the Crags' caves, some small, some cavernous, dry, or wet, with endless connecting passages one could easily get lost in. The best fishing on Phe'lak was but a dive off the cliff beyond the Mouth. The adults organized fishing teams, so they always had a fresh catch. Willie, her ma, and Sunny made up such a team.

An endless forest sprawled on the west side of the Bladeds all the way back to Karia. The palace underpass, from where the refugees escaped, exited into one end of those woods. They burst with good hunting, nut trees, and a fruit tree here and there.

But the woods crawled with enemy search teams, K'tul and Tjourhien! Yandar never ate flesh, but they ate fowl in such great need. So the kids braved those woods every sundown and brought a good catch each night without fail. And many nuts the cooking teams ground to make bread. Willie and Sunny raided an enemy campfire or two that yielded treasures: dried fruits and medical salves their medics used on the wounded.

But Ma had mindspoken her in her private frequency! Because the K'tul were empaths and telepaths and could hear Yandar mindspeak, the genetics team had developed each person's private mind code from their DNA. They all had to memorize the list, but Willie put it off, telling herself that some other person had the papers, then another… when in truth, she hated memorizing.

Although she didn't need to learn that entire list. She already knew her ma's and Tommy's. Now she only needed Sunny's. She remembered that the orphan kids had the list. They all sat together, finishing their desert, easily the largest group in the cavern.

Nearly every Karian adult and many teenagers fought and died in the war, leaving behind many orphans. The King ensured they left not a single one behind in their flight from Karia. He said that if they saved anything, it had to be the kids, their future, and their scientists and engineers.

He forbade this last group from fighting in the war. He brought them all to the Crags. They made up the refugees' second-largest group. Practically the entire Karian University sheltered here.

Seeing all the orphans together made Willie think: Was she an orphan, too? She lost her gramma, and her dad before her. And before Da, her granda and six uncles. Was that enough to qualify her? Not that you got a badge or anything other such. Only the camaraderie and commiseration of others like you.

But she fared better than most. She had her ma, Nara, and her little brother, Tom, and now, could she dare say, Uncle Triex, too? Oh, how she wished the Yendal Prince would marry her ma! He was a Lord! They said he had been Viceroy of Yenda! Even king for a spell. He was Hrysa's uncle by rights—or was it adoption?

More than any titles, Willie liked the man and wanted him to be her father. She and Tommy could call him Da. They had already bonded to him. She marveled at how easy that had been. They said bonding to a Yendal was easier because they were telepaths with stronger psychic abilities[*] than Yandar folks.

---

[*] Not true. Triex and his brother Fatie were the strongest telepaths ever.

She had heard rumors that Parian cordonite families would soon adopt all the orphans. Willie didn't know what a cordon was other than it was a place in Paria where displaced people lived. She imagined it beautiful and grand. It had to be with so many good people there, generous enough to adopt all the Karian orphans!

"Hey, Willie, up in the clouds? Come back to earth? What's up?" That was Jordan.

"You got the list? I need to learn a few frequencies."

"Your boyfriend's? Sunshine boy's?"

Heat rose to Willie's face. She should teach Jordan some manners. But she let it slide. Ma said all the boys had a crush on her, and being mean was their way of showing it. Some way! If that was the measure, Sunny must really love her. They fought all the time.

She located the list in a boy's hands and snatched it. She sat at the edge of the bench and memorized Sunny's private frequency, then Uncle Triex's. For this to work, both sender and recipient needed each other's codes*. Did Sunny have hers? Did Uncle Triex?

She returned the paper and ran from the cave. She made her way to the Mouth, then onto the long cleft beyond it. She meant to sit and mindspeak Sunny in peace. She walked to the edge where they often sat together, gazing at the stars and dreaming of peace. He often told her tales of a faraway world he called Tuncay. Where did he learn all those stories?

Willie peered beyond the edge, trying to imagine where Sunny had gone, where he spent his night and missed all the festivities. It was dark, and she went on night vision. Willie wasn't sure, but they said that Yandar got their night vision after Worldmaker Yanara's Big Bend plunged Yand into darkness for fifty years. Willie couldn't imagine that. Half a century in darkness?

The tide below had receded but still looked high from what Willie could see. Waves crashed on rocks at the foot of her cliff. On impulse, she decided to fly and see things from above, whatever the darkness afforded her night vision.

She meant to hop into a high launch and lazily spiral down, but missed her footing and fell! She backwinged frantically, scrambling to right herself. She failed and continued to plunge. The rocks approached fast; she would crash...

---

* Not true. Only the mind speaker needed the other person's *private code.*

There came a loud woosh, a mighty downstroke of wings, and two strong hands grabbed Willie by limb and clothing. Another powerful stroke of those amazing wings righted her—them, herself and the wings' owner—with the waves. With a few more strokes, her rescuer lifted them back to the top of the cliff.

Willie's heart raced so hard she thought it would fly from her chest. She and her rescuer had tumbled a full cartwheel in that maneuver, barely above the waves! Might as well say *in* the waves, as drenched as she was. Now she found herself on her feet, right side up, with an adult looming over her. Uh oh! She'd done it, now! Sure to catch hell from her ma. And that wasn't all! Her rescuer was…

It was Hrysa! Oh, gods! The queen of the land saved her. Could this be more humiliating?? If the orphans caught wind of this… if Ma… if Sunny…

Willie cringed and shrunk from the proffered hand. "Come, sweetie," Hrysa, ah, the queen, said. "You'll catch your death flying blind in the dark. You must master your night vision. We can't have you stumbling about and falling. You must've caught quite a fright."

"I, umm," Willie started, but the words wouldn't come.

Hrysa looked genuinely concerned. "Come," she said. "This will delay me, but I'll take you to your mom first. You are Willow, no? My uncle's new ward?" With a smile and a wiggle of her eyebrows, "And soon-to-be daughter, if I read the signs right?"

What? Willie was so flustered that she only caught half of Hrysa's words. But… *soon-to-be*… and *daughter*…

"Going somewhere, m'girl?" a rich, deep male voice came from behind Willie. She had her back to the Mouth, so she had to turn to see the approaching figure. It was… no, it couldn't be…

Ah, shucks, this isn't my night, now! If it wasn't the Phe'laki General, Hrysa's grandad. "I, ah, I, emm…" Willie stuttered, thinking the General had addressed his question to herself.

"Grandad!" Hrysa exclaimed at the same time. "I thought you were enjoying Captain Chimeran's company—"

"And took the opportunity to steal away? Like a thief in the night? Are you not our new queen, now?"

25

"I made arrangements, Grandad," Hrysa replied. "I can't leave my dad, as injured as he was, so completely on his own—"

Ah, Willie thought, this confirmed both rumors about their King: that he'd been gravely wounded during Princess Silvia's abduction and that he chased after the K'tul to get her back.

"How can you leave your people?" asked the General.

"—and my sister to the K'tul—"

"—leaderless—"

They went on like that, talking past each other, interrupting, and increasing in volume. Willie attempted to slink away, but the General caught her by an arm.

"Who have we here?" he asked. "Ritchie's granddaughter? Were you trying to follow your queen? See what I mean, Hrysa?"

"No," Hrysa exclaimed loudly, while Willie shook her head. "I found her diving off the cliff. She delayed me—"

"Otherwise you'd be off by now—"

"Yes." After an awkward silence, "I'm not abandoning our people leaderless, Granda. I left notes—"

"You left notes?!"

"Yes. To Pete. I made him viceroy in my absence. I said I'm going to aid Dad in ridding us of that K'tul spaceship—"

"You know your dad doesn't mean to rid us of it," General countered. "He means to *hijack it* and take it to the stars."

"Yes."

"Then how will you return to us? Ah, you don't plan to come back. You think *your mother* will come back."

What? Didn't Queen Asimia die? Willie wondered.

"Won't she, Granda?" Hrysa shouted. "You know she was better when I saw her in the Burning Woods in Snowwind's realm."

Burning Woods was the part of the forest to the west of the Crags that a greyk'tul witch torched while chasing Hrysa. The orphans gave it that name—or was it Sunny? —when they first heard Hrysa's escape story, that the caves now buzzed with. *Snowwind's realm* was a separate dimension in which some unicorns could exist. *Was that where Queen Asimia had gone?*

"That was only yesterday!" Hrysa continued. "With Silvia and the null gone from here, Mom will recover. She will return."

"And you?" shouted the General. "Will we—*will I*—ever see you again?"

"I left you a note."

"You left me a note!?" The general bellowed, scaring Willie. If fire and lightning could fly from a man's eyes! "And what did you tell me in that magnanimous note?"

"Not to hate me," Hrysa shouted back, then paused and stared at her grandad. "I must do this," she said with less volume. "Our people are in good hands, Grandad. My note to Pete explains what I must do and makes him viceroy. Do you not remember what Dad said on our mind-chat last night? That Pete is a natural leader? You know the man. You know he is that, and I am not."

What did she mean she was not? She was the queen! Willie would object if she could find her voice. Maybe the General also wanted to, but Hrysa didn't give them the opportunity. She continued making her points as fast as she could.

"I left a note for Triex as well. And Fatie. I stashed them in Nara's sleeping spot. Triex is to lead the relocation, following the plan he laid out to us the other day. Ah, it was only last night! Fatie can aid him, but he and Pete must first retrieve the scientific equipment from the Heel."

The relocation was easy to understand—to the Parian cordon. And Willie knew that the scientists and engineers hid most of their equipment in the Heel, a cave a few miles down the mountains, so they wouldn't have to carry them up the Bladed Hills on their backs. The forests were too thick for low flight, and they didn't dare fly above the trees, as the K'tul watched for that.

These instruments were irreplaceable. They couldn't leave them behind. Lord Fatie concealed them with a spell, the rumor went, although Willie didn't think the Yendal Lord was a mage. Under pursuit, Hrysa spent a night in the Heel without noticing the numerous equipment, and neither did the greyk'tul, who entered the cave, hunting her.

Hrysa continued, "And you…" But she trailed and paused.

"And me?" asked General. It seemed his anger had subsided as Hrysa spoke. "What have you planned for me?"

"Like we discussed last night, Granda. Go to Paria to help my uncles with the relocation and check on Cousin Emmiat at the hospital. I mean, go *be* with her, lay your claim, and ensure she heals well. We can't leave her alone now, injured and forlorn!"

Eh? Willie pondered that while Hrysa paused and gazed at her grandad. Was she giving him a chance to object? Willie didn't understand this part too well. She knew that Lady Emmiat was Silvia's nanny, and the K'tul nearly killed her when they abducted the princess. But what did it mean to lay your claim?

Hrysa continued, "Then after that—"

"What after that?" the General interrupted.

"What troubles you most besides my safety and Silvia's and our folks'? I mean the Phe'lakir! The K'tul's assault on them."

General hung his head. The Phe'lakir was the native people's collection of tribes. The General's mother, Clanswoman Marka, led them. *The K'tul laid siege to the Phe'lakir!?* Willie hadn't known that part. *That explains why they didn't come to help us.*

But General spoke: "Haven't we done this before, you tricking me to go? Like when you sent me from the walls?"

"And that worked. You rescued Mom and Silvi—"

"To a measure! Neither your mom nor Silvia are with us!"

"And how is that your fault? No. Let's not deliberate it. Go back inside. Find Pete. Lay a plan to save our people. Take care of Paria and make the trek to the Phe'laki Heights, to Marka." Phe'laki Heights, the highest mountain range on Phe'lak, was home to the Phe'laki Clans. "Help the Phe'lakir survive until stronger help comes to our aid from Yand. Or my mom regains her power."

"Oh, my!" cried the General. "Do you really believe that help will come from Yand? Or that your mother will regain her power?" He stared. When he spoke again, his tone had turned from anger to acceptance. "That can only be if Silvia leaves our world."

Willie barely caught his last words. They came as a low whisper. But she understood their meaning. Because of the null, Queen Asimia would only regain her power if Silvia left their world.

The General was easily half-again Willie's height and more than four times her weight. She looked up to see his face, expecting the grandeur of the fabled warrior. But in that moment, her night vision revealed only a man, a grandad, resigned and hurting.

"And you say you are not a good leader! You humble me, my girl," he said. He took Hrysa in a bear hug, lifting her off the ground. But he put her down and asked, "You put all that in a note?"

"Yes," Hrysa replied, wiping her eyes. "I left it for you with Captain Chimeran."

"You don't expect me to take a second wife, now, do you? Just because I talked to the woman?" Did the general smile?

"Hmf!" Hrysa replied. But, ooh! That was scandalous!

The General backstepped to give Hrysa ground to launch. "Fly, my Hrysa," he said quietly. "I'll be right behind you."

"What?"

"If I'm to go to Paria, we might as well jog there together."

"I'm *flying,* Granda!"

"Right. I'll see you at the K'tul base one hill west of Paria, or however your dad described it." He winked at Hrysa, and Willie saw that despite the darkness. "Don't think I can't find it."

Hrysa launched herself into the air, beat her wings two times, hovered for a moment, then turned abruptly and dove beyond the cliffs. Willie started after her, but General grabbed her wrist firmly and shooed her toward the cave. He watched until she reached the Mouth. Then he grabbed a rope on the grappling hooks at the cliff's edge and climbed down into the waves that crashed loudly below.

The celebration was at its height when Willie returned to it. It would go on all night. She considered mindspeaking Sunny, but she caught sight of her ma looking frazzled. She followed with her eyes and caught a meaningful eye contact between Ma and Professor Pietro—should she think of him as Viceroy, now?

Prof. or Viceroy? She settled on Sir. Sir rose from his place with the science group and joined Willie's mom. The two slunk out of the cave. If they said anything to each other, Willie couldn't hear it. These private codes made it impossible to eavesdrop. How would a kid survive that? She needed a workaround.

She followed them to the families' sleeping tent, where her ma had claimed a spot for them. It was the closest to the warming fire, granted them to honor Ritchie's family. Willie slipped inside and hid behind a rock in the shadows, peering around it now and then to see. Thankfully they spoke aloud, although quietly.

"What is it, Nara?" Sir asked.

"Have you found a note? Mine said there're four such."

"No. What note?"

"Here."

She handed Sir a crumbled piece of paper. Oh, how Willie wished she could read it from her corner. But she knew what it said. She'd heard it with her own ears from Hrysa's mouth.

But Sir hadn't. As he read on, he started to object. "What the hell? Please excuse me, I meant, what is this? Hrysa left?! To follow Snowfox to the K'tul spaceship? Whatever possessed her?"

"Read on," Ma encouraged him.

"What? Me viceroy? No! No way. We'll get us through this crisis, and then I'll settle at the Parian U. until they come and get me from Tuncay. Oh, don't look at me like that, Nara! OK, I'll stay! But I don't want to be viceroy. Don't we have another if it's a viceroy we need? Wasn't your suitor Viceroy of Yenda during the Yandar-K'tul wars back when? I ought to know. I was on Yand then. I fought in that war, I'll have you know!"

"Wasn't that two hundred years ago?" Ma objected. "And he's not my *suitor!*" This last earned her a glare, but she ignored it and continued, "I don't think he wants such a position anymore. And don't say *Fatie can be king.*"

Fatie had been King of Yenda during the Yandar-K'tul wars two hundred years ago, as Willie remembered her history.

"He doesn't want that either," Ma went on. They're past all that. Both of them. They abdicated for good."

"But I'm a scientist, not a viceroy!"

Instead of answering him, Ma went blank for a few moments. "It's Triex," she said when she re-engaged. "He wonders if we got our notes."

"Let's go on group-speak," Sir said, but another thought hit him: "Triex knows about the notes?"

"He said Hrysa just mindspoke him."

Sir did something, and, all at once, Willie could hear everyone on a mindchat. She tried to guard her thoughts, but it was no use. *"Willow!"* Sir bellowed, turning to her menacingly. *"You mean to eavesdrop so rudely? Might as well come out in the open and hear this."*

"I, umm, I'm so sorry—"

"Not sorry enough!" Sir continued berating her. *"You'll live to regret this! What do you think should be punishment enough, Nara? Triex?"*

Ma turned ashen. "Please, Pete," she began speaking aloud with a wavering voice, but Uncle Triex interrupted. If he sounded amused, Willie was too discombobulated to tell.

"Same as this rascal over here, I think. Come, Sunny!"

Sunny!? Oh, what had he done now! And got caught, same as herself.

"And what's that?" Sir asked without a hint of malice in his mindvoice.

"Enlist them in our service. The first members of Ops SpyNet. We began operations today."

"Oh, no!" Ma objected. *"Please, Sir..."* she trailed off.

But, *'Sir?'* Ma called the professor, *'Sir,'* same as Willie? Or did she mean Uncle Triex? Oh, that was worse! Ma called Uncle Triex, *'Sir?'* Weren't they practically engaged?

"WILLIE!" Ma's mindvoice boomed in Willie's head, deafening her. She'd clearly heard her thoughts. Oh, no! Had Sir heard? Had Uncle Triex? *Sunny!?*

Sir seemed familiar with Uncle Triex's idea of a spy network. However, he disagreed with the activation plan. He wanted to first safely relocate to the Parian cordon and adopt the children into Parian families. He thought they should staff the operation solely with adults. Only when and if absolutely necessary, he would allow the children's participation. And only for benign activities.

Uncle Triex argued that relocation could spread into months, and they couldn't wait that long. They needed eyes and ears on the enemy *now, during* the relocation! Plus, children were small and easily blended into shadows.

Sir countered that they couldn't risk the safety of their children. He shared King Snowfox's view that the kids were the future of Yandar and Yendal survival on Phe'lak.

Us scraggly kids! Willie thought. *If the King said it, and now Sir... are we important!? Not a burden or nuisance, or endless guts and bottomless stomachs as the cook aunties call us?*

Sir and Uncle argued for a while. Ultimately, they agreed to initiate Ops SpyNet immediately, but only with adults. Right. Like Sir could prevent Uncle Triex from doing whatever he wanted. Or control the kids. Sunny would have apoplexy!

Ma had taken Sir's side of that argument. She wanted no kid involvement at all and wouldn't change her mind no matter how much Uncle Triex reassured her that he wouldn't do anything to risk the child. Willie thought he meant *her*. But he said *the* child, not *my* child, or, better yet, *our* child. Did they break up, then? It was all Willie's fault! She shouldn't have eavesdropped. She shouldn't have gotten caught while eavesdropping.

Captain Chimeran entered the cave, waving a piece of paper. It was all Willie could do not to stare at the flyers' golden wings, silver hair, and dark complexion, all signs of her mixed DNA. Folks of mixed DNA were scarce, like chimeras. The captain was the only one Willie had ever seen. She led the handful of military flyers who had accompanied the refugees to the Crags for protection. They also had three Phe'laki warriors—two now that the General had left.

The captain's entrance allowed Willie the opportunity to disappear into the shadows. She slunk back to a corner, hugged her knees, and tried not to listen to the adults' conversation.

Suddenly, a mindvoice interrupted her thoughts. *"Willie?"*

It was Sunny! *"Where are you?"* she exclaimed.

"At the cordon, with my brother."

"You have a brother?"

"Yes. Triex."

"You mean Uncle Triex? Isn't he My Lord *to you?"*

"What 'my lord?' Triex?"

"Yes, that *Triex! Your Lord!"*

And there they went, fighting again. They couldn't even say two words to each other.

"I'm back out tomorrow," Sunny said, changing the subject. *"We're bringing a fishing group from the cordon to the Keys. I could pop out to the Crags to see you if you want."*

Willie felt heat rise to her cheeks. Sunny thought she wanted to see him! *"And what makes you think I want to see you?"* she blurted. He was always so presumptuous, too overconfident.

Sunny giggled. *"Or you can fly down to the Keys to see* me."

"I don't need to see you, Sunny!" Willie shouted in his head.

"Fine, sheesh, don't deafen me!" Sunny retorted. *"I can hear you, fine! Let me come up and show you how to guard your thoughts and mindspeak. Or else we'll never join my brother's Ops SpyNet. Don't you want to?"*

Aghh! Now Willie had to tell him that kids weren't allowed in the Ops!

Hrysa Saving Willie at the Crags

Future Time: Continuing from Chapter 2. Willie's POV.

3. Sunny

*T*he rest of the evening passed without further ado. Despite his boasting of teaching her this and that, Sunny didn't show up. Willie retired to her sleeping spot in the family cave with her mom, curled up beside the warming fire and went to sleep.

Well into the night, a pair of arms lifted her and carried her to another, smaller cave. It, too, had a warming fire at one end, but no other people. A private cave! How did they rate that? Being a hero's family didn't qualify them. Everyone here was such. Uncle Triex must have made up his mind about Ma!

Willie drifted back to sleep until a conversation in hushed whispers reached her ears. It was Ma and Sir. And another—Lord Fatie. He had gone to Paria with Uncle Triex shortly after the coronation and had just returned! They must be discussing the plans for relocating to the Parian cordon. Willie nearly awoke all the way from her excitement. But she couldn't hear Uncle Triex's speaking voice. Lord Fatie had returned from Paria alone.

He spent most of his day at Lady Emmiat's bedside in the Parian hospital. Willie heard the tales of the lady's injuries. So horrific! She fought Silvia's abductor with all her strength, but the K'tul overpowered her and sliced her throat! Lord Fatie said it took many blood transfusions to keep her from dying. She still fought for her life when he left her. And if she survived, she would never speak out loud again. The doctors couldn't save her vocal cords.

That K'tul attack had been so savage! Willie had seen the burns on General George—from mage blasts, they said. The two Yendal Lords, too, had many wounds! She shuddered to think that. Her ma noticed and came over to fuss over her and Tommy, speaking soft words to them and caressing their hair. She then did something remarkable: she spread *a blanket* over them.

It was more than a month since Willie felt such comforting softness. Lord Fatie must have brought the blanket from the cordon.

What a marvelous place the cordon must be, Willie thought again, to have enough blankets to spare for the Karians. The refugees had nothing but a cloak or a makeshift covering of rushes the aunties weaved. Or what loot they raided from enemy camps in the woods.

"Willie," a mindspeak caressed her mind in her private frequency. It was so melodic and beautiful and unmistakably low and male. But it was not Sir or Uncle Triex. She knew their mindspeak. *"Please call me Uncle Fatie,"* the voice said. Ah, it was his Yendal Highn—Uncle Fatie. *"And soon, I think just Uncle will do,"* he concluded with what sounded like good-natured amusement.

"I brought the boy," His—Uncle Fatie said aloud. "Not sure how he followed us to Paria, but it's too dangerous for a kid to hang about us right now."

What boy? What kid? **Sunny?** *Then the lump beside me...*

Uncle Fatie went on. "It's too dangerous to transfer anyone to Paria right now. They have checkpoints and guards watching everything and everyone coming and going. We thought they'd be in disarray now with Silvia's abduction, but not so. They organized."

"How so?" asked Sir.

"All the Parian authorities are K'jen. They have nothing to do with the greyk'tul's affairs, at least on the surface." It was greyk'tul who kidnapped Silvia. "The K'jen control of Paria is indisputable and complete. Their leader is a top witch, S'tihsa. We've met him before. He assaulted us in the palace underpass as we made our escape.

"The cordon knows him well. They call him Snakeman. Or Snake. He's treacherous and evil. He's the one who directed Paria's stealthy capture and led the siege on Karia; and who—" He let that drop abruptly with a look at Ma. *What? Was Snakeman the witch who took Gramma's wings?* Horror spread to Wille's limbs, but she had no time to react, to cry out loud as Uncle Fatie continued.

"With his plans foiled in Karia, Snake has returned to Paria. We'll find what we can about his operations there. But let's hold this discussion until the morrow when Triex joins us. I mean the relocation details and Hrysa's departure."

"Why didn't Triex join us tonight? Are you here for the equipment?" Sir asked.

"Indeed. We managed to pass only one horse through the Ivory Gates, and rather than double on it, Triex decided to stay the night and pass in the morning with the work crews. I plan to retrieve the equipment from the Heel now while it's dark. We must ready them to transport tomorrow. It'll take a few trips so we best get started. We don't have much darkness left."

"For sure. I'll organize my techs to help you. But, now?"

"Yes."

"Ah, well, most are indisposed now. The liquor flowed, my friend. You missed much. But *I'll* come with you."

"No, you won't. Snowfox dragooned us not to risk you."

"I'll come," the lump beside Wille piped up. It was Sunny!

"Me too," she added.

"No, you won't. Neither of you," Sir contradicted with an inflection in his voice that allowed no buts or ifs or maybes. And when Willie tried to utter something of the sort, Sunny elbowed her hard, and she subsided.

"You'll go on sleeping until the sun shines in the sky. I want no more disobedience from you. Got that, young man?" Sir told Sunny sternly. Amazingly, Sunny nodded and resumed his mild snoring. *Fake snoring.*

In the end, Uncle Fatie drafted two of Captain Chimeran's military archers and the two Phe'laki warriors to help him. And Sunny did follow him to the Heel. At least, so Willie surmised. She closed her eyes and pretended to sleep, but sleep took her for real. When she awoke, it was morning, and Sunny was missing from her side. The only tiny lump that remained beside her was Tommy.

Uncle Triex arrived on horse early that morning before the last expedition returned from the Heel. He entered the cave while Willie and her ma tidied their sleeping spot, careful not to wake the baby. Tommy hated to be called *baby,* but he was a toddler of three, and seven entire years younger than Willie. He would remain *baby* for a long time to come.

Uncle Triex walked up to Ma and kissed her on the cheek! Shock of all shocks! That surely meant he would propose!

Catching her staring with huge eyes, Uncle Triex ruffled her hair and gave her a crooked smile. "What do you think, Willie?" he asked, with a wink. "Shall your mom and I get hitched before or after we move to the cordon?"

Ma made a fake effort to protest, but he pulled her to him and hugged her with one arm! "No worries," he told her, "I'll propose properly. Give me a chance to catch my breath and see Pete and my brother."

"I'm here," Sir's voice preceded him as he walked into their cave, "and your brother hasn't returned yet from the Heel with my equipment—"

"It was a lot of stuff—"

"I know, I know, but I worry. It's light out. Should we go after him?"

"No, give him a few more minutes."

"And don't you think it'd be better to hold the wedding at the cordon? Something to celebrate in our new home?"

"Hmm, I don't know."

"What is it?" Ma asked, looking alarmed. "That *hmm* didn't sound too good."

"Not entirely sure. But the K'jen rule the world in Paria, and they have the cordon under strange rules. I think it may be better to bring married people rather than singles."

"And why is that?" Ma persisted.

"There is a rumor that Snakeman will start a census—"

"Oh no!" Ma cried out. "How will we—"

"And you think it's better to find families rather than unattached folks—women—is that it?" asked Sir. "Do you worry they'll take our single women?"

Uncle Triex inclined his head minutely. Ma regarded him with horror in her eyes. *Take* could have many meanings, but never a good one when it came to K'tul.

"No, Nara, I didn't mean like that!" Uncle Triex, a strong telepath, told Ma, having heard her thoughts. "Not for their wings! But it couldn't be good. The entire K'tul army is all men. They have no women warriors. They brought a few female civilians, but they're wives of their high elite males."

"You mean they brought none suited for a brothel?" asked Sir, shocking Willie from her fear about her ma's wings.

"Well, as a matter of fact, they *have* brought a few such, but why take the risk with our women to find out? They already speak of raids at the cordon, albeit as if they are rare events." Sir's jaw was on the floor.

Ma was faster to speak. "Then why not stay here? Why volunteer for the abuse?"

"Because the abuse at the cordon is rare and predictable. We will manage it. Leave it to me and my brother and our SpyNet."

"I can't see how we'll manage," Ma objected.

"You'll have to trust me. I'll get into Snakeman's ear. I will feed him whatever I want—lies and half-truths. I will muddle our census and gaslight the witch until he doesn't know which side is up. I will turn greyk'tul against K'jen and watch them tear each other down. And through all that, we can make ourselves a life under their thumbs and noses until stronger help comes to find us."

"Stronger, you mean Asimia?" Sir asked, finding his voice.

Uncle Triex nodded and added, "And Yand."

Willie was too shocked to consider fear. Ma remained speechless. But Sir's expression now morphed to… scandalized? "You've been to a K'tul brothel?" he asked in utter dismay.

"I've been to two," Willie's new dad-to-be answered matter-of-factly. Ma schooled her expression, but her thoughts overflowed her guard. Scandal. Confusion. Revulsion. Regret. Jealousy?

"Not in that way, you two!" Uncle Triex objected. "Sheesh. You take me for a K'tul lover? Such thoughts in front of the girl!"

"Did they have females there, or only men?" asked Sir.

"Females, too," Uncle confirmed. "K'tul mostly, but a few Yandar. It's what made me take the rumors seriously. And what made me go there in the first place. To see with my eyes."

"Oh," Sir remarked. "And there are two such places?"

"Two that I found in the short time I had last night. What do you say, Pete? Will you marry us?" He indicated Ma and himself, but Ma pulled back from him as if his arm had become… sullied.

"What," he asked her with a frown, clueless. Sir chuckled. A large commotion from the Cavern alerted them to the return from the Heel. Willie looked expectantly beyond the cave's opening, eager to put the awkward talk of brothels behind her. Sunny hopped through the entrance. All the adults left the cave, Ma ordering Willie to mind her sleeping brother. Sunny gave them a backward glance as they filed out, some more solemn than others.

"So you went after all, you rascal," Sir told Sunny, ruffling his hair as he passed him. "We'll reckon this later."

"What's with Sir?" Willie asked Sunny.

"What's with your *ma?*" he asked in return.

"Uncle went to some weird place in Paria she didn't like."

"What weird place?"

"I don't know. Where were you last night?"

"Me? I went to the Heel to help my brother Fatie," he replied defensively. "See? They needed me." He turned his back to show off his backpack. "It's full of syringes and other small science stuff."

"What science stuff?"

"And before that, I slept here with you, idiot! Come, let's go get some breakfast. I'm famished." Before she could react, he grabbed her hand and dragged her behind him.

"Sunny, wait! Tommy's sleeping; we can't leave him alone!"

They were already in the cooking cavern before he slowed enough to comprehend her objections. "Oh," he said. Meanwhile, Tommy's wails could be heard by all. Ma started toward them, shouting her name that special way: "Willie!"

"Easy now, Nara, let the girl eat. I'll get your little one," an auntie offered. "Let me?"

Ma agreed and returned to Uncle Triex, Sir, and Lord— Uncle Fatie with a last wag of her finger at Willie. Sunny pulled Willie's sleeve, handed her a plate, and piled food onto his.

"Eggs?" she asked him hopefully.

"Nah, leftovers. Didn't you have a feast last night?" They did. So this morning they had bread rolls stuffed with whatever remained—fish of various sorts. And a freshly made sweet porridge.

They hid in the shadow of a boulder close to the adults and ate their breakfast. Sunny wolfed down his porridge and went for more. He returned with an extra giant gab in his spoon for Willie. He splattered it on her plate with a wink before she could protest and sat back down. "Nice and sweet," he told her. "What'd I miss?"

She shrugged her shoulders. But yuk! He'd added more sweetener to the goo. She gave him a sour glare with a frown, and he stuck his tongue out at her. He already began to annoy her. But they both wanted to listen to the adult talk. So, between spoonfuls of porridge and exaggerated bites of fish rolls, they settled in and trained their listening ears to the adults.

Snakeman would not allow the fishing camp at the Keys that the cordon elders proposed, so Uncle Triex had to find a way to infiltrate the K'jen's highest echelon and become Snake's trusted advisor. When Snakeman got to trust him, and only then, Uncle

Triex would propose the fishing expedition once again. He thought he needed a week.

A week! Willie choked. That dashed her hopes of waking up the following day at that marvelous place. Sunny bent to her ear and whispered, "Why do you think the cordon is so marvelous?"

"You need to ask? They have blankets and eggs."

"And? So? Don't we have blankets and eggs here?"

"Didn't they bring them from the cordon?"

"And? SO?"

"Shut up, Sunny! Don't you want to hear?"

"I already know all this."

"But I don't!"

When they could only pass one horse at the Ivory Gates last night, Uncle Triex snuck out and continued on foot. He went to the K'tul military base outside of Paria. That's where he discovered the second K'tul brothel. The first one was at the Parian docks, close to Snakeman's headquarters, which the top K'jen had restyled from the prince's palace into a temple. Much incense burned there.

Uncle Triex presented a vivid image of that temple, complete with the repulsive smell. But Willie's cheeks flushed at the word brothel, not the questionable fragrance. What did Sunny think of *that?* He had not responded in any way. Maybe he didn't know what a brothel was. He was a year younger than herself, after all.

"And how is it you know?" he asked with a whiny tone.

"Aghh, get off my head."

"But you're so loud!"

"No, I'm not! You're eavesing—"

"Yes, you are! And that's not a word."

"It is, too."

No. Yes.

"Hey, you two! You're both loud enough to wake the dead!" Sir bellowed out loud in a menacing tone. "Enough! It's bad enough you're eavesing! Do it quietly. And didn't we say mindspeak **only** in our private frequencies?" That was enough to properly terrify—and quiet them. "And you want these two for your SpyNet?" Sir asked Uncle Triex with a disapproving shake of his head.

"Ahem," Uncle Triex cleared his throat and continued, ignoring Sir's jab. "As I was saying, that was not the important thing at the K'tul base—Crater 1, they call it."

"What was not the important thing?" Sunny asked in Willie's private frequency. *"The brothel?"*

But Uncle Triex continued. In yesterday's logs, he found an entry for Courier 13, an atmospheric ship departing for Hellbound, the K'tul spaceship in their skies. It had to be the one transporting Silvia. King Snowfox had stowed aboard that courier. He had spoken to them two nights ago while on board awaiting its departure. He planned to hijack Hellbound and take Silvia away to end the null. That nothing of the sort happened was not a good sign.

Everyone rushed to object, saying it was way too early to expect results. They reasoned that King Snowfox would need time to get his bearings on Hellbound and measure the enemy. And he was wounded! He may need to heal some to mount his attack.

The depressing news didn't end there. Although Hrysa left for the K'tul base to follow her dad to Hellbound, Uncle Triex found no trace of her there. Again everyone erupted. Maybe she stowed aboard the courier. No. The courier left the base before Hrysa left the Crags. Maybe she took another courier.

"No, there was no other. Many transports, but these ships are incapable of exiting the planet's atmosphere."

"Maybe..."

"Look, I checked the roster. The last courier was the one that left yesterday morning with Silvia and Snowfox on board."

Bleak silence. And there was more. There was no sign of the General, either. "Maybe they'll turn up in the cordon," Sir finally offered. Uncles Triex and Fatie stared at him. More silence.

"Let's plan from here," Sir concluded. "I'm sure they will join us when they can."

"Fine," Uncle Triex agreed. "We," he pointed at Uncle Fatie, "will begin SpyNet immediately. With just the two of us at first," he hastened to add before Sir could object. "We'll warm up Snakeman and make him see the benefit of a fishing project at the Keys. We need a code name for him, Fatie."

"Why? What's wrong with Snakeman?"

"Everyone knows that. They'll know when we talk of him."

"Right. What about *Foureyes*?"

"Perfect. Fatie, you're Strike, and I'm Arrow. Hrysa is still the Brog, Fox is Talon, and George Rock. We need a name for Pete. How about Ink? Shall we go?"

"Ink," Dad objected. But Uncle Triex was eager to begin Ops SpyNet! So was Sunny. He scrambled to his feet to follow, but Willie pulled him back down. She guessed there was more to hear.

"But one more thing," Uncle Triex added. "First, can you marry us," he indicated Willie's ma and himself, "and organize some adoptions? I brought papers. This way, we can bring the kids first, straight into families. The easier to assimilate."

"One hundred plus kids? Easier?" Sir objected.

"Yes. Easier. I didn't say easy. And we must complete all relocations before the census."

"And how soon is that?"

"Soon. We'll delay it as much as possible."

"Fine. Yes, and yes."

"Wait," Ma objected. "What yes? You mean marry *me* to him?" she pointed at Uncle Triex. "The gentleman hasn't proposed."

Uncle Triex went to a knee.

"This is the best part," Sunny whispered in Willie's ear. "Watch and learn."

"You watch a learn. I'm a girl."

"Oh, yeah. I'm watching."

Willie wouldn't believe it if they told it in fairy tales. An hour later, her ma and Uncle Triex got hitched. The few issues got resolved quickly. First, Ma freaked out that she had nothing to wear, but that mattered not. She married the man in her leathers. They lacked provisions to throw another feast. Still, no one cared since they had eaten their breakfast of glorious leftovers, and the groom was to depart promptly for his new spy project.

Then Sir made a meek fuss about the papers not being proper as they didn't address Uncle Triex's other wife. Willie's new dad said it mattered not since she was stuck on the moon with their son, Tiger, that moon's King.

Willie had to conclude that nothing mattered much those days. Sunny bounced off the walls and ate every minute detail with his eyes. Finally, Sir got pacified. They held the hasty, abbreviated ceremony right there in the common cavern as folks hurriedly assembled to attend the event. It was over as the stragglers filed in.

Her new dad handed Sir some papers, kissed Ma on the lips and Willie on the top of her head, ruffled Sunny's hair, and made his exit with his brother, Uncle Fatie. Ma cried the rest of that day.

Two weeks passed before Willie's new dad and Uncle Fatie convinced Foureyes to allow the fishing project at the Keys. Luckily, the catches started bountiful and continued like that.

Uncle Fatie lent his exotic cooking to the K'jen Premier Glory's (Mr. Snakeman's) kitchen, especially to the rare crustaceans the Keys were renowned for. He didn't spare the special marinade he prepared from the homemade cordonite brew (moonshine). They had the chief K'jen witch eating from their hands.

Another week went by before Unc—Dad felt it was safe enough to experiment with the first transfer. The Crags Assembly decided the Prince's family should go first. The Prince was Willie's new dad, Triex. They called Uncle Fatie the Old King, although he was neither old nor fat. He was as young and fit as his brother.

Sir volunteered to go last with Captain Chimeran's archers, which made sense since he was now the Viceroy. The assembly accepted his elevation readily, even when he did not. He attempted to unload it on Uncle, then on Dad, but neither wanted it. They said they could do much more if they stayed away from administrative duties, whatever that meant.

One fine evening, Willie and her ma got a private group mind chat from Dad, alerting them to prepare for the transfer in the morning. "Get the kids ready, love," he said. Love was Ma? When did that happen, and Willie missed it? Did people start loving each other when they got married? Hmm.

Besides Willie and Tommy, the kids included Sunny and two orphan babies Ma and Dad meant to adopt. Where was Sunny? Dad wanted to adopt him, too; in fact, he was the first one Dad wanted, but Sir objected vigorously. Sir wanted Sunny as his own! Willie couldn't fathom that. She thought Sunny annoyed Sir! Sir must have annoyed Sunny, too, because he wouldn't hear of such arrangement.

"I already have two moms and a dad," he would yell and run off. Or, "No! I don't want you for my da," and disappear. When he returned, Willie would ask him where he'd been.

"Paria," he would say, or "the cordon" or "the Crater."

But most nights, he slunk into the common cavern, where Sir waited for him with a plate piled high with Sunny's favorite foods, always with a few sweetments.

"Have you had something to eat today?" Sir would ask. Sunny would always nod yes but then devour the food like he hadn't. And Sir would sit with him and ruffle his hair while he ate.

Without fail, however, when he finished his dinner, Sunny would leave Sir and sneak into Willie's sleeping blankets, beginning to softly snore the moment his head hit the pillow. Willie marveled at such exhaustion.

That night, Sir brought Sunny's food into their private cave, and Sunny ate it like a starving wolf while Sir conversed with Willie's mom. Sunny's antics diverted Willie, so she didn't hear what they said.

In the morning, Dad came to collect them. He had a cart waiting for them at the Keys, but they had to make the trek there on their own wings or the horse Dad brought. Tommy and the two orphans, only a year or two older than her little brother, had to ride with Dad while Willie, her ma, and Sunny flew overhead.

Well, not exactly overhead. It was complicated. Flying was dangerous as it attracted attention from K'tul and their missiles. They had to fly close to the water line and follow the coastline in a zig-zaggy way. Ma was dubious about that, but Sunny was fearless and had done it before. *Countless times,* according to him.

They followed Sunny and arrived at the Keys before Dad and the babies. Sunny made them land on the outskirts of a large village by a rickety little cart with only one horse. A big man stood by it. He turned to them as they landed.

He was so big that Willie took him for Phe'lak at first. But he was Yandar and evenblood like herself and Ma. Of the three Yandar races, evens (even as in evening) were the darkest, but still, their complexion glowed. The man wore his dark red hair in many braids arranged on top of his head. It added to his height. It was so beautiful that Willie stared until Ma elbowed her.

"You must be the first group," he said, approaching them.

"We are," Ma replied. "I'm Nara, Triex's wife, and this is my daughter, Willie. The boy is our Viceroy's ward, Sunny."

"Very pleased to meet you, my lady," the man responded.

My lady? But, yes, Ma was now the Prince's wife. And *Viceroy's ward?* Not son? When had they made that arrangement?

Her Lady, Willie's ma, replied, "My husband brings our three babies—"

"One baby, my lady, the other two are spoken for."

"I don't understand, Sir, spoken for?"

"There is much demand for babies—children—in the cordon. The first two months of our forced segregation, the K'jen couldn't decide what to do with us. They attempted to exterminate us like rats. They poisoned our water. Most of our children perished. Especially the Yendal, being so much smaller and maturing slower. But you must know about Yendal babies, my lady."

"Indeed, I do," Ma confirmed.

"So, my lady, everyone vies for your kids. We started a lottery. Two couples won the rights for the two you bring, but one ceded them when we learned they are siblings so that they can stay together. Are they both Yandar?"

"Ah!" Ma exclaimed, suddenly more amenable to this turn of events. "Yes, both are Yandar. But we have about one hundred kids, and half are Yendal. I take it you have many Yendal families?"

"We do."

"My husband and our Viceroy will work with your Elders to equitable placement. These first two are two and three years old. And please, call me Nara."

Two and three years old? Even the two-year-old was bigger than Tommy, and he was three! And what did they mean by Ma knew about *Yendal* babies? Willie wondered. Could Tommy... But their bio dad still lived when Tommy was born, and he was married to their ma. Oh! Should she think of him as only *her* bio dad?

"I'm Yanus, my lady—I mean, Lady Nara. I was a fisher before the war, so I now lead this expedition to ensure our catches are good enough to pacify the chief witch. Your husband is the most capable Prince we've ever met. Most of us knew him from before the war. I'm sure the Viceroy is as capable?"

"More."

"Hmf!" Sunny scoffed as Willie thought *'more?'* to herself. Who was more capable than her dad?

The adults chatted for a few more minutes until Dad arrived, bringing the horse and the babies.

Sunny, Willie, Nara, the Mouth Cave, the Crags

Past Time: One month after Chapter 1, at the Worldmaker Palace on Yand. Asimia's POV.

4. Singular

*O*ne fine morning about a month after that fated lunch with the dragon, Asimia sat at the kitchen counter with Fox and Luc. She had much on her mind, but the two wolfed down their breakfast and rushed out to hitch a teleport ride to the pastures. They wanted to check on the little colt's progress growing his horn.

Asimia lingered, finishing her coffee alone and musing about her problem: how to manage two chaste marriages to two men. It bothered her since her betrothal. It became impossible to ignore after her first time with Snowfox—and every time after that. And her weddings approached.

To complicate matters, her two betrotheds demanded to live with her. Even Luc, who was the Ruling Prince of Orange. Snowfox already lived with her. She couldn't throw him out of his home just because she married him! She had tried in vain to convince them otherwise, but they felt so strongly about it that they put it in their marriage contracts. Take it or leave it.

What if she left it? Would they tear the papers? She didn't think so but didn't want to test it. It'd cause another mess. But if she accepted it, would living in close quarters cause them to kill each other? Fox said so once, but Asimia didn't think he meant it. He and Lucent seemed to be a little friendlier to each other now.

She searched for a word to describe their predicament. *Strained* was too weak. *Explosive?* Better. *"Powder keg?"* offered Alex with his mouth full. *"Shall I bite them?"*

"No! No biting!" she absent-mindedly told her cat.

The two were more than a girl could ever dream of. Both tall and handsome, Fox with aqua-blue eyes that only the waters at the west of Comi Keys could match. And only in their days of glory, before the K'tul polluted them with mage fires. A silverblood to his core, he was so bright that he'd put your eyes out in darkness. He lit up the night like a million moons and stars in the skies of Yand.

He was an exceptional archer, rivaling their dad, the legend of the Yandar-K'tul war. Fox had commanded the Western Archers during that war. The final battle nearly took Asimia's life. It was Snowfox who carried her to safety, nulled from their mother, and stabbed through the heart by their dad. She lived only because of Fox. She loved him regardless. Always.

Their bond was so strong as to rival Stardust's to Yileen. But Asimia was in a strange predicament with Fox. She managed to overcome her inhibition from growing up with him as sibs to become intimate. But she had to give that up when they married!

Lucent, a goldenblood, shone like the sun! Where Fox lit up the night, Luc blazed brightly around the clock. He'd blind you if something excited him. He was striking with amber eyes and strawberry hair. His wingspan rivaled Fox's, second only to Mom and Granda Blaze, the dragon! But Luc would be forbidden, too.

And if that worry wasn't enough, there was also this: With two exceptional men to dream about and occupy her mind with their woes of chastity, her errand heart turned to another! It was so outrageous! She shouldn't even allow a stray thought, yet her entire mind bent toward this third man on its own.

Infatuation, she told herself again like a million times before, *a crush.* But… He was a grown man when her betrotheds were still teens, although he had not more than two decades on them. Tall and dark, with dark wings that purpled at times and bluish-green eyes, so rare in evenbloods.

His name was Dr. Pietro, a prodigious professor at the U. He achieved tenure at the youngest age ever recorded. He was renowned the worlds over, a fabled geneticist. Asimia, her brothers, and Luc had taken his class, and sometimes attended even now after they graduated.

Forbidden fruit, she told herself. Best to leave him alone. Don't play with the good man. He's always too busy with his scholarly affairs, anyway, his multitudes of techs, labs, and discoveries. No time for even a glance at her. This poor little worldmaker girl who pined…

Sheesh, stop it! The matter at hand? Forbidden fruit. Not the prof. The husbands. The chaste marriages. She needed a solution before she married them, and certainly before the three embarked into the great unknown on their interstellar trek across the heavens.

A loud pop interrupted her thoughts, unmistakably the mage signature of a palace teleporter. Grandma Stardust materialized out of the sparkly pink smoke. No, it wasn't her. It was her herald.

"Her Majesty the Queen, prepare all." Another loud pop, more pink smoke, and now Grandma appeared in truth, in all her splendor, amid the scrambling kitchen staff.

"Sheesh! Did we need the herald?" Asimia exclaimed. "Calm down, everyone," she told the staff. But they didn't. Chef Piere hurried over, sketching elaborate bows and curlicues with one arm while squeezing his belly with the other.

"Your Majesty, at your service! May we prepare you a light breakfast? An early lunch?" All the while streaming orders with his fingers to the folks behind him.

The brandy appeared. "Coffee is better?" Asimia suggested.

"No need for anything, everyone, as you were," Grandma ordered the staffers like she addressed an army assembly. Then to Asimia. "Can you oblige me with transport to Tuncay?"

"Tuncay?" The request surprised Asimia as Grandma lived with a wormhole master. "Where's Uncle Yildiz?"

"The moon. Your folks' unicorn mares foaled."

"They did? Both of them?" This was cause for excitement.

Grandma nodded yes. "One just now—"

"Shall we go see?"

"Ah, no? Tuncay first, please. Give your uncle a little time to get the foal on its legs."

A staffer awaited with the gilded pot of coffee and china. Another still waited with the brandy and elaborate sniffers on a tray. Asimia motioned to the first, and the woman hurried to pour her Queen the perfect cup of joe. The other began to fill the goblets, but Grandma wrested the bottle from him and topped her coffee with the golden liquor. She guzzled it down.

"That bad?" asked Asimia.

"No. Just need the fortification to face my daughter."

"Did Mom summon you?"

"No! Nothing of the sort."

"Grandma, can you help me out?" Asimia blurted. "What does the word chaste mean to you?"

The abruptness of the change in topic surprised Grandma. "I mean, in a contract?" Asimia added.

49

"You mean, like in a marriage contract?"

"Yes."

"Like in *your* marriage contract?"

"Yes! What does it mean?" Asimia exclaimed, exasperated.

"It means no children. What else? Oh, you thought… no! You didn't! Why marry two husbands if you can't…"

"But Grandma, how to have no children if not…"

"There are ways. It shouldn't be so difficult for you. You are a worldmaker, my sweet. You are fertile in twenty years."

"Huh? What does that mean?"

"You can conceive in one year every twenty. That's why your mom had you after twenty years of childless marriages to two men and Sunstorm twenty years after you. But don't tell your dad."

"Oh," Asimia suddenly understood. "Why not tell my dad?"

"For the obvious reason."

"What obvious reason?"

"Men like to think they are… potent."

"And he is. He fathered two children—"

"In twenty years. Two in twenty. Ravenclaw fathered three in three—" Ravenclaw was Asimia's three evenblood brothers' bio father. He was also her dad's friend.

She rallied to her dad's defense, "No, it took Ravenclaw *four* years. And you said it was my mom's biology and not Dad's—"

"Yes, exactly."

"And are you sure all worldmakers—"

"No. But Yileen was like that, as were Yolinda, Yira, and Yanara. Why don't you ask your genetics professor?"

Asimia hadn't expected this turn in the conversation and flashed bright pink like a beacon of adulterous thoughts.

"What?" Grandma asked. "I meant your professor, Dr. Pietro. That dashing, prodigious geneticist boy."

"Boy!" Asimia exclaimed, scandalized, causing Alex to hiss.

Grandma stared. Then, "You like him!" she exclaimed.

Can you turn more pink than flame red?

"Oh, no, now!" Grandma continued once she confirmed her assessment. "Don't do it! Leave it, Asimia. You want a third husband? Trust me, two will keep you on your toes."

"I'll take you to Tuncay now," Asimia attempted to end the conversation, getting up from her chair.

Stardust also rose but grabbed Asimia's hand. "Control your blushes, sweetie, and ask the geneticist for birth control. The twentieth year is long and lasts about three or four. You're eighteen, right? You're getting married during your fertility. And forget about entangling the man. I will not allow risking him in such a voyage and depriving Yand of him, even if I allowed you a third marriage. The young man is singular."

"Singular? How?"

"There is only one of him. I selected a veritable gaggle of scientists to follow us to our new celestial home. Yildiz teases that I emptied the U. and the Academy both. But not randomly. I marked duplicate talent. For example, we have several exceptional physicists. I inked three names in my roster. I did the same for other essential disciplines, subject to the various deans' approval.

"Dr. Pietro is singular. Get what you need from the man, and leave him behind in his peace. Don't discombobulate him, darling."

Asimia nodded. "Can I see your list, please? And I think I'll go to Yenda first to see the foals before I go see the geneticist."

"Of course. I have a copy for you here. Give Yildiz a minute to get the new filly on her legs and take Lucent with you. You ignore him shamelessly. It'd do you both good to spend more time together—alone. He's good. I didn't accept the match for nothing."

Asimia nodded again. "Should I leave you on Turunc? Can you call Mom from there?" Grandma nodded.

She dropped her grandmother on Turunc and returned to Yand instantaneously, not wanting to risk another null with her mom when she came to pick up Grandma. So Asimia returned to her kitchen with the staff still on high alert.

"Shall we prepare a basket for the dragon, my lady?" Chef Piere asked. I do believe it's our turn today."

"No, Piere, thank you, but Uncle Yildiz is busy with the foals on the moon today. Did you hear? My folks' mares foaled."

"We heard, my lady. That is the most exciting news!"

It was indeed! Asimia wormholed to the pasture and found Fox and Luc arms full of mud and unicorn. They couldn't contain their excitement when they heard the news. "I'm going," she told them. "Come, let's all of us go."

Snowfox begged to be excused. "I'll finish up here," he said, "then I have a little more work in the smithy to polish up that new bow. I want it ready to show Da next time he visits."

But Luc was so eager to go that he forgot he was covered in mud. Asimia popped them at the Unicorn Inn by the unicorn pastures on Yenda, surprising the proprietor. "Shall I prepare a room, my lady?" he asked, eyeing Lucent's messy appearance.

Asimia giggled. "Yes, please. What do you think, Luc?"

"Ah, I was hoping to see the foals, Simi!"

"And we will. Let me check." She mindspoke her uncle. "He says not to bring contamination from Yand. Wash thoroughly first; only then can you see this little beauty." It made sense. They lived in fear of spreading disease to the few remaining unicorns.

It was why they isolated this last remaining Yendal herd while growing two new ones on Yand and Tuncay. She even scrubbed Alex to endless growls and hisses. Lucent hurried to clean up and joined Asimia on the balcony. He put an arm around her waist. "It's so beautiful here," he remarked.

"Yes. I don't know why I don't bring us here more often."

"We could honeymoon here," he remarked hopefully.

"Yes," Asimia agreed. "Grandma went to Tuncay this morning to arrange the engagements and weddings, including ours."

"Oh! Ah, that's great. That's so exciting."

"You sound more scared than excited, Luc."

"It'll be fine, dear heart. I worry how it will work out among the three of us. And that chaste thing. How we... I mean, emm..."

He struggled and let it trail. Asimia felt the urge to share. "Ah, my grandma explained it means no children and not no..."

She didn't know how to explain without being too explicit. But he understood. "You mean we can have marital relations but not get you pregnant?"

"Yes. Exactly."

"And is that possible? Will I get instruction?"

"No, silly." Asimia couldn't help but giggle while Lucent blushed bright enough to burn the balcony and the inn. She explained all the things she learned that morning from Grandma.

"Oh," he said, "I can go see Dr. Pietro. He'll need some DNA from you, Simi. Maybe a few hairs."

"No, I'll go," Asimia countered. "It's embarrassing to send one of my husbands."

She teleported them to the new stables in the valley below. They found Uncle Yildiz with the vets and their teams. Lucent couldn't contain himself. He nearly ran over, but Asimia took his wrist and whispered: "Let's stay calm. They're all apprehensive."

He nodded, and she released him. The team parted to allow him a space by the birthing bay. The new filly was indeed a beauty! She shone brightly white dabbled in silver. What an amazing mare she would make! But she was still wobbly and couldn't stand on her own. Unicorns were slower to stand than horses, but it'd been hours!

They spent many hours there. It was well into the afternoon when they remembered lunch, and only because Asimia's stomach rumbled. She had to extricate Luc, who conversed intensely with one of the vets and his two medics.

She teleported them to their room; they cleaned up and went downstairs to grab their lunch. They meant to scrounge something easy, inhale it, and return to the pasture. But the chef awaited them with a spread and a parade of serving staff. "My lady," he said, "we see you so rarely these days. Allow us to serve you a proper lunch."

"Come, darling," Luc chimed in. "Let's have a proper meal. We've inhaled breakfast without as much as tasting it, and I need to spend the night at Orange tonight. We'll still have time for another look at the filly after we eat."

"Who inhaled breakfast?" she teased him. "And won't they have a feast for you at Orange? But let's eat our lunch. Uncle will take the foals to Tuncay soon now that the new one found her legs."

"What a beauty!"

When they finished their meal, Luc pointed at a group of people below their balcony. "Can you guess what they want?"

"I don't know, but I bet you do. And it reminds me, what did the vet want? He seemed so serious."

"Indeed. He's the one to accompany the fillies to Tuncay. He wanted to petition to join our expedition but didn't know how. Plus he worried we would leave before he returned from Tuncay."

"Oh," said Asimia. Does his entire team wish to follow us?"

"Yes, and I wonder if these good people below also wish something like that."

"Let's go see," said Asimia, rising, but he took her wrist.

"Easy, my heart. Let's not spook anyone here. Besides, eat your dessert. You're looking thinner these days."

"I haven't had much appetite lately."

"I noticed. But leave this delectable Bakewell tart? Yum. Here," he offered her a forkful from his plate. She giggled, making him beam. His smile was so warm! "I love your giggles, my heart, to watch you smile," he said.

"Ma Mandolen feeds Mom Yanara pretty much all her food. Don't you start on me!" she teased him with mock severity.

A few forkfuls later, Luc called the proprietor and asked about the people outside. "Oh, please, my lord, lady," the man said, "pay no mind to them. Enjoy your dessert. They can wait."

Luc took charge. And at that moment, before Asimia's eyes, he transformed from a carefree youth to a ruling lord. "Ask them to prepare their petition and send a spokesman," he ordered the proprietor. "My fiancée is lunching with me, and we need to return to the new fillies. We have limited time, but we will be glad to hear them. Tell them to make a list with their skills."

The proprietor's countenance changed, too, becoming reverent. "As you wish, my lord," he replied and withdrew to carry out his order, bowing first.

"A list with their skills?" asked Asimia.

"Yes, indeed." The bright smile returned. "How many folks can you bring in a wormhole? We can't bring them all. We need some equitable measure for choosing who goes and who stays. This will also ensure we bring the proper science, engineering, and craft to our new home without depleting Yand and Yenda."

"Indeed. Do you have a list of our wants? Or is it needs?"

"Both." He brought two papers from his pocket inscribed with the Orange colors. One was titled NEEDS, and the other WANTS. Under NEEDS were the names of doctors, agro engineers, and other essentials. Under WANTS, the names of disciplines Luc found nice to have but not essential to survival, like Chef Piere.

"Can we please move Chef Piere and his staff to the needs?" asked Asimia. "Life can get very boring without them."

"Ah, no worries. We'll take many from the wants list. Seriously, darling, how many can you bring in a wormhole?"

"Not sure. I brought a hundred to Avalanche Pass during the war, so at least that many. I would say a few more. We could count on half as many again, maybe two hundred on a good day."

"Ok, good, it helps me to know that."

"Uncle is a wormhole master, too. He can bring a few—"

"Can you synch wormholes?"

"I don't know. We could practice—"

"Yes, good. Please do. And see how many he can bring."

"Yes, Sir!"

Lucent paused and stared for a moment. Then he relaxed and beamed at her. "I'm sorry, sweetheart, I got carried away."

"No, we need to plan. I'm such an idiot. You're a ruling prince, and Fox a military commander. I should have asked you two to organize."

"No worries. We have been. I made the lists when I was in Orange. We need official Worldmaker paper before we post them."

"Post them?"

"Yes. How else will the folks know what we need and what positions are still available? We'll amend the lists periodically as positions fill up. And we better include an application procedure."

Asimia remembered her grandmother's scientist list. She showed it to Lucent. "Wo!" he exclaimed. "She's more ambitious than me! She's emptying the U and the Academy both."

"That's what Uncle said, too!" Asimia exclaimed. "She's the Queen, no?" Luc nodded and requested a writing implement from an attending staffer. He then delved into reconciling his lists with Grandmom's, scratching out the redundancies.

They enlisted many folks from the eager crowd that day, easily counting to a hundred strong. Lucent allowed a bit of growth to that number, and by the time they left Yenda, the number of Yendal would-be migrants had doubled.

Asimia had one more task to do before the end of that day. She should have gone in the morning but put it off until after the unicorns. Now she dropped Lucent at the prince's palace in Orange and teleported back to Dragonslair, her residence, rather than at the U. *Gods!* What excuse could she find now? No one would come to her aid. She had to do this on her own. Fine. She sat at the kitchen counter and downed a few stiff drinks. There. That was better.

She teleported to the U. without Alex, much to the cat's objections. She popped out in the hall before Professor Pietro's office door. She rapped timidly. Nothing. No answer. Well, she tried. Relieved to a measure but mostly disappointed, she made ready to teleport when the door swung open, and there he was: the prof in all of his... well, emm, usual self.

"My lady," he exclaimed, surprised to see her. "Please come in. To what do I owe this pleasure—I mean honor?"

"Ah, I, emm, I..." Asimia stuttered, "I was about to leave—"

"No, please stay. I was a bit preoccupied, that's all. You have my full attention now. What can I do for you?"

What indeed? He was more handsome and tall in the flesh than in her daydreams. He was easily Snowfox's height, and Fox rivaled their dad and Grandad Blaze, the dragon.

"I'm not so tall as that," said Dr. Pietro.

He could read her thoughts? *Oh, my! Run for the hills.* She turned to go in a panic.

"Please stay," said Dr. Pietro, with a beseeching look on his face. "I didn't mean to intrude in your thoughts."

"But you did?"

"Couldn't help it. I'm a telepath. Please guard what you don't want me to hear. What can I do for you?"

"I, emm, I'm in need of—"

"Birth control?"

"What?" Shock and awe! "How did—"

"Stardust sent me a memo."

"She did?"

"With her herald." This with an amused smile.

No! She killed me with her herald. "And what did she say?"

"That you're too shy to ask, but you need birth control because you marry in your fertile period/year and can't have a worldmaker baby because she'll kill you, you not being such a potent worldmaker."

Oh. My. Gods. Could it be more humiliating? If only the earth would open up and swallow her. "Surely she didn't say that?"

"Yes, she did."

"With her herald?"

"Yes."

"Oh, my gods! I'm so embarrassed!" She must have turned bright pink, or flaming red, because her cheeks burned.

"Please don't be. You would have asked me yourself."

"Yes, but I would have—"

"Beat around the bush first?"

"Well, yes."

"And now there it is. Request made, and you don't need to stress, my lady."

"Please, I'm Asimia. After all this mess, you might as well call me by my name."

"What?"

"Please call me Asimia, Dr. Pietro."

"Fine. Then I'm Pete. Please call me Pete."

Ok, now that they got through the icebreaker—iceberg?— what came next? "Emm—"

"She sent me your hairbrush, but blood is best—"

"Of course."

He pressed a button on the wall behind his desk. "Darryl," he yelled, "Bring a syringe. I need a vial of blood from my guest."

They remained speechless, gazing at anything in the room but each other, until a tech arrived, scrambling with a tray that featured a syringe, among other such. "My lady Worldmaker," the tech pronounced, nearly spilling his tray of instruments. Dr. Piet— Pete righted his hand, saving the precious load.

Asimia offered her arm, and the tech filled his vial with her blood. "What do you want us to do with this, Dr.?" he asked.

"Nothing. Prepare it. I'll do the analysis myself."

"Yourself, Sir?" After a severe glare from his boss, he added, "Yes, of course," gathered his jaw from the floor, inclined his head, and backed out the door.

"Emm, that was it; I best be on my way…" But the Prof— Pete offered her his hand. He didn't say or demand anything. He only offered. She glanced up at him and found his eyes pleading.

"Take my hand?"

She did. He lifted her palm to his lips and kissed it, then cupped his face in it. He closed his eyes and whispered. "Yes, you best go before I break your vows."

Didn't Snowfox say the same thing??

"Break my vows?"

"Kiss you."

"Break them. I haven't taken any vows yet."

Oh, no! Did she say that? He squeezed her in his arms and kissed her passionately. "I love you," he whispered amid kisses. "From the moment you walked through my classroom's door two years ago. Will you take a third husband?"

Oh, my! Asimia hadn't expected this at all! Shocked out of wits and speech, she surrendered to his steamy attention. But hey, she thought. This is great. This is how crushes break. Got what you want, now move along. How did Grandma say it? Get what you need from the man and let him be?

But the crush didn't break with the torrent of kisses. She tried but couldn't leave the man be. In utter dismay, she realized...

"I love you," she whispered, "from the moment you threw that piece of chalk at me for daydreaming in your class."

"Figures," he said. "But you can't take me with you..."

"No."

"Stardust explained it to me in a postscript. I am singular."

"She won't allow me a third husband, either."

"That figures, too."

"How so?"

He let her from his arms. "I should have made my move and proposed the moment you turned eighteen. I blew it. I didn't think I could... You best go now. I'll let you know when I have your stuff."

Asimia returned to her kitchen and got drunk. The following morning, Wolfpack came from Tuncay to arrange for a switcharoo with Mom. That was the crazy name the Dragoons had given the simultaneous exchange of locations via wormholes.

Asimia spent her day on Tuncay with Drace and Squirl while her folks visited Yand. Her non-bio twin, Hawk—she and Hawklord were born a month apart to their two moms—went to Yand with her folks. Something about signing the papers (getting betrothed) with two young ladies in Riverqueen.

At nightfall, Wolfpack brought Fox and Luc, and the news that Mom decided she wanted to spend the night on Yand. The three of them partied with Drace and Squirl, and let's just say the liquor flowed freely. It was a respite Asimia needed sorely.

The next day dawned, and thank goodness they had arranged switcharoo time after coffee. Much coffee. Back on Yand, her boys spent their day doing their usual stuff. She lunched with Uncle Yildiz and the dragon. She then visited extensively with Aunt Shadow, who was very tight-lipped about the folks' visit. Asimia let it slide again. They had dinner with Fox and Luc and then retired to their respective rooms—Aunt Shadow to the infirmary.

Alone in her room, Asimia slipped out of her clothes and into her nightdress when Pete's mindvoice reached her. *"Asimia?"*

"Pete?" she replied.

"I wanted to see if you returned safely."

"I have. Where are you?"

"In my bedroom."

"Are you alone?"

"Yes, as always. Singular... alone..."

She teleported to his coordinates to find him sitting at the edge of his bed in nothing but his boxers. The room was sparsely furnished and lit, but tidy and clean. He stared at her. She let her nightgown drop and straddled him. He took control of her body and kissed her breathlessly. "Should we not wait until after you took your pills? I prepared them."

"How long does it take?"

"A week, two to be certain."

"Do you know that other method of interruption at the end?"

"You mean withdrawal? Yes, but not in this position."

"I love you in any position. Guide me."

"I love you in any position now and always and forever. I can wait for centuries or millennia until our circumstances change. Until I am no longer singular, and you can take a third husband."

"That much? That long?"

"Yes. Just don't forsake me. Don't forget me in any heaven and sky you end up calling your home."

"Never. Ok, then. Always and forever begins now." She laid her head on his shoulder, and he rocked her all night long.

Asimia and Pete in his House

Future Time: Continuing from Chapter 3. Willie's POV.

5. Inside the Line

Willie spent her day with Sunny, helping the fishers haul their nets and traps while Ma played with the babies. It was a team of five adults, including Dad, but Dad was nowhere to be seen. Two tended the lines, and the other two labored with the nets and traps. Yanus proved to be quite adept at keeping the work going and the fish coming. Willie marveled at the size of the catch!

"They laid the traps last night," Sunny informed her. "Don't you know anything?"

"And how would I know that," she retorted, although she did. They did the same at the Crags. Now these ten traps teemed with lobsters.

They took a break for lunch. The Parians fussed over the babies, caressing their cheeks and playing peek-a-poo but also commenting on how skinny the poor things were. Not to worry, the aunties would fatten them up before you knew it.

Sunny took Willie beyond the cove, zig-zagging the coastline amidst the rocks to harvest smaller crustaceans. By sundown, they had their pans filled to the brim. Sunny slurped a few raw and showed Willie how to crack the shells and drink the insides. She was amazed at how good they tasted. They rejoined the adults to find that Dad had returned. It was time to go.

Their cart groaned with the catch. "Will they let us keep some of these?" Willie asked Sunny.

"They always do. Whatever their chef rejects for not being good enough for the K'jen royalty." There were enough winks in that sentence to send him tumbling on his side.

"What does that mean," she asked, but he wouldn't say. She chased after him, chanting, "What? What?"

"Hey, you two!" Ma called. "They're calling us. Gather up."

Their little rickety cart had a false bottom. It was for the scientific equipment, Sunny explained, but they were to hide in there instead this go-around. He said her dad was testing. "Testing what?" she asked him.

"If the K'tul find the false bottom, silly," he replied.

That didn't sound good. It filled her with fear, not that she could do anything about it. They climbed in, Ma first, then Yanus lowered the babies into her arms one at a time. Willie followed them. Sunny made to close the hatch, but Dad shoved him down after the others.

"You're responsible for their safety, okay?" Da told him.

"Yes! Sheesh!" Sunny replied to Dad's glare. "But they counted me on the way up. We're asking for trouble, just saying."

"Do what I tell you, this once! No arguments!"

"Fine!"

"Good. Everyone settled? Give the babies their bottles, love. They need to sleep when we get to the gates."

"I'm doing my best, love," Ma replied.

"Their chef is Uncle Fatie, haha," Sunny told Willie.

"What?"

"That's how we get to eat. Much of this catch is not good enough for Snakeyes and his cronies."

"Oh," Willie exclaimed, but Ma got her attention, ending that conversation. She had Willie and Sunny help feed the babies their bottles. The adults closed the hatch and loaded the carriage above them with the fish. The smell! Ma gave Willie a dab of peppermint paste—where had she gotten it—and another to Sunny.

"Yanus brought them," Sunny informed Willie when he caught her staring at the bottles. "There's spare milk, too, over here if you want some. They have goats at the cordon."

Ma shushed them. Dad hitched the second horse to the wagon, and they started to move. Willie could see the outline of two of their adults on her side through a tiny hole that Sunny had cut into the rickety carriage structure. The men walked by the wagon rather than on it. She wondered how good K'tul were at telling weight.

They went slowly for about an hour when commotion from outside drifted to their ears. Dad's mental voice reached them in private mindchat: *"We're at the Ivory Gates. It's busy; everyone is returning for the night."*

Sunny winked at her and added, *"They work the fields and orchards; that's how we have bread and fruit."*

"Shut up, Sunny," Dad told him. *"Pay attention, this is very important. Be ready to evacuate Willie and the babies if we get stopped, but only on my mark. Got that?"*

"Three babies, Uncle? What if they cry?" Sunny objected.

"You know what to do. Just do it! Now hush!"

"Fine, fine! Just saying!"

"Nara, you best come up on top. They need to count six; you'll stand for Sunny."

"No, love," Ma objected. *"Let the boy come on top; I'll stay with the babies so they don't cry!"*

"Everyone!" Dad mind blasted. *"Do as I say! Now, Nara!"*

Reluctantly, Ma climbed up the false bottom through the fish, and Willie bet that no amount of peppermint paste in the world would take that smell off her. There came a few mild thuds as she rearranged the sushi, as Sunny called their catch.

They progressed even slower after that. Thankfully, the babies had gone to sleep after drinking their milk. Sunny planted his eye in his keyhole and narrated to Willie what he saw. *"Farmers, a group of five, no, six, pickers, a dozen or so, wait, there's more, sheesh, Snakeman must crave them oranges,"* and more of the like.

He paused abruptly and turned to Willie. *"They're all passing us,"* he said. *"That's no good. Get ready."*

Willie's heart jumped to her throat. *"For what?"*

But Sunny had turned his back already and reglued his eye on the peephole. Dad's voice, calm and collected, spoke in K'tul.

"For what, Sunny?" Willie insisted.

"Shush, quiet. They're on to us."

K'tul voices barked at Dad as he continued to converse with them in their language that Willie didn't understand. But Sunny did. He flinched. He winced. He smacked his mouth with both hands to stop himself from exclaiming out loud. "Get the babies," he signed in guard sign, the stealth communication method the Phe'laki Guard used because they could not mindspeak, lacking psychic abilities.

But Willie had petrified in fear. "Get the babies, and don't mindspeak," Sunny signed again, this time right in front of her eyes.

"Three babies!" she signed back, objecting.

"I'll get Della," he offered. Della was the three-year-old girl. "Get the other two." But when Willie inched a shaky hand toward Tommy, the little toddler began to whimper.

"No, quiet," she hushed him, like the baby could read guard sign. He was ready to wail.

Sunny fumbled on the floor in the darkness of their confined space, searching for something, pulling at the boards and throwing slivers of broken wood about. "It's here, somewhere," he signed, "help me find it."

"What are you doing?" Willie replied, terrified.

"The trap door. Willie. We must open it!" He started to kick the floor. A baby cried weakly. The conversation outside paused. Dad's voice piped up again, this time hurried.

Sunny looked at Willie in sheer panic. She rocked Tommy to hush him. Loud thuds outside. Banging at the sides of the carriage. The K'tul looked for their hidden compartment!

"They wrote down a boy. They're looking for me."

"I'm scared!" Willie signed back.

There came a crush, and the head of a giant hammer broke through the side of their wagon by Willie. She dove to the other side and fell onto Sunny, spilling her brother on him and Della. The babies whimpered louder. "I'm scared. Mommy!" Della cried.

Loud, angry voices answered in K'tul. A spear thrust through the opposite side of the carriage and nearly skewered Willie. She rolled back and forth as it gave chase, Sunny frantically pushing and pulling her out of its way. He'd spilled Della, and she Tom. All three babies wailed. Sunny kicked the bottom again as he rolled with her. From the compartment's other side, the hammerhead drew back. A K'tul head burst through the gaping hole.

Willie shut her eyes, waiting for the hammer to smash her head. She twisted instinctively to protect her brother. But the hammer didn't land on her. With a last mighty kick, Sunny cracked the bottom, and Willie fell through it. She hooked a wing talon and hung… sliding, falling. Sunny dove on her, his arms full of babies. *"Blink,"* he mindyelled. The world went blank.

Willie didn't dare breathe. Babies whimpered beside her, or was it underneath her? And did that mean they still lived? All of them? Sunny shook her. "Willie? You good?"

"Yes, where are we?" she breathed.

"Inside the Crimson Gates, behind a rampart."

"Where is that?"

"Paria's third ring. The cordon is inside. But I can't bring us all the way. I don't have safe coordinates."

"Can they see us from above?"

"They haven't yet."

"But I hear them marching!"

"Shhh!"

"What do you mean, coordinates? How did we get here?"

"Can you keep the babies quiet until your dad finds us?"

"And how will he find us?"

"I'll call him now." And before Willie could stop him, he mindcalled Dad. But Dad was still at the Ivory Gates' checkpoint, negotiating with the K'tul sentries. She could hear him in her mind. How? The Ivory Gates were far from here. It went: Ivory, Azul, Crimson, Ebony, and Gold—the five rings of Paria. Karia had seven. A yellow and a Silver went between Ebony and Gold.

Sunny said they were at Crimson. Ah, Willie realized, Dad was mindspeaking at once so they could hear him.

"Some mistake, Sir," Dad told the K'tul soldiers. *"You see? There was nothing below, only more fish. And now you broke our cart! We must mend it quickly if we are to make his Premier Glory's dinner. You don't want to make him wait? Let us pass!"*

Another voice, Uncle Fatie's(!), chimed in. *"Indeed, these are late. Step aside, soldier. What is your rank? Your name? I'll take charge of these folks. His Premier Glory is getting hungry. We don't want to make him cranky!"*

Uncle Fatie had come to save them! Sure enough, the wagon began moving again, although groaning.

"Willie?" came Ma's terrified mindspeak.

"Shush, she's fine, love," Dad told her. *"I can hear them."*

But Ma broke into sobs. *"Shhh! You're a warrior, Nara!"* Dad admonished her. *"Compose yourself. I'll go get the kids. Yanus, take charge of the wagon, bring it to safety."*

"Yes, my lord," Yanus replied.

"I got it from here," added Uncle Fatie. *"Go get the kids!"* And as Dad hesitated, *"Go, man, Hurry. And don your robe."*

His robe? What robe?

"Where are you?" Dad directed his mindspeak to them.

"Inside the Crimson Gates. I don't know where to go from here," Sunny answered him. Was his mindvoice wavering?

"You all good? Send me coordinates. Ah, good. I see. I'll be there in a few minutes. Stay put and make no noise. I mean it."

"Yes. Hurry, Uncle," said Sunny, sounding scared now.

"Hurry, Dad, I'm scared," added Willie.

"Hang on, I'm almost there."

"Don't be scared, Willie," Sunny told her in her specific frequency. He grasped her hand, but she pulled it away.

"I'm not scared!" she projected forcefully when, in truth, she was terrified. Oops! Was that his specific? She didn't want Sunny to take her as a coward. But his hand trembled when he touched hers. She looked at his face and saw so much fear in his eyes. Sunny was more scared than herself! He was a smallish kid, younger than herself, trying hard to screw his courage on.

"Oh, I'm so scared, Sunny," she whispered breathlessly. "Please hold my hand!"

It was all he needed. He grasped her hand so hard that she gasped in pain. She was about to say something, but at that moment, torchlight fell on them from above. K'tul voices carried to their ears: sentries patrolling the crimson walls above their rampant. Sunny pulled them all, Willie and babies, bodily against the crimson stones and shielded them with his body. He was too small to hide them all.

"Hang on," Dad's mindvoice boomed, sounding closer. But they couldn't hang on. The two-year-olds started whimpering again, soon to break into a full wail.

"We gotta move," Sunny projected, dragging Willie by the sleeve. But it was too late. Two large K'jen soldiers jumped from the walls and landed right in front of their faces.

Willie screamed. The babies wailed. The K'jen reached with their clawed hands to pry them from their corner. "What have we here?" one of them hissed in broken Yandar. "Pups! Tender ones!"

K'tul ate kids! Guttural panic overwhelmed Willie. She screamed mindlessly, echoing her high-pitched terror around the walls. *"Maaa!"* She needed to protect the babies, but fear consumed and paralyzed her and made her useless.

The toddlers slipped from her hands and scurried in all directions, wailing to the moon. *"Willie, run, hide, m'girl,"* Ma's mindscream tore Willie's chaotic mind. Sunny darted past her, grabbed her hand, and dragged her behind him as he tore after the todds. They dodged K'tul together, pounding the cobbled pavement, panting hard, and screaming the babies' names. But the K'tul overtook them.

In his last act, before clawed hands grabbed him, Sunny gave Willie a mighty shove at the toddlers and cried, "Run, Willie, run! Dive through the Green Line!"

But what green line? She stumbled from Sunny's push and fell on her face. As she scrambled to regain her feet, she spied green paint splotched on the street! A boundary? The cordon on the other side? With a second wind of terror kicking in her breast, Willie beat her wings and scooped the babies in a sweeping motion by whatever of their little bodies she could grasp. She dove over the paint to crash to the ground again. More cobbled street. She tasted dirt.

What happens now? Am I safe here? She tried to roll to her feet, but her arms and body were full with wailing babies.

"Sunny!" She yelled out loud, louder than she had ever heard herself scream before. But the K'tul had him. "They took Sunny!" she yelled at the top of her lungs. "Help us! Somebody help us!"

"The boy, Triex! They got the boy!" came a mindvoice, distant but powerful and angry. It shook Willie. ***"They've taken my son!"*** It was Sir!

"You stay put now, Pete," Dad yelled back. *"I got this."*

But he didn't have this. K'jen descended on Willie. *"Daa!"* she yelled. *"Save us!"* And a miracle happened. Doors opened to her right, spilling pale lamplight onto the street. A pair of adult hands scooped Willie as others ripped the babies from her. Then, as quickly as they had appeared, the hands dragged her inside a house while another adult slammed the door shut, bolted, and attempted to barricade it—but not fast enough!

K'jen soldiers kicked the door in. Everyone in the room scrambled back, but it was no use. The K'jen herded them all outside, where another K'tul held Sunny by the throat. Sunny had gone limp. "What do you think, O'rksa? Can S'tihsa make a bite out of them?" a K'jen barked in his broken Yandar, pointing at the babies with a naked scimitar.

The K'tul who had Sunny—O'rksa?— spat, "This one here has too much vinegar. He bit me." The others laughed.

They speak in Yandar to scare us more, thought Willie. But she was plenty scared; she didn't need more. Just then, A K'jen officer pushed through. He had many stars on his chest and a whip in his hands. He cracked it over the K'jen sentries, spitting orders in their harsh tongue. He yanked Willie and the toddlers from them.

"What is the meaning of this mess?" He barked at the K'tul. The third K'tul still had Sunny. "Why are these kids outside the line?" He glowered at the K'jen sentries while lowering the wailing toddlers and Willie to the ground. He gave Willie a slight shove toward the adult Yandar. "And what of him?" He shouted, pointing at the listless Sunny. "Give him here."

"Ah, excuse us, Sir, but no. We must bring this trespasser to his Premier Glory to make an example out of him."

"An example of someone as puny as him?" The K'jen officer burst into laughter. "You nuts? You think you can keep your hide after I finish explaining the mess you made here to my boss?"

"Who's your boss?"

"Snakeman."

"You lie. Liar! We best arrest you, too. Maybe you will be good enough for a skinning. The pup's wings and your sickly hide."

The K'jen officer fished something from his pocket. It was a token with a scary lunging snake on it. At the sight of it, the K'jen gang dropped Sunny and backed up. "Please, Sir," they implored the officer. "We didn't know."

"Scat!" he spat after them. "I'll make a personal inspection of this mess inside." He turned his malicious face to the kids. Willie cringed, expecting a quick or savage death. Instead, Sunny, who had miraculously returned from the dead, grabbed her elbow and pulled.

"Come," he said. "Don't you know your own dad?"

The Parian adults led them back inside a house and quickly to the back door. More adults met them. Some took the babies from Dad's arms, rocking and shushing them.

"Come, my lord," an older Yendal woman said. "Your new residence is ready. We've expected you an hour ago."

"We had trouble. Take the kids. I'll stay here in case any more devils show up. Yanus should arrive with the cart soon. They should be unloading the catch at the palace now." He shook his head. "Temple," he corrected himself. "My wife is with them. I may wait for them to arrive before I join you."

"No, Da, please," Willie begged under her breath. Dad got promoted to Da. But he gave her a stare.

"Go with these good folks, kids," he said, "and be at ease. You're safe now."

"Come, Willie," Sunny encouraged her, taking her hand. Da looked at him and winced—Sunny had a cut on his forehead.

"The boy's hurt; please see to him," he told the woman. "I'll never hear the end of it from his dad."

"Who's his dad, my lord?" asked the woman as the others turned to go, bringing the babies in their arms.

"Hey, that one's mine," Da shouted after them. "Don't give him away, now. My wife will have my head!" And to the question about Sunny's dad, "Why, our Viceroy." With that, he turned to go.

"Well, well, Sunny, you're the Viceroy's son?!" the woman exclaimed. "Why didn't you say so? We might've fed you better."

"I'm not his son!" Sunny objected. "I'm only his ward."

"Oh. I bet. Does he mean to keep you close? To control your schemes and machinations?" Her tone had a mock severity. "Is that where you go every night? He feeds you better than Auntie Avalee? And why doesn't he adopt you?" And more.

"No. Yes. I mean, no!" Sunny blurted, struggling to match answers to the woman's barrage. It was comical enough to make Willie giggle. She suddenly realized they spoke aloud, without whispers, mindspeak, or guard sign. And the woman Avalee seemed unafraid and was, in truth, affectionate toward Sunny.

They marched for a few minutes toward the back of the cordon, passing through dark, empty streets and darker houses. At the cordon's depth, a few lamps shone dimly through a window here and there. Finally they arrived at a house that had a little more light.

"This it?" exclaimed Sunny, and made to run ahead, but the woman—Untie Avalee—held onto his hand.

"Not so fast!" she told him. She ushered them inside, where the other women already had the babies. Soon Da came through the door with Ma in tow. Willie jumped into her arms. She smelled so fishy! But Willie didn't care.

Another woman brought a sleeping Tommy and passed him to Ma's eager arms. Ma kissed the baby and cried while Da patted her back and whispered, "It's all good, my love; we made it! All of us." But Ma glared at him so hard that Willie shrank back.

"All good, Master Triex?!" Ma bellowed. "My Lord Triex?! Or should I say My Lord Triexador the Magnificent?"

Sunny took Willie's hand and pulled her to a safe distance in the depths of the room. Two lamps lit it, not too brightly, but Ma's eyes sparkled with anger even in the dimness. But she held back. "We best clean up first," she said. "I stink, as do you! And all the poor kids. We'll talk after that."

"This way, my lady," said Auntie Avalee. She led them to a room with a large tub into the floor with circulating water.

"All of us?" Ma asked.

"You can take turns if you wish, my lady," Auntie replied.

"Nah, no time for that," Ma countered, stripping Tommy's clothes off him. Then, without warning, she shucked hers, too.

"No! Oh, no, no!" Sunny exclaimed, turning his back and covering his eyes.

"In you go, darling," Ma directed Willie while lowering herself and Tommy into the gently bubbling water.

"No, Ma!" Willie balked. She pointed at Sunny with her head. "He… emm, no! Nah!" she shook her head for emphasis.

"Look, honey," said Ma. "He's got his back to us. Hurry and slip into the water." She turned to Sunny. "No peeking now!" He shook his head no, as vigorously as Willie had shaken hers.

Untie Avalee chuckled. "Come, boy," she told Sunny, leading him out of the room. He stumbled behind her with his eyes still closed. "Sensitive age, my lady," she shouted to her back.

"May we please beg for a change of clothes?" Ma called.

"We have them ready for you, my lady, but I may amend them. We didn't expect you to be this thin."

They had sweet soap to scrub the fish smell off their bodies. Ma's temper subsided a little. They left the room as Sunny entered it, escorted by another woman and protesting as he went.

A big commotion followed them—Sunny ensuring no one remained in the room while he bathed. As it was, after he dried and

reclothed himself in new threads, Auntie had to clean more dirt off
his face with a washcloth. And he still smelled of fish. "Sheesh,"
Willie told him. "You still smell. Didn't you use the sweet soap?"

"There was soap?"

"You're hopeless!"

"Am not!" While Willie deliberated the benefits of soap with
Sunny, adults gathered in the front room. It was the biggest room in
the house and had a hearth in it. Sunny dubbed it The Hearth Room.

Uncle Fatie was among the adults, still in his K'jen uniform.
It gave Willie a fright at Sunny's amusement. Yanus and Da, both
cleaned up in fresh clothes, conversed quietly until Ma entered the
room. Da approached her solicitously, but she glared at him.

"How long will she be mad for?" Sunny asked.

"Shh," Willie shushed him. "Let's listen."

"But they'll bring food now."

"To us, too? But not fish, I hope! I'll never eat fish again!"

"Mmm, yum! Sushi!" Sunny teased her.

"Stop it! Ooh, you got stitches!" Willie just noticed that he
had three stitches on his forehead.

"Hurt like hades, too. Still does." He stared expectantly.
"What?"

"Oh, I don't know. It may feel better if you kissed it."

"What? No way. Yuk. Kiss *you?*"

"Why not? And not *me!* Idiot! The stitches!"

"Yuk. No! Sunny. Never."

"Pipe down," came Ma's warning mindspeak. *"They'll
serve dinner now. You can sit with us or eat quietly in your corner."*

"You can see us?" Sunny asked, genuinely surprised.

*"Yes. Me and everyone else. No need to hide. We'll send you
to your room if we don't want you to hear something."*

"We have a room?" Sunny asked. *"Together?"* But food
began parading, diverting his attention.

The adults sat around a long table as two Yandar women
deposited dishes laden with yummy stuff. A Yendal woman brought
plates, and a fourth, also Yendal, cups. The brew was not far behind.

Ma fixed two plates and brought them to their corner. She
said, "There's plenty of food, and not all fish. Eat your fill, but
waste nothing." Not that there was any chance of that with Sunny
around. "You can have seconds if you want them and a sweetment."

Everyone ate in silence for a while. But then Da started to toast their successful First Transfer, and Ma finally lost her top. She erupted! **"Successful!"** she roared. "We nearly lost our kids! Ours and the sweet babies before these good people adopted them! We're not doing this ever again!"

"But honey—"

"There is no but and no honey! We must find another way."

"I can't say I disagree with Nara, Triex," Uncle Fatie took Ma's side. "It was nuts!"

"It was our first time, man! They'll relax. You'll see."

"And why would they? Do they have anything better to do than harass us?"

Da was about to retort but stopped with his mouth half opened and stared at his brother. "That's it!" he exclaimed. "You're a genius! We need to give them something better to do!"

"Like what? You got any ideas?"

"Yes. Let me think on it and make a plan. But I heard today that the greyk'tul who kidnaped Silvia have gone Renegade and are organizing themselves at the Crater."

"Oh? More trouble for us?"

"Unless we divert it. Make it trouble for Snakeman instead! Make his cronies busy and take their eyes off our business."

"I—" Uncle Fatie began but was abruptly interrupted by a violent rap at the door. The adults scrambled, but before anyone made it off their seats, the door flew open, and… a dark creature from one of the gods' hells hopped inside the room.

"SUNNY!" it bellowed. But as Sunny made to bolt, it turned to the adults at the table. "You will do **NO SUCH THING AGAIN! EVER!!**" It spoke to Da: "You get me, Triex? **Where's my son!**"

It was Sir!

"Pete?!" exclaimed Da, Ma, and Uncle Fatie.

"Do what?" asked Da.

"Your so-called transfer!"

"For gods' sake?!" Da bellowed. "How did you get here? Didn't we agree—"

"Not in your fish cart!" shouted Sir. "I flew. The same way Snowfox did when he first brought you here a month ago. If he can do it, why not I? I have the advantage over him. He glows in the dark when I'm a dark man in all the blackness of this blessed place.

So you bring us from freedom to this?" And much, much more. He traversed the room while he talked to… stop before her and Sunny.

Sunny stared petrified with eyes like saucers. "My boy?" Sir exclaimed. "Are you hurt?" His tone dramatically softened when he addressed Sunny. He scrutinized him and settled on the stitches on his brow. "You got stitches! You're hurt! Come here!"

He scooped Sunny into his arms. Shock of all shockers, Sunny went limp in Sir's embrace. The adults finished scrambling from the table and followed Sir to the corner. Willie made to vanish, but Da lifted her in his arms and brought her to the table.

Fatie dragged the frazzled Sir to the table as well. He went on to introduce him to the Parians as their Viceroy, Pete—Dr. Pietro—the renowned geneticist.

To Willie's amazement, Sunny relaxed on Sir's lap. He laid his head on Sir's shoulder and sucked his thumb like a baby! She settled on *her* da's lap but didn't lay her head on his shoulder nor suck her thumb. As she caught a glance in Sunny's direction, he winked at her and said in her mind: *"We can hear better this way."*

"I have a better way for the transfer," said Sir. I'll explain after this scamp goes to sleep." Sunny started to snore softly.

Everyone was all too familiar with Sunny's schemes and didn't get fooled by his fake snoring. However, Auntie Avalee led Sir, who brought Sunny in his arms, to a bedroom. Tommy already snoozed there, under the watch of a nanny! Da followed with Willie, depositing her on the soft bed beside Sunny.

"Shall we betroth these two?" asked Sir.

What? No! Willie thought as Sunny put in her mind, *"Yuk, no way! When all hells freeze over."*

"You think? Da replied. "Sometimes it seems they may yet kill each other before we reach that point."

With a chuckle, Da and Sir departed. Sunny continued his fake snores. On impulse, Willie laid a soft kiss on his stitches.

"Oh, yuk!" he exclaimed. "Ptoo! Ptooewy! What did you do that for?"

"Did you not ask me to kiss you?"

"I did not do such a thing! I'd never!"

"Sheesh. Hush! It was only the stitches. Good gods!"

"Ah, ok, then. But don't do it again."

"Never!" Willie vowed.

Willie and Sunny with the Fish Cart at the Keys

Past Time: At the Worldmaker Palace on Yand. A month after Chapter 3 Snowfox's POV.

6. Snowfox

*O*ne bright morning a month later, Snowfox visited his aunt Shadow at the infirmary like he always did on his way to the training field. This morning, he had a surprise for her. Her fiancé, Flash, lay half-asleep on a cot beside her medic bed. They had given him a room in the Kids' Wing, but he still slept beside his beloved.

Aunt Shadow had recovered some from the horrific injuries she suffered in Asimia's defense. She could walk on her own with a cane, although slowly, but still didn't have the use of her wings.

He found her awake, reading a book. She glanced from its leaves to welcome him. "Did you know the phrase *tornado attack* originated from our first queen, Stardust's great-grandmother?" she rasped. Her vocal cords had not yet recovered fully.

"Did it? That long ago? And there I thought *I* invented it?"

They chuckled softly. Aunt went into a coughing fit. "How would you like to come inspect a few of those in the flesh?" he asked her. "I'm on my way to the field for a little serious practice."

"You've found your replacement?" asked Aunt. He had retained his command of the planet's Archer Ops, although he had attempted to yield it at the end of the war. His grandmother, Queen Stardust, wouldn't hear of it. Now he trained his successor, a woman of mixed DNA. She was also reluctant to assume the mantle, as every other one of his attempted recruits.

"Chimeran?" he offered, not too confidently.

"Oh."

"You disapprove?"

"No one else?"

"No. They all wish to follow me to the stars." He smiled. "But seriously, what's wrong with Chimé?"

"She's fierce. And command material, for sure. But as a trainer? She's always the last to launch and struggles to find her line. Her banks are untidy, and she tends to shoot first, aim second."

"That bad?"

"No. She'll do fine. I'm excited. Shall we take the horses?"

"No. You shouldn't ride yet. I'll fly you."

"What? How?"

"On my back. Come, you'll see." He pulled her gently upward by both arms, until her head rested on his shoulder.

"No coffee, first?" Her mouth was next to his ear.

"I thought we could get some breakfast at the canteen? We can watch from there, in the shade."

"Won't they need you on the field?"

"I can shout in their brains right enough from the bleachers."

She laughed. "Oh, boy, this is going to be fun."

He maneuvered his back to his aunt and guided her arms around his neck. She caught on.

"I hold on for dear life?"

"Yes. Vice grip."

He half-rose from the bed, lifting his aunt onto his back. He hoisted her legs about his waist, securing them with his forearms under them. He closed his hands tightly around her knees.

"Ouch," she exclaimed. "Don't break them again. They've barely mended." That *ouch* woke up the medic from his snooze. He had a glance their way, freaked out, and scurried out the door.

"Oops, sorry, Aunt." Snowfox apologized, loosening his hold a little. "Is this better?"

"Yes, but barely. Is this a good idea, my darling?"

"Yes, it is, you'll see. Here we go."

"My gods, Fox," she whispered, "when did you grow this much, and I missed it? You're every bit as tall as your dad and at least as strong!"

"Yes, and may pass him. You think he can survive that?"

"Him? No way. We'll never hear the end of it."

Chuckling softly, Snowfox walked outside. He fell onto the doctor, who hustled ahead of the panting medic.

"No, you don't! Put her back down now. In her bed. Now!"

"We're taking a short flight, Doc. No worries."

"My lord, Flash!" the doctor yelled past Snowfox's shoulder. "My lord Snowfox is taking your fiancée. Help, please!" As Flash stirred to the doctor's summons, Snowfox beat his wings and rose vertically off the ground.

His foxes jumped about him. *"You guys stay,"* he told them.

"Take us, Fox," they both yelped, barking.

"The kitchen is fixing delicious snacks for you," Snowfox replied, having anticipated their antics. *"And juice. Go see!"*

"Just fish," Snowdrift complained, jumping higher.

"Behave, and I'll take you to Tuncay this afternoon."

"Tuncay! Tuncay!" the foxes picked up the chant. Satisfied that his foxes would behave in his absence, Snowfox righted himself, veered left, left-banked sharply, and launched to the sky.

"Ah, this feels so good!" Aunt shouted in his ear. You've always been the best flyer, Fox!"

"Nah, Wolfpack puts me to shame."

Aunt Shadow giggled. "Where's Asimia?" she asked. Shouldn't you two be spending all your time together now?"

"You've noticed?"

"Her frequent absences?"

"Yes. She's sneaking around with Pete."

"Who's Pete?"

"Professor Pietro, the geneticist."

"What? How do you mean? I knew she went to ask him for…" She let that trail as if not wanting to embarrass her nephew.

"Yes, she did. For birth control. But you know it's more than that. She's having an affair with him. Haven't you guessed?"

"I wondered. But no, I didn't know for sure. It doesn't bother you?" She sounded curious and amazed.

"It does. It tears my heart out."

"Then do something. Why do you let it continue? It's so unbecoming of her station… and yours. End it, Fox!"

"I will do no such thing."

"And why not? Are you not her husband?"

"No. Not yet. And when I am… I do not own her, Auntie. Nor do I want her to stay with me out of anything else but her own free will and choice. I will make sure she knows that."

"But how did such a thing come to pass? Does she not love you? Is she not bonded to you?"

"She does, and she is. But we were sibs a few months ago."

"You think that's the reason? She's inhibited?"

"Yes. Mom explained it to me. You don't wake up one morning and think of your brother as your husband."

"And when did you know you loved her this way? I mean, like a mate, not like a sister."

"I'm not entirely sure. I always adored her. About two years ago. I think. Grandma appointed Dr. Pietro as head geneticist at the U. with tenure—a title he fully deserved. He quickly became renowned the planet over and the moon. Every youth from every prominent family flocked to take his class. So did we.

"All five of us went. And Luc, too. That's where we first met him. So there Professor Pietro was, tall, dark, handsome, exciting. A dashing, unrelated, eligible *man,* when I was her brother, a teen with not much to offer her that she didn't already have."

"Oh," Aunt Shadow said. "She loved him that long?"

"Yes. More than two years now. When she turned eighteen, I proposed to her, hoping I was first and not second. I was first, but she didn't want me. I confused her utterly. I was still her brother, despite that she loved me—how she loved me."

"But she loves you, now? Like a husband, I mean?"

"Indeed she does."

"Are you sure?"

"I am.

"How? Oh, You've clipped her wings?!"

They used that expression to indicate the first time of intimacy. They never meant it in a vulgar way.

"I have."

"Honey, how do you know—"

"That it's not guilt? Because she hadn't gone to him yet. I mean, before our first time."

"Your first time? You mean… you and her… many times?"

"We sleep together every night, Auntie. And no, it's not guilt. She loves me. But here we are."

They arrived at the training field. He had spiraled over the city to lengthen their flight, thinking his aunt may enjoy being airborne again, albeit on another's wings. Plus, it allowed them to finish their conversation and get all this stuff off his chest.

"You think she's cooling with him?" Aunt asked as Snowfox planted his feet on soil.

"Nah, no." Aunt attempted to climb down from his back, but he held her firm. "Hold on, I'll take you up the stairs. I reserved us the best balcony seat."

He climbed the two sets of stairs to the top level of the canteen's dining hall. They had rebuilt the canteen bigger and grander after the war destroyed it to rubble. They added another story and a semicircular balcony affording a view of the entire training field that sprawled beyond the building.

He walked to a reserved table in the best private corner of the balcony and lowered his aunt by a chair. He hustled to pull the seat for her, but another beat him to it. It was Flash. "I took the straight flight route," he said, smiling. "Or has she gained so much weight from all my feedings?"

"Hmf," Snowfox remarked. "She weighs nothing, and you feed her air. I thought I'd bring her here away from prying eyes and feed her a hardy breakfast with real food in it."

Aunt Shadow laughed. "And here it is," Flash remarked, pointing at a serving staffer approaching them with a large tray.

They spent the entire day at the field. Snowfox became personally involved in training the new recruits and witnessed firsthand how poorly suited Chimeran was for the job. *I need to train the trainer,* he thought to himself. *How long do I have?*

Sweaty and smelly, he rejoined his aunt and Flash on the balcony. He thought to offer his back again but saw how exhausted Aunt was, so he agreed to the military teleporter mage. He summoned the man, and a pop later, they found themselves in their courtyard outside the infirmary. Flash scooped his fiancée in his arms and headed there while Snowfox made for the kitchen.

"I'll send a tray," he called behind him as his foxes ran to greet him, jumping around his legs. "You have to let me walk!" he told them. "Make sure she eats every bite!" he yelled back at Flash. "She needs her strength, and gods know the world needs *her.*"

He worried plenty about this point. With his folks on Tuncay and he and his grandma, Queen Stardust, leaving Yand, they emptied the planet of its military leadership. *But Hawk is coming,* he reassured himself like every other time he had these thoughts.

Plus, when Asimia and the null left, Mom could return— although he knew in his heart that his mom, ma, da, and brothers would not return. Yand was no longer their family's home. Tuncay was. The war uprooted and displaced them, even when they survived it.

He passed by the kitchen and ordered food for Aunt Shadow and Flash to the infirmary, and he hit the shower. When he came out, smelling clean with that citrusy stuff Asimia kept, he found her and Uncle Yildiz waiting for him in the kitchen, sipping on cocktails. Simi got up and gave him a sweet kiss on the cheek like she missed him. Like she meant it. She fixed him a drink.

"Ready for Tuncay?" Uncle asked him. "Or would you rather take your lunch first? The staff say you haven't yet."

"We lingered at the field. I was testing Chimé."

"And how did she do?" asked Asimia.

"A little better than miserably. She's a fierce warrior and maybe command material, but no trainer. I think Hawk will have to assume that role for a while after we leave."

"Let's take Chimé with us, then," Asimia offered. "She turned in her petition, no? By the way, do you know what happened with Hawk's betrothals? Did he break them?"

"Ah, that would be yes and yes. Chimé and all of my archers turned in their petitions. And many more flyers. We'll empty the world. Stardust will not allow it, even if we could take them all. And you're not really surprised about Hawk, are you?"

Asimia shook her head. "No, not really. He's utterly stuck on the one he lost in the war. But let's ask him about the archers."

"Of course. And I'll see if I can pry a bit more information about our folks, too. They insist on meeting me at the Keys as if hiding something or something is happening at Highwings they don't want me to see. I worry they had an accident, and Wolfpack may be injured. I haven't seen him for a couple of weeks. Uncle Yildiz, have you heard something?"

"There was a fire, and Wolfpack burned his hands and face."

"What? And you didn't tell us, Uncle!" Asimia erupted while Snowfox lost his voice. He struggled against a flood of emotions as horror spread through his heart to his limbs.

"Please," Asimia begged their uncle. "What happened?"

"Look, I don't know much. Your folks don't want you to worry; Wolfpack is mending well. I bet we'll see him today."

"I better," Snowfox muttered. "Let's go, please."

"Eat something first, Fox," said Asimia, offering him a few bites from the small plates on the counter.

"Ah, leave it, love. Let's go, please, Uncle. Have a good day, Simi, and I'll see you tonight?"

"I wish I could come. Please don't linger long. I'm worried about Wolfpack. Hurry back with the news."

Snowfox stared. Did she mean that? *Hurry back?* She looked sincere, except he knew how she would spend her afternoon. His foxes, Snowdrift and Hunter, jumped into his backpack, their usual mode of transportation. "Of course, love," he told her, then dove into Uncle Yildiz's wormhole.

Wolfpack waited for them at his barrack at the Keys, with Mouse and the wolves. Snowdrift and Hunter delighted to see them and took to jumping around them and yelping excitedly. "Come, boys, kits," Mouse called to the wolves and foxes, leading them and Uncle Yildiz outside to give Snowfox and his brother privacy.

The barrack was such an improvement from the tent Snowfox had shared with Wolfpack and Mouse a few months back when he helped settle this fishing village. But Wolfpack lay semi-reclined on his bed in shadow when the room was not. Had Mouse spelled him? So Fox wouldn't see him clearly? He cautiously approached his brother's bed, fearing what to see… and oh, gods!

He had seen countless battle wounds in the war, and surely this was one such. *"Mage* fire!" he murmured. "You thought you could keep it from me? What the heck happened?"

He helped his brother sit up, supporting him in his arms from his back. The motion caused Wolfpack pain. ***"Mom!"*** Snowfox mindyelled in his mom Yanara's brain. He forgot himself momentarily and let his rage pour through that mental call.

"Snowfox?" came her answer. Momentarily, the room filled with his folks, plus Dr. Gregory.

"Everyone out," the doctor shouted, and surprisingly, everyone obeyed—except for Snowfox.

"What happened, Doc?" he asked when everyone else had filed out of the room.

"There was a fire. My lord Wolfpack rushed in to save your… father…"

"My father! Rats in hell, Doc! Dad always saves us!"

"Not this time, Fox," Wolfpack whispered with burned vocal cords. "Leave it, please. I promise to tell you all the details later, at a more appropriate time. I should be at the infirmary, but I snuck here to see you and to offer you my petition. I wish to helm your expedition."

"Oh, my dear gods! You're a mess. Now I'm thinking of canceling the blasted trip. Can't leave *you* behind, my baby brother, and Yand and Tuncay in such predicaments." Emotion overwhelmed him. "You get better, and I'll move back in with you here at these Keys, and we can be happy and carefree again. Only worry about fish and mudslides, not geneticists and potential celestial disasters."

"It's ok, Fox. The doc assures I'll be on my feet in a month." The doctor nodded vigorously. He was their family doctor, the one who delivered every one of them kids, except for Fox, whom Mom adopted as a newborn. That made him family, not only a physician.

"And then I will come with you," Wolfpack continued, "on your celestial voyage. The passage to your destination will not be so easy, bringing so many folks and stuff. Believe me, you'll need *me.*"

"But the dragon found the way easy. He said—"

"They went on a wormhole of the strongest wormhole master ever to grace the universe, our gramma Yira, with only two passengers in it. How many do you bring?"

"We have more than two thousand petitions."

"How many wormhole masters."

"Two."

"How strong is Uncle Yildiz?"

"He doesn't know. Only once, he brought a vet, you, Mouse, a couple of med staffers, two unicorn mares, two foals, and himself. He travels alone or with one passenger or two the rest of the time."

"We need to test him. And Simi, too. And you'll need *me.*"

Wolfpack's voice faded and trailed. "I tested the way to Grandad's planet," he continued quietly. "I wanted a preview. It was not difficult for me, but I felt a temporal aspect as I entered Draco. It makes me worry when we bring hundreds of people in a wormhole."

His body went limp in Snowfox's arms. "Oh, my!" Snowfox exclaimed. "Is that how you got hurt?"

Wolfpack remained quiet, breathing with difficulty. The doctor brought him an oxygen line. Snowfox didn't press the point. "Oh, how to embrace you?" he asked instead. He wanted to hug his brother, to comfort him and himself, but anywhere he attempted to hold was an open wound. The shoulders, the arms. He couldn't even caress his brother's face.

He reached an arm behind Wolfpack's back and eased him onto his soft pillows. Not knowing what else to do for his brother, he knelt before his bed, cupped his face in his hands, and cried.

"I have pain meds, Fox," the doctor whispered, tapping him on the shoulder. Snowfox parted from the bed, and the doctor helped Wolfpack swallow his meds.

A few moments later, Wolfpack's mindvoice reached Fox: *"The anomaly didn't do this to me. Please don't despair, my Fox. Simi loves you. I know this as a brother and as a pathfinder. Give her a moment to breathe. She's adjusting. And you know she loved Pete before she knew she loved you this way.*

"And Pete is honorable and levelheaded. I know him well. He wouldn't do anything to hurt her. Or you."

Snowfox lifted his head and looked at his brother. *"I'm doing my best,"* he said softly, *"finding my way, too."*

"I know you think you're doing your best, but you can do better. You need to take charge. The expedition needs a leader. A real army commander, and I don't mean Gramma Stardust. Run it like a military expedition until we get there and for the first two or three years after landing. Then switch it to the Queen."

"Stardust?"

"Simi. And you need me to helm the wormholes. Or you risk never getting there if some issue arises from that temporal event. That risk could be dire. You may lose many people, if not all. Can you live with that? Promise me so I can go to sleep and get some relief from this pain. Or I waste the good doctor's meds."

"I promise."

"Mouse!" Wolfpack mindyelled, and Mouse stepped inside and whisked him, herself, the doc, the doc's entourage, and the wolves back to the med center at Highwings.

Uncle Yildiz entered the barrack and clapped Snowfox on the shoulder. "Cone, my boy," he whispered. Compose yourself, and let's not cause your folks more pain. I'll tell you all in due time."

Snowfox spent the entire afternoon with his folks but struggled to stay composed. At some point, Drace and Squirl made their appearance, their mage signatures so similar that Snowfox couldn't tell them apart. One of them fetched Sunstorm and his nanny, Enamelia.

But the baby! He did much to brighten Snowfox's misery. He was a year old now and got more scampish as he went. He pointed at his big brother and leaped into his arms. He patted Fox's face with both tiny hands and planted exaggerated smooches on his cheeks. Oh, how he was going to miss his boy!

"Fly? Fotsie fly?"

"Can we?" Snowfox asked, looking around to see which adult would give his permission. He settled on Dad.

"Yes, but not on your back. He can't hold on properly. You have to sit him on your shoulders and grasp his legs. Do you remember how I carried you? Here, let me remind you." To endless giggles and squirms from the baby, Dad instructed his eldest son how to give their youngest a proper flight ride.

When Uncle Yildiz returned them to the residence on Yand, Asimia all but jumped into their arms. "I'm going crazy over here, she exclaimed. How's Wolfpack! Come, tell."

They had landed in the courtyard, and she ushered them to the kitchen. The foxes bounded after them. Yildiz begged to be excused and left them. Snowfox recounted Tuncay's news—all that he knew—to Asimia. They both thought there was much more to Wolfpack's story but decided to hold their peace for now. Not that there was anything they could do at this distance.

Lucent joined them for dinner. Snowfox had skipped lunch and refused the snacks they offered him at Tuncay, being out of sorts. So he was hungry now but couldn't face another fish.

"Please, Pierre," he begged the chef. "Something light tonight, and no fish for me."

"Hold all the fish, please," added Asimia.

"For me, too," Lucent agreed. "You two look upset."

Asimia patted his hand and said, "Something, some accident happened on Tuncay, and Wolfpack was hurt—"

Lucent turned to Snowfox with dismay and concern plain on his face. But didn't get his question out. Snowfox was faster. "Shall we leave it till morning? I'm exhausted and still want to discuss some business with you tonight.

"Yes, of course. What business?" Lucent had spent his day at Orange conducting the province's business.

"Not that kind of business," Snowfox replied, "but now that I'm thinking of it, have you tapped your successor?"

"Yes. Not officially, but yes." Luc had planned to pass the principality's reign to his sister, but two days ago, she foiled his plans by declaring her intent to follow him on his journey. In fact, his whole immediate family threw in their petition, along with their entire household. Luc turned to his paternal uncle, but the man was reluctant and took his time thinking about it.

"That's good. Your uncle?"

"As a proxy to his son until the boy's majority. We gathered the tutors. The poor kid will know no childhood."

"Are you worried?" Asimia asked.

"Yes, my sweetheart. He's an untested small boy. Who can guess how he'll grow?"

"But meanwhile your uncle is most capable," said Snowfox.

"Indeed! More than myself."

"Look," offered Asimia. "Once we settle in our new home, I can bring you for spells to check on the boy."

"That's a great idea," added Snowfox. "Retain the rights."

Lucent nodded. "I have. And I like to lay a claim to a large province on Phe'lak to call Orange with my sister as Ruling Princess. Flat and mild will be best."

"Granted," said Snowfox, registering that Luc had asked *his* permission. Not Asimia's. He glanced at Asimia, but she didn't give the minutest flinch. In fact, the opposite. She appeared... relieved?

Take charge, Wolfpack said. *The expedition needs a leader and your family a head.*

"I claim leadership of our expedition. I propose the name The Grand Yandar Migration. Any objection?"

"About time!" Lucent exclaimed loudly. "We needed something to lift our spirits. He turned to a staffer. "Could we please kindly have something appropriate for a good toast?"

"What's wrong with the brandy?" Asimia asked.

"We drink that all the time—"

"Asimia? You?" Snowfox asked.

"About time, my love." She raised her glass. "To our leader, Commander Snowfox, the Legend of Avalanche Pass, and all of Yand." She amended, "Indeed, just Legend."

"Indeed," seconded Lucent. "And to the Grand Yandar Migration!"

"Good. Then this is my first act as leader. I appoint Wolfpack, the Pathfinder, to helm the wormholes. For he always finds the true path and is the keeper of time."

He didn't know what made him pronounce this last quality, 'keeper of time.' But somehow it felt appropriate.

"True Path" and "Keeper of Time," Asimia and Lucent seconded. The kitchen staff erupted in whoops, exclamations, and much clapping. The chant "Keeper of Time" dominated, timid at first but grew to thunderous. Alerted to the chants, Flash joined them from the infirmary, bringing Aunt Shadow. "Keeper of Time," they, too, joined in. And "Snowfox, Legend!"

"Asimia?" Snowfox asked his beloved. She had been the assumed leader of this expedition, ranking them all militarily as the planet's worldmaker. She was also the lead wormhole master. Now he stripped her of both.

"I'm so relieved, my love," she said in his head as the chanting drowned spoken words. *"Who better to lead us? The legendary Commander Snowfox and the Singular Pathfinder and Keeper of Time, Wolfpack. But I'm worried that he's so hurt."*

"Right. We'll wait for him to recover. Don't fear on that front. Doctor Gregory assured me he'll make a true recovery. But how is it that this time attribute comes to our minds?"

"About Wolfpack? I don't know. He only just mastered wormholes, and with difficulty. But you saw him during my rescue. I would have been lost without him. Did you not feel his power? And something unmistakably temporal about it?"

"I did. All of that. Good. Then it's settled." Then, "Good, everyone," he shouted above the uproar. "Piere, please serve a good round of the toasting wine to all. Then I'll ask you to withdraw and allow me some privacy with my family."

After a few rounds of hearty toasts, kitchen staffers brought the dinner dishes and spread them artfully about the counter. With everything set, they began to exit the kitchen. Flash and Aunt Shadow made to follow them, but Snowfox stopped them.

"Please, I need a witness," he told them.

"Let me bring your Aunt to the infirmary, and I'll return shortly. Do you need the scribe?"

"Eventually."

"You realize now the petitions will double," Lucent commented with a huge smile. "No, triple, quadruple."

Asimia giggled. "Yes, indeed," Snowfox agreed. "Which brings me to my second act as leader. We will test our wormhole masters' capability, determine how many folks they can bring in each wormhole, and allow that to guide our numbers. And we'll use Luc's system for prioritization of disciplines."

Asimia nodded vigorously. "Another huge relief, my love. It's also the combined mass, not only the number. But yes. We absolutely need to do that."

"Good. I'm famished. Shall we eat while we turn to our next subject?"

"Yes. What's the next subject?" asked Lucent.

"Our wedding vows. We need to amend them."

"What?" Luc nearly choked on his olive bread. "I'll need more liquor for this part. Sheesh, Fox, you sent everyone away."

Asimia glanced at Snowfox nervously, got up from her perch at the counter, and went to the bar corner. Alex followed her, stretching and yawning irritably. The foxes, too, bounded after her. She returned with two bottles. She handed one to Luc. "Keep it," she told him with a pat on his shoulder. Then she turned to Snowfox. "Eat a few bites first."

And so he did. He cleaned his plate in no time flat. Lucent got a head start on the drinking. Both he and Asimia regarded Snowfox apprehensively. "I claim this family as my own," Snowfox declared, slowly, deliberately.

"Well, about time!" Lucent exclaimed, looking relieved. "Was that it? You killed us!" Then he turned to Asimia, "Sorry, sweetheart, did you wish to claim the head?"

"No," she declared, shaking her hands before her for emphasis. "This is very good."

"Do you give us a name?" Luc asked him, looking expectant.

"I was hoping we could still use our wife's title. It's so much better than mine. What do you say, love? Can we be *The Worldmaker's Family,* with me at the head?"

"Yes! That's perfect, Fox!" Asimia agreed.

"Good. Then let's continue with logistics. My birthday is coming up in two months. I propose we hold our wedding the day after. Naturally, the engagement will go before that, at any time now. Agreed?"

"Yes."

"Now our contracts. First, the word chaste. I amend it to mean no children and only apply to Asimia. Luc, you—"

"Wait, what do you mean apply only to Asimia?" Lucent interrupted him.

"I mean, she got birth control from our friend Pete, the geneticist." He saw Asimia wince.

"I know that much," said Lucent. "But... if Asimia has no children, how could we... wouldn't it mean that we would have no children either?"

Snowfox stared. "How old are you?"

"Huh?"

"Let me finish this part. Lucent, I will allow you a second wife, and this is how—" You could have children without Asimia, he was about to say, but Lucent erupted.

"No! What are you doing, Fox? I will take no other wife. I want no one else."

"Fine. I'm covering all possibilities. Now is the time since we're amending. I declare that any and all extramarital children fathered by Lucent are the children of my family and have Asimia as Mother and Lucent and Snowfox as Fathers."

"There won't be any extramarital children, man! Did you not hear me?" The Prince of Orange was scandalized.

"It gives you latitudes, Luc. Accept it. No one is forcing you to do it."

"Ok, fine."

"Asimia."

"Yes?" The love of his life looked at him apprehensively.

"I will allow a third husband—"

"What?" both Asimia and Lucent exclaimed together.

"Snowfox," Asimia muttered, "I want no third husband—"

"Stop this nonsense," shouted Luc. She wants no other—"

Snowfox put his hand up and silenced them. "Let me finish. Forever is a very long time. So you two think in those terms.

Asimia. A third husband, but not in long distance. You know who we can take with us and who we cannot. Don't destroy the man. He deserves the chance to have his own family. And we can bring him to visit us on Phe'lak for prolonged periods, but not more than a year or two.

"I mean for now. We will amend this when circumstances change. Is it acceptable?"

"Fox—"

"Is it acceptable?"

"It's more than generous. You humble me."

"What just happened?" asked Lucent. "Did our wife accept a third husband?"

"No," said Asimia.

"Not now," Snowfox said at the same time.

Lucent breathed a sigh of relief.

"Ok," Snowfox marched on. "That leaves me. I will take no other wife and father no extramarital children."

Asimia winced. Lucent objected, "But didn't you say... I mean, what if—"

"Right. The next clause covers all what-ifs. Any extramarital children, even accidental, belong completely to this family. Better?"

Luc accepted that.

"Now for our honeymoons. There will be two honeymoons to span one week. We can't linger longer than that. I'm eager to depart on our expedition. Are you not?" They both nodded.

"Ok, Lucent and Asimia, you two go first and take four days. Take him somewhere nice, love. You neglect him shamelessly."

"Wait!" Luc exclaimed. "You're giving me first rights?"

"Yes. Do you not want them?"

"I do! Oh, I do, but—"

"Then accept before I change my mind."

"I accept!"

"Asimia?" She nodded yes.

"Asimia and I will follow with three days. I would like to go to a picturesque village by Avalanche Pass. Do you think you can take me there, love?"

"Yes, my love," Asimia confirmed, wiping a tear. And in his head, *"You're a much better man than I deserve!"*

Snowfox Carrying Shadow, Worldmaker Palace

Future Time: At the cordon in Paria, continuing from Chapter 5. Willie's POV.

7. SpyNet

Willie wasn't sure how long they slept, but Sir entered the kids' bedroom at some point and lifted Sunny in his arms. No one summoned her, but Willie couldn't let Sunny face the music alone. Could she? So she followed Sir, curled up in her ma's lap, and pretended to snore softly, listening to the conversation.

Most of the adults had left, and only her parents remained with Uncle Fatie and Sir. They debated *how* Sunny moved the kids out of the wagon in the face of danger. Oh! Uh oh!

She stole a glance at Sunny. He had gone limp and comfy on Sir's lap, looking to be sleeping. But Willie knew he was awake. So did Sir. "Come, my boy," he said, "I know you're awake. Please tell us how you spirited yourself and the kids from the wagon when the K'tul discovered you."

After some cajoling and a few false starts, Sunny admitted that he *blinked.*

Blinked? Willie was not the only one confused as to what that meant. Teleport? No, Sunny didn't know how to teleport. Alright. Whatever it was. How far could he go? Could Sunny blink to the moon? No! Sunny shrunk back from that. But could he blink to the Crags? Yes, easily. That's how he came and went all the time.

There were a few demonstrations. Sunny first blinked only Sir, then everyone else wanted to blink to confirm. Finally everyone blinked away, including Willie. One moment she was in the house in Paria, the next in one of the base caves at the Crags, in water.

Before she could register her fright—or drown—she was back in the safe, warm room in the Parian ghetto. Ma fetched towels for everyone to dry themselves. Thankfully it was only their feet.

Ok, Sunny could blink to the Crags but not to the moon. How many folks could he bring? He had just brought Ma, Da, Uncle, Sir, Willie, and himself, six total. Sunny shocked everyone, declaring he could blink a hundred more. The adults dismissed that as another of his bravados.

Sir decided they had enough to work with and should let the kids sleep. They brought Willie and Sunny back to their bed, closed the bedroom door, and continued their discussion.

They went on for quite a while. Leaving Sunny behind, Willie stole to the door, cracked it open, and listened. Sir concluded Sunny did not teleport but either tunneled or wormholed. These traits were scarce, especially to wormhole, which required a particular meta gene. He would confirm if Sunny had that gene with DNA analysis when he got his equipment from the Crags.

Another amazing thing Sir said was that only the high royalty of Yand bore that trait. That sent the adults on a mad detective scramble to figure out Sunny's origins. No one knew his parents or where he'd come from. They remembered seeing him for the first time sometime in the first year of the siege.

Willie remembered vividly. She found Sunny one day in the palace's outer courtyard during a particularly brutal K'jen mage attack. It caught many folks outside the main palace structure and the safety of its walls. They put stricter rules in place after that. It was the same day Willie's ma burned for the first time. Ma went back to fight on the walls after that time, but not after the next. King Snowfox forbade her. She still nursed Tommy at that time.

Willie spied Sunny cowering behind a column by the palace entrance, trying to screw on his courage to dart inside before they closed the doors. But the blasts and fireballs kept coming, and he had an injured wing. After a particularly savage barrage, he cried out in fear, and it was all Willie needed to find *her* courage. She hopped to his column and dragged him up. They dove together through the palace doors just before they shuttered.

She caught hell from the adults. Sunny told her he hadn't really been scared. He would've hopped and dove and saved *her* in the same way. He was embarrassed she had witnessed his fear. He glued himself to her after that. He held her hand and cried along when they brought Ma bloodied and burned from the walls. They became inseparable.

The only Yandar high royalty on Phe'lak, Sir went on, had been Asimia and Snowfox. Their two daughters, too, but the girls were too young to figure in Sunny's parentage. The Yandar royal family had adopted Snowfox, so he didn't share their genes. That left Asimia.

Sunny had to be her son(!) with limited possibilities for his father. The boy silvered a lot—he glowed silver-white in darkness like King Snowfox. If Sunny was Asimia's son, his father had to be one of two possibilities: another silverblood—Snowfox or another. Or a person of mixed race that didn't golden or even much. No pure golden or evenblood could have fathered the boy.

"I, for example," he said.

"You what?" asked Ma.

"I couldn't have fathered Sunny with Asimia," explained Sir. Everyone stared at him.

"What are you saying!" Ma erupted. "Why would you father a child with Her Majesty!? You speak of her as if she were—"

"My friend," Sir finished for her. "I was speaking in the genetic sense, my dear. I'm an evenblood. You see? Genetically impossible to be Sunny's biological father."

"Oh," Ma said. "Can you find his parents with DNA?"

"Yes. Ah, it depends. No! No, I better not. I have a small sample of Asimia's DNA left, but I'm keeping it to make more serum to reverse her worldmaking gene's position to end the null."

"Right." Uncle Fatie agreed. "That's more valuable than knowing Sunny's precise parentage. I'm sorry we lost the first preparation you sent us with Sunny."

Oh! Willie thought. *That had to be the errant Sunny had disappeared to the day before the coronation! Sir sent him to bring the serum to the inn where the royal family had overnighted on their flight from the Crags. It was the same time the K'tul abducted Silvia.*

"Yes, but knowing if Sunny indeed wormholes is important," Sir countered, interrupting Willie's musings. "For example, where did he come from? Yand?"

The word Yand startled everyone. "Can he wormhole back? To get help?" Da exclaimed.

"He can't even go to the moon, man," Fatie countered. Then he turned to Sir, his voice sounding perplexed. "Is this why you want the boy so much, Pete? To keep beside you and study him?"

Sir stared wordlessly at Uncle Fatie. "No!" he shouted after an uncomfortably long silence. "You think I keep the boy under my thumb? Why, I lost my mind tonight when I thought… **when you**

nearly got him killed!" He bellowed that last part, glaring at Da. "To think that the K'tul had him in their claws—"

"Fine, fine," Fatie interrupted the tirade. "No need to lose it again! I only wondered."

Sir calmed down a little. "I can't tell you exactly why, but the rascal wormed himself into my heart. I love the scamp as my own! Who gives a rat's a-s who his bio parents are? Or what vestige of heaven the little scamp descended upon us from?"

"Oh, he said he loves me!" Sunny whispered in Willie's ear, making her jump. The *scamp* had crawled stealthily behind her.

"But that makes no sense!" Ma objected, a few mental steps behind the others. "Why would our king and queen have a son and not acknowledge him? He can't be Snowfox's son. Maybe an extramarital—"

"No, Nara!" Fatie interrupted her. "You were around them nine years ago, as were we. We would know if Asimia had a child in that timeframe, extramarital or not!"

"Ah, so you're nine!" Willie whispered to Sunny triumphantly, as it proved he was truly a year younger than herself.

"What if I am?" Sunny replied. He turned bright pink and stuck his tongue out at her.

"But *could he* have come from Yand?" Uncle Fatie continued. "Or rather Tuncay? Yanara and Frost are the premier royal couple, and they've had two silverbloods, Asimia and Sunstorm. Why not a third?"

"No, I don't think so," Sir replied. "Wouldn't we know if they had a child nine years ago?"

"And how would we?" Uncle Fatie persisted. We've had no contact with them for the past decade. It's *entirely* possible we missed a third child."

"Didn't Fox take Silvia to Yand when she was four to hunt her a shibal companion? She's two years younger than Sunny, so my son would have been a toddler then, and Fox would have met him. So. No."

"Oh, right!" Uncle Fatie had to agree. "I forgot that trip."

"Plus," added Dad, "even if somehow Fox missed Sunny's existence, someone had to bring him to Phe'lak. Who? The Pathfinder? Why would Wolfpack do that?"

"Could he have blinked on his own?" asked Da.

"Didn't we cover that? He can't even blink to the moon!" Sir replied. "Wait, when was the first time any of us saw Sunny? I know, the first year of the war, but I mean precisely?"

They all looked at Ma. "What?" she said. "Why is that important? Fine. Let's see. I believe it was during one of the first long bombardments, but I was fighting on the walls at that time, like you two," she indicated Dad and Uncle. "Not sure about you," she directed that to Sir. "I think he ran to the palace for shelter."

That's how Willie remembered it. "That's when I saved you," she told Sunny, who had fallen uncharacteristically quiet. She stole a glance over her shoulder and found him pink and fidgeting. "What? You nervous?" she asked him. "They won't throw you out."

"They might," he countered, but not with his usual vigor. He looked ready to bolt. But Sir continued, diverting her attention.

"He ran to the palace during bombardment? Where was *I?*" Ma shrugged her shoulders. "How would *I* know?"

"My, my," Sir went on, turning to look toward their ajar bedroom door, causing Willie and Sunny to shrink back behind it.

"Ok, enough," he pronounced after a prolonged silence. "We've exhausted this trail. My son didn't come from Yand. Couldn't come on his own, and there's no way Wolfpack dumped his baby brother into a war zone and left him."

Sunny caught his breath through his teeth. "Wolfpack dumped me!" he muttered. "My other parents threw me away, and now Dad doesn't want me…"

It was so absurd that Willie could only stare open-mouthed.

"Let me see what I can glean from DNA about his parentage," Sir concluded. "I have some of Fox's and every other Karian silvering male's. I won't sacrifice Asimia's. I want my equipment and team transferred here from the Crags, pronto," he told Dad. "Now about Sunny's blinking ability. We can use it."

To Willie's astonishment, Sir proposed a new method for transferring the refugees. After much debate and what seemed like forever, Ma, Da, and Uncle agreed: Sunny would blink every single person and piece of equipment from the Crags to the Parian cordon.

The Fish Cart Returning to Paria

The logistics were much more complicated than the concept. Everyone agreed they needed to keep Sunny's blinking ability secret, fearing it would inadvertently leak out. If the K'tul heard of it, they would arrest Sunny and torture him in their abominable experiments for extracting new methods to power.

Willie's parents and Sir lectured her and Sunny to no end and dragooned them to keep this vital secret. Sunny would not blink under any circumstances except under Sir's direction and supervision. Willie got it. Sunny's life depended on it. If Sunny got it… that was an entirely different matter that only he knew.

They spent the next two months transferring people and stuff with the new method. They enlisted the doctor to help them without telling him the truth. They said they needed people to stay calm in the cart under the fish. Could he make sedatives for them? He was happy to oblige.

They brought the empty fish cart to the cove at low tide, placed the passengers in its false bottom, and fed them the pills. Once they fell asleep, they drove the cart around the bend, and

Sunny blinked them to the Blue House in the ghetto. Blue House was the name Sunny gave their house. It was blue.

They drove the empty cart back to the fishing project at the Keys. At night, the Parian fishers loaded their catch and drove the cart first to Snakeman's Temple, then to the Blue House in the cordon, and left it in the courtyard. Nara met them with Willie and Sunny. After the fishers departed, they *"unloaded"* the transferees, who, in truth, still snoozed inside the Blue House.

If any of the household people suspected anything, they said not a thing about it. The following day Yanus came to pick up the empty cart from the Blue House's stables. And the new load of Karian refugees was ready for placement.

They transferred the orphans first. It was a bit trickier with the adults, as some refused the pills outright while others argued about it. But Sir didn't give them a choice. He was the Viceroy, after all, and they had to obey him, something he used often. Willie suspected he had come to enjoy his new rank.

Sir took over the Transfer Ops from Da and Uncle Fatie. He wouldn't allow his son to shoulder the danger without him. This way, if something bad happened and Sunny perished, the Viceroy would die too. It made zero sense to Willie, but who could argue with Sir? He was the smartest person in the world and knew so many different ways to say the same thing.

This freed Da to devote his time to Ops SpyNet. Willie wasn't entirely sure what that entailed, but every night, she and Sunny overheard many tales of the K'tul base outside Paria, Crater 1, and the renegade greyk'tul and their affairs. And much about Snakeman, who they also called by his code name, Foureyes.

They didn't involve the kids, as Dad had initially intended. Sir had objected strongly against it from the beginning but more now that Sunny belonged to him. The Parians who adopted the kids would not even hear of it. Dad agreed readily, surprising Willie.

Da was the top operative of Ops SpyNet. He told false news from one K'tul faction to the other, making them believe wrong motives toward each other. *Gaslighting,* he called it. Willie wasn't sure what gas they were lighting, but in the two months she worked with Ops Transfer, Ops SpyNet began to bear fruit.

K'jen sentries that had incessantly plagued the cordon turned their attention toward watching the greyk'tul at the Crater. This allowed the cordonites to come and go easier. And the number of gratuitous K'jen raids decreased dramatically.

As a reward for some juicy information about the Renegades recruiting troops from the provinces, Snakeman made Willie's da Ghetto Consul. This meant the cordon got some autonomy and Dad a new, higher seal that he used to garner things for the community.

The first thing Da did under his new authority was to expand the green line in one direction to include a large field. Willie and Sunny took time off from Ops Transfer to splotch green paint on the new street, along with many other kids. It was a day of celebration. They used a big part of the new field to make a stadium where kids could play. Sunny dubbed it *The Training Field.* The large building on its inner edge became a school!

Dad had the entire community labor for days to fortify their new green line. He lorded over them like a true overseer as they worked to dupe any K'tul eyes that watched how he used his new role. As a result, the cordonites installed a fence of pointed pikes with twisted barbed wire on their top without alerting the K'tul.

The information about the Renegades had been false, a part of Dad's campaign to gaslight their overlord. Willie came to understand gaslight as confuse, or misdirect. Mr. Foureyes bought it: he mobilized his arsenal of K'jen mages against the Crater, which had become the Renegade's military base. They had fireworks shows for nights on end. It was so spectacular they had to suspend Ops Transfer until things calmed down.

Uncle Fatie convinced Snakeman to allow him to operate an inn at the docks. He reasoned that His Magnificent Premier Lord Glory could entertain his officers there as a pretext for more spying on the greyk'tul. Uncle Fatie guaranteed that the greyrobes would flock to that inn if he (Snakeman) made him (Uncle Fatie) chef.

Snakeman gave him the Sea Urchin, a disreputable dive in the back streets of the pier. Perfect for Uncle's purposes.

The Blue House became the central residence of the ghetto. It was enormous, with a courtyard, stables, and separate kitchen and staff wings. The main house had many bedrooms in a dedicated wing. Ma and Da shared one, Uncle Fatie took another, Tommy shared one with his nanny(!), and Willie had her own adjacent to the Hearth Room.

Sir begged for a room for himself and Sunny, surprising everyone. The Elders had offered him a nearby house, but he argued they needed to economize space with the new folks arriving from the Crags. But they all knew his true reason was to accommodate Sunny, who wouldn't leave Willie even for a moment.

The next focus for Da was to gain control of the hospital. It had been Paria's primary medical facility before the invasion and still functioned properly. But it lay outside the cordon. Slowly at first, then more boldly as Snakeman granted him more and more airs, Da wiggled and extended the green paint in twisted ways until, miraculously, it enclosed the hospital! He called this method *gerrymandering.*

It worked brilliantly. They controlled the hospital! Da made the cordonites build a fort around it, much like they did with the field. When K'tul sought aid for ailments or injuries, they had to petition at the entrance. Da distributed tokens to rank, and they went by that for admission priority!

The separate clinic building on the hospital's campus had enough space for the scientists and engineers to move in, stealthily at first, and set up laboratories and offices. It became like a regular university. Willie remembered the Karian U. only vaguely, but this had to be a good approximation.

Sir claimed a large wing where he accommodated his techs and precious instruments and equipment in a large lab with adjacent offices. Willie wasn't sure if he remembered to do the DNA analysis on Sunny's origins. She didn't ask.

They had a happy surprise. Lady Emmiat recovered! Four months after her horrific ordeal, her body healed, if not her spirit. Her vocal cords no longer functioned, as the doctors had predicted. Like all Yandar, she could mindspeak those bonded to her, but she was not bonded to anyone in the cordon. Luckily, Da, Uncle Fatie, and Sir, who had been friends with the woman, were telepaths. She could mindspeak with them. Plus she was fluent in guard sign.

Uncle Fatie brought her to the Blue House to live with them, but it didn't last long. One bright day, Uncle returned home in the middle of the afternoon, bursting with news and loudly summoning Lady Emmiat. It was happy news, and he wanted to show her rather than tell her. He brought her to the Urchin, which he had refurbished with cordonite and K'jen(!) labor, and there… surprise! The lady's husband had returned from the dead!

Sunny had dragged Willie to the inn in stealth—kids weren't allowed to that part of the city, but he miraculously knew his way about without blinking. They witnessed the reunion. The lady's husband was Phe'laki. He had burned badly in the war—hideous scars covered his face! How could anyone recognize him? But his wife did, instantly!

"I told you he'd find us," Uncle kept telling the lady.

Lady Emmiat's husband had to spend time in the hospital, where the doctors restored sight to one of his eyes by removing scar tissue. Uncle Fatie granted him the inn's operation, which freed the uncle for more Ops SpyNet. The man, Russel was his name, moved to the inn to run it, and his wife, Lady Emmiat, followed him.

A year after the Karian refugees began their perilous relocation from the Crags to the Parian cordon, the place was unrecognizable. It had become more of a village than a ghetto. Da was the Consul of their little town, and Snakeman had promoted him to his first advisor—his *First,* they said.

Snake gave Uncle Fatie titles, too, but Uncle worked more on the greyk'tul part of Ops SpyNet. Sir was not only their Viceroy but had also become the U. Provost. He kept the room at their Blue House, although he spent much time at the hospital-clinic-turned-U. Sunny went on sleeping in Willie's bed every night.

It was Willie's eleventh birthday. Da and Ma decided not to make it a village affair to avoid attracting attention from the K'tul. But they did plan a family gather.

That morning, Ma presented Willie with a new dress—pink with dainty white flowers. Willie loved it so much! She hadn't had a new dress since the war began more than three years ago! She put it on immediately and thought she'd never take it off again. She'd even sleep in it that night. She couldn't wait to show it off to Sunny!

Before she darted out the door, Ma had another surprise: ribbons for her hair! She washed and fluffed Willie's unwieldy locks until a halo surrounded her face, dark and twinkling with little stars—Ma had sprinkled stardust in it. Where did she get it? She then weaved in the colorful ribbons, like pops of color in the luscious darkness, without reducing the volume.

Willie could not contain her excitement! What a surprise this would be for Sunny! He'd surely love it. The moment Ma released her from the chair, she darted from the room, yelling at the top of her lungs: "Sunny!"

He was at the U. in his dad's office and would come as soon as his dad released him. Sir heard their exchange and sent him home immediately. He blinked right beside her! It was so sudden that it made Willie jump. But another surprise! Sunny wore the new outfit his dad had specially tailored for her birthday. Wow!

She stared, lost for words. What a transformation! He looked princely! They'd look amazing together, he like a prince, she a princess in her new dress and divine hair.

But Sunny had one look at her and balked. "What the hell did you do to your hair?" he shouted. "No! I don't like it at all. Yuk. Looks like the spikes of a porcupine. I'll call you *porcupine hair* now." He went on to chant, "Porcupine hair, porcupine hair."

"Oh, you monster!" Willie yelled and stormed to her room, crying. By the time Ma caught up with her, she had undone her exceptional coif and replaced it with two messy pigtails.

"Willie, what have you done? That was expensive stardust, and the ribbons weren't free, either," Mom exclaimed in dismay.

"I don't care!" Willie wailed. "He calls me *porcupine hair!*"

"Who? Sunny? I'll be…" Ma declared, letting that trail off. "We'll see what his dad has to say about that. About time we put some bounds on that boy." But Willie went on wailing, and Ma relented. "Come, my girl. There's no going back to the beautiful hairdo. Let me at least fix your braids."

Reluctantly Willie let her Ma redo her hair. She made a few beautiful braids, not only the two Willie had struggled with.

"You look great, my darling," she declared when she finished. "Don't let that little monster tell you otherwise. Why do you listen to him, anyway?"

But Sunny snuck into the room. "No!" he shouted when he took in the scene. "What the heck is this?! Pigtails? I liked the porcupine hair better!"

"Come here, you scoundrel!" Ma said and lunged for him, but he dodged and ran out as Willie broke into new sobs. "Come my darling. Let me—" But Willie didn't let Ma finish. She bolted out the door. She didn't care what hair she had. She didn't care if Sunny liked it or not. She wanted to die from embarrassment.

She launched and flew(!) through the streets, causing a commotion wherever she passed. Dad and Sir forbade all flight at the cordon. It was one of the rules Da had negotiated with Snakeman, and their peace depended on keeping the rules.

She flew low, skimming cobblestone streets and skirting houses. She found herself at the edge of the cordon when Sunny called in her mind: *"Willie, stop. Please, I didn't mean that."*

Oh yeah he did. He always meant what he said. All the mean things, the nasty, *outlandish* things he said to her. Tears blinded her eyes, so she couldn't tell exactly where she'd flown to. She landed. Excess momentum carried her forth to crash on the pavement. She pulled to her feet… to find… a K'tul! Blue-skinned, horned, and baring his fangs! And wearing grey! A *greyk'tul.*

"Sunnyyy!" she yelled out loud, heart in her mouth.

Sunny? No, leave him. Best on her own. *I flew over the line,* she realized in utter fright. The K'tul, too, had his feet firmly planted on the other side of the ghetto.

For a moment that lasted an eternity, Willie stared at the K'tul, trying to screw on her courage to turn and dive back over the green line. But the demon reached a clawed hand and grabbed her by the throat. "Well, well, look at this! What have we here?" He said in Yandar with barely an accent. He lifted Willie off the pavement and brought her eyes level with his. "The provost's daughter?"

"No, moron," A voice came from behind Willie's shoulder. It was Sunny. Oh, he had flown after her! *"I'm the Provost's son. She's the Consul's daughter."* And he dove onto the K'tul, beating at his hand that held Willie while mindyelling, ***"Daaaa!!!"***

"Daaaa!!!" Willie joined him. They yelled together, forgetting their unsettled score. The K'tul laughed maniacally. Before Sunny could hop out of his reach, the demon grabbed him with his other hand. He now had both of them by the throat.

"Daaaa!!" they both continued to yell.

Sir arrived on his wings! He had a glance about him, taking in the tableau. It played clearly outside the green line of safety.

"Let the kids go!" he projected in mindspeak and aloud.

"Or else what? What can you do to me? I'm Greyk'tul, First's First and Renegade Leader! Haha! Nothing? I didn't think so. Your kids are outside the line, Provost! Or are you the Consul?"

"Provost," a voice came behind Sir. "I'm the Consul." It was Da! He'd run from the blue House! "What can we do for you, Master Greyk'tul? Don't I know you? Aren't you the one—"

Uncle Fatie rounded the corner from Paria proper. *"He's Mn'ianka,"* he confirmed in mindspeak. *"Can't mistake the horns."*

"Haha, I am that, and I have horns. I do what I will, and how can you stop me? You feed lies about me to S'tihsa!" the K'tul hissed in a dangerous, low whisper. "I take your kids and anything else I want. I am Mn'ianka, Mn'esya's twin!"

He stepped to the side and inclined his head minutely to his left. A smaller greyk'tul stood there, also horned but purpled-skinned and twisted, exuding danger. You could feel it. "And that one is K'nista, my mage. You've met him before."

"Give us the kids and go from here," Da boomed.

"We'll settle the scores later," Uncle Fatie added.

"We'll settle them now!" Mn'ianka hissed. "I have terms."

Dad and Uncle Fatie exchanged looks.

"Let the kids go. Negotiate!" Uncle barked the last word, and to mindspeak-specific chat, he said: *"I got this. Triex, Pete, take the kids home."*

"Terms!" Mn'ianka barked back. "I demand the right to inspect your goldie females under eighteen."

"Granted!" Uncle Fatie spat back.

What? But the K'tul put Willie and Sunny down, and the two dove for the green line and into their respective dad's arms. Dad passed her to Sir, and Sir beat his mighty wings and flew them to the Blue House while Dad ran after him.

Yes, Sir flew again(!), against the rule. He arrived at the house first. Willie burst from his arms into her ma's as Sunny burrowed tighter in Sir's. Soon Dad rounded the corner, panting hard. Uncle Fatie stayed behind to negotiate with the K'tul.

Mn'ianka Menacing Willie and Sunny, at Ghetto

Past Time: At the dragon's lair on Yand, continuing after Chapter 6. Snowfox's POV.

8. To the Stars

Snowfox stayed away from Asimia's bed that night. And the night after that and the week that followed. He tried hard not to listen to her private thoughts or her comings and goings, but his heart turned to her on its own. And so he knew she wasn't in her room all those nights he didn't spend with her.

Not that he'd expected anything different. But to have it flown in his eyes… It hurt like the blazes. She was nice enough toward him during the days, although strained. They drifted apart by the hour. The geneticist had won.

He won this battle, he told himself. *Not the war. She's marrying me, not him.*

But it stung! *Cut her loose,* Wolfpack had told him. *Let her fly; see if she comes back to you. You don't want her any other way.* The problem with that was that he did. He wanted her any way she would grant him. And he wasn't even sure she would come back.

He spent longer mornings at the training field, driving the troops to exhaustion and himself to madness. He lingered at Tuncay late in the afternoons and into evenings, making not only himself, but Uncle Yildiz crazy, too.

One such evening, Uncle approached him as he bounced Sunstorm on his knees, his baby brother cooing and patting his face. "The dragon wants you," Uncle said.

"Oh? Now?"

"No, tonight. After dinner but before midnight. He wants his sleep, too. And bring some wine, the blueberry."

"Gladly. I should have gone to see him anyway; I need to talk to him about our star course."

"Ah, for that, maybe we can meet there tomorrow at noon? I want to hear it."

"Of course. I'll bring Luc, too. You don't think Grandma—"

"No. She's too busy setting her affairs to order. And she's expecting a challenge from Hawk."

"Oh? Why doesn't she pass the reigns to him peacefully? Does she need to kill him first?"

Uncle Yildiz chuckled. "Apparently. But it's tradition."

"Right. But if she wins, you won't be coming with us?"

"We're coming, my boy, don't fret."

Snowfox skipped dinner. Sometime before midnight, he had a household mage teleport him to the dragon's lair. He found the dragon in open air, curled up under the dragontree, sleeping. But surprise! In his paw, also curled up and sleeping, was Asimia, with Alex in her arms. The rascal cracked an eye and growled.

"I'm only pretending," the dragon whispered in Snowfox's mind, *"but she sleeps in truth. Come, don't wake her so we can talk for a while."*

"How long?" Snowfox asked, amazed at the sight. His foxes jumped from their backpack and quietly went to join the cat.

"That she's been coming to sleep here? With me? A couple of weeks. Since you put her out of your bed."

"I didn't—"

"Oh? She made all that up?"

"What?"

"You sent her to the professor—"

"I did no such thing! Is that what she got from that? I only gave her her freedom!"

"And is her freedom yours to give?"

"Grandad," Snowfox exclaimed, exasperated. *"I don't know how to navigate this. I may be an adult now, but I'm not yet twenty. I've loved only* her *my entire life. My heart is raw. I can't hardly breathe. What can I do? What* should *I do?"*

"Can you take this man with you?"

"No."

"No, you can't? Or no, you won't."

"No I can't."

"Oh. And she knows that?"

"Yes. And not from me. From Grandma Stardust. Should I take her home?"

"I like her here."

"Simi?" he caressed her hair.

"Fox? How are you here?" she replied sleepily, rising to an elbow and dislodging her cat and his foxes.

"The dragon called me. I'm not spying on you," he hastened to add."

"I know, love. I think we need to talk directly, not in veiled speech and innuendos. I'll go first. I love you."

"Do you?"

"With all my heart. All my life. But only as of late like a—"

"Husband?"

"Lover."

"Oh."

They talked for a while. She fell in love with Pete back when she thought Snowfox was her sib like her other three non-bio brothers. She never suspected that her feelings would turn romantic or that Snowfox's already had. He hadn't given any indication.

But she loved Snowfox like a husband and lover now. Her life had no meaning without him. Their bond was so strong that it defined her. She would perish without him.

Then couldn't she forgo Pete? No, she couldn't. She loved him too. And she had never loved Pete as a brother, so it was easier with him.

She handed Snowfox two pieces of paper.

"What's this?"

"My betrothal contract to Pete."

"What?" Shock of all shockers. And there, Snowfox thought they had made some progress.

"You know we can't bring him along," he objected.

"I know. But I can't leave him behind without the promise that when our circumstances change…"

Snowfox recovered somewhat from his shock to discover his amiable feelings for discussion had soured. Only a sense of betrayal remained. That it was he who gave her this idea didn't help. What was he thinking? It was easier to say it than to face it.

"Did you know?" he asked the dragon suspiciously. "Is this why you summoned me?"

"No. Nah, ughuh! No. I thought it would help if you found her here and not with him. This is cruel. Exceedingly."

"Why show these to me, Asimia? Did I need to see the papers? I thought we'd already settled the matter. Is there something more you need me to do? Disappear perhaps?"

"I need you to sign these. Wasn't it your idea?"

"What? I will do no such thing."

"Fine, I'll have Gramma Stardust—"

"Give me." That would be humiliating. He snatched the papers from Asimia's hand and fished his pockets for a writing implement. She handed him an ink pen. He signed them both, handed them back, and turned to go.

"Snowfox, wait," she called after him. "I want you to know this was the last thing. I'm done with Pete—"

"Oh? Until when? When he comes to find us on Phe'lak for your wedding?"

"No. Only to visit. And *if* he comes."

Snowfox missed the last part, the *if*. "But you won't have to wait that long," he blurted angrily. "Aren't you going to give him his copy?" he indicated the papers in Asimia's hands.

"No. *You* are."

He stared. Was there a bottom to this? "I will do no such thing, Asimia!"

"Fine. I'll get Stardust's herald."

Snowfox snatched the offered copy from Asimia's hand. "Ok, I'll take it. Tomorrow good enough? Or should I go now?"

She nodded. "Tomorrow is fine, or the day after. Fox—"

He put his hand up and silenced her. "Noon tomorrow we meet here to plot our course. Luc—remember him?—Yildiz and the three of us. See you then. I'll take the paper to Pete after that."

"Wait, let me take us home, Snowfox," Asimia called after him, but he had already launched.

"Nah. I'm not going home," he shouted over his shoulder.

He flew to the training field, to the canteen, and landed on the second-floor balcony. It was late, but a few folks still hung around, drinking and telling tales. Chimeran was among them. She called him over to their table, but he only nodded and went to the bar. The bartender had long left, so Snowfox fixed himself a stiff drink. Then he sat in misery, drinking it.

Chimeran approached him stealthily and made him jump when she put a hand on his shoulder. "That bad?" she asked.

"Hmm," he only replied.

"I know what you need. A few of us are happy to oblige."

"What? No! Where did you get that idea?"

"From the looks of you."

"That obvious?"

"Yes." She took the bottle from his hand and poured more into his glass. "You know, you ought to take a second wife. And maybe a third."

"Chimé, please!"

"And don't tell me you only love *her*. The entire universe knows that. But some of us don't give a rat's a-s about love. We'd settle for action with you. And you may learn a couple of things."

"If you aim to scandalize me, I'm too drunk for that."

"Already? No, seriously. There's this one girl who pines for you. You know which one I mean. Up in the mountains in the west. She sent her regional mage to petition to go with you. To the stars, I mean. And you know the poor man had to trek. No extreme teleporters left up there."

"We ought to fix that. And I know. I received their petition. The whole squadron wants to follow me. Luc said they have no different skill than you guys here—"

"Idiot! You think her bow was the only thing she offered?"

"Chimé, please!"

But a couple of bottles later, Snowfox found himself crying on Chimé's shoulder. She called the military mage, and he obliged with the extreme teleport to the silver mountains in the west.

In the morning, Snowfox woke up in a strange room, in a woman's arms. *Asimia?* He thought experimentally. But this woman neither felt nor smelled like his betrothed.

Slowly, tentatively, and with much misgiving and dread, he reckoned with his surroundings. The young lady was RC! He lay in her arms, in what had to be her bed in her bedroom. His foxes were nowhere to be seen.

"Oh, sh-t!" he moaned. Disgusted with himself, he crawled to the bathroom and puked out his guts in the toilet while berating himself. He wasn't even fully awake.

"Morning, love," RC's melodic, rich contralto voice projected from behind his shoulder. She put a hand on his forehead while he carried on with his business. "How much did you drink?"

"Not sure. Listen, RC—"

"No need to say anything, Fox. I know you don't love me."
To his attempt to protest, she added, "I mean, *that* way."

"I was going to say yes."

"Yes, what?"

"You can come on the expedition." She caught her breath
loudly. "But you marry Harry before we depart, and I cannot take
the entire squadron."

"We figured that," RC replied. "We'll draw straws. What
made you decide? Last night?"

"No. I planned to tell you."

"Liar. But no matter. You done? I'll make some coffee."

"Nah, I best get going. What time is it?"

"Close to noon."

"Ah, hell!" He crawled around the woman to look in the
mirror over the sink. "I don't suppose I can have a comb?"

"Here, I'll do your braid. But it'll take more than that. Jump
in the shower while I summon the regional."

She meant the mage. "He's not—"

"Nope. You'll take the scenic route home, I'm afraid. Unless
you think your lady will oblige you?"

Snowfox winced. "Long way home will do."

When he got out of the shower, he found a cup of coffee on
the counter and inhaled it, hoping it would settle his stomach. It
didn't. As he sat patiently (not so much) in nothing but his boxers
while RC fixed his braid, he realized there was no way to make his
noon appointment. That reminded him that he still had to bring the
blessed paper to Pete, and that thought soured his stomach more.

He mindspoke Uncle Yildiz and begged him to move their
meeting to tomorrow and to please let everyone know. He pulled on
his pants, searched in his pocket to make sure he hadn't lost
Asimia's precious paper, put on his shirt, and looked for the mage.

He waited in the kitchen. RC gave him a hug that he returned
awkwardly. "When do you want us to come to Dragonslair?" she
asked him.

"We'll summon you. Chimeran is also going, bringing
another half squadron from the east."

"Yeah, she said. Why do I have to marry Harry?"

"Ah, please, RC, my life is such a mess right now. It'll make it so much easier for me if you marry the man."

"I get it," she replied defensively. "But why Harry?"

"Isn't he... aren't you two..."

"No."

He shook his head. "Ah, I can't deal..."

"No matter. Come, Johan," she called the mage, "Commander Fox is ready for his ride. Go easy on him." To Snowfox she said, "You know where to find me if you ever need... mm, a shoulder again."

Snowfox winced, and allowed the regional mage to take him on the longest teleport ride to Dragonslair. Thankfully, the man dropped him off at the residence and turned straight back. Snowfox ducked into his room, closed the curtains, and hit his bed.

He slept for hours. Two things happened the moment he cracked an eye. First, his foxes. Snowdrift licked his face while Hunter worked on his feet, flipping the covers. Then, the attendant. Alerted by the foxes' excitement, she swung the door slightly and peered inside. Then she announced loudly to the entire universe that her lord had risen. *From the dead?*

"Hey, hey, girl," Snowfox told Snowdrift. "Hunter, boy? Where did I leave you two last night?" He retraced his steps, beginning with visiting the dragon. He'd taken them along—they curled up with Alex—but couldn't recall beyond that.

"At the lair. Simi brought us back."

Snowfox inhaled his breath sharply. *"Oh, sorry! Did you guys have dinner last night?"*

"We did, but you didn't. How was RC?"

Another wince. *"Please guard your thoughts, Snow. She was fine. And lunch today?"*

"Breakfast. We waited for you to wake up for lunch."

"I still have an errand. You want to come along? We can have a big lunch after?"

"Yes!" Snowdrift replied excitedly.

"Yes! Yes!" Hunter agreed.

He bounced from Snowfox's legs and fetched the backpack. He climbed into it. But before they could sneak out, Doc came and offered medical aid. Fox refused. Then a kitchen staffer brought a tray, but he sent that away, too, promising to come to the kitchen soon for lunch. The woman informed him it'd be dinner, deposited her tray on his table, and left. There was no sign of Asimia.

"She's on the moon," the dragon informed Snowfox's brain. *"Oh? Doing what?"*

"The unis? You made a mess." Understatement of the century. *"She knows the western mage brought you."*

Of course she did. *"I'm about to make more mess,"* he told Grandad. Not that he meant to. But he didn't know how to avoid it.

He poured his foxes bowls of juice from the pitcher on the tray and a glass for himself. He downed it while they slurped. He donned fresh clothes, gathering his wits. It was early evening. If he remembered correctly, the U. offered an evening genetics class.

His foxes finished their juice and climbed into the backpack. He secured it on his back, grabbed an olive roll from the tray, and headed to the U. He flew rather than teleported to give his mind a few extra minutes to clear. He sketched a few circles over the city, taking his time and procrastinating—delaying the unavoidable.

He landed in the new Constantine Wing, which the city had constructed after the war reduced the main campus to rubble, like every other building in Dragonslair. A pair of students pointed out the classroom, and he parked himself outside the door.

A few minutes later the door flew open, and college kids poured out. But the Prof. lingered inside. Snowfox found him standing at the chalkboard with a writing implement in one hand and a gaggle of attentive students about him. Tall, dark, and handsome.

And fit. How could a college professor be so fit? Granted, Dr. Pietro was young, no more than fifty, when the average faculty age was well into the hundreds. He was a prodigy, singular, irreplaceable. So how did he get army training? *But he's allowed to train, just not engage in battle,* Snowfox mused.

The Professor noticed him and dismissed his students. "Come, Fox, I was expecting you," he called.

"You did?"

"Yes, indeed, but earlier. Everything alright? You brought my papers from Asimia?"

Snowfox produced the paper from his pocket. It was crumbled and soiled. He smoothed out a corner with the heel of his hand and handed it. Professor took it with a wry smile and an eyebrow. "It's gone through some hell, I see," he remarked. "Never fear, it'll see worse," and he started to tear it.

Snowfox grabbed his hand. "No! Hold! What the hell?"

The motion freed the geneticist's wrist from his sleeve to reveal a hideous scar. Dr. Pietro yanked his hand and tried to pull cloth over the scar, but Snowfox wouldn't yield. Unmistakably, this was a war wound. "You fought in the war!?" he asked the good prof.

"I did. So did you and the rest of the world. So?"

"So you shouldn't have! You're chief essential! Who let you? Stardust? Hawk?"

Anger rose in Snowfox's breast. They never allowed their essentials—irreplaceable scientific and engineering personnel and others bearing unique skills—to risk themselves in such peril.

"They didn't know. Don't go blaming them."

"How could they not know? Before or after the bend?"

He meant his mom's bend that destroyed the K'tul spaceships. Before the bend, they fought aerial battles against those ships, while after, they fought on the ground whatever enemy troops remained. Either was dangerous, but the aerials much more. Most of Yand's Flyer Force perished in those maneuvers.

"Before, during, and after. Does it matter?"

"You fought in the aerials?"

"Under your brother's command." Snowfox's brother Hawk commanded the Eastern Flyers. "And you the West," the professor finished. "It's done. Leave it." He resumed his sardonic smile. "Can I have my paper now? I need to destroy it in front of you."

"What? Why?"

"Because Asimia wanted you to witness it."

"Huh?"

"From my mouth to your ears so you can believe it. I lay no claim on her. She's all yours. But I will love her until I die, you should know."

Snowfox stared, reevaluating the man. He didn't know what to say. "Keep it," he said finally. "You may change your mind later. Love doesn't come and go by will alone. In a couple of centuries—"

"Indeed."

The professor stared, clearly not expecting this response from Snowfox. He accepted the paper. "Do you mind if I have it redrafted? It looks like someone... drooled on it... or worse?"

Snowfox turned bright pink.

"But come to my office. I have a surprise for you."

The professor led Snowfox from his classroom and down a long hallway. At its end was a stairway leading down. To Snowfox's surprise, it led to a campus underpass. It was a new construction. A few twists and turns later, they came to another staircase leading up. They climbed it and emerged in a long hallway with offices sparsely distributed right and left, Dr. Pietro's among them.

"Pete," a very familiar voice greeted the geneticist. Wolfpack! Snowfox pushed through the door, and there was his brother(!) looking considerably better than the last time they met. He still sported light bandages on his face. "Look, Fox," he called when he saw him. "We've charted a tentative course."

Beside him by the whiteboard was the Quantum Mechanics physicist who tutored Snowfox and his sibs since he was two. The silly kids called him Professor Warbles because his specialty was bending spacetime. An ancient woman sat on a stool beside them.

With a careful hug for his brother, Wolfpack introduced her: "This is Professor Khin—"

"Ah!" Snowfox marveled. *"The* Professor Khin?" He knew the name, as did all of Yand. She was the most renowned astrophysicist, famous for her... well, about everything.

"Famous for her many theses and papers on wormholes, spatial and temporal or both, anomalies—" Wolfpack continued.

"I know!" Snowfox interrupted him. Warbles taught them much about the esteemed Professor Khin and her theories. "Very pleased to meet you, Madam Professor. What an honor!"

The legend was that Professor Khin retired after the first K'tul war and the Big Bend that ended it. She vanished, causing a stir the planet over. Some said the bend erased her, but that was not true. She had been sighted, albeit sparsely, and even attended a symposium here and there.

Mom had looked for her for help with wormhole theory back when she struggled to keep the K'tul spaceships from breaching her planetary shields. But Snowfox didn't think she found her. And now the Professor stood in the flesh before him with a writing implement in one hand and ink smudges on her face. She was no taller than his little brother, who, at sixteen, wasn't taller than a tall Yendal.

She seemed approachable and friendly. She giggled. "Emerita now, my boy. But please, call me Khin. Or it'll be a long, boring trek across the stars."

Snowfox couldn't believe his ears. He gave Wolfpack an inquiring look, which he returned with a positive incline of his head.

"Ah, I never expected such honor!" he exclaimed but caught himself. "How are you not singular and essential?"

"Hmf!" she declared. "I *was* until I trained my successor. *He'll* be the singular when I go. Some of us plan such things orderly, unlike some others." She directed a glare toward Dr. Pietro.

"Well, some of us have fifty, not fifteen hundred years," the geneticist replied with mock severity.

"Look over here, Fox," Wolfpack directed his attention to the whiteboard. They had drawn the constellations of the Bears (Ursa Minor and Major) and the Dragon (Draco) and decorated them (muddled them) with many equations and wormhole schematics. They also drew other figures here and there, that Snowfox recognized as types of celestial bodies or other space phenomena.

"Welcome to the expedition, Dr.—I mean, Khin. What do you have for me, Wolfpack?"

"Me too, Fox," Warbles added. "I'm coming, too."

"Ah, welcome…" Snowfox searched for the prof's name.

"Warbles will do, you rascals!" The physicist declared, with a pretend glare at Snowfox and Wolfpack. "That's what everyone calls me now."

"Please, forgive us, Dr. Elliot," Snowfox triumphantly recalled the physicist's proper name. "We were kids. But…" he shook his head and smiled. "My uncle Yildiz mentioned that Her Majesty, my grandmother, emptied the colleges. Is anyone left?"

"Apparently just me," said Pete acerbically.

Wolfpack pulled Snowfox by the sleeve. "Looks like we'll need a few wormholes."

"You mean three? Don't we have three wormhole masters?"

"Yes, but I mean, we may need a couple of legs to our trip. Three wormholes but more than one hops—one may be temporal."

"You mean we can't ride one wormhole jump and get there like when we go to Yenda? Or to Tuncay, a star system away?"

"Tuncay is in the next star system in a straight space-shot. Not another few galaxies away in another constellation. Remember when mom fell in Cepheus' supermassive blazar?"

Fox flinched. He couldn't forget that! "Do we face the like?"

"Not exactly, although we need to consider that, too. We can't wormhole through quasars or other such celestial features. Our people will perish if our wormholes fall apart. They'll burn. Only Mom can survive that type of environment."

"Yeah, Mom and you. Didn't you pull her out?"

Wolfpack looked thoughtful, puzzled. "I'm sure I can't survive that environment. I think I used temporal properties—"

"Huh?"

"—and that's my main concern. Did I mention it before, Fox? When I scouted the space we must traverse, I encountered a temporal anomaly. I passed it, but I worry about Simi and Uncle—"

"Allow me," Dr. Pietro cut in. Wolfpack nodded slightly. "The wormhole gene. I've researched its distribution among the Yandar and Yendal populations. Only members of the Yandar royal family possess it. By royal, I mean descended from the dragon."

Snowfox made to object that Wolfpack was not, but Dr. Pietro raised his hand and halted him. "Wolfpack's gene differs from your mother's, uncle's, and Asimia's. It's in the same vicinity on his DNA code as his pathfinder gene and has an extra allele beside it. A variant for time. Temporal."

"Look over here, Fox," Wolfpack attempted to divert him to the board again.

"Wait," Snowfox objected. "I think the rest of our leading team needs to hear this. Are you all available for the next couple of hours? Dinner at my house?"

Everyone looked at each other, then began to nod yes except Dr. Pietro, who looked everywhere but at Snowfox.

"You, too, Dr. Pietro," Snowfox told the man.

"Call me Pete. Are you sure?"

"Didn't you and my little brother just tell us that we're about to dive into temporal space, and only Wolfpack has the gene?"

"Yes."

"Then I'm sure." Dr.—Pete still looked uncertain. "Before I change my mind," Snowfox encouraged him.

"Very well," Pete agreed.

Fox summoned Simi, Luc, Uncle Yildiz, and Grandma Stardust to dinner at the residence. Wolfpack transferred their little college group to the courtyard outside the kitchen before anyone else arrived. Snowfox alerted Chef Piere that they had esteemed guests for dinner.

"Who, my lord?"

"My grandma and these here—"

"The queen is coming to dinner!? Set the dining room!" Pierre bellowed to his staff. "Hop! Scramble!" They did. Lovely.

But the esteemed guests preferred the counter in the kitchen. Uncle Yildiz arrived, bringing Grandma, then Luc, on an extreme teleport from Orange. Only Asimia was missing.

"Simi?" Snowfox ventured timidly. *"Are you coming, love? We're all here. You'll want to hear this."*

"We're coming. It's a bit delicate. I can't rush it."

A wormhole blinked in and out, and Alex jumped out of it, but no one else. The rascal hissed and growled at everyone, then padded off to settle by the hearth. The foxes followed him. Another wormhole sputtered, stuck. Asimia walked out of it, ushering someone behind her, gently pulling his hand and encouraging him.

A man stepped out, and the wormhole closed abruptly behind him. It was Grandad Blaze, the dragon of Yand! He blazed so brightly that all had to shield their eyes. Asimia whispered something in his ear, and he dimmed down considerably.

"Come, Granda." She ushered him to a seat at the counter. The scientists rose and saluted him reverently. Wolfpack flew into his arms.

"My little Pathfinder!" Grandad exclaimed.

"I'm so glad you're here, Grandad," Snowfox said. "The good professors and our Pathfinder have charted a course through the space we shall travel, but you have already crossed it."

"Indeed, what an honor!" Khin exclaimed, taking Grandad's hand. Are you coming with us?"

"No, he's *singular* beyond!" Snowfox objected, eliciting smiles and chuckles from everyone. "But he'll come to visit for a spell." He turned his gaze at Pete as he said that. Then to Asimia, who took it to mean, *could you bring him?*

"I will bring you, Grandad!" she said.

"I better," offered Wolfpack.

They spent hours reviewing the course the scientists, pathfinder, and dragon presented. Asimia projected it into the space over their heads, filling the room with stars, celestial bodies and phenomena, and wormhole pathways. It was difficult to account for temporal space, and since the Pathfinder didn't fear it much, they resolved to be aware of it but not allow it to divert them.

Star-struck, they all watched Asimia's projections eagerly, with interruptions only as staffers paraded their dinner or brought another round of the good brandy. Snowfox lifted his glass in an exuberant toast: **"To the stars!"**

"To the stars," shouted all, raising their glasses. The kitchen staff, who had watched the show enthralled, took up the chant, "To the stars, to the stars!" rocking the kitchen and the entire wing of the residence.

Close to morning, they had exhausted Grandad Blaze, and he started to phase. Asimia wormholed him back to his lair and returned without delay. She offered everyone else teleport rides to their homes. To Snowfox's surprise, she also sent Pete home with a mage and only said goodnight to him with a peck on the cheek.

After a few careful hugs, Wolfpack wormholed away to Tuncay, and only Lucent remained. Asimia turned to her two betrotheds and said, "I'm sleeping in my bed tonight. You're welcome to join me."

Luc's eyes widened so much that she felt the need to explain, "We're only sleeping, so come in your pajamas. I mean the full attire, not only boxers. And be mindful of the cat. He kicks and drools in his sleep and sometimes bites." She turned to her room with Alex in tow, who stretched and yawned as he went; Snowdrift and Hunter followed them.

Snowfox was familiar with the three companions' sleeping antics, but Luc wasn't. "They bite?" he asked.

"Only the cat," Snowfox told him, turning to go get his PJs. "My foxes only drool and squirm, especially when they sleep with Alex. He bosses them."

Lucent grabbed Snowfox's wrist. "Wait," he said, flustered. "I don't have pajamas. Only boxers."

"No worries. Come on, you can have a pair of mine."

Snowfox, Asimia, Lucent Toast to the Stars

9. Over the Moon

A month later, Wolfpack made a full recovery, and a season of pageantry ensued. First came Asimia's engagements to Snowfox and Lucent. They kept it simple, as the Tuncan delegation was eager to return to their moon, where… they held two more engagements! Drace to Squirrel and Wolfpack to Mouse.

Oh, how Asimia wanted to attend her brothers' double event! So did Snowfox. The fireworks had to be spectacular with all three Dragoons involved. But how could she with the dratted null? Fox could have gone with Uncle Yildiz but chose to stay with her.

A state affair followed on Yand: Grandmother-and-Queen Stardust tied the knot with her long-suffering fiancé, Uncle Yildiz. It was a planet-wide celebration lasting two weeks. And that was the abbreviated version to avoid delaying what came next.

However, what came next did delay longer than anticipated. Asimia's twin, Hawklord, Second High Prince of Yand and heir to Yand's throne, laid his challenge (glove) at Gramdma's feet—but took two months to prepare for the duel. Stardust deemed it beneath her dignity to abdicate her throne and transfer the title to Hawk. She needed first to humiliate him publicly.

But she didn't! Hawk bested her(!) and became King of Yand—although he was bloodier than Grandma at the end of the match. Asimia wondered: Grandma had never lost a duel! She was unparalleled in swordsmanship on planet and moon. How did Hawk learn to disarm her? It didn't help that every time he scored on her, Uncle Yildiz winked at Asimia.

The Tuncan family attended the event, but for Mom Yanara, again, because of the blasted null. Oh, how Asimia missed her mom!

At the end of the match, Grandma lifted Hawk's arm and pronounced him King of the Land. Then, smiling, she kissed him and handed him her crown. The crowd erupted, although it was difficult to tell whether the cries were celebratory or anguished.

Stardust had been queen for more than a millennium, and her people loved her well. But they also loved their new King.

He was the dashing prince who saved them from the K'tul in the bloodiest wars in Yandar history that nearly decimated the planet. When all was almost lost, Commander Hawk rallied his Flyers and mounted bloody aerials against the K'tul spaceships, pitting arrows and flesh against celestial cannons. And after Mom blasted those ships from Yand's skies, it was this young prince who led the cavalry on the ground, exterminating the landed invaders.

Plus he was so young, handsome, and single. Everyone titled wanted him for their daughter or son or even for themselves.

Hawk took a lap of victory on his splendid unicorn, Flyer. Joy and pride for her twin overwhelmed Asimia. As the planet's worldmaker, she had the honor of crowning and pronouncing him king. There wasn't an eye left dry in the world or a throat not sore from cheering—or a rose petal unplucked on all of Yand. Yand's citizens had brought them all to the military field and showered them on Hawk.

When the adrenaline subsided, Asimia teleported the family to the residence, where an army of doctors and medics awaited with med bags filled with tricks and bandages.

Grandma Stardust and Uncle Yildiz had their belongings already moved in. "I told Snowfox not to fret. See? We're going on the migration!" Uncle told Asimia with a wink. "And she," meaning Grandma, "not bloodied much. I think the boy took the worst? She's fierce as ever with that blade of hers," and more such. He was giddy, and they hadn't yet opened the sparkly the palace had sent.

"I hope Hawk didn't notice all this prearrangement, Uncle," Asimia told him. "He did perform magnificently. Where did he learn all those new moves?!"

Two weddings followed the duel. A week later, Aunt Shadow felt recovered enough to marry her fiancé Flash. The affair took place at Riverqueen, where the couple made their permanent residence. It was a subdued event at Aunt's insistence. The Tuncan attended, again, minus Mom. It was great to see them so often.

Dad was beyond elated to see his twin sister on her own two feet in a semblance of her old self. Despite her many scars, she radiated happiness and was stunningly beautiful in her red wedding gown. She had refused offers to fix her face with worldmaker magic.

She didn't want to risk inadvertent calamities that usually followed worldmaker bends. She wore her scars as badges of honor.

Baby brother, Sunstorm, was a big hit at the wedding feast. He stole the show, like always, with his exuberant antics. He could say a few words now, giggling and begging for pick-up from every adult who paid him attention. His nanny had her hands full, although she had plenty of help. The little toddler had enthralled Fox, who called him scamp and brat affectionally and bounced him on his knee, earning endless giggles and face pats from the tiny hands.

Asimia felt a pang of guilt in her stomach to watch them. Snowfox loved babies and wanted a few of their own. *We'll adopt,* she told herself. And maybe she could have... she patted her belly.

Asimia's turn to tie the knot with her two fiancés came a month later, the day after Fox's birthday. Aunt Shadow and Flash had worn red at their wedding, the traditional silverblood colors, although Flash goldened. Red enhanced Aunt's silver complexion. Grandma Stardust and Uncle Yildiz, both goldenbloods, wore white, the dominant custom for the golden and even races.

Asimia was marrying a silvering man and a golden. So they did both. She and Snowfox wore red, while Lucent blinded everyone in head-to-toe white. Both her men were visions to behold.

King Hawk declared the wedding a royal affair and ordered a week's holiday for the planet. Yenda followed suit. Only *one* week, because that would last to the end of the newlyweds' honeymoons and the beginning of assembling the migration.

The wedding exceeded the highest expectations. Three separate processions led the bride and her two grooms through overcrowded streets, made to groan from the swell of migrants that had already begun to assemble. They led from the Worldmaker Palace, where all three resided, to the Palace of Yand, now home to King Hawk, the bride's twin. He performed the ceremony, which made it sweeter.

No one had seen a more esteemed escort than Asimia's. King Fatie and Viceroy Triex of Yenda counted among the Tuncan dignitaries and rode immediately behind her on unicorn mares. Flanking her was Grandmother, Emerita Queen Stardust of Yand, and Ma Mandolen, Warleader of Yand. Uncle Yildiz, the Dragon of Yand's flesh and blood and the Queen's husband, rode beside his wife. Such splendor!

Asimia rode her magnificent unicorn stallion, Snowwind, and people later remarked that she eclipsed them all.

Snowfox also rode his unicorn, Lightning. His procession preceded her own and Luc's. Asimia caught a glimpse of him when he mounted up at the residence. He shone like a thousand moons, handsome and commanding in his red attire. His foxes crowded before him on his steed. On his right rode Dad, the legendary Commander of the K'tul Wars. Beside Dad came Aunt Shadow, Regional Commander of the West Territories.

To Fox's left rode their brothers, Dragoon Dragonlord (Drace) doubling on his unicorn, Thunderclap, with his fiancé, the Yendal Dragoon Squirrel (Squirl). Beside them came their younger brother, Wolfpack the Pathfinder, on his magnificent unicorn mare, Horsie, with his Yendal fiancée Mouse, the third Dragoon, side-saddle before him. His wolves soft-padded by Horsie.

Alex insisted on riding with Mouse! He wanted to be in the *first* parade with the foxes and the wolves.

Lucent had the entire Orange Princehood contingent for escort, his mom and sister prominently to ride beside him. Asimia didn't see this magnificent golden-endowed procession but heard tales later. Luc and his family outshone the sun!

After they spoke their vows and the ceremony concluded, the endless parade of well-wishers—and those who wanted to kiss the bride—began. Asimia's mind disengaged, waiting for it to end so she and Luc could start their honeymoon. A rich voice jolted her from her daze. "Congratulations, my dear."

It was Pete. She looked up and faced his eyes filled with warmth and love. If there was pain or regret, they didn't show.

"Thank you," she replied as his kiss burned her cheek. There was so much more she wanted to say to him, but she kept it all to herself. He passed, and she remained.

She asked Lucent if he was ready for their honeymoon. He was eager to go, but his folks expected to see him at the feast at the residence to toast and celebrate. Could they depart after dinner? Snowfox bent behind Asimia and whispered, "At your own risk, man. You'll miss the opportunity to depart today."

Luc gave Asimia an inquiring look. "The hard liquor will flow freely, my love," she told him. "how much can you hold?" He squeezed her tightly about the waist. There was no escaping this fate. They had to mingle with the guests.

Snowfox had been right. By the time their esteemed guests had their fill of feast and newlyweds, Lucent was drunk, and she more so. So were most of their guests.

This was not an issue for the planetside folks. She and Snowfox had assigned designated extreme teleporters who didn't drink a single sip during the banquet. They stood by. Now, they obliged the inebriated revelers with their return trips home, mainly to Orange and Riverqueen. These dedicated staffers would have plenty to drink once they discharged their duty.

But it was different for the otherworlders—those who hailed from the moons Yenda and Tuncay. No teleport could bring these folks home. Only a wormhole. And their rides, Uncle Yildiz and Wolfpack, were also drunk, like herself. Not wanting to risk wormholing into somewhere unnatural, these folks agreed to spend the night and depart for their moons in the morning. They accepted accommodation at the residence.

The sleeping arrangements were comical. To settle the numerous guests, Dad claimed his old bedroom that they had given to Lucent, and all the boys slept with him. It was like the good old days of their childhood. Only now it included Luc, Fatie, Triex, and Squirl. Hawk also decided to stay—he'd already missed his Tuncan family and wouldn't pass up this sleepover for the world. The new King of Yand was still a teen, after all.

The girls, Ma Mandolen and Mouse, slept with Asimia in her room. At some point close to morning, Mouse rose from the bed. Assuming she went to the bathroom, Asimia kept from rolling onto her warm spot and waited for the girl to return. When Mouse did not, Asimia rolled over and went back to sleep.

A while later, a panicked mindscream shook her awake. It was Wolfpack. *"Asimia! Hurry! Help! I'm losing them!"*

He sounded so far away! And there were strange echoes, muffling, then amplifying. Terrified, Asimia jumped from her bed, dislodging Ma and Alex. She ran outside in her pajamas, the cat on her heels. *"Wolfpack!"* she mindyelled. *"Here! I'm here!"*

But there was nothing. No Wolfpack or Mouse. Only her brother's wolves, howling to the moons, sending chills into her heart. She reached for Snowfox and found his foxes yelping and barking—but no Fox! She had the ability to reach her husband a star system away! He had to be further!—or— *"Fox!"* she mindyelled with all her might as fear gripped her and froze her limbs.

Boys and men poured from Dad's room. Other guests, slower, began to open doors from the west, south, and east wings. Dad reached her first, Luc behind him, shouting, "What is it, love?"

"Da, can you feel Snowfox?"

"No! Nor Wolfpack. **Dragonlord!**" Dad yelled for reinforcements, but Drace was already beside him with Squirl.

"Where's Mouse?" the Yendal asked, bewildered. *"Mouse!"* he mindyelled his sister, but no one answered him.

A wormhole crashed with a loud bang of cold air. It was twisted, distorted. Asimia dove into it before anyone could grab and hold her back. She extended her arms, reached with both hands, and caught something! Wolfpack's hand! It was frozen.

She yanked with incredible force, lending magic to adrenaline, as another hand grasped her pajama sleeve from behind her and pulled along. The wormhole collapsed. It ejected them back to the courtyard, where the three—Asimia, Wolfpack, and another—crashed to the ground. The third person was Uncle Yildiz. But no one else was there. The courtyard was empty.

"What the hell," she shouted, "what—"

"Temporal," Wolfpack yelled, popped another wormhole and pushed them through. They dropped at the exact spot, only now the yard was filled with people—everyone but for Fox and Mouse.

Wolfpack was cold and shaky. "Hurry," he yelled through chattering teeth. "I need your help or lose them forever. My wormhole won't reverse chirality. I couldn't transfer them. They're hanging at the edge of Temporal Space. I need you to hold their end open. We'll ride the one-way backward. On my mark!"

"Can it be done?" Uncle yelled, his alarm plain. Grandma grabbed her husband's sleeve and held on for dear life.

"I'm not losing you again," she cried. "I'm coming with."

"Me too," Ma yelled, grabbing at Asimia's arm but missing as Asimia danced around her. Dad had a vice grip on Asimia's hand.

"No!" Yildiz yelled, shoving Grandma violently and yanking his arm free.

Wolfpack popped a wormhole. "It's temporal," he cried. "I'll augment it with a straight-time. Hold your wormholes. Now!"

That was the mark. "Let go, Da," Drace told their dad, waving his hands in a negate spell. Asimia dove into Wolfpack's wormhole. Uncle Yildiz and no one else followed behind her.

They fell into darkness. It was like no other wormhole Asimia had ever experienced. *Temporal,* Wolfpack said. But it was endless! Suddenly at its distant event horizon, a figure! She doubled her efforts. Instinctively she reached to the nearest quasar for cosmic rays to form micro black holes for a wormhole.

"No!" Wolfpack mindboomed, deafening her. *"You'll collapse my temporal, and we'll lose them forever! Hold the course!"* Like there was anything else Asimia could do. She held.

The figure at the end grew, resolved into two. It was Snowfox and Mouse. Unmoving! Mouse had her arms around Fox, and a bubble of something surrounded them. Air! The Dragoon girl had wrapped them in a nimbus filled with the life-giving stuff! But it was shrinking. As she and Wolfpack approached the two, their air diminished to nothing.

"Is there a planet with a breathable atmosphere? Can you deposit us?" Asimia mindyelled Wolfpack in desperation.

"Yes, look," he replied, projecting an image into her head. Exotically beautiful, a planet-size object buzzed electrically. Fully developed auroras flashed on its horizon, like crowns on a princely brow. It was spectacular to behold, but their need was greater.

"Now!" Asimia urged her brother.

"It's peculiar, rogue. Not tethered to a star," he hesitated. *"Its magnetic field is hundreds of times stronger than Yand's."*

Of course. It was what caused the auroras. *"I'll compensate for gravity,"* Asimia told him. *"Now, or we'll all die!"*

"I don't know if I can break us from there," Wolfpack yelled while diverting his wormhole to the peculiar planet. How did he do that? It was a new path, Asimia realized, a straight-time. She lunged for the figures at the end, her momentum throwing them all from the wormhole into darkness. Her feet touched solid ground.

The gravity crushed her. She compensated quickly and opened her eyes to spectacular light shows. Wolfpack and Uncle Yildiz squeezed their sides and panted hard beside her. In her arms, Snowfox and Mouse didn't stir. They remained still and frozen with the coldness of death.

She frantically patted their cheeks, and Wolfpack and Uncle Yildiz followed suit, rubbing their arms and legs. Wolfpack's face was right beside her. She slapped him hard, repeating a few times.

"Hey," he objected.

"Are you sober now, Pathfinder?" she yelled. "A pathfinder lose his way?" He didn't reply. "Can you go back?"

"I'll have to—"

"Do that! Go back now and fetch five air packs on temporal. Or your brother and fiancée are dead. You want to live with that?"

He popped away but reemerged in the next heartbeat—impressively temporal. He brought five air packs. "I know how to get back," he yelled, "but it's not easy. Don these."

They haphazardly fitted Snowfox and Mouse with air packs. A sparse groan was the only indication that the two lived. "But you can do it!" Asimia yelled back at the Pathfinder.

"Yes. You'll have to hold this end open if I'm to manage the transfer. Mouse! Come, love." He donned an air pack and lifted his fiancée in his arms. Asimia and Yildiz donned theirs.

"Tell us what to do," Asimia yelled, lifting Snowfox into her arms. Uncle Yildiz wrestled her for the honor, but she wouldn't yield her new husband. She was acutely aware of how much she loved him, how meaningless her life would be without him. She might as well die if they couldn't recover her Fox.

Wolfpack quickly gave them two options: a temporal wormhole on top of a one-way. This maneuver would return them home in their proper time. Or they could forego the temporal and only ride the one-way backward to end up home but at a different time. He would then bring them back to their proper time with a temporal. It was how they recovered him the first time.

They opted for this last. Time was ticking. Ready? Three wormholes opened simultaneously… and collapsed. They stood on the same earth, on Peculiar. "No!" Wolfpack cried. "You ride my wormhole. Hold yours until I say. Again! Ready?"

This time, only Wolfpack opened a wormhole. They tried to step inside it, but only the Pathfinder succeeded. *"Now, your wormholes!"* he commanded in their minds. Two wormholes opened, sputtered... collapsed again.

"Try only one," he amended. *"Asimia! Now!"* This time Wolfpack's wormhole remained open, and Uncle Yildiz, dragging Asimia with Snowfox in her arms, stepped inside it.

"Sustain it, Simi," Wolfpack mindyelled. *"Use your infinite strings. Fix the chirality so we can transfer."*

But Asimia's hands were full. *"My pocket, Uncle,"* she yelled. Her uncle searched her pajama pockets for her infinite string stabilizer crystals while retrieving his own. He shook them violently, a set in each hand, then spun them, forming a micro-tornado, a top. Asimia's were Alices—had no chirality—and his double one-ways.

Wolfpack's Pathfinder sword and brow gem burst into twin blue waves that merged, blinding with a radiance rivaling this world's auroras. Balancing his beloved in one arm, the Pathfinder produced his own infinite string contraptions from a pocket, Alices like Asimia's, and spun them, whipping up a second blue wave. The sword, the gem, and the crystals merged, exploding in a spectacular blast—like the birth of a star.

It blew them. They moved, albeit slowly, agonizingly. Inch by painful inch, they crept backward—against the chirality of the one-way wormhole! Or had it reversed? Uncle Yildiz pulled Asimia when she faltered, still twirling their combined infinite string tops. The double wormhole closed with a deafening boom. It hurtled them into the residence's courtyard, many years into the past.

"Don't move," Wolfpack yelled. He gave another blast of his sword and infinite strings, opening a new wormhole. It was temporal, and encompassed the haggard little group. It threw them onto the same spot but at their proper time. People, three wolves, two foxes, and a cat scrambled around them.

The doctor and an army of medics descended on them. They snatched Snowfox from Asimia's arms and Mouse from Wolfpack's. Before either of them could react, a barrage of questions assaulted them, Ma's above all. "What happened? Oh my! Fox! Mouse!"

"Wolfpack wormholed drunk," Asimia fibbed, making it up on the spot, "and wormholed to Frozen Moon instead of Tuncay." Frozen Moon was Turunc's sixth moon. It was frozen.

"Asimia!" Wolfpack objected.

"Stick to this story!" she rebuked him forcefully in guarded mindspeak. *"Uncle Yildiz!"* Uncle got the point. They shouldn't alert the Tuncan about the danger in their expedition's planned course. It would create a mess. They might enlist Mom Yanara to help, which would be a disaster, and not only because of the null!

"We found them freezing on that moon," Uncle confirmed.

"Wolfpack!" Ma yelled. "With me!" But she would have to negotiate his wolves to get to him.

"Leave him, Ma," Asimia cried. "Let him see to his fiancée first and me to my husband. Berate us later! Please!"

The doctor jabbed copious needles into Snowfox and Mouse to get their blood flowing, warm them, etc. He ordered a scalding hot bath. He meant to thaw them. The Tuncan followed the medics anxiously. Asimia hopped after them, determined not to let her new husband burn. His foxes, agitated and yelping, followed with Alex.

A hand on her shoulder diverted her attention. It was Lucent. "Asimia," he started, but seeing her anxiousness, he amended, "ah, see to Fox, then meet me in the kitchen."

"Can you please see the folks to their moons?" she asked.

"Will the Tuncan go? And send them with Wolfpack? Do you trust him to wormhole? He's not that drunk in truth, is he?"

"No, but we best send Uncle Yildiz—"

"To keep the pretense," Uncle finished for her. "I'll round them up, my girl, but don't expect them to go until Fox recovers. You don't look too good yourself. Let's have us a warming brandy."

Grandma Stardust pulled her husband bodily toward the kitchen. "Lucent, bring her," she ordered. "Let the med staff do their thing. She and Yildiz can do better with some mulled liquor in them. Pierre! Pronto!" she yelled to the chef like she owned the place.

Lucent put an arm around Asimia's shoulder. "Come, my dear heart," he whispered. Seeing her disarray, he pulled her into his embrace. "Oh, how I love you, my sweetheart! Come. I know Wolfpack is not that drunk. Where did he take you?"

Asimia burst into tears. "Oh, I'm such an idiot," Lucent continued, leading her toward the kitchen. "You have all the world on your shoulders with the expedition, and now this. Try not to worry, love. I have us ready to go on two or three days' warning."

"Ah," Asimia cried, "there are two thousand folks on the field expecting passage to the promised land… and we can't even bring ourselves through…"

"No, my love! We'll work out the kinks of the transfer. And we won't bring two thousand. We'll bring five hundred. I distributed tokens. We'll take only the greens."

Asimia regarded her husband in new amazement. Why did she underestimate him so? He ruled Orange, the largest and most productive province of Yand. This amiable, happy-go-lucky nineteen-year-old brought his state forth from the brink of the war's annihilation. Orange hadn't missed a harvest due to his governance.

"We must bring the military—" she began.

"They're all green, my dear heart."

"And RC—"

"And her precious baby. Yes. They, too, are green, as are the folks in your household, Stardust's, and mine, with their families. Also the scientists, engineers, and other essentials. The rest are orange or red. Some oranges go now, and some on a second pass."

"A second pass?"

"Oh, love! I'm bonded to you. I have an idea what trouble befell Wolfpack: a temporal anomaly in the middle of our planned route. He knew about it, right? Did we not decide a few weeks ago that it didn't warrant much worry? It must have gotten stronger. We'll compensate for it, or find another course. I'll bring Dr. KhinMarMar and Warbles to regroup with us tonight. And your Pete. Who knows? We may need to decipher some DNA."

"What? Luc—"

"Yeah. I know."

"What? I was going to ask, who's KhinMarMar?"

"Oh. That's Dr. Khin's full name. Khin means khinesis— movement, and mer—sea or wave. Oh! That's like *moving a double wave!* Or moving *in* a double wave?"

"Huh?"

"A diviner named her at birth. Do you think the sage woman mistook a wormhole for a wave?"

"A *double* wormhole?" asked Asimia.

They stared at each other, marveling. "Come," Luc urged, entering the kitchen and leading her to the counter. Grandma and Uncle had the mulled wine ready.

"But this meeting with the physicists, Luc, you'll delay our honeymoon?" Asimia muttered quietly. "Are you giving it up?"

"It can wait another day or month or century. We can take it on our new world, my dearest heart." To her unsettled expression, he added. "All I need right now, all I ask of you, is my wedding night… if you would like…"

She folded into his arms and kissed him soundly. "Yes," she said. "Come to my room tonight. You won't need your PJs, but do mind the cat." The cat had returned from the infirmary and growled.

Luc smiled and gave her a gentle kiss. Grandma poured a glass of the warm liquor down Asimia's throat, then extricated Luc, and the two went to see to the final but endless migration details. Uncle went back to his bed, although it was now morning. The Tuncan didn't need him for transport. They decided to stay.

Asimia ran to the infirmary. She found Fox and Mouse submerged in a piping-hot bath, breathing through tubes attached to oxygen tanks. Wolfpack was in the water with them, rubbing Mouse's arms and legs, as was Ma Mandolen, doing the same to Fox. The foxes and wolves whined and yelped outside the door.

Asimia climbed into the tub and took over from Ma. It took a few hours to bring Fox and Mouse to normal body temperature. Doc added sedatives in their IVs to keep them sleeping and speed up the healing process. He assured everyone that they were out of danger.

With that, the Tuncan acceded to return to their moon. Asimia, Wolfpack, and Uncle spent the rest of the day exploring the anomalous space that faced them, trying to find a simpler way to navigate it. But in vain. In the early evening, Lucent brought Drs. Warbles and KhinMarMar, so Asimia and her fellow wormhole masters took a break from the endless treks and sat with the physicists to discuss science of wormholes and temporal anomalies.

Kitchen staffers served dinner at some point, keeping to simple finger foods, and the group worked while eating. Asimia saw that Fox's foxes and Wolfpack's wolves got their dinner at the infirmary. Alex ate with them, of course. He liked to boss them.

Wolfpack thought something had ensnared the peculiar planet toward Batentaban, the Chi-Draconis star. It captured it in a quantum of temporal space! Any interactions with it accelerated its temporal shift. He could tell the anomaly was variable and growing overall. It was much stronger now than when he first found it.

Dr. Khin could see no way their wormholes caused the acceleration. It took something much stronger. A few natural phenomena could cause it, but not in this timeframe. What then? A bend? How? Who? But they could find no answer.

Still, they needed to navigate it. Dr. Khin offered wormhole theories[*] to expand their arsenal of Alices and navigation of reverse chirality. Wolfpack wanted to try her ideas immediately, but Lucent forced them to call it a day—a night—and resume in the morrow. He reminded them of Snowfox and Mouse in the infirmary.

Before they adjourned, Dr. Warbles got them to agree to collect data from the peculiar space to see if they could explain it with anything more scientific—purer physics than wormhole theory. That earned him fierce glares from Khin and an assignment from Luc to assemble a science team to do that. And the physicists left.

Luc led the way to the infirmary. They found Snowfox and Mouse sleeping soundly and looking well. Wolfpack stayed behind, but Luc escorted Asimia to her room. He carried her through the threshold, deposited her gently on the bed, and shooed the cat away. But Asimia had a better idea. She teleported them to Dad's rebuilt observatory-turned-bedroom and opened the dome. Her new husband loved her all night long under the stars.

Close to morning, while lying lovingly in each other's arms, Asimia felt a pang of guilt. "I'm sorry, my love," she whispered.

"What about, my dearest heart? Wasn't this good for you?"

"Mmm," she replied, among soft kisses. "I didn't mean *that,* silly. I meant about the moon," meaning their ruined honeymoon.

"What moon?" asked Luc. "Ah, yes, the moon," he added, catching on. "No worries, my dearest. I'm over the moon."

---

[*]**About Wormholes:** A *one-way wormhole* has fixed chirality—it is traversable only in one direction. An *Alice wormhole* is non-orientable—it reverses its chirality once something enters it. The wormhole masters use their infinite string devices to stabilize their wormholes. Asimia used her Alice wormhole to reverse the chirality of Wolfpack's one-way so they could return home. The Pathfinder was the only one who mastered temporals.

Asimia and Lucent in the Telescope Room

Future Time: At the cordon in Paria, continuing from Chapter 7.
Sunny's POV.

10. Burning Woods

Sunny's heart beat so hard he thought it'd fly from his
mouth. He could hear Willie's loudly in his ear as they both dangled
from his dad's arms. He was even too scared to worry about the
indignity of that. Dad rounded the corner, and there was the entire
household awaiting them in the backyard of the Blue House. Their
collective anxiety and fear was like an extra punch in the gut.

The moment Dad's feet touched the ground, Willie flew into
her mom's arms. Aunt Nara grabbed her daughter and hustled
inside, shooing staffers out of her way. They all followed her. Dad,
with him still in his arms, followed, too. Oh! Sunny realized. He had
promoted Sir to Dad. There was no going back now.

Uncle Triex burst through the kitchen door and nearly fell
onto them. He squeezed his sides, panting hard and dripping sweat.

"See that he hasn't taken any injury, but take him out of my
sight before I make sure he does!" Aunt yelled at Dad through
clenched teeth. "He caused this mess! He hurt my baby! He brought
that K'tul's attention onto us!"

"Look, Nara," Dad objected, "He's taken such a fright. Let's
have the medic see to both kids, and we'll figure it out after—"

Uncle Triex interrupted him with a terse glare. "Best take
him, Pete," he said, "we'll talk later when Fatie returns. Let's see
what he has to say." Dad turned toward their quarters, Sunny still in
his arms. A woman followed—aghh, she was a nurse!

To Sunny's relief, the nurse's examination was brief, and she
didn't jab him with any needles. She only lingered about his neck,
where the K'tul, Mn'ianka, had squeezed him. He felt a few bloody
nicks there that were sure to turn into bruises.

"These will turn bright blue on him before they darken," the
nurse pronounced, "on account he silvers."

Worst fate ever! But the woman smiled! Oh, she smiled at
Dad! "He's fine other than that," she continued. "I see no lasting

harm. But an *even* child would do better by you, my lord, I think. A few of us wouldn't mind obliging you."

"Thank you kindly," Dad interrupted her. "I'll consider it."

With a pat on Sunny's head, she turned to go. "Take care of the little rascal. I'll see to Willie."

Sunny scrambled to get down from Dad's knees, but Dad held him fast. "What?" he complained, "I'm good. You can let go."

"Oh, I can let go now? I think we'll have a little chat first."

Uh, oh! Trouble! Sure enough, Dad went on.

"Why did you hit Willie?"

"I didn't hit Willie! Honest, I didn't, Dad. I only called her porcupine hair and pulled her pigtails. That's all."

"You what? Oh, and that was all?"

Sunny shook his head repeatedly to confirm.

"*Porcupine hair?* You called her *that?* Oh, my!"

Sunny continued to shake his head.

"Now, why would you do that? And you pulled her braids?"

"Only a little..." Sunny's voice started thin and got squeakier the more he tried to explain. "Her braids were worse than the porcupine—"

"Enough! You rascal! You brat! Didn't your mother teach you anything? Some manners? Some decorum! Even when you don't like something, it's not always wise, and certainly not nice—"

Dad stopped abruptly. Sunny's lower lip quivered, and his eyes welled in tears. "My Ma..." he squeaked, then burst into sobs.

Dad's countenance changed. "Now, now, my lad," he exclaimed. "I'm such an idiot. What have I said to you? No matter. No worries, my Sunny. I know you lost your mom in the blasted war that made you an orphan." He bounced Sunny on his knees, caressing his hair and wiping the tears from his face. Sunny buried his head in Dad's shoulder.

"Tell me why you hated Willie's hair so much. You liked it, maybe? A bit too much, maybe?"

"It's her birthday, Dad. She'll be a year older."

"So?"

"And I'm not! She's two years older than me now!"

"Isn't your birthday next month?"

"Yes, but I'll never catch up. She'll always be older!"

"Right. You've figured that out? So what? Does it matter?"

"Her hair is so beautiful, and she's so much older now; she won't want me anymore!" Sunny's sobs intensified. He was bawling by the time Uncle Triex walked through the door.

"This can't go on, Pete. Willie is wailing. She's more discombobulated than him," he pointed at Sunny. "We can't keep them like this. She's eleven now—"

"They're still children, man, but here, I've drafted papers. It's not like anyone would argue about it!" He handed Uncle Triex a wad of papers. Uncle looked them over briefly, found a writing implement in his pocket, and put his signature on the top page.

"You rascal," he told Sunny, "I best not regret this! Nara will have my head!" Then he turned back to Dad. "The boy better sleep here with you from now on until—"

"No!" Sunny objected violently, dislodging himself from Dad's lap. "I sleep with Willie!"

"It's not up to you, scamp!" Uncle replied severely. "You'll mind your elders or—"

"Or what?" Dad challenged his friend. "How will you enforce it? How far are you willing to go? Can you keep a blinker from your daughter's bed? We've betrothed them. Is it not enough?"

What? Whew! What did Dad mean *betrothed?*

"Dad, I don't want—" he started, dismay plain in his voice.

"Shut up!" His dad silenced him with a menacing tone. "Can you stay calm for a spell? Who asked you, anyway?"

Sunny cringed and shrunk.

It was a long while before Uncle Fatie returned from his negotiations with the Renegade K'tul leader. Mn'ianka searched for Hrysa, Uncle said. But there was something else, too. They found something or someone and were uncharacteristically cryptic about it. Uncle Fatie didn't hear any details but guessed it was Asimia. He lingered at the base to catch anything more, but in vain.

Despite Dad's objections, the adults decided to hold Willie's birthday party and then delve into Ops SpyNet business. It was a small gathering, a handful of kids and a couple of adults, Yanus among them. Sunny didn't know how to approach Willie. They exchanged tense glances all day long until evening arrived, sealing Sunny's fate: Willie no longer wanted him.

Depressed, he crawled into his dad's bed that night and curled up, sucking his thumb. Dad found him like that and covered him with the blankets. "Well, I'll be…" he muttered, shaking his head. "How can one so small be so forceful?" He caressed Sunny's hair, then left, presumably for the Hearth Room, where the adults held their meetings. Sunny was too tired to stir but turned his keen listening ear through the cracked door.

Yanus's voice carried above the others. He brought news of K'tul activity by the Keys. Renegades and redrobes searched for something around the ruined Halfway Inn. One of Yanus' lads tried to creep close to them to hear, but they barked their words in K'tul that the boy didn't understand well—none of his lads did.

Hmf! Sunny thought. I *should go.*

"But one thing for sure," Yanus went on. "The K'tul aren't working together as we feared at first. The greyk'tul threatened the K'jen with violence a couple of times."

"You think they traced Asimia?" asked Uncle Fatie.

"Nah," Dad disagreed. "I would feel her if she returned,"

This piqued Sunny's curiosity enough to make him crawl to the hearth room's door to peek at the adults. They were giving his dad weird looks.

"What?" asked Dad. "I'm bonded to her. Are you not?"

"We are," Uncle Fatie replied, pointing at Uncle Triex. "And to Fox, Hrysa, and Silvia. But I don't sense anyone, do you, Triex?"

Uncle Triex said no. Everyone in the room took to feeling for the royal family. In vain. Sunny stretched his own senses, and lo! Silvia! It gave him such a fright that he forgot he pretended to sleep.

"Dad!" he cried.

Dad ran to him. "What is it, son?"

"Silvia is on Hellbound!" Sunny shouted.

"Can you feel her? Asimia? The others? You're not in bed?"

"Yes. No, only Silvia. I could hear you, I wanted—"

"Eavesing again? Leave it us, eh, my boy? No. Wait. Why couldn't *we* feel Silvia?"

"I don't know, Da."

"And she's on Hellbound?"

Sunny nodded. Dad took him back to bed and tucked him in, bidding him stay this time. He returned to the hearth room to inform the other adults that Silvia was on Hellbound, still alive a year after her abduction. It caused quite a commotion. The adults had many questions and theories and wondered if they should attempt to rescue her. Then they turned to the fates of Snowfox and Hrysa. Maybe that was who the K'tul hunted about the Keys?

Asimia's case was different. Snowwind had taken her to another dimension. They argued on that forever. Sunny listened for a while until he got bored. He climbed out of bed and went to Dad's desk to look for the papers Uncle and Dad had signed that morning.

He found the document in a side drawer. He read it. The more he read, the more his eyes popped. It was about a betrothal between Willie, First High Princess of Yenda and Third of Highwings, second degree. But someone had scratched out the word *Third,* scribbled *Second* above it, and initialed it TM and NR.

Yandar and Yendai took their most influential parent's first name for a surname or, if more influential than their parent, a descriptive title about themselves. Nara was Nara, Ritchie's daughter, initials NR, but Triex was Triexador the Magnificent, initials TM. Pete was Pietro the Geneticist, Singular, initials PGS.

He read on. Betrothed to him, Sunny, First High Prince of the Parian Cordon. Initialed PGS. What? No! Oh, no, never! This wouldn't do at all! Sunny fished an ink pen from the front desk drawer, scratched all that nonsense out, and scribbled Fifth High Prince of Yand and First of Tuncay over it. He pondered that briefly and augmented it to say, *probably King of Tuncay.* He scribbled his initials, SY, although he didn't know where the Y came from.

The paper was his and Willie's promise to marry each other without exclusions of other. He objected to that, too, and, since he was on a roll, amended it to say, *to the exclusion of all others.*

There! He had to show Willie. He nearly yelled out her name but remembered where he was and that he needed stealth. He nearly blinked out when another paper caught his attention. It was wrinkled and soiled with ancient dirt or… whatever.

He unfolded it carefully, smoothing out the edges so it would lay flat, and read it. Among many other various stuff, it said this: Asimia, Worldmaker and First High Princess of Yand, blah, blah, and Pietro GS blah, blah, betrothed to marry blah blah when he comes to Phe'lak to stay. What? He read it again. Oh! Wasn't Asimia… and Pietro… now his dad!

"Willie," he mindyelled with all his might and blinked vigorously into her bedroom, crashing at the end of her bed. She lay

on her stomach, crying. Seeing her like that, he forgot all the stuff he came to tell her.

"Willie, don't cry!" he murmured in utter dismay. "I don't hate your porcupine hair. Well, actually… no! Wait. Don't start bawling. I hate your braids only. It's ok."

She stopped short of bursting into sobs. She flipped the covers and patted the mattress beside her, curiosity at the papers overcoming her anger at him. Sunny was cool with that. It was acceptable. "What you got there?" she asked him.

The two poured over the two sets of papers. They had plenty to fight over their own contract—if not for the other. It was juicier.

"Is PGS and Pietro your dad?" asked Willie.

"I think so…"

"He and our Queen…" Sunny only shook his head yes, his eyes still wild, matching Willie's.

"And you think they… did it?"

"Did what? Whew! Oh no! You had to think that!? What's wrong with you? That's disgusting! No, never!"

Willie giggled, and he joined her. "But what's all that stuff about you?" she continued. *King of Tuncay?"*

They went on like that until they fell asleep from exhaustion. At some point, strong arms lifted Sunny and carried him to another room, another bed. A minute later, still asleep, he blinked back beside Willie.

When he woke up in the morning, back in his dad's bed, the whole world was on fire. No. But you'd think so. *"What's going on?"* he asked Willie's head.

"You slept in," she replied. *"There's much news. Dad reported from the K'jen temple that the K'tul found a unicorn and are trying to capture it."*

What? Oh, no! The only unicorn left on Phe'lak was Snowwind! Sunny had taken the others to the moon. Plus if they found Snowwind…

"Where?" he asked. *"We have to save him and Asimia."*

Willie burst through the door. "Can you feel her, Sunny? How are you bonded to her?"

"I'm not bonded to *him*," he replied. "Oh, you didn't mean the unicorn; you meant my sister?"

"You have a sister? Who?"

"Asimia."

"There you go again, Sunny!" Willie shouted angrily. Fine, let's go save them, but you stop your crazy fibbing."

Sunny put on his trousers—he had slept in his shirt—took Willie's hand and blinked them to the Keys near the Halfway Inn, a bit off the main road. They crept the rest of the way on foot, hiding in whatever shadows they found.

The inn was a ruin of ash and debris and crawled with K'tul, grey and red. Both factions were loud and hostile toward each other. Sunny understood the K'tul language well; he pulled Willie behind a boulder and listened.

Snakeman wanted the fey horse and the witch, but so did Mn'ianka. One of the greyk'tul referred to Mn'ianka as his boss. The redk'tul insisted they had jurisdiction since the villages—they meant the Keys—were under the Parian province, but the greyk'tul countered that Crater, their base, had already claimed them.

They went at it as they searched—for what? There was nothing here. This was the inn from where Snowfox sent Asimia off on Snowwind to preserve her life from the null. Sunny witnessed that, hidden in the shadows. It was when he brought his dad's anti-null elixir—only too late. Asimia had been too far gone for the remedy to work.

Could the K'tul have thought the horse hid here, shifted in that other dimension? But that event was a year ago! And it would mean the K'tul knew about unicorns' ability to shift!

Sunny and Willie watched the K'tul for a long time. Willie squirmed beside him, and he told her many times to cut it out. They used their specific mind frequencies so the K'tul wouldn't hear their mindspeak. Around noon, they were tired and hungry, but Sunny wanted to check another location.

He blinked them to the Burning Woods, where he saw Snowwind with Asimia and Hrysa the day after Simi's send-off. They found themselves closer to Karia than he had intended. The woods crawled with all sorts of K'tul. Black was prominent, but also many red, and a sparse grey. He pulled Willie behind a tree. A large group of blackk'tul carried on, yelling and… tracking? It was hard to tell what they did. They looked at the sky more than the earth.

Oh, Sunny thought! ***Hellbound*** *is in the sky.* ***Wolf!***

There came a loud boom, and two greyk'tul teleported in. One was Mn'ianka, the other his mage, K'nista. *The boom was to scare the others*, Sunny thought, *like an evil herald.* It sure scared the heck out of him. The redk'tul fared no better. Willie, too. She grabbed Sunny's hand and shook it. *"Take us home, Sunny!"*

Sunny blinked Willie and himself back to the Blue House. They caught hell. Not only was Willie's mom ready to take Sunny's head, but Dad was also ready to pounce. But Dad's pounce felt more protective than angry. He scooped Sunny into his arms and declared, "I'll deal with my son, if you don't mind, Nara."

He brought Sunny to their room before Aunt could reply. "What happened, son?" he asked, abandoning the pretense. "Did you sense Asimia? I didn't."

"Only her unicorn. Many K'tul hunted him—even now—"

"Which means Asimia could not be that far behind," Dad finished for Sunny. "I'm sure I would sense her, but you seem so disposed… Come, let us go get our lunch and see what other intel the others brought. You best act like I've dealt you a wallop."

"What? You mean…"

Dad only nodded yes, with much eye and eyebrow action.

"Should I cry?"

"Yeah, I think that'll help."

Sunny started to cry. Dad brought him to the kitchen, where lunch awaited. Sunny tried to worm his way to Willie, but Aunt Nara blocked him no matter where he approached from. Willie exchanged meaningful glances with him. *"I'm grounded,"* she told his private mindspeak. *"I'm never to see you again, and they may dissolve our betrothal."*

"Never!" Sunny vowed forcefully in her mind. *"They can't keep me away from you!"*

He sat beside his dad and ate his lunch quietly, listening to the adult conversation. It happened in mindspeak since Uncles Fatie and Triex were remote.

Uncle Triex reported from the K'jen temple that Snakeman was having apoplexy. He was hell-bent on capturing the Yandar witch, Asimia. But his brother on Hellbound, meaning Wolf, wanted her for himself, and how to conceal her from him? Uncle Triex advised his faux liege, Snakeman, to catch her first, then figure out how to evade Wolf.

He intended to buy the Yandar cordonites time to rescue their Queen. Dad agreed vigorously. So did Sunny, although nobody asked for his opinions.

Uncle Fatie reported from the K'tul base, Crater 1, that the renegades were also in an uproar. Mn'ianka and K'nista set out to hunt the precious prize but didn't say where—they were secretive about the whole affair. They wanted Asimia for themselves, thinking she would make a great bargaining chip for their cause. The horse was expendable. Mn'ianka ordered his troops to dispatch it the moment it made its appearance.

"But that's so stupid," Sunny burst out loud. "Then Simi would be stuck forever in the other world!"

"Shush!" his dad quieted him. "You heard all that?" Dad had an amazed expression on his face.

Sunny shook his head, squeaking. "Didn't everyone?"

"No! It was in private frequency that excluded you, you scamp! How did you break the code?"

Sunny raised his shoulders and flipped his hands. He didn't know. "I didn't do anything, Da. Honest." But suddenly, his senses exploded. "Asimia!" he yelled and blinked.

He found himself behind a tree—the same spot he and Willie had vacated an hour ago. His dad crouched beside him with a hand on Sunny's wrist. He'd figured out how to ride the blinks: touching the blinker.

A few yards away from them, two K'tul grasped Asimia(!) by the arms. She crumbled between them, small and translucent. Her wings fell limp to the ground behind her. No longer was she silver-white, but ashen-grey.

Snowwind shifted in and out, bucking and kicking the K'tul and jabbing them with his horn. But he couldn't stay in this realm long. The K'tul slashed him with scimitars and knives. His hide was more red than white.

Dad made to burst from their cover. *"Stay, Da,"* Sunny yelled in specific mindspeak. *"I'm smaller. I'll blink her out—"*

"No!" Dad yelled forcefully, also in specific. *"You will not do such a thing. You'll stay here! You hear me? I'll grab her and—"*

But Sunny untangled from his dad's hold, beat his wings, hopped to gain height, and dove for Asimia and Snowwind. Dad broke cover and lunged after him, but not fast enough.

The trees were too thick to afford Sunny much height. He missed his dive and nearly crashed to the ground. He tumbled, unleashing a burst of white-hot blasts, blinding the K'tul and throwing them off Asimia and the unicorn. Dad shielded his eyes as he ran after him. Asimia collapsed in a tiny broken heap with Snowwind nudging her, pushing her away from the immediate fray.

Silver-white fire buzzed about Sunny's body. It exploded from his hands, danced like lightning, and blasted forth to concuss all. K'nista threw a shield sphere around himself, Mn'ianka, Asimia and Snowwind, abandoning the others. Sunny dove for Asimia. K'nista's electrified shield threw him back violently. He fell into Dad's arms. ***"Blink!"*** Dad ordered forcefully.

"No!" Sunny yelled, but blink he did.

They popped into their room at the Blue House. The door burst open behind them, and Aunt Nara dove through with Willie on her wings. "What—" Auntie yelled, but a loud mindspeak boomed into their minds, interrupting her. It was Uncle Triex.

"You can't stay there, Pete! The whole K'tuldom is coming after you. Throw them off the cordon. Now! Or else we lose all!"

Sunny still shook from excess adrenaline. "How?" he yelled at his dad. "How did you make me blink?"

"No time, lad," his dad replied. "Deliberate later; save the world now! Blink us here."

"Don the red uniform first," Uncle Triex's disembodied voice instructed Dad. *"You must look like a K'jen."*

Aunt Nara grabbed a red uniform from the wardrobe and helped Dad into it. Dad gave Sunny a set of coordinates. Sunny blinked mindlessly. Willie's anxious face was the last thing he saw of the room. She waved her arms and begged him to take her along, but it was already too late, even if Auntie had allowed her to go.

Sunny popped back into the woods with his dad, close to the melee. But there was no Asimia(!), and many of the K'jen devils and K'nista had gone with her! Mn'ianka was still there, razing hell. A redk'tul heap littered at his feet in a pool of purple, and he still worked his scimitar. He had many more to get through.

"They got Simi, Dad! We must get her back!" Sunny mindyelled, struggling to break from his dad's grip. But Dad held him firmly. And where to blink? He needed coordinates! Ah! He could trace K'nista's teleport! It was fresh!

"Don't blink out, son! Hold!" Dad mindyelled, squeezing him hard. *"Triex got this. Can't you hear him? Snakeman has Simi in the K'jen temple, and K'nista is there. They won't kill her. They both want her alive! You and I must focus here!"*

He took Sunny's chin in his hands and turned his face to look at him. *"We must divert these K'tul, or they'll raze the village."* He meant the cordon. *"You with me?"*

Sunny could only give his dad a blank stare. Dad shook him hard. But Sunny had nearly phased from the flood of adrenaline. His heart raced dangerously. With a mighty effort, he felt for Uncle Triex's mindspeak. It was as Dad said. The K'jen had Asimia in the temple and argued with K'nista on possession.

"They must see us," Dad commanded, still shaking him. *"You understand? On my mark, break from cover and run like your life depends on it—because it does! We'll do it in bursts. Take cover, then run... then... Got it?"*

"Yes."

"Mark."

They burst from cover and tore through the woods.

"K'nista! To me! Now! The marauders!" Mn'ianka's mind summons echoed behind them.

A loud roar and a deafening pop followed Sunny and Dad as the top devil, K'nista, teleported in and ran after his First, chasing them. Explosions and fire boomed and crackled behind them as Sunny pounded after his dad on a maddening course, zig-zagging to avoid the hell that pursued them.

Missiles and blasts chased them unrelenting. *The **K'nista** **show** all over again,* Sunny thought with his heart in his mouth as he blindly ran after Dad, hopping and half-flying to keep up. With an incredible feeling of dejas vous, Sunny ducked behind a tree—straight onto his dad—and gasped for a heartbeat.

Then came the next mark, and he burst back out into the dancing inferno and ran. Again and again! It was the same thing K'nista had done to Hrysa a year ago that Sunny tried to save her from—did save her from. The Burning Woods burned for a second time as Sunny and his dad ran through the fires.

Who would save *them* now? He burst from cover again—no! His dad, panting and gasping, pulled him back. *"To the Crags. Blink!"* he ordered, and Sunny obliged.

They landed by the hearth in the depths of their family's cave. But it'd been a long time since that hearth burned. It was dark and cold in the cave. Sunny tried to take a step… and collapsed. His dad caught him instantly, before he reached the ground.

"Are you hurt?" he asked anxiously. "Let me see."

Sunny had a shuriken stuck in his thigh. Dad inhaled his breath at the sight of it. "I don't dare pull this, lad," he told Sunny. "It'll bleed."

Sunny was squeamish but tried not to show it. What if Willie saw? "I don't think I can run anymore, Da."

"I'll carry you. I don't expect us to stay here long."

Dad couldn't find any other injury on either of them. But their clothes were singed and smelled.

"He cooked us," Sunny declared. "Like he did to Hrysa."

Dad stared at him. "Hrysa?"

But they had run from the fire into the freeze. Sunny's teeth began to chatter. He squeezed tighter into his dad's arms, who took his red jacket off and covered him up with it. "Don't you go into shock now," Dad ordered.

"What shock? Am I dying?"

"No. But we'll both freeze solid in here. Hush. Catch your breath. Let me check with Fatie. *"Strike!"*

"Ink. Are you at the Crags? Are you safe?"

They used their code names!

"Safe enough. Can we come home now? I'm losing… you know who, and he's the only one who… you know." He didn't say his name or blink. A strong mage like K'nista and Snakeman may be able to hear their private mindspeaks. Better not risk it.

"Is the boy hurt?"

"Yes. One shuriken in his thigh. He'll need... you know."

This last *'you know'* was for Sunny's benefit. But Sunny understood that the ***you know*** meant surgery, and began to whimper.

"I don't need surgery, Da," he begged. "Just pull it out."

"They're inspecting the cordon—taking count." Uncle Fatie continued. *"They'll be looking for you, too. Best be there. Did they get a good look at you?"*

"Yes," Sunny mumbled out loud.

"We led them on a merry chase toward the Keys."

"Ok, good. I asked Doc to meet you back home. In your room, please, don't let Su— the boy run around."

"But I'll have to go find Willie," Sunny mumbled aloud.

"He won't go anywhere," said Dad. *"It's his leg. He won't be able to walk anyway."*

"Oh, that's not good. They may do a lineup. Devils 5 and 1 will probably come in person." The numbers indicated K'tul military rank. Uncle meant K'nista, 5, and Mn'ianka, 1. *"He'll need to be able to stand."*

"No, I can't," Sunny whimpered aloud. "It hurts, Da!"

"He'll stand." Dad contradicted him. *"We best get going and fix him up so he can do it."*

"I told Triex to expect you. Snakeman sent him home."

"Oh? That's not good."

"It's neutral. Go. Before it rains K'tul in the cordon."

"Right." "Sunny, blink us to our room," he said aloud.

Sunny did. The doctor waited inside their room with his evil bag in hand and a sinister smile on his face. What was that object in his hand? **A syringe?**

"Willie!" Sunny wailed at the top of his mind's lungs. The door flew open, and Willie hopped onto him, hugged him, and gave him a sweet peck on the cheek.

Hmm. All you have to do to get a kiss is get a shuriken in your leg? He'd normally object and wipe it off, but it felt so good, and he was so tired. He passed out.

When he came to, his shuriken was gone, and bandages had replaced it. He lay in Dad's bed, Willie sitting anxiously beside him.

Sunny, Pete Escaping K'nista, Burning Woods

Future Time: At the cordon in Paria, Continuing from Chapter 10. Sunny's POV.

11. Temporal Blinker

"**W**here's my dad?" Sunny asked Willie.

She shrugged her shoulders. She didn't know. "They had a meeting while you slept, then rushed out like crazy people."

"Where did they go? Never mind. *Dad?*" he yelled in mindspeak.

"Disengage, Sunny. This is not a good time," Dad replied.

"Where are you? Coordinates, Da. We need to save Simi."

"Leave it to us—"

"No!" Sunny exclaimed and forcefully barged into the mindlink to probe with his meta senses. It took all his strength, but he found his dad crouching behind an object in a dark room... no. The room was not dark. Many artificial lights lit it. But Dad was in darkness behind a... curtain? Furniture? Another Yandar and two Yendai crouched beside him.

Uncle Triex was in plain view in the light, surrounded by K'jen. Sunny winced and nearly blinked to that room but registered that Uncle wore a red K'jen uniform. He conversed with them as if... what? He was one of them?"

"He only pretends," Willie told him aloud, making him jump. "They're trying to rescue our Queen. Da said not to interfere."

"But—" Sunny objected, ready to blink.

"Sunny!" his dad interrupted him with that commanding tone. *"See to Snowwind. They cut him badly, and he'll perish if we don't help him. Can you do that?"*

"Yes. Where is he?"

"Same place in the woods. They left him there to bleed out."

"What? Oh, no! No, no, no!" Sunny yelled, unsure if aloud or in mindspeak, and blinked to the woods. Willie had grabbed a handful of his sleeve and came along. At the same location where the K'tul had Asimia, the unicorn lay injured on his side, bleeding from a thousand cuts. His breath came labored and weak as if dying.

"Snowwind!" Sunny exclaimed in utter dismay. Driven purely from adrenaline, he blinked the horse, Willie, and himself to their family cave at the Crags. As darkness and cold enveloped them, Sunny reached out to the doctor at the hospital. *"Doctor, Sir?"* he mindcalled. *"Can I please bring you? Bring your needles and meds and your bags."*

"Didn't I just fix you?" came the doctor's perplexed reply.

"Please, doctor, may I have coordinates."

"May you—" the doctor obliged Sunny's head with coordinates. Sunny blinked in and out and brought the doctor to the Crags. The man laid a glance at Snowwind and caught his breath.

"No time to lose," he declared, directing Sunny and Willie on how to help him treat the unicorn's wounds. Two hours and many salves, injections, pills, and bandages later, the doctor pronounced that was all he could do for the horse.

"Will you stay with him?" he asked. "We should bring him to the village if to survive, but we don't dare do that, do we? Your dad," a look at Willie, "would have my head."

"We'll watch him," Sunny assured the doctor, who returned a questioning look. But Sunny didn't add anything further. He blinked the doctor back to the clinic and returned to the Crags.

"Come, Willie, I know where to take Snow."

"Where?" she asked. "I'm scared when you leave me alone!"

"To the moon. And it was only a second."

He watched Willie's eyes pop out. "The moon? No! Nah…" she started but ended with a "…yiiikes!" as he hugged her by the waist while bending to the horse.

"Blink!" he cried.

They found themselves in a large courtyard of a country estate, with a sprawling residence in four wings around them. "Oops!" Sunny yelled. "I missed. Must be on account of my leg hurting so much."

He blinked them again. Now they emerged outside the stables before the open double doors. The residence was behind them. They could see far off to the right if they turned around.

Willie was bewildered. "Is this the moon?" she whispered in a thin voice. She twirled around, taking it all in. Eventually she grabbed Sunny's sleeve. "I'm scared, Sunny! Let's hide!"

With a last gentle caress of Snowwind's silver muzzle and a soft pat of the silky mane, Sunny left the unicorn to lay on the ground and followed Willie behind bales of hay. From there they could see through the open stable doors that many horses occupied the stalls. One was Hrysa's unicorn Silverstream.

"Silverstream, girl!" Sunny called to her out aloud. Willie covered his mouth with her hand. The mare gave a vigorous whinny and began to snort and kick. Snowwind answered her and attempted to scramble to his feet.

"Oh, no!" Sunny whispered through Willie's fingers. "He'll hurt himself." He pulled her hand off his face and shouted, "Help! Lucent! Come quick! It's Snowwind! He needs help. He's badly hurt. Help!" And more. Aloud and in mindspeak.

Stable hands emerged from everywhere and saw the injured horse. Sunny and Willie shrunk behind their hay, hugging each other tightly, as a mad scene unfolded around Snowwind. A young lad broke off and tore for the mansion, soon to return with Lucent.

"It's our lord the Second King," Willie mouthed to Sunny in amazement. "This is really the moon!"

Sunny shook his head many times up and down to indicate an emphatic yes. He recognized the man as King Lucent, although he wasn't sure how he knew him. But there was no time for discussion or deliberation. A vet and several medics arrived and bent to minister to Snow.

"Oh, no!" Sunny mouthed to Willie. "They'll give him more pills and kill him! Do you have the bottles the doctor gave us?"

Willie produced two bottles from her pocket. Before Sunny could think of how to get the meds to the vet without revealing themselves, Willie threw the vials at the vet without breaking cover. One hit the man on his back, and the other rolled by his feet.

"What by the gods…" the man exclaimed, turning to find the vial that hit him as King Lucent fished the other from the ground. Both men turned and stared hard toward the direction the pills had come from.

"Time to go." Sunny grabbed Willie's hand and blinked them out. He had meant to return them to the Blue House, but that was not where they ended up. Not only were they not home, but this was not a house or a village. This was a beach.

"Rats! I missed again!" he exclaimed. But where was this?

"What's this, Sunny?" Willie whispered in his ear. "Where are we?" She looked all around her. "I'm scared!" she declared. "Take us home, please!"

"Ah… I'm trying," Sunny objected. "But…"

"What? Are we lost?"

"Ah… I don't know. No! I… Yes, maybe!"

"Sunny, please! What is this place? Is this your home, where you came from?"

"No, of course not! This is a beach."

They stood in what seemed to be endless sands. But this was not the coast of Paria. That coast was not this sandy. Sunny had never seen such a long, glorious, smooth stretch… no, wait. Yes! He had! But not in any of the beaches of Phe'lak. There was another place… but the sands there were golden. These here were reddish, not as in blood, as in terracotta.

And it was wavy. So much so that it made Sunny dizzy. He swooned, and Willie caught him. The ground was definitely not flat. Ripples of sand sketched through it, larger the further from the water. A few more yards inland were dunes.

"Shall we hide behind that dune?" he squeaked to Willie.

"This is not home, Sunny! I don't want to hide; I don't want to stay here."

"But I'm dizzy. I don't know where to go."

"Do you think this is the other side of Phe'lak? It's not Paria. Or are we still on the moon?"

Sunny shook his head. He didn't know. He searched his mind for coordinates. "I thought I used the Blue House's coordinates. But when we blinked… Did you feel something else? Like another one?"

"You mean another blink?"

"Yes."

"No. I close my eyes when you blink."

"Ooh, Willie! You would still feel it with your eyes closed! *I* sure did."

"You mean somebody kidnapped us? I see no K'tul."

She cupped her free hand over her eyes and scanned the horizon. "There!" she called. Sunny turned where she pointed. In the distance, he spied a group of people splashing in the water and others… flying! These were Yandar! Flying free!

"They're flying, Sunny!" Willie exclaimed. "Let's go see!"

She beat her wings and tried to launch the two of them for flight, but Sunny had his feet firmly planted in the sand. She let go of him and took only herself in the air, hovering about him, dislodging sand that flew in his eyes.

"Owoo," he yelled. "Stop that!"

"Come! I want to see!" She took to low flight, calling behind her, "Follow me, Sunny. I see children!"

But Sunny's leg hurt like the blazes. He couldn't even beat his wings from the throbbing pain. When Willie let go of him, he wobbled backward and fell. Thankfully the sands were soft, but he felt it. He cried out in pain, but Willie was already far.

He shaded his eyes and watched her fly then dive into the water! He lost her among the other folks. "Willie!" he yelled aloud and in mindspeak.

"Come, Sunny! There are kids here. Two girls like me!"

"What girls? I can't move! Your mom and my dad will have our heads. Come help me find coordinates to get us home!"

But she splashed and giggled. Defeated, Sunny flattened himself on his back and gazed at the sky. It was glorious! Diffuse pink clouds scattered here and there, and lights! Rainbows and auroras! And not only one! Many of various colors and hues. Circular, they danced like fluid crowns adorning the brow of this peculiar world.

Now *that* was a word. *Peculiar.* Why did he think that?

And the sun… that was not Eltanin, Phe'lak's star.

How long did he stay like that? He couldn't tell. It felt strange, as if time was different here. Slower? Temporal?

Approaching giggles diverted his attention. He raised himself on an elbow and watched three figures flying low toward him. They swooped and skimmed the water, then the sand. One was Willie. She had new ribbons in her hair, emerald and crimson. She landed before Sunny and offered him her hand. "Look," she called, turning and pointing at two little girls who hung back shyly.

The girls looked to be Willie's age, both evenbloods. They, too, had many ribbons in their hair, one crimson and gold, the other emerald and silver. To see the three girls, three *evens*… they were so beautiful! But when the girls came closer, Sunny realized that one was not entirely evenblood. Her tone and aura rippled in waves, the colors of a rainbow, but always settled in a dark, even complexion.

And the other girl… this one was… Willie's twin?? She looked so much like her!

Oh, no! Sunny thought! *We've died and gone to heaven!*

From the distance, a woman separated from the group in the shallows and flew towards Sunny and the girls. She landed a few meters away, walking the rest of the distance. *Thoughtful of her not to dislodge the sand in our eyes.*

The woman came closer, and Sunny saw how pretty she was. Tall and graceful, with a striking resemblance to Willie's "twin"— and Willie!

"Ritchie," the woman called in a rich, resonant contralto. "Where have you gone to, sweetie? Who's your new friend?"

Ritchie!? Wasn't that the same name as Willie's gramma that the K'tul executed in Karia? Did the woman mean Willie's doppelganger girl?

Before Sunny's unbelieving eyes, *his* Willie dove for his hand, yelling. "Take us home, Sunny!"

Did the name Ritchie spook her, too?

Sunny blinked. They were not home. This was not the Blue House. They were at the stables on the moon. Silverstream whinnied him a greeting. Snowwind galloped in the pasture beyond.

*Galloped? But he was injured! This was a different **time!***

Squeezing Willie's hand like their lives depended on that act, he blinked again. Back to the red beach. But now all the people had left. And the time felt different than their earlier arrival. It was an earlier temporal time!

Panic gripped him. He was lost. One more blink. Stables. Clearly back on Sentinel One, Phe'lak's first moon. Phe'lak dawned on the horizon.

He blinked again. Back to the beach. No. Not the beach. They were in the peculiar planet's atmosphere! And wo! A K'tul spaceship lurked behind a moon(!)—clearly visible to him and Willie, but could the planet see it?

His mindscreams filled Willie's brain, feeding them back to him, amplified, along with hers. *"Blink, Sunny!"* she mindyelled, tearing every molecule of his consciousness. She projected a vivid image into his head.

"The Crags," he yelled with all his might. "Blink!"

They landed on hard rock. *Was this the Crags?* It was! They made it! In their cave! Discarded bandages from tending to Snow littered the place, so this had to be the correct time, at least approximately.

"We're are at the Crags!" yelled Willie. "It worked! Stop blinking! We can fly home from here."

"I can't fly, Willie," Sunny yelled back at the top of his lungs. "My leg hurts so much, I'm going to puke!" and proceeded to demonstrate what he meant. He couldn't contain himself any longer. He burst into sobs. Puking and crying, he mindyelled his dad.

"Da! Save us!"

Willie joined him. *"Ma! Da! Can you hear us? Come get us, please! We're lost at the Crags!"*

When he next felt conscious, Sunny lay in his dad's bed with Dad snoozing lightly beside him and hanging precariously from an edge. He stirred the moment he felt Sunny.

"You awake, son?" he asked.

"Where's Willie?" Sunny squeaked. He couldn't feel her beside him. Dad took his hand and guided it to the other side of the bed. She had rolled over and clung to the other edge. Sunny made to turn her way, but Dad scooped him in his arms.

"How do you feel? How's the pain?"

Sunny took inventory. Relieved, he realized the pain was gone. "Fine," he squeaked.

"So you want to tell me what happened to you two? You've been gone for two days. I lost my mind searching for you. Then you materialized at the Crags, minus the horse. What happened to him?"

"Didn't Willie say?" Sunny asked apprehensively. They had worked up a story while they waited for the adults to come and save them from the Crags. And they waited for hours! When the rescue finally came, it was in the form of Yanus and the fish cart. Yuk!

Sunny barely clung to consciousness by the time the master fisher stashed them under the fish, and now hardly remembered the excuses the man gave them for taking so long: The K'tul watched the cordon closely. K'jen came and went. They had a lineup.

"Did you have a lineup, Da?"

"Yes. Did Yanus tell you? We told the K'jen you died in the plague that's striking our young."

That made Sunny jump. "What?"

"Relax! There's no plague. It was a ploy to explain your absence to the K'jen. It made them less enthusiastic to search for you. What's a couple of pups to them? But Yanus said you were out of it the entire trip?"

"I was, but I heard him tell Willie about the lineup."

"So tell me your adventure. I want to hear it from you, my little scamp."

"Ah, emm," how did the story go now? "I brought the doctor, and he fixed Snowwind, then we stayed with him in his realm to feed him his pills. For—"

"Two days," Dad finished for him. "Right. But how do you know how long *you've* been gone?"

"Didn't you say…"

"I did. For me, it is now two days after the K'tul took Asimia from the Burning Woods. But what day might it be for you? I'm not sure it's the same."

"Da—" That objection came out whiny and a bit loud.

"Shush, quietly, please. Let's not stir everyone again. We just managed to settle them down."

"What happened to Asimia? Did we get her back?"

"No. We didn't get her back. Snakeman has her in the temple under so much guard not even Triex or Fatie can get to her. But she lives. I can feel her."

Sunny felt out experimentally. "Me, too."

"No, don't do that!" his dad admonished him. "They'll be watching for that."

"But Da—"

"I know. It's hard to bear. But bear we must, and not do any more stupid things."

"I'm sorry, Da, I didn't mean to—"

"I know, son. I meant *me* do stupid things. I let my feelings take over whatever reason I had left. I should have never sent you, an injured boy with strange abilities, to tend to a shifter horse.

"He would have died, Da. He was so near death he couldn't even shift! We couldn't just leave him to die."

"And have you saved him?"

"Yes. He was galloping in the future—"

"Future!" They stared open-mouthed at each other.

Sunny went first. "I'm sorry, Da," he muttered, tears welling in his eyes. "I couldn't… it got away from me, like always…"

"I should have guessed," Dad replied, squeezing Sunny tighter in his arms. "You can't control it, can you?"

Sunny shook his head no.

"Ok, no matter. We'll figure it out. Doc stopped by and rebandaged your leg. There's no infection, but you split your stitches and made it bleed."

"Is that why it hurt?"

"Does it hurt now?"

Sunny checked his leg again. The pain hadn't come back. "No. Nah. Only throbs a little."

"It hurt before not only because you split the stitches, but also your pain meds wore off. Come. I want to hear all about it, but let's go to my lab first to start some tests. It's time to figure out your genes, my Sunny. I resisted long enough."

Sunny's eyes popped. "With needles?" he squeaked in a breaking voice full of dismay and dread.

"Only a very tiny one, I promise. Can you blink?" "No," he amended urgently. "I'll carry you."

But Sunny was still stuck on the needles. "Please, Da," he breathed in a fading voice. "I promise I'll be good—"

"What? This is no punishment, son! I promise I won't hurt you a single bit, and you'll get to watch all the exciting stuff my instruments do while analyzing. We can't have you blinking around the universe and who knows what time. Ok?"

Sunny stared, ready to bolt.

"I know another temporal blinker," Dad continued, "and he can control it. No, not only control, master it. Once he waded hundreds of folks through an extraordinary temporal goop. I don't see why you can't learn to control your own ability. At least to a measure where I won't have to lose my mind every time you blink."

"You mean the Pathfinder? Me like him?"

"You know the Pathfinder? How?" Dad asked, amazed.

"I think he's my brother," Sunny blurted without knowing why he thought that.

"Your **brother?**" his dad exclaimed. "I'll be! And how could that be now? Let's see. Can you describe the Pathfinder?"

Sunny searched his memories. He thought so hard he might as well pass out. But he couldn't produce an image. He shook his head no.

"No, you don't know? Or no, you don't remember?"

Sunny shrugged his shoulders. "Right," said Dad. "Ok. Well, then. Let's go figure it out, my little mystery-full-of-surprises!"

"But what about Asimia? Weren't you rescuing her?"

"We'll have to trust Triex and Fatie. They sent me away. I *interfered,* they said. Hmf!"

Sunny arranged the covers over Willie, careful not to wake her, and then tested his leg to see if it hurt when he put weight on it. It did. "Here, take another pain pill," Dad told him, getting one from a bottle on the night table.

"Should I blink? I don't think I can walk. Maybe fly?"

"No! No blinking. No flying either. I'll carry you."

But how to accomplish that? They tried a few methods in vain. First, Dad wanted to carry him on his back, but the moment he put pressure on Sunny's leg—to hold him, Sunny cried out in pain. Then he thought of carrying Sunny in his arms, but Sunny didn't want to be carried like a baby. Strapping Sunny on his back was too scary; on his chest made Sunny fly upside down. They could flip him. Nah. It would scranch his wings!

They took one of the horses in the end. Dad mounted up and had a stable hand lift Sunny, placing him side-saddle in front of him. He even had a small cushiony pillow brought for Sunny to sit on. They rode through the streets of the cordon like that, with everyone staring at them. Sunny beamed to no end.

"You happy?"

"Yep."

They made it to Dad's lab at the college. His techs had a look at them and made their excuses just as Dad attempted to issue orders. He thought of yet another trait to test for. Sheesh. At this rate, he'd probably drain all of Sunny's blood!

"Did you really spend time in Snowwind's other dimension?" Dad asked him. "Can you shift, son?"

Sunny said nothing but cast his eyes to the ground. Dad may change his mind. But no!

"You can, can't you! Why should that surprise me? No, wait, don't start crying! It's ok, I'm not mad at you! I'm only trying to fathom… what… who you are."

Sunny tried hard not to cry, but his lower lip trembled on its own again. What if Dad didn't want him after discovering what and who he was? What if he was some thief or murderer?

But Dad pulled a chair and sat, bringing Sunny onto his lap. "Listen good, my sweet boy. It doesn't matter to me who or what you are. You're my son, and I love you. You got that?"

"You do?"

"Yes. Is that so hard to understand?"

"You won't let them execute me?"

"Now wait a minute here. That is too preposterous even for you! Who would dare execute you?" Then Dad noticed the tears already running down Sunny's face. "Oh. My! You really believe that? Why, my silly boy?"

"Because I blink and I'm different, and I don't remember where I came from."

"Ah. So you truly don't remember? It's ok; tell me what you *can* recall. We'll piece together whatever else we can from what's inside you." He tapped Sunny's nose. "I'm a geneticist, right? Singular, essential, and all that stuff. And I'll want you no matter what we find. Deal?"

Sunny accepted that. Dad got up, fished into a drawer, and produced a glass slide and a small pin, sealed in a tiny sterile case. He washed his hands thoroughly, gloved them, and broke the seal, liberating the needle. He showed it to Sunny, who had already cowered away from it. "Wow, look at that, Sunny," Dad exclaimed, pointing out the window. "Is that a bird or a dragon?"

Sunny rushed to peer to see the dragon but instead felt a tiny bite on his finger. Dad took that finger and smooshed it onto the slide. "All done," he declared. "Tell me your story while I get this test going."

So, while Dad got his instruments whirling, spinning, humming, buzzing, spewing numbers, and more, Sunny explained that he blinked randomly, often in his sleep. Dad didn't as much as flinch at that, so Sunny went on with his full story, what he remembered of it, anyway.

At some point when he was a baby, he blinked into danger and led a K'tul* to steal his niece's unicorn, Silverstream, so his other niece locked him.

That brought a reaction from Dad. "Silverstream?" he asked mildly, as if not to spook him. "Isn't that Hrysa's unicorn, son? Who might this niece of yours be? And the other one who locked you?"

"Hrysa and Silvia."

"Hrysa and Silvia??"

"Yes."

Then, when he was seven, he dreamt that Silverstream was galloping into danger. He blinked to follow and save her but found himself at the palace in Karia in the middle of the war. The palace was under intense bombardment, and Sunny had to crawl from pillar to pillar, desperate to make it to safety inside the castle, before they shuttered the doors. Debris hit his wing as he ducked behind a column.

Willie saw him and darted to him to save him. He hit his head as they dove for cover, and he couldn't remember much after that. He still didn't know where he came from or how to get back. He thought he came from Yand, but could he blink that far? *In his sleep?* Wasn't Yand hundreds of light years away?

Flashes of broken memories randomly flooded his brain. Some made no sense, like Asimia and Snowfox were his siblings. And also the Pathfinder. He knew he had a bio mom and dad but didn't remember them. He also knew, although not sure why, that he was a High Prince of Yand and Tuncay.

"Ok," said Dad. "This is enough to get us started."

They spend much more time at the lab. Dad took Sunny to the cafeteria and bought him lunch. They had chocolate smoothies! And ice cream, and many other sweetments! Dad seemed to delight watching him stuff his face—and pockets—with the divine stuff and take not a single bite of fish!

---

* Not entirely true, but this was how Sunny made sense of the events.

When they returned home, Sunny ran to Willie and emptied his pockets. But Dad had a more civilized box of goods—lunch box, he called it—that Sunny and Willie shared together. Sunny could hear his dad's thoughts: *How could Sunny eat more? And where does he put all that?*

Many days passed without Dad saying anything about what he might have discovered in Sunny's blood. Sunny and Willie eavesdropped to many conversations on nights on end, but Dad never mentioned his discoveries about his son. The adults always talked about Asimia and what the various K'tul factions planned to do with her. Why, there was even a new courier from Hellbound.

The mention of the courier conjured a vision in Sunny's mind: He hung in the heavens in utter blackness with only pinpoints of stars surrounding him. Below was a planet with auroras circling its crown and an incredibly heavy spin! It was the same red planet he'd brought himself and Willie to. He imagined the red beach with the people and the two evengirls. Ah, they were princesses! He'd come to save them!

He instinctively reached out to them… grasped a hand… it was Willie! She quivered in fear. *"Look!"* she called into his mind, pointing at a faraway object. He looked, and…fear gripped him instantly, paralyzing and suspending him in space.

He couldn't move to approach the object for a better look. He squinted and projected vision, a spell that allowed him to "see" without his corporal eyes. He filled his brain with the dreaded outline of a K'tul spaceship—a courier!

"A courier!" he exclaimed out loud, making Willie jump.

"What?" she whispered tensely. "Shush, I want to hear."

"Did you see that? The ship?"

"What are you talking about, Sunny? Fantasizing again?"

"Oh." Well, that was a relief. His imagination often got the better of him. He thought he'd blinked again when, in truth, he'd only conjured up a story triggered by the adults' mention of the courier. But it was so vivid! And that K'tul courier no longer hid behind the moon. "Where are your ribbons?" he asked Willie.

She reached into her pocket and pulled a wad of crimson and emerald strings and twisties. "You want them?" she offered. "Ma doesn't want me wearing them."

He took the ribbons from her. "Why not?" he asked. Then, "See? We've been there in truth. These here are proof."

"Of course we have. Now shush," she replied. "Can you sit quiet and listen for once?"

With much effort, Sunny disengaged from his fantasies of saving princesses from K'tul and a courier ship attacking their planet. He returned his full attention to the business of eavesdropping. The adults went on without Dad ever mentioning anything about him, genetic or otherwise. Like Sunny didn't exist.

"Stop being so dramatic," Willie rebuked him. *"Your dad has other things to worry about, too. He loves you. You know it!"*

"I don't know, are you sure?"

"Yes. He dotes on you, gods know why."

Many more days later, Sunny began to think that Dad's DNA analysis had yielded nothing. Not a single clue of Sunny's being. But one night, as he pretended to sleep, Sunny noticed Dad scribbling in his notebook at his desk. Then, he did something unusual. He pulled the drawer out, revealing a secret compartment underneath it! He deposited the diary there, replaced the drawer, and locked it. He put the key in his trousers' pocket.

Sunny waited for his dad to fall asleep. He went and kissed him on the brow to make sure. Hmm, maybe one more kiss. When Dad didn't stir, Sunny fished the key from Dad's pants and recovered the notebook from its hidey hole in the desk. He curled up on the bed beside a sleeping Willie and read.

Sentence after juicy sentence made Sunny's eyes pop out. One passage was exceptionally sweet. It went like this. "My son's genes are like the pearls on an infinite strand. They come endless, one more, another, and one after that, as bright and precious as any individual pearl on that string: wormhole master, shifter, mage, temporal.

"The only ones missing are pathfinder and worldmaker. But maybe I have missed those? Or they haven't activated yet? It wouldn't surprise me."

Sunny and Willie at the Peculiar Planet

12. Sword of Kings

Snowfox woke up in the infirmary to sweet caresses and a kiss here and there. He opened his eyes tentatively, not wanting this bliss to end. "Mmm, Simi," he whispered.

"I'm right here, love," she replied, doubling the kisses. "You gave us quite a scare.

"Mouse?" he asked.

Asimia scooted back and helped him lift his head off the pillow. Mouse lay on a cot nearby, with Wolfpack sitting on the edge. "Hey, you good?" Snowfox asked his brother.

"Yeah. Mouse, too. But we have to solve this problem before we take another step."

"No kidding." Lucent entered. "Why are you two not on your honeymoon?" Snowfox asked him, with a head nod at Asimia.

"He yielded it so we could take care of our little problem," Asimia replied.

"Told ya not to dawdle, man. You should've left last night."

"You mean the night before? It's been two nights since our wedding," Lucent corrected him, placing a hand on Asimia's shoulder. "Do you feel up to facing some breakfast? Doc said there's no reason to keep you here any longer."

"Coffee," Snowfox begged and attempted to sit up. That made him dizzy; Asimia pushed him back gently.

"Or you can stay here for another hour or two," she said, "to recover enough for our honeymoon." She teased him lightly with a soft kiss on his nose.

"Nah, I'm yielding it, too," he responded with a tender caress on Asimia's arm. "Too much going on, love. Can you forgive me?"

"Of course, love," Asimia replied. "Let's jump into married routine, beginning tomorrow—you get your wedding night tonight. We can have honeymoons when we reach the promised land. I hear spectacular vistas await us."

Snowfox looked at Lucent. "Ok by me," Luc confirmed.
"We assume our sleeping arrangements beginning tomorrow night."
        "Which are…"
        "How about like Mom?" Asimia replied. "Alternate nights?"
        "Makes sense. You good with that, Luc?"
        "Yes. More than I expected."
        "Why?"
        "I don't know. Being the second husband, I guess."
        "Second husband, not second class. Mom said another thing,
right Simi?"
        "Yes. We're equals in marriage." Lucent stared as if
processing that. "Come, let's take it to our office," Fox switched
subjects. "The Kitchen? Wolfpack? Mouse?" he called the two.
        Luc attempted to help him, but Asimia already had an arm
around his waist. He stood carefully and tested his legs. They didn't
buckle. Then his head. It didn't spin. His legs again. They worked.
        "It's great not to be frozen," he declared.
        Three people awaited them in the kitchen, sitting together on
one side of the counter, drinking coffee. A pot of the divine brew
rested before them, wafting its aroma toward Snowfox.
        "Mmm," he muttered, closing his eyes.
        "Bring this man a cup before he perishes," Asimia ordered a
passing staffer, but another already approached with a tray of cups.
        "Breakfast is nearly ready," the staffer announced.
        The guests were Warbles, Khin, and Pete. Snowfox took a
few gulps of his coffee, his eyes never leaving Pete. He shook his
head and turned to a stool Asimia had pulled for him. She helped
him sit, then sat beside him across from the professors. Luc sat on
Fox's other side as Wolfpack and Mouse joined them.
        "Wolfpack and I thought to invite the good professors back,"
Luc informed him. We need to confer again."
        "Right. But why Pete?" Snowfox mouthed his reply.
Warbles and Khin, yes. But Pete made his heart skip a beat or two.
        "Wolfpack's wormholing gene is different than Asimia's or
Yildiz's," Luc replied. "We need to understand the difference."
        "Right. But are you sure that's the reason Pete is here?"
        Luc glared at him. "Look, man." He whispered. "Wolfpack's
the only one who can break through that… whatever that temporal

jam was that froze you and Mouse. Simi and your uncle cannot. We need Pete's help. Don't make a scene, please."

"Of course not," Snowfox agreed. "Pete," he addressed the geneticist. A pregnant pause followed as if everyone expected him to... what? Cause a scene? He'd moved from that, hadn't he? "Welcome," he amended whatever he was about to say. "Welcome all, Dr. Khin, Dr. Wa—Elliot." Everyone exchanged greetings.

"Pete, the other day in your office," Snowfox continued, "didn't you say Wolfpack's gene has a temporal aspect to it?"

"Yes, I did say that. It's an entirely different adjacent allele."

"And that's important, no? How?"

"A normal wormhole cannot traverse through a temporal rift in space." Pete paused for a few seconds, gazing at Snowfox. "Only a temporal wormhole can do that. A wormhole master not bearing the temporal gene cannot form temporal wormholes."

He looked around him. "Was that clear?"

"As daylights," Khin replied. "I can confirm the first aspect."

"Me too," added Warbles.

So much agreement among scientists was unnerving to Snowfox. "Are you saying our fate is sealed? Are we doomed from the start? Should you analyze my brother's blood or something? Make an infusion—I mean transfusion of this gene?"

"A splice," Pete corrected him. "I already have." Did he attempt to hide an amused smile? But did he say he already had? "Are you trying to get rid of me, my lord?" the geneticist continued, still staring at Fox. "I won't stay long. I will make my report, offer my remedies—potential remedies, I should say—and go."

"Please, Pete," Asimia interjected before Snowfox could reply, "stay for breakfast. It should be ready in a minute."

"It's Snowfox," Fox told Pete.

"What?"

"Please call me Snowfox. Or Fox. You keep reminding me that you are my friend."

"Indeed, I am that."

"You were saying, Pete?" Wolfpack encouraged the geneticist. Pete began to talk just as the staff served their breakfast. He pushed his plate aside, but Wolfpack gently pushed it back. "Let's eat first, shall we? Mouse and Fox missed an entire day of meals, and Mouse can't afford to miss another."

"Indeed, little brother," Fox responded. "I'm famished."

They ate their breakfast quietly. No. They all talked with their mouths full. Before Pete could resume, the two physicists burst out with a myriad of ideas on how to study the anomaly. Their test protocol was so comprehensive that Snowfox had to remind them they didn't have infinite time. What could they do in the next couple of days?

"Two days?! Nothing. Absolutely nothing in two days."

"What about a week?"

"No, nah," they definitely needed two months, at least one.

"What if we bring the instruments to the anomaly?" Wolfpack suggested. Warbles popped his eyes out, and Khin giggled like a little girl. Obviously that would do.

They settled on one week and would even try to shorten that time if things went well. But *could* Wolfpack bring them to the anomaly? Wasn't that impossible?

"No. I can bring you there, fine. Just can't bring you back." "On my own," he hastened to amend. "It took me, Simi, and our Uncle to reverse my wormhole's chirality."

"I don't think that's what we did," Asimia contradicted him. "The polarity wouldn't reverse. We climbed the chirality backward."

"Oh, my!" Khin exclaimed. "And that didn't kill you?"

"It could've," said Wolfpack, "but I don't think that's what we did. Oh, I know. That's what I initially thought, but we reversed it, Simi. Your Alice on top of mine."

"Oh!" exclaimed Asimia. "But it was near impossible! How can we manage so many migrants? Does it mean we can bring the folks to Phe'lak but not bring them back?"

Everybody stared at her. "We didn't mean this to be a one-way trip," remarked Snowfox. "We'll find a way. That's what we're doing with the data collection and genetic engineering, no?"

"I can come and go," asserted Wolfpack.

"Alone." Fox corrected him. "You couldn't bring Mouse and me back..." he shuddered. "I wouldn't like to repeat that."

"Me neither," added Mouse.

"Ok. How do we bring the science team to the anomaly in wormholes that are near-impossible to reverse?" asked Snowfox.

"We **must** study the anomaly!" Warbles objected.

"And I won't risk you," Snowfox replied.

Uncle Yildiz entered the kitchen. "You'll teach *us,*" he told Warbles, indicating Wolfpack, Asimia, and himself, "and we'll gather the data for you. We'll be your techs." He grabbed the attention of a kitchen staffer as he spoke and ordered food. He dove in it the moment it arrived. "Busy night," he muttered as he chewed.

"And my splice will help," Pete added, the discussion finally returning to him. But before he could elaborate, Snowfox got an urgent message from the military field. It was Chimeran. *"Fox, come quick. The Northwesters arrived, and RC is pregnant."*

Bombshell! Every bit of discussion subsided along with every heartbeat. Asimia flinched so hard, she might as well fall from her seat. She stared at him. Her shock and anger assaulted Fox. He was too shocked to respond. But his heart twisted, churned.

"I'm busy, Chimé, can't it wait?" he told his lieutenant mechanically.

"Sure thing, Boss. I thought you wanted to know."

Sure thing, but she had done the damage. Asimia's gaze had settled on wounded and confused. *"Simi, I can explain…"*

But Asimia turned from him. She rose from her seat and backed away slowly, then turned and practically ran out of the kitchen. He got up to follow her, yelling, "Asimia!" but Lucent grabbed his arm and pulled him hard. He hadn't expected that and fell back onto his seat.

"What have you done, man?" Luc shouted.

"Nothing!" Snowfox blurted, rising again, this time forcefully enough to counter Luc's pull. He saw Pete rise from his seat, pointed a finger at him, and warned, "Don't you dare insert yourself into this!" and ran after Asimia.

He found her in Mom's private garden in the West Wing. She faced Mom's swing with her back to him. She had her face cupped in her hands and cried. Sobs racked her body. It took Snowfox aback to see how much pain he had caused the one he loved the most in the world.

"My love…"

She raised an arm behind her and stopped him. "Go. Leave me," she told him among sobs. "Don't make more of this than necessary. I need a few minutes, then I'll return to join you."

"No, my love, please let me explain," Snowfox attempted. "There's no reason for this… you have no fear of…"

"Shut up, Fox! You made the mess, now own it. Don't pretend like this is nothing. It's unbecoming and craven. Have I not owned Pete? Or have I humiliated you before the entire Yandar military? Indeed the entire world? Our expedition... the scientific community!"

But... was that what it took to make it right? To declare... to sign the papers*? But he knew it wasn't that. She'd been discrete while he... not only hurt his beloved. He humiliated her. A pregnancy among the flyers would not remain secret for long. It would soon reveal his indiscretion and may already have. Chimeran had already guessed...

"I made the mess, my love," he began. "I'm not denying it. But I have no... designs on RC. It was all a mistake. She has no rights to claim—"

"Claim what? You? Or father rights for her child?" She turned to face him. "No, I don't expect her to do that. She's honorable. But clearly Chimé thinks... and so the entire world will know soon, if not already. Give me a few minutes to compose myself. I'll return, and we'll never talk about this again unless you decide to claim the baby."

She paused. Then more quietly in a strained voice, "I would support you. We want children. This would be your precious gift."

Snowfox stared dumbfounded, not knowing how to respond. Wolfpack's mindvoice rang in their heads, *"Guys, stop fighting. We'll figure it out later. Come back while we have the profs. We have much to discuss and decide our options."*

The door to the garden flew open, and Luc burst through it. "What's all this?" he shouted, rushing to embrace Asimia. "What's the matter, my darling? There's a child? RC's? We wanted children, right? It'll be fine, we'll adopt the baby—"

Asimia pushed back from Luc and wiped her face. "Let's return to the kitchen," she said. "Wolfpack is right. The profs' time is precious." She turned hand in hand with Luc, avoiding even a glance at Snowfox.

"We'll talk more tonight," Luc acceded. *"And I want in that conversation,"* he projected in mindspeak toward Snowfox. *"My right since it involves a child. **You** wrote the rules!"*

---

* **To declare** and **to sign the papers** means to get betrothed.

But what just happened? He'd have no opportunity to explain? What Asimia must think! His heart was in knots, but Lucent didn't give him the time for self-inflicted misery. He elbowed Fox along. They returned to the kitchen together like nothing had happened.

They found the others in deep discussion and arguments. Uncle Yildiz was the only one still eating. He was on his second plate. "Much work coming up," he told Snowfox with a wink, mistaking a passing glance for a question. And Pete had left.

"I sent Pete back to his lab," said Wolfpack. "He has some more work to do preparing the splice. We must administer it to Simi and Uncle before embarking on any wormholes." *"And I didn't want to complicate matters further,"* he added in guarded mindspeak.

Snowfox looked at Asimia, who returned his gaze and nodded.

Pete returned a couple of hours later with the first dose of his temporal gene splice. He administered it to Asimia and Uncle Yildiz in the form of an injection in the arm. He insisted they needed a few more jabs in the arm for the elixir to give optimum effect. But the six-hour intervals made them balk. They couldn't wait idly. They decided to undergo the gene regimen while learning to navigate the anomaly and collecting data. And they dove in.

That kept Asimia busy all day, so Snowfox couldn't talk to her further. While she risked her life transferring to and from the peculiar planet and the anomaly, he spent his day checking on the troops at the field with his brother Hawk, the new king. Mouse shadowed them, so he couldn't talk to RC, either. He was too worried about Asimia to be able to focus on anything else. The wormhole masters' progress diverted his attention.

After receiving their temporal splice from Pete, the first order of business for Asimia and Uncle Yildiz had been to master the temporal anomaly on their own. Going there was straight forward, but returning was a different story altogether, a mess. Wolfpack had to rescue them the first few times, despite the splice and additional dosages throughout the day. They needed to do something different. Wolfpack got an idea: more props.

Mouse sacrificed her stunning brow sapphire, and Wolfpack retrieved fresh infinite cosmic strings from Cepheus' Blazar. Aunt Shadow blew crystal sheaths around those strings using Mouse's molten sapphire flux. Mouse and the dragon spelled the amulets. They chanted for hours. The finished products looked like marbles. They distributed them to the wormhole masters, so each had one new Alice and a one-way set to add to their originals.

Pete kept up his jabbing regiment, splicing Uncle and Asimia every six hours. They got three good jabs that day.

Snowfox and Hawk offered to assist in some way, but they had nothing useful to offer. They left the field and huddled with Warbles and Khin, learning as much as they could about wormhole theory and space anomalies. They sometimes met the scientists in the palace, where Hawk had his own staff of physicists assisting. But more often they met in Warble's office or lab at the U. Back and forth. Good thing they had teleporters.

By late afternoon, armed with the new infinite string contraptions and past their third jab of Pete's miraculous elixir, the wormhole masters called a success: Asimia and Uncle Yildiz returned home from the anomaly without Wolfpack's help!

They were exhausted, with numerous burns on their hands from the vigorous twirling of their cosmic string props. But they didn't even take a breather. They dove into stage 2: turned themselves into scientists. They donned scientific instruments from Warble's lab and a few more exotic ones from Khin. After learning various techniques for operating them, they embarked on endless wormholes and data collection.

They kept Warbles, his team, and Khin hopping at every new data dump. It went well into the night. Khin got the U.'s and Turtle Island's giant telescopes working to add to the cache of information.

What they found was remarkable. First some good news: The anomaly was localized around the strange planet and was not spreading. But, and this was a big deal, it was variable. It loosely attached to the star Chi Draconis, named Batentaban after the Yendal astrophysicist who discovered it. It sported spectacular auroras like halos on its crown and many brightly-colored rainbows.

The planet's orbit was so elliptical and dipped so far toward the next major star in the constellation, Delta Draconis, that it appeared to be flying off from Chi to Delta in some scans. The two stars were too far apart for that to make sense.

Since Wolfpack was still the only one able to wormhole past the peculiar planet, he took up this exploration exclusively. He spent the better part of that night wormholing to Delta and collecting data. Altais was the Delta star's name, and it came clean: It didn't block the wormholes from reversing chirality or cause the temporal anomaly that plagued the space around the peculiar planet.

Did they get any sleep that night? Hmm. Fox wasn't sure, but he was able to eat dinner with them at some point before they resumed their activities. All three ate like starving wolves, rivaling his foxes, Alex, and Wolfpack's pack.

The next day proved easier for them after a fourth jab of the temporal elixir, which they took with breakfast. And easier yet after completing the treatment with six injections in all. Easier, Simi said, but not natural. Natural remained only for Wolfpack. Simi and Uncle had to settle for good enough. However, a big worry remained: It was enough to transfer themselves back and forth, but was it sufficient to transfer hundreds of migrants?

At the week's end, Dr. Khin declared she understood the mystery. A rogue temporal wormhole had caused the anomaly. The phenomenon was so unusual that it surprised even her!

But how could it be? The only other wormhole master Snowfox knew was Mom, and she had no business going to Draco, let alone unleashing a temporal wormhole. Plus, Pete didn't mention Mom had the temporal gene. Wolfpack was the only one. Could it have been Wolfpack from another time? But why? And from when?

The group assembled that night in the kitchen to ponder this. Khin explained that the spectral instrument had captured traces of this wormhole. The temporal aspect was confusing, but that was often the case with temporal matters. She was sure the wormhole trace originated in the future yet executed in the past. Asimia examined the data thoroughly but she gleaned nothing of the caster's identity. No signature whatsoever.

So, what future? How far ahead? Centuries. Was that possible? It was. That confirmation came from Wolfpack. It made Snowfox wonder if his brother had traveled that far ahead in time.

"Wolfpack," he began, "could it be you in a future time?"

"Well," Wolfpack replied, "if it were me, I'd have no knowledge of it, would I, since it hasn't happened yet."

Right. So what to do? Wolfpack had a suggestion. Leave the mystery of who caused the anomaly till later. It would inevitably reveal itself when it happened in the future.

"Let's focus on the now," he said. "We still need to see if we can pass the anomaly without it leaving us with no way back."

And so they tested that. All three wormhole masters could get through the anomaly to Altais. Check, albeit with difficulty for Uncle Yildiz and Asimia. All three could return to Yand on their own! Check. All three could transfer one hundred to two hundred people. Check. They brought hundreds of Yendal would-be migrants from their moon to Yand. But beyond the anomaly?

Ah, no. They had no easy way to test that one. They would have to risk hundreds of people. Wolfpack to the rescue again.

"If that becomes a problem," he offered, "you can divert your groups to the peculiar planet, and I can transfer them to the Delta system (Altais). We can resume our journey to Phe'lak from there in our three wormhole groups."

Yes! That would work! Everyone cheered.

That night, Snowfox screwed on his courage to claim his wedding night. He'd stayed away from Asimia's bed during that hectic week and slept in the company of one of his brothers to maintain accountability for his whereabouts. When all the cheers and toasts subsided, and the hard-working team departed for their respective beds, Snowfox took Asimia's hand.

"May I claim my wedding night, my love?" he asked, holding his breath. "If you would have me?"

"What took you so long," she replied.

They slept in the next day. When they awoke, he was ready to go again. Another hour later, exhausted but happy, they luxuriated in each other's arms when Wolfpack's mindspeak shattered the bliss. *I'm bringing Mom.*

"What? When?"

"Momentarily."

And he did. Snowfox knew this not only because he could feel his mom but also because his mom nulled Asimia. His wife struggled to breathe!

"Wolfpack!" he mindyelled. *"What the hell!"*

"It's ok, love," Asimia told him. "I really want to see Mom! How can I leave this world without seeing her one more time? Without saying goodbye?"

"Agreed, love. But we can't leave this world with you nulled, either. We best wait a few days before we depart."

"I only need one."

"Nah, remember the last two times?"

"Those were complicated. I had injuries besides the null."

He helped her dress. She struggled even with such a small action. He carried her down the stairs and through the courtyard to the kitchen.

They found their mom Yanara surrounded by their entire Tuncan family: Dad, Ma Mandolen, the Dragoons, and Wolfpack, who brought them.

"We're taking no chances," said Drace. The last time Mom came to visit was when K'nista kidnapped Simi while she and Mom nulled each other. No chance of anything like that happening with the Dragoons around. Not that they expected any K'tul after Mom blasted them all to hell—their planet, Ketal.

Dad held Mom in his arms, with Ma Mandolen crowding him anxiously. He deposited Mom down as Fox did the same to Asimia, and mother and daughter embraced and cried in each other's arms. They both suffered immensely living apart from each other. This reunion was so heartfelt that neither minded the null.

Uncle Yildiz and Grandma Stardust entered the kitchen. They looked sleepy, but Grandma rushed to Simi and Mom nonetheless. She hugged them fiercely. "Oh, my beautiful girls!" she lamented. "How I will miss you, Yanara!"

Grandma had adopted Mom from the moment of her birth and loved her dearly. But their relationship was complicated. Only recently Grandma was able to express her love for her worldmaker daughter. Snowfox thought that Uncle Yildiz's return from the K'tul captivity had much to do with that.

"You have my brother bring you to visit," Mom told her fiercely. "Promise me!"

Stardust nodded a few times, making Snowfox cringe. Despite their progress with the anomaly, the return trip would not be easy unless something drastic changed the temporal space.

Mom didn't stay long. Wolfpack returned her to Tuncay, accompanied by Drace and Squirl to protect her while the null lasted. Mouse remained behind to guard Asimia. Everyone else stayed, too.

Dad had a hefty, leather-wrapped bundle that could only be a sword from the shape of it. "What's this, Da?" Snowfox asked him.

"A gift for you travelers. Your moms and I thought that in addition to a military leader," he inclined his head to Snowfox, "your expedition needs to settle the matter of queen." "Or king," he hastened to add.

"Oh, don't look at me," Stardust protested. "I was queen for a thousand years. I no longer wish it. I want a few centuries of quiet time with my love."

Her love, Uncle Yildiz, wrapped an arm around her waist and gently kissed the top of her head.

"Hear him out," Ma encouraged. "This is special."

"I've forged this sword," Dad continued, placing the bundle on the counter. He unwrapped it and wo! It was a sword like no other, even sheathed! It buzzed and vibrated from inside its scabbard. An exquisite ruby adorned its hilt. Snowfox wanted to see the blade, but Dad would not unsheathe it.

"This is all I can do," Dad continued, chuckling lightly. "You see, I've forged into it pathfinder qualities with Wolfpack's, Pete's, and the dragon's help. Once I affixed the ruby and sheathed the blade, I can no longer free it from its scabbard."

Everyone marveled as Dad went on. "I hoped it would show you your true path like Ice shows Wolfpack." Ice had been Dad's sword that he stabbed Asimia with to end the null at the end of the Yandar-K'tul war. He gifted it to Wolfpack after that event. In the Pathfinder's hands, Ice morphed into a Pathfinder sword.

"But since Wolfpack will break your path," Ma Mandolen picked up the story, "we thought to try something different: allow the sword to pick the next king or queen." She looked at Snowfox and Asimia as she said that.

"Oh?" asked Asimia. "How do you figure that, Ma?"

"Let's see who this sword allows to draw it," Dad replied.

Asimia stared at Dad for a few moments as if trying to understand the meaning of his words. She lifted the sheathed sword from the counter. It was nearly as big as her. She took a few steps back to give the blade enough space and drew it. Just like that. Null and all.

Everyone gasped. She let the sheath drop, gripped the sword with both hands and raised it above her head. The ruby gave a blinding blaze while the blade burst into flames. Chef Piere entered the room to inquire about breakfast, took in the scene, and fell to his knees. "My Queen!" he hailed. The rest of the kitchen staff followed suit, taking a knee—or two—and chanting, "Hail the Queen!"

The entire family, Granma included, took a knee to Asimia.

"Please, rise, all," she told them, looking flustered. "I didn't want to be queen. Da, are you sure this is a true test?"

She resheathed the sword and replaced it on the counter.

"Let's test it," Dad replied. "Can any of us draw it?"

Snowfox shrunk to a far corner and watched his family, as one by one failed to lift the sword, let alone unsheathe it. It might as well bear the weight of the universe in their hands. He refused a turn. He didn't want to be king. He had yielded his right to the Yandar throne to his younger brother Hawklord. He didn't wish to assume another. Military Commander suited him much better.

Wolfpack popped out of wormhole, returning from Tuncay. To everyone's eager stares, he said Mom was recovering well. "But the sword has another property," he declared. "It recognizes a true heart. Once it chooses the monarch, queen here, it will also pick her mate or mates. Only one of true heart can bear the sword as Asimia's mate. Asimia?"

"Hmm?" she replied, staring hard at their brother but also at Snowfox. He tried to disappear. "Shall we forgo this?" she offered. "I have no doubt of my husbands," which Snowfox knew was untrue by the glare she had just given him if nothing else.

"One can carry the sword for you," Ma suggested. "Unless you prefer to carry it yourself through… how many wormholes? And I hear a peculiar space…"

"Wolfpack!" Asimia yelled at their brother, who lowered his eyes guiltily. Yep, he'd spilled the beans. But Asimia should remember Ma was a formidable interrogator.

"Very well," she acceded. "Lucent?"

She offered the sword to Luc, who had dimmed so much he might as well silver, like himself, Fox, and their wife. As everyone else in the room, Luc failed to draw the blade earlier. So what would this mean? *"Will she divorce us?"* he asked Snowfox.

"Courage, man!" Snowfox urged him. *"At least one of us should pass this test. We can't leave her husbandless."* Was that a word? *"Or to carry this humongous thing across the galaxies!"*

Luc may have failed before, but now that Asimia passed the sword to him, he was able to hold it! Elated, he retrieved the scabbard from the counter and started to strap it onto his back with Ma's help.

Dad had hung back regarding the scene, smiling—well amused, thought Fox. But now Dad turned to him. "Don't forget *Fox,* my darling," he told Asimia.

Uh, oh! Fox didn't want that.

But, "No, never," she replied. She took the sword from Luc, assuring him it'd be only for a moment or two. Then, "Catch," she yelled at Snowfox, tossing him the enormous weapon, hilt first, while its blade flamed. She threw it with the ease of a dart or shuriken. Instinctively Fox caught it in one hand.

Everyone gasped. The sword gave a blinding burst of blue flames, turning its ruby into a sapphire. The gem exploded in waves of light so intense that everyone had to shield their eyes.

"I think he passed," cried Dad. *Did he sound relieved?* "Lucent, you want to take it from him before he blinds us all?"

Lucent obliged him. In his hands, the blade calmed to what Fox took to be its normal radiance. "Do you have a name for this marvel, my dearest heart?" Luc asked Asimia.

"Eaglewing!" Fox and Luc's wife, Queen Asimia, shouted. "The Sword of Kings!"

Asimia Tosses Eaglewing to Snowfox

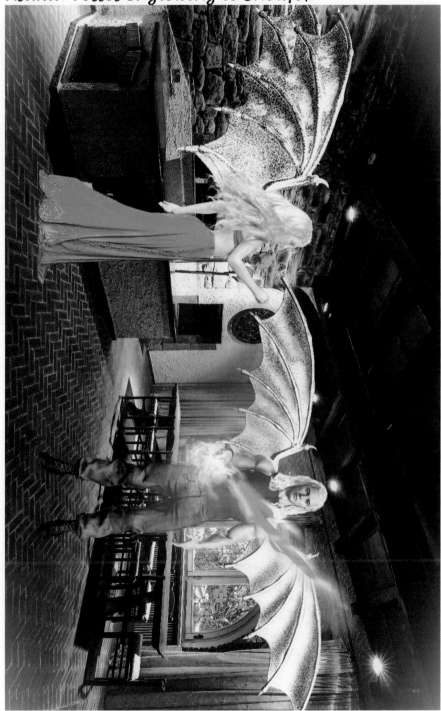

Future Time: At the cordon in Paria, Continuing from Chapter 11. Sunny's POV.

13. Kiss the Sky

*A*s the days passed, Sunny became obsessed with his visions of the weird planet. It took over his obsession with his dad not sharing his findings about his DNA. It filled his head with fantasies and daydreams. He often blinked Willie to the Crags, and they sat together on the Runway—the long shelf in front of the Mouth cave—and deluged her with his stories.

There was a princess… No. Two princesses… and they lived in this magical world with unicorns and dragons and… He often paused for the next inspiration to strike. It went on forever, with many variations.

There were always dark turns at the end. The K'tul came with their spaceship and destroyed the princess's world. They cut up the unis, ate the dragon, and took the princesses prisoner… until a gallant knight, no, a prince, swept in from the depths of space to save them. The valiant prince was surprisingly young; and silvered.

Finally, Willie had enough. "Can you stop fantasizing about saving some princesses in who knows where or when? They don't even exist."

"Do, too."

"Do not!"

"How can you say that? You saw them too!"

"All I saw were some Yandar people and two girls. And they were evens, like me. Not silvers."

"I never said my princesses silvered."

"But you keep going on and on about how beautiful they are. How bright their eyes and bouncy their locks… I thought you meant like our Queen Asimia."

"Hrysa is our Queen."

"No, she's not. Queen Asimia came back. So you like evengirls now?"

"No! Yuk!"

"But you said…" she shook her head, knowing she could never win an argument against him. He always knew how to twist out of anything. "And I saw no spaceship," she continued, finding something more to contest. "You dreamt that courier up all from your head."

"Did not."

"Did, too. And that strange planet, too."

"But you were on that planet. Twice."

"I was on *a* planet. I saw no auroras from space."

"You'll make me push you!"

"You wouldn't dare, Sunny! I'll tell your dad!" She jumped to her feet and made to launch.

Sunny grabbed her elbow. "Come, then," he shouted in her face at the top of his lungs. "I'll show you!" And he blinked them to… what was that? Hell?!

The courier was there. The same one he and Willie spied behind a moon back when… when was that? Not too long ago, subjectively, but Sunny didn't know this world's current temporal time. It felt further in the past than when they met the people on the red beach and about the same when the ship was behind the moon. He wasn't sure what time of day it was, either. It was dark, but they hung in space where it was always dark.

Explosions riddled the planet below, and something had disrupted its auroras. They discharged wildly. Instead of void around Sunny and Willie, roily, churning dark stuff enveloped them.

He had brought a nimbus of air with him—how did he know how to do that?—because he had meant to stay a while and show off the various things to Willie. The roily stuff made the bubble burst, and all their air ran out. It ruptured violently, blasting them outward into the void. It would devour them.

They flipped and tumbled together, grasping for each other's hands, but the incredible violence separated them. Willie hurdled away from him, beating her wings wildly. But they would burn! They would break!

"Willie!" he screamed and screamed her name.

"Blink, Sunny," she shouted back, *"blink us."*

"Blink!" Sunny cried, fixing Willie's last thoughts into his mind. That set her coordinates, and his wormhole opened at her

location. He dove to reach her, but the distance was too great. He didn't make it. Her wormhole closed and swallowed her.

"**No!**" he cried aloud. Where had he sent her?

"Blink!" he shouted again with all his might. He found himself at the Crags, and Willie not there. "Blink," he repeated desperately. Did he move? He stood at the same spot, on the Runway, but now at a later time of day, in darkness. Willie wasn't there either. *"Willie!"* he mindscreamed the world over, not caring who heard him.

All the adults in his life answered him from the cordon: Dad, Willie's mom, his Uncles Fatie and Triex. But he shut his mind's ears and didn't hear what they said. He needed to think.

Think. Think. Ah! Trace her wormhole. He started to blink but halted. He forced himself to retrace his own steps first. He traced his first blink back into the roiling chaos. Was it the correct temporal time? Desperate, he tried to trace his second blink, the one that sent his Willie, his one and only Willie to...

Please, gods, he begged. *I will never be mean to her again. Or pull her hair,* he added to sweeten the deal. *I promise, cross my heart.* He blinked and dove after Willie's wormhole. He found himself in a narrow metal corridor inside a metal ship. Was this the courier that circled the planet—or hid behind the moon?

"Willie?" he mindsent quietly.

"Sunny," her fear-saturated mindwhisper replied.

"Keep sending. I'll find you."

"Come quickly. There are many K'tul here. I think one of them is Snakeman. But they have no princesses."

She fell quiet. *"Keep talking, Willie. I'm almost there."*

"They'll hear me! I'm scared, Sunny!"

His blasted corridor continued forever. But eventually he reached what could pass for a door. It was metal and shut. He stopped. Beyond that door, he felt a space like a room, with Willie inside, and many K'tul. *Rats,* he thought. *I blinked Willie into the Snake's nest!*

But what to do? He couldn't open the door. Ah, vision! Although distorted from all the metal and Sunny's fear-impaired, less-than-perfect concentration, the spell revealed the K'jen leader himself. He sat at the far side of the chamber with many other devils around him. And Willie had been right. There were no princesses.

"Sunny," Willie whispered into his mind. *"Can you forget the princesses and take me out of here? Please?"*

"Yes," he replied. But how to get through the door? He didn't dare blink without a solid hold on his Willie again. He'd never find her if he blinked uncontrolled. Could he sustain the opening and make it wide enough to reach her? Too much to risk.

Snakeman made up his mind for him. The chief K'jen turned suddenly and fixed Willie's location with a stare of fire. Sunny scrambled to conjure a disorientation around her, but Snake was faster. He lunged at Willie and grabbed for her throat!

Sunny dove through the closed door and fell on top of Willie, rolling her away from Snake's claws. She screamed incoherently. He joined her. He blinked the two of them, screaming, and no one else to the Crags. They fell from his wormhole, rolling on the sharp rocks, scraping legs, knees, arms, wings, faces…

He came to a sharp stop and yanked Willie up from the ground. Then he pushed her back down. She fell on her behind, which made her stop screaming. She looked at him, uncomprehending at first, then started to bawl.

But her sobs did nothing to temper Sunny's anger. It burned him. "Don't ever do that to me again!" he shouted. "Don't disappear like that. You scared me to hell!"

"*I* disappeared? It was you! *You* sent me to hell!"

"Did not!"

"Did, too! I don't ever want to see you ever again!"

T hey would have gone like that forever, but a pair of strong hands grabbed Sunny by the shoulders and yanked him around to face away from Willie. It was his dad. He looked near apoplexy. He crushed him in his arms to the point where Sunny couldn't breathe.

"Can't breathe, Da!" he squeaked. That bought him about one millimeter. He gasped for air.

"What did you do? Where did you go? I've lost my mind!" and much more that Sunny missed on account of gasping for air.

When Dad finally put him down, Sunny wasn't sure what to do—start talking or bolt for the hills. He noticed it was dark, so he missed his blink aim again. He had meant to bring them back during the same daytime, if not at the exact time. But something told him it was worse than that—something in Dad's reaction.

"What?" he braved in a barely audible voice. "How long was I gone for this time?"

"You don't know, do you!" As he spoke those words, Dad's demeanor changed. It became angry, menacing! No, not really. But to the scared Sunny, Dad sounded exceedingly severe.

In response to Dad's question, he shook his head in the negative. "A day?" he choked out in his scared voice.

"A day, huh?"

Oops, Dad's countenance worsened the more they spoke. Sunny better stay quiet until… maybe after dinner. He tested his stomach. Yep, he was hungry.

"This is the last time I'm doing this, Pete!" Uncle Triex's voice sounded from behind Sunny, making him whirl in surprise. "Let's take these two home first while Fatie still distracts the K'tul. Then we'll have that discussion."

Oh, no! What discussion? Are they kicking him out? For good? He'll be on the street again? He'll never see Willie again? Or his dad? "Da…" he moaned.

"Shush, hush," Dad told him, bringing him back into his arms, but gently this time. "You've never been on the street, you little scoundrel. And Willie isn't going anywhere, nor am I."

But it was too late for consolation. Sunny burst into sobs, crying, "Willie!" He wailed that out loud, reaching for her from his dad's arms. She was in her own dad's arms, her head buried into Uncle Triex's shoulder and her arms tightly about his neck. He could hear her cry.

"You think your kid will let you fly him, or should I take him on the horse?" Uncle Triex asked Da.

"What do you say, scamp? Does your leg still hurt?"

"No," Sunny's tiniest voice squeaked.

"Will your wings get scrunched?"

"Nah… I don't think so."

"Are you afraid of heights?"

"No, Dad!" That burst out loudly, with his normal voice.

"Not embarrassed?" Sunny shook his head. Somewhere in that discussion, Uncle Triex had descended the cliff, mounted the horse, and had Willie before him side-saddle. He turned the horse around a few times, sending inquiries into their minds.

"Well? Sometime this year? We'll miss our window!"

"Ok, last point. The horse has Willie on it."

Sunny had to think on that. He peered below the edge to see the horse that bore his Willie and her dad. It reared and neighed in anxiousness.

"Can you fly close to the horse?" he asked his dad. "We don't have to go so fast, do we?"

"Hop on."

Sunny quietly scampered onto his dad's offered back, locked his arms around Dad's neck, and held back even the minutest yelp as Da grasped the tightest grip about his legs. Then Dad launched for home, following a close course about the horse. *If the K'tul watch…*

Thankfully, the K'tul didn't watch—because Uncle Fatie distracted them most of the night. An explosion or two made Sunny's heart jump as his dad flew him. *"Hang on, my boy,"* Dad encouraged him at every unnatural boom. And Sunny did just that.

Dad flew tight to the horse. They arrived together, and Dad swooped from the heavens—no, from his low flight—to land outside the Blue House's stables beside Uncle's ride. Sunny's feet hit the ground before Willie's.

Willie's dad didn't allow his daughter's feet to suffer such a slight. It was beneath a princess, no? Uncle carried Willie in his arms. And to Sunny's utter dismay and humiliation, his dad lifted him and brought him like that, too—like a baby.

They made for the kitchen's back door, but Auntie Nara met them halfway there and wrestled Willie from Uncle's arms into her own. Not that anyone would do that to Sunny, but he felt his dad's grip on him tighten.

Auntie Nara was besides herself. She rocked Willie in her arms and sobbed as she walked. Tommy's nanny came to meet them, bringing a balling Tom. "Take him back in, Wandel," Auntie directed the woman. "They'll hear him all the way to the snake's nest," she meant Snakeman's temple, "and raise the entire village."

"Are you all right now, my lady?" the woman inquired anxiously while turning to precede them to the kitchen. "You found them, my lord?"

"As you can well see," Dad tersely replied before Uncle could, making the woman flinch. Through this exchange, Willie hugged her mom tightly and remained quiet. Sunny thought she had sobbed herself out. *He* did, although his fright remained.

A kitchen staffer met them and asked about dinner. Auntie recovered enough to allow them to serve it, although she was torn between that and giving the two a bath. *Together?? Never!* Dad to the rescue. He proposed a snack for the kids and a good wash, and after that, they could sit for a proper dinner. He hoped Uncle Fatie would return, too, by then.

He also cautioned Aunt Nara against any immediate admonishments or punishment for the kids. It could wait. Sunny loved most of that part but wasn't sure about that *could wait.*

He wolfed down his sandwich, inhaled a couple of tall glasses of milk, and sheepishly followed his dad for his bath. A staffer had already drawn it in their bathroom, so there was no wiggling out of it. He made everybody turn around while he shucked his clothes and slipped into the warm water.

Dad helped him clean up his face and shoulders, then undid his messy ponytail and washed his hair! He took forever, rubbing sweet soap into it, all the while muttering under his breath how it was more *even* than *silver* from all the dirt! He tugged so hard that Sunny thought he'd have no hair left by the time he cleaned it to his satisfaction.

"There!" he finally concluded and left Sunny to finish up on his own. "Don't take too long," he instructed—after *he* took hours. "And don't go anywhere," he added, walking out the door.

But all that tugging and rubbing about his head made Sunny sleepy. He fell asleep in the tub. He woke up from his dad shaking him, none too gently. "Ah, sheesh, Dad, don't drown me!" he yelled.

Dad called for a bath towel, and a woman came with a humongous one open before her. She stood slightly to the side and turned her back to Sunny. With his eyes closed, Dad gripped Sunny from under his arms, lifted him from the bathtub, and wrapped him up in the awaiting towel. Aiming for the towel was a comical dance since neither adult could see. Finally, all wrapped up and dry, Dad squeezed him in his arms.

"Where did you go, my boy?" he whispered after the woman left the room. "You were gone from the bath when I came to get you. The tub was empty. Then you materialized in it right before my eyes! Are you my Sunny? From our proper time?"

Sunny had no idea what the proper time was. But he was Sunny, and this was the same bathtub… so, yes. "I blink in my sleep, Dad," he breathed miserably in his dad's ear from where his head rested on Dad's shoulder. "Even in bathtubs."

"I watched it happen, son. I need to fix your blink gene. It's the wormholing gene. It's discombobulated. Did someone lock it, and you found a way around it? Hmm?"

Sunny shook his head up and down.

"Was it a strong wormhole master?"

Another shake.

"When? You're so young. When did you first unlock?"

Unlock meant to turn on a gene for the first time. Sunny wasn't sure. "I don't know, Da," he squeaked. "I was a baby. One?"

"A baby! One year old? What tweaked you that hard to cause you to unlock?"

"I wanted to sleep with Silverstream."

"Silverstream? Hrysa's unicorn, again?"

"I'm sorry, Da, I can't help it."

"I know. Come. Let the nice woman dress you and tell me all about it." The woman had preceded them to their bedroom and had arranged Sunny's clothes neatly on the bed, waiting for him.

"No!" Sunny exclaimed. "I'll dress myself."

Dad deposited him on the bed, still completely wrapped up in his towel, and shooed the woman out.

"Ok. Tell. Where did you go?" he asked again, ruffling Sunny's wet hair. "First, when we found you at the Crags. That was a big deal. You were gone for two days again. Then, in the bathtub. You couldn't have gone for more than a few minutes in that one. But I'm sure your relative time is different. Can you tell how long you were gone for?"

Sunny looked up at his dad. "Relative is like subjective?" he squeaked. Dad nodded. "I don't know, Da. I went to the weird planet both blinks today," he hesitated, "my *relative* today, but it was two different times. The first time, when I blinked from the Crags, a K'tul courier attacked the planet. The second time, in the bathtub, the ship was in the sky but hadn't attacked the planet yet."

"Wait, my boy! You mean you went to the same place but at two different *temporal* times? And you could tell they were different? The second time you blinked, from the bathtub, you went to an *earlier* temporal time?"

"Yes," Sunny squeaked, suddenly scared.

"Don't be afraid, son. I'm piecing it together. The first time you blinked, from the Crags, you went to a *later* temporal time?"

Sunny nodded.

"And what happened at that later temporal time?"

Sunny recounted his adventure, that he blinked to the planet to rescue the princesses and show Willie. He sobbed anew when he got to the part of losing Willie and fearing he'd never recover her again, then finding her inside the K'tul spaceship. Dad bounced him on his knee and comforted him, telling him it was all over now, and he did get her back. Dad was keenly interested in the K'tul ship. And the planet. Was it the same planet Sunny always talked about?

"Yes, Da. With the auroras."

"Oh, my!" Dad exclaimed, finding something important in Sunny's story. Which part? The K'tul ship? The planet? The auroras? "But who are the princesses you wanted to rescue?"

"Willie and I met them on this planet *before,* but they weren't there now. I don't know who they are, only their names."

"Wait!" Dad interrupted him. *"Before* or *after?* Ah, by *before,* you mean you met them in an earlier blink?"

Sunny confirmed. He knew the sequence of his blinks but wasn't sure about the temporal sequence of events unfolding on or around the planet. He blinked to different temporal times at random.

"Hmm," Dad pondered. "The temporal time when you saw the princesses had to be later than the spaceship attacked the planet."

"Why?"

"Eh? Oh, right. We can't conclude that categorically. But I think…" he let that trail, unable to reason further with the information they had. Sunny felt so miserable, ready to balk.

"Ok, son. Let's leave it for now. Tell me about the blink in the bathtub. The K'tul courier hung in the sky…"

Sunny continued, "Yes, the courier was in the sky but hadn't attacked the planet."

"And it felt to you like an earlier temporal time?"

"Yes. It felt like the *earliest temporal time!* The courier hid behind a moon; you wouldn't see it from the planet. I thought if I destroyed the courier in that earlier time, it wouldn't exist to attack the planet in the later time. But I didn't know how to destroy it, Da! Then, suddenly, a blink mouth opened. Three people floated there, surrounded by an air bubble. Two men and a small woman—"

"Small like a teenager, or small like a Yendal?"

Sunny shrugged his shoulders. "The K'tul ship saw them!"

"How did you know!?"

"They dropped their celestial cannons from the ship's belly and trained them on the people!" Sunny got scared all over again.

"Don't fear, son. What did you do? Did you do something?"

"I threw a temporal block to stop the people from exiting their open blink so the K'tul wouldn't blast them."

"A block or a backward blink?" asked Dad.

"A blink?" Sunny squeaked. "Backward?" He wasn't sure.

"Reversed chirality?" Dad explained. Sunny didn't know *chirality.* "Spun the opposite way? *No!*" Dad cried. "That wouldn't explain it. You *fixed* the chirality! You did throw them a block!"

"I think so," Sunny squeaked in his tiniest voice. "They struggled but couldn't pass my block to exit their blink. I was about to reverse the blink and send them back, but you shook me awake."

"Ah!" Dad hit his forehead. "So the blink remained frozen on that chirality. What have I done!"

Sunny burst into tears. "Not you, it was me, Da," he muttered among the sobs. "And I saw their air bubble burst. They'll die now! They already died, didn't they?"

"No, hush, son, they won't die—didn't die. I think I know that event and the three people. I was on Yand when it happened. They found a way to come back. But why did you use a *temporal* block? Why not straight."

"I don't know…" Sunny wailed.

"Can you fix those coordinates in your head?"

"I don't know," Sunny replied, ending his wails in hiccups. "I'll try." He thought intensely for a few moments, "Not sure about the temporal coordinate."

"Kiss the sky, son. Fix what you can. We'll work it out."

"Kiss the sky?"

"Yes, you've never heard that expression? It's like fixing the space-time about you and taking an image of that in your brain. Our stealth flyers invented this technique during the K'tul wars on Yand to mark their locations along the mountain passes when they flew in the dark. Night vision wasn't enough to give clear coordinates. The method only uses the time of day, but I think it might work in the temporal sense for you."

"Oh," Sunny squeaked, turning to look at Dad's face. There was so much sadness in his dad's eyes! "How do you know about the stealth flyers, Da?" he asked. "Did you fight in the war?"

"I did. In the East, under Commander Hawklord. He's the King of Yand now."

"But you're a scientist!" Sunny objected. Yandar treasured their scientists and protected them at all costs. They never allowed them to take part in battle—to risk their lives. Plus, Dad was special. *Singular,* they called it. No other was capable of replacing him.

"I'm also a Yandar man, right?" said Dad. "If we didn't fight the K'tul scourge, there would be nothing left for me to practice my science. So I couldn't hide and wait for the end."

"Dad, how did the war end?"

"Our senior worldmaker, Yanara, bent our sun and destroyed the K'tul spaceships."

"Wo!" Sunny exclaimed. "She bent the sun?!"

"Indeed. And she was pregnant at the time."

"She was? But the boy survived?"

"He survived, although some of us later worried about any potential damage that event may have caused him. On the molecular level, I mean." A fierce stare at Sunny, then, "And how did you know it was a boy?"

Sunny stared at his dad, lost. "I don't know. But wouldn't a girl null the worldmaker?"

"Indeed she would. Asimia, her daughter, did null her. They nulled each other."

"Dad," Sunny switched subjects, having sensed some dangerous turn about the boy the sun may have damaged. "When did you know you loved Asimia?"

"Ah, you little scamp! You figured that out?"

Sunny shook his head up and down several times, as was his habit for indicating *yes* rather than nodding.

"I loved her from the moment she walked into my classroom for the first time. She lit up my world. I hadn't met a being like her before, nor since."

"But why didn't you marry her?"

"She was only sixteen then. Do you understand the age of majority? Of legal consent?"

"Yes," Sunny replied apprehensively. "That's when Willie and I will marry—when I turn eighteen. She'll be nineteen then, maybe twenty." He cringed to say that. "But Asimia—"

"When she turned eighteen, I hesitated, doubting that her mother, Worldmaker Yanara, or her grandmother, Queen Stardust, would accept someone like me."

"What do you mean, Da? You're the best scientist!"

Dad chuckled lightly. "Even if I am—"

"Are you much older?" Yandar took spouses close in age.

"No, that wasn't it. I only have a couple of decades on her. That's well allowed. But I lack titles."

"Oh? You mean like you had to be a prince?"

"Yes. And I knew the Prince of Orange was besotted with her, waiting for her to turn eighteen to propose."

"That was Lucent, her second husband?"

"Yes, indeed. And how would you know him? He was on the moon when we first found you at the palace."

"He's the Second King of Highwings, Da. Doesn't everyone know him?"

"Yes. But not everyone calls him by his first name."

"Oh. But Asimia wanted you, right?"

"She did. It's a long story, champ. Leave it for later?"

"Ok," Sunny agreed. "But please don't be so sad. It would make me cry again."

"It would, wouldn't it?" Another tiny yes squeaked from Sunny. He patted his dad's cheek to comfort him. The emotion that contact returned was immense—sadness, worry, longing for Asimia.

"Dad, what about Asimia now? Will we get her back?"

"Ah," Dad replied haltingly. "Snakeman placed her in stasis at the temple, but Triex overheard that Wolf wants to transfer her to Hellbound. It'd be impossible for us to recover her from the ship, so we're working on a plan to recover her before that happens."

"Should I blink her out, Dad?"

"No! Don't do such a thing! They'll grab you too."

"They can't hold me. I'll blink back out."

"And into where and when? No. I can't risk you, son. You're precious." Did Dad wipe a tear? "You're everything," he added.

With newfound clarity, Sunny realized that Dad sacrificed his own wishes and desires for his son's—Sunny's—safety. He hadn't expected that and didn't know how to react. Should he cry? Thankfully Dad went on. "You better sleep with me from now on."

"But Willie—"

"No buts. We can't have the girl dragging along in all this danger of your sleep blinks. I'll go with you. No one will miss *me*."

"*I'll* miss you, Da," Sunny croaked meekly.

"You'll be with me, silly!" Da replied and turned his attention away from Sunny. Uncle Fatie had returned home.

U ncle Fatie burst into their bedroom like a creature from some god's hell, interrupting Sunny's conversation with his dad. He scrambled to cover, although the towel still covered him head to toe.

Uncle sported a few slashes on his red K'jen uniform, looking like he had gone through a few explosions and maybe hand-to-hand. His sword was plain to see, scabbarded by his side. All the shuriken were gone from his chest belt. Sunny was fascinated with weapons, especially with swords and flying darts. But Dad wouldn't allow him such a dangerous activity, as he put it.

Not that the K'jen authority allowed them weapons. Bows and arrows were the only exceptions that Uncle Triex negotiated from Snakeman as part of *fitness training*. It wouldn't do to have His Exalted Premier Glory's workforce become fat and sluggish.

"Hey!" Uncle Fatie yelled at Dad. Hearth Room, now! And he turned and left as rushed as he'd arrived. Commotion followed— household staffers scrambling to accommodate their lord.

Dad mindcalled Uncle Triex, *"Triex, I need to invite Khin and Wa—I mean Elliot to dinner."*

A few moments later, Uncle Triex's mindvoice replied. *"Do you have to? Fatie wants to debrief. Oh, never mind. Nara said fine, although she would have appreciated a little more time to prepare."*

Dad mind-shouted, *"Khin, Elliot. My house for dinner in half an hour."* He amended, *"The Blue House. Casual but urgent."*

They both confirmed. Warbles had already started his dinner but didn't mind putting it aside. Nara always had better.

Next, Dad mindcalled the doctor and asked him to bring sedatives—but no needles. He said that part with a finger tap on Sunny's nose.

Finally, he ordered his tech Darryl Jr. to fetch the block kit pronto. To Junior's silence, he yelled, *"Yes, I meant the whole thing. And no needles."* Then he remembered that Darryl had dropped the Jr. eons ago when his dad, Darryl Sr., died in the plague.

Back to Sunny, "Come my boy, let me show you how to kiss the sky before the house fills up with scientists." He filled Sunny's head with images. "Fix that," he instructed.

Sunny tried. Then Dad retrieved it from Sunny's brain. But it was incomplete. "No, he said. You left out the time. Here, see?" He added details to indicate the time of day, but not only by the clock. With the sun's position in the sky. "Can you recall that?" he asked.

Sunny tried again. Yes, he could! Dad was thrilled with him. "That's my good boy," he said. "Now, is there an image like that in that beautiful little mind of yours from your most recent blink?" Sunny was amazed to discover that there was. He conjured it. "Ah!" Dad exclaimed. "Splendid! Let me fix it in my brain." A few moments later, "Now the previous blink."

This was more difficult, but Sunny managed to recall something. Dad struggled. After a few minutes, he gave up. "Not as sharply focused, he explained. You were scared, weren't you?"

"I lost Willie, and Snakeman took her, Dad," Sunny replied, his lower lip already trembling.

"It's all good, my boy," Dad said, caressing his hair. "Superb, in fact. We'll take it nice and slow. I think we have all the time in the world unless some past event that wasn't compatible with the Grand Migration's success erases us. And I'm sure Khin will have many methods to teach you better than me."

"Teach me what?"

"To kiss the sky. It's how we'll find your peculiar planet at will—and the K'tul ship that plagued our migrants. We'll destroy the K'tul and save your princesses."

Sunny, Willie, the Courier, the Peculiar Planet

Future Time: At the cordon in Paria, continuing from Chapter 13. Sunny's POV.

14. Slide the kiss

Momentarily, Uncles Fatie and Triex joined them in their room, taking seats about Dad's writing desk. Good thing Sunny got his pajamas on. He guessed Uncle Triex didn't want Aunt Nara to hear Uncle Fatie's stories—and Uncle had lots of stories to tell.

Sunny listened enraptured as Uncle recounted his diversion tactics during Sunny and Willie's rescue from the Crags. Uncle Fatie, in his red K'jen uniform, got into an intentional scuff with a ranking greyk'tul at the Renegades' base. It was a shouting match with Uncle threatening to blast the entire Crater and level it— pretending to be a K'jen witch.

"Was it Mn'ianka?" asked Sunny eagerly.

"Who? Ah, no."

Before the greyk'tul drew his scimitar, Uncle retreated but didn't go far—just to the Crater's perimeter, where a band of cordonites—Captain Chimeran and her recruits—awaited with homemade Molotov cocktails and aerosol bombs. They created a ruckus. With the Molotovs' fire and the aerosols' smoke, the attack passed nicely for a mage strike.

Then the clever uncle dispatched the captain and her merry band to the safety of the ghetto. He mounted a horse, and gave the vengeful greyk'tul a meandering chase through the city's underbelly, to end at Snakeman's lair—emm, temple.

Snakeman, of course, took the skirmish to mean that the dratted Renegades chased his man again, with mages, mind you. Snake swung into action. It kept both red and grey K'tul busy all night while Dad and Uncle Triex brought Willie and Sunny safely back to the cordon. When the K'tul concluded their epic battle, sections of Paria burned—but not the cordon. Uncle Fatie had to restrain Snakeman from flattening the Crater.

"You should have let him, Uncle!" cried Sunny, clapping his hands. His uncle beamed at the encouragement.

"We'll get them next time, right, champ?" he told Sunny. "For now, I wanted to preserve that divine courier that berthed yesterday in one of the Crater's bays."

"Oh?" Dad's ears perked up. "Another one? Or is it that same one? No matter. Can we hijack it?"

"Well, that's why I didn't let Snakeman blow the base. But no, this is a new one. The first one left with Snakeman's reply to Wolf's request to transfer Asimia—basically saying, if you want her, come and claim her."

"You mean to say Wolf sent a new courier after Snakeman refused him? He still means to claim Asimia?" Dad exploded.

Uncle Fatie flinched like he had let something slip that he wasn't supposed to. He turned an inquiring glance toward his brother. "Yes," Uncle Triex confirmed Dad's suspicion. "Wolf sent another courier to transfer Asimia to Hellbound. But don't get all worked up, Pete!" He intercepted Dad's new outburst, raising a hand. "I'm still working on a plan to recover her. Hold your temper. I'll delay this one, too, as long as I can. We'll get her; you'll see."

Uh oh. Dad didn't see. He was about to have apoplexy again.

When Snakeman placed Asimia in stasis a few days ago, it sent Dad into fits—he couldn't feel her in stasis, nor could Sunny or anyone else. They went through sheer panic, thinking the K'jen had killed her, and endured excruciating days until Uncle Triex was able to lay eyes on her stasis pod, with her unharmed in it.

That got Dad to calm himself and return to his usual logical self for a spell. But now, with this second courier from Hellbound… here we go again.

The planning for recovering Asimia accelerated. They had to get her before the K'tul took her to Hellbound. If not, they would have to hijack a courier from the K'tul base to get to the spaceship, where it orbited the planet beyond the atmosphere.

Sunny knew another way to get to Hellbound: blink. But Dad forbade that, fearing for Sunny's safety. Like that ever stopped Sunny. But maybe if he learned to control his blinks… surely Dad wouldn't object then. They could put it into their rescue plans.

"Meanwhile, could you prepare a new second dose of the worldmaker gene splice for Asimia?" Uncle Triex continued. "We couldn't find that first syringe at the Halfway Inn, although we searched again. The K'tul must have destroyed it during Silvia's abduction, like we guessed before. K'nista destroyed the inn."

"I wish we had the presence of mind back then to secure it," Uncle Fatie added. "But Lady Emmiat was in such emergency... and we didn't expect to see Asimia again." He stopped and turned his attention toward the door. "Ah, was that the doorbell? Who might that be?"

Ah! Saved by the doorbell. Dad shook his head, saying, "We haven't finished this, not by far. We'll continue this discussion right after this next bit of business. Are we clear?"

"We are." Uncle Triex replied. "Our goal hasn't changed by Wolf sending another courier. It only accelerated. Like I said, I'll slow the transfer, and we'll get Simi back before she boards that ship. You have my word."

"And mine!" Uncle Fatie affirmed. "She may be your sweetheart, but she's our sister. You best remember that."

Wo. Who won that exchange? But a staffer rapped politely on their door and announced the doctor's and Darryl's arrival. They arrived together—albeit from different locations. Another staffer ushered them into the room. Sheesh. Sunny was in his pajamas. Dad, diverted from his troubles about Asimia, welcomed the two, shooed the Uncles out, and took a few minutes to torture Sunny with humongous needles.

No, not really. There was only the tiniest pinprick like before, sweetened by flying unicorns rather than dragons this time. And Dad smooshed Sunny's fingers onto a couple of slides. Then he dispatched the new slides with Sunny's blood to the lab with many severe instructions for his poor tech.

Meanwhile, the doctor fed Sunny pills. Sunny didn't want to take them, but Dad told him that he had asked the doctor to flavor them with cherry and make them sweet. Yum. They tasted like candy. As a reward for being so brave with the needles and the pills, Dad allowed Sunny to come to dinner in his pajamas. Great! Plus they wouldn't have to go through the dressing rituals again.

"Willie," he mindyelled loud enough and non-specifically to deafen everyone. *"We're doing jammies. Wear your blue with the dragon."* They had two sets of matching pajamas, both blue because Sunny refused to wear pink, one with a flaming dragon, the other with a prancing unicorn.

"Mom won't let me," came Willie's disappointed mindvoice. *"Oh, come on, Nara! Don't be such a spoilsport for once,"* Dad admonished Willie's mom.

The physicists arrived, and the group ate dinner in the dining room, not the kitchen. Willie did wear her jammies, although she got confused and put on the ones with the unicorn. The staff fussed to no end. They hadn't seen so many scientists together in the house before. They even brought sweetments!

Dad held back any conversation about Asimia or Sunny-and-Willie's adventures to avoid any eavesdropping, inadvertent or otherwise. They only talked about science! All night long!

After dinner, everyone retired to the Hearth Room for the private discussions. Dad allowed the staff to serve a round of drinks, shooed them off, and locked the doors. And that wasn't enough privacy—he clearly didn't want any of this out of the room. He seated Sunny onto his lap and whispered in his ear, "Son, do you know how to block the sound of passing out of this room?"

Sunny thought on that, then shook his head up and down. He obliged his dad. Nothing unnatural befell anyone, and no one blinked. He truly only blocked the sound.

"Well, Pete," Dr. Warbles started with a pause as he lit his pipe. "You brought us here in all haste. Do you mind sharing?"

"Well, where to start?" Dad started. "Surely you remember the planning phase for the Grand Migration a couple of centuries ago on Yand? We all took part in that planning."

The doctor and physicists affirmed. "Good," Dad continued. "Then you must also remember that I augmented Asimia's and Yildiz's wormhole gene with a splice I developed from Wolfpack's to enhance their temporal abilities. Doc, you assisted in administering it. The splice enabled them to navigate that anomalous space around Chi-Draconis."

"Indeed," Dr. Khin again affirmed. "All of us worked with the expedition leaders," she indicated Dad, herself, Dr. Warbles, and the doctor, with a circular arm gesture, "What of it?"

Dad recounted Sunny and Wilie's blink adventures, today's and when they met the princesses on the peculiar planet. Oh, my! Like dropping a bomb. After a million exclamations, interruptions, retelling, discussions, and arguments, Uncle Triex intervened.

"Excuse me," he said. "I think Pete invited you for your knowledge of the actual voyage of the Great Migration, as we," he indicated Dad and Uncle Fatie, "migrated less than two decades ago. We experienced nothing anomalous when Wolfpack brought us.

"But we do remember that during the planning phase of the expedition, a severe difficulty plagued the wormhole masters. Temporal space and one-way wormholes that wouldn't reverse chirality. Did I guess right, Pete? You want to ask how these original migrants fared during the migration?"

"Shoot Pete," said Dr. Khin. "How may we enlighten you?"

"Did you stop on the peculiar planet?" asked Dad.

"Not our group, but the others, yes. Wasn't that the plan all along?" Dr. Khin replied.

"No. I thought the plan was to pass through the anomaly and go straight to Altais to regroup."

"Right. But only if Asimia and Yildiz could pass their groups through that temporal space. Excuse me, Pete, but even with your splice, they found it insurmountable. They could pass themselves, but not two hundred souls. Only *we* made it straight to Altais," she pointed at the doctor, Dr. Warbles, and herself.

"All three of us came in the first group that Wolfpack helmed, with Lucent in command. The other two groups, Yildiz's and Asimia's, didn't make it straight. They landed on the peculiar planet, and Wolfpack had to transfer them all. I remember Wolfpack commenting that the temporal anomaly had increased in intensity."

Sunny cringed to hear that. He felt certain the adults would figure out he was the culprit, and… but Dad gave him a calming pat.

"Ok," Dad said. "You, Wolfpack's group, went straight to Altais. But when you passed by that anomalous space, did you see a K'tul courier ship?"

"That's not how it works, my dear, and you should know it. You can't see outside or through a wormhole. Wolfpack is this amazing temporal god or something. He passed us straight through the anomaly. We exited on a nice planet orbiting Altais."

"So you saw no K'tul behind moons or hiding in auroras or in plain view blasting their cannons?"

"No, not us. Again, we're the wrong group, Pete," said Dr. Khin. "We all came with the Master, the Pathfinder, the time god—"

"You need to ask someone from the other two groups," Dr. Warbles interrupted her. "They had some trouble, right, Khin?"

"Emm?" she replied. "Did they?"

"So the other two groups stopped on the peculiar planet?"

"Yes, indeed," said Dr. Warbles. And one of the two groups had more trouble.

"Which one?" asked Dad.

"The third one, I seem to remember, Asimia's."

That bit of information dropped like an anvil. Dad winced and brought his hand to wipe his face. Sunny grabbed it, pulled it back down to himself, and squeezed it in his. "Dad, Asimia transferred," he told his dad. "She was alright, you know this."

"Yes, of course," Dad told him. "Still hard to hear, champ."

"Your son is right, Pete," Khin added. "She and her group transferred safely to Phe'lak in the end." But as she finished that sentence, she winced. "You think that planet is where your kid goes when he blinks? This little wormhole master. And he saw K'tul lurking there? You sure it's the same planet?"

"Did any people in the other groups see auroras on this peculiar planet?"

"Yes!" Dr. Warbles exclaimed. "Folks gushed about auroras! And the immense spin. Your Sunny saw auroras, right? How many such planets do you surmise exist in the same ballpark space?"

"Right. The one such planet existing is paradoxical enough," added Dr. Khin. "We all wanted to go study it, but Wolfpack had his hands full with the temporal anomaly."

"Hmm," Dad mused. "Do you figure it resolved by the time *we* transferred?" he indicated himself and Uncles Fatie and Triex, "or did Wolfpack find another way?"

"I can't see another way from Yand to Phe'lak," Dr. Warbles contradicted that notion.

"And such natural phenomena don't resolve in a scant two centuries," added Dr. Khin. "Something else must have happened."

"Like something not natural?" Dad asked. "A bend?"

"Yes." That caused another hour of deliberations. Did someone create the peculiar planet's supermassive spin and auroras? Was the planet truly rogue, or did someone move it?"

"What someone?"

"Your kid?"

"You mean to say my little one can do all that?"

Sunny shrank into his dad's arms, and Dad squeezed him tighter. "No. The spin and auroras have to be natural," Dad told them. "And my son didn't move any planet. I don't think he's a wordmaker. At least not by the current state of his genes. His blinks may have added to the temporal phenomena but not created them."

Sunny shrank more, making himself really tiny on his dad's knees as the scientists pondered that. Apparently, *adding to the temporal phenomena* was a tall order. "Ok, Pete, spit it out," Dr. Khin exclaimed. "Your kid is a wormhole master, and what else? Not a worldmaker, you said? Are you sure?"

"A *temporal* wormhole master," Dad corrected Dr. Khin. "Not entirely sure about the worldmaker. A mage, certainly—a dragoon, at that. And his temporal gene is…" he searched for a word as Sunny neared panic. "…large…"

Shock and awe befell the scientists. "But," Dad hastened to add, "all his meta genes are locked, mangled, or damaged. We must help him unlock and realize them."

Uh oh! What did Dad mean by *realize?* But Dad went on. "Let's come back to this. We need to know about the K'tul courier; do you know anyone who came in the other two wormhole groups?"

Dr. Khin and the doctor shook their head, but Dr. Warbles knew one such: "There were many. I don't recall now who they all were. Plus, as you know, we lost most original settlers in the plague two hundred years ago, and now in the war. But I do know one."

"Well, do tell sometime this century," Dad encouraged him.

"Your tech, Darryl. He was in the second group."

"What? I thought he was born on Phe'lak."

"No. But he was a child during the migration, maybe as old as your son."

"Oh. You think he'd remember?"

"Doesn't *he?*" Dr. Warbles indicated Sunny, making him flinch. Dad noticed and patted him gently on the shoulder.

"No," he told Dr. Warbles. "He doesn't."

"But that's because of PTSD," declared the doctor. "A normal nine-year-old would. Summon your tech, Pete. He'll know."

While Dad summoned poor, long-suffering Darryl, Dr. Khin pulled her chair really close to Dad's so she could easily caress Sunny's cheek. That couldn't be good. No way.

Sure enough, a barrage of questions followed. What do you do when you blink? How do you do it? *I say, blink.* No, not what you say. How do you form the micro black holes? Where do you harvest the cosmic rays? What does it feel like as you go through the blink? Does it have chirality? And many, many more things that Sunny never thought of. She reduced him to a whimpering wreck.

He twitched so much in his dad's arms that Dad interrupted Khin's interrogation. "Look here, Khin. I'll have you know I pumped my Sunny with all sorts of cocktails to block his adrenaline flow from causing him to blink in his sleep." The doctor nodded in agreement. "And we don't yet know if all that was close to enough. Don't tweak him. Or we'll find out before we're ready."

"I finished, anyway, Pete," she replied.

"Oh, and your conclusion?"

"I think you better test his temporal allele. It's misfiring."

"I already started Darryl on it. But now we called him back."

They waited for Daryl to inhale his dinner. When he finally arrived, out of breath and a bit disheveled, they interrogated him until they squeezed the last drop of info a nine-year-old had stored in his memory. That's how old Darryl was during the Migration.

He migrated with his parents in Group 2, which Yildiz helmed, with Queen Emerita Stardust in command. Yildiz couldn't pass the temporal anomaly and had to land them on the peculiar planet. It was so beautiful! Those auroras! Some of the folks did see a K'tul courier ship, but when they told Queen Emerita, it had gone.

"No, it didn't," Sunny interrupted Darryl's narration. "It hid behind the moon."

"It's ok, son," Dad told him. "Let's see what else Darryl remembers of how it happened. Go on, Darryl."

They all thought they hallucinated the courier. The Pathfinder appeared abruptly and took them all away to Altais. It took both wormhole masters to manage the transfer.

Darryl wasn't sure but thought the temporal anomaly had gotten worse. When Dad asked him to describe the anomaly, Darryl remembered feeling temporal disorientation, like a glitch—an abrupt skip in time. And no. No one saw any young princesses.

What about the third group and their wormhole master, Asimia? Sunny felt his dad's heart flutter at the mention of Asimia's name. The answer was *no.* She couldn't pass the temporal space either. Wolfpack had to transfer the third group as well. And Group 3 had more trouble. The Pathfinder brought the bulk of them but had to return to retrieve the others. Queen Asimia and King Snowfox were among the stragglers.

"So what happened?" Dad bellowed at Darryl.

"The Pathfinder recovered only *them,* Sir. He left some folks behind, I think. Not entirely sure."

"What?" Dad and the physicists exclaimed together. The Group 1 migrants looked at each other. Apparently they didn't know this detail. "Do you remember this?" Dr. Khin asked the others.

The doctor shook his head while Dr. Warbles replied, "Yeah, maybe, emm… sort of. There may have been some trouble, but the Pathfinder made nothing of it. Neither did Asimia or Snowfox."

"So how does Darryl know it?" They kicked that around for a while and settled on the concept that it must have been a temporal fold—a ripple in time that time-separated Group 1 from Groups 2 and 3. Then something else brought them all back to the same time reference since they continued their journey together.

That was a lot to surmise. Sunny felt lost at this detail but didn't have much time to ponder it. Dad insisted that whatever had troubled Group 3 on the peculiar planet was most significant but didn't know exactly how yet. He needed to think on it.

Darryl finished his narration, "Once all our three groups assembled on the planet at Altais, we embarked on our last leg to Phe'lak in our three wormholes without any further trouble.

"We landed on the brightest, purest shore you ever saw. King Snowfox named it Paria, declaring he had brought the migrants from the depths of the universe to defend this promised land. He vowed to give more than take, and to befriend all native peoples."

"Right, Right," Drs. Khin and Warbles declared. They remembered that.

"Right," added Dad. "That's our Snowfox." He dismissed Darryl again and called the adults to regroup.

Dr. Khin was ahead of the others. "We need to train your son to control his wormholes. We have much work to do in the past. Otherwise, we may have never completed our migration."

"What? How do you mean that?" asked Uncle Triex. "Didn't the migration already happen? All of you original settlers transferred fine, regardless of a bit of trouble here or there. Or you wouldn't be here. Even Darryl said so." That elicited smiles and rolling of eyes.

"Indeed we did," Dr. Khin replied, "but I think only because some critical events occurred to make it so. You heard Darryl's account. They saw a K'tul courier. Trouble befell the third group. If necessary events didn't come to pass properly in the past, then we'll disappear from here."

"What do you mean?" Auntie Nara exploded as Uncles Triex and Fatie stared in confusion.

"She means," Dr. Warbles jumped in, only a tiny mental step behind Dr. Khin, "that we are here because a certain sequence of events occurred in our past in a way that favored the migration to succeed. What if Group 3 didn't get out of trouble? What if whatever saved them didn't happen then or hadn't originated in that past time? What if one of us, say, a temporal blinker…"

He paused for emphasis and pointed at Sunny with his eyebrows, making Sunny's heart race. He was so scared. What should he do? Blink? *"Don't blink, my boy. Don't panic,"* Dad told him. *"Daddy's here. No one will harm you. Shush, relax, and listen. Should we get Willie?"*

"We better…"

"Nara!" Dad's voice rang, startling everyone. "Come closer, please. Sunny draws comfort from Willie's proximity."

Nara returned such a glare that made Sunny nearly blink, but Uncle Triex intervened. "Come, honey," he told his wife, "let me have the girl for a spell."

Reluctantly, Auntie Nara passed the sleeping Willie to her dad, who pulled his chair to butt right up against Dad's. Sunny felt immediate relief. He lay his head beside Willie's and relaxed enough to sleep but didn't.

"I'm only pretending, too," Willie sent to his specific mind frequency. *"We can hear good this way."*

"Go on," Dad directed Dr. Warbles.

"I was saying—" Dr. Warbles started.

"That the critical event, or events, that saved Group 3 and enabled the migration's success could have originated from the future and haven't come to pass yet," Dr. Khin finished for him. "Sorry, my dear," she told him. "I want to get some sleep tonight.

"And since only one of us can blink…" meaningful stares at Sunny and his dad, *"you,* Pete, better teach your son to control his blinks. Ah, what am I saying? You'll need me, emm, us, for that."

"You think we'll have to intervene in the past to avert some disaster we don't know anything about but could have happened if we didn't, emm, don't? And that Sunny will be our temporal wormhole master? Like Wolfpack?" asked Dad in one breath.

"Precisely!" Dr. Khin exclaimed. "Although I'm not sure if *like Wolfpack* is absolutely required. Wolfpack is singular, correct? That's a tall order for a small sleep-blinker boy."

"Ah," Dad objected, "he blinks in his sleep because his allele is mangled. And how do you know that the opposite isn't true, and if we meddle in the past, we may *cause* certain events—Group 3's trouble—and prevent the successful migration?"

"I don't know one way from the other," Dr. Khin replied. "But how do you feel about a K'tul courier ship—and its celestial canons—leveling a planet that's been discombobulated with temporal anomalies? I put my money on *we need to intervene."*

She fixed each one with an iron gaze. One by one, they indicated their agreement.

"Good," she concluded.

"We'll need to collect every data possible," Dr. Warbles added. We must find originals of the third wormhole group. And any written records. We don't dare send Sunny back—"

"No!" Dad interrupted forcefully. "I won't risk him." "We can't," he added.

"Splendid," Uncle Triex declared. "Ops SpyNet to your service."

"Ok," said Dad. "Let's organize a learning course for my boy." He caressed Sunny's hair gently. "In the meantime, I will work on boosting his malfunctioning genes and keeping him calm."

"I'll take over the physics and spatial coordinates theory," offered Warbles.

"He already knows that, I think," Dr. Khin interrupted. He blinks all the time. It's the temporal part he lacks—"

203

"—and navigating the stars—" Dr. Warbles continued.

They dueled like that back and forth, driving Sunny to near-blink. "How will I ever learn all that stuff?" he blurted, forgetting that he pretended to sleep. "Is that the kissing the sky?"

"Exactly, my dear sweet boy," Dr. Khin replied, reaching over Dad to ruffle Sunny's hair. "We better enlist one of the astronomers for that. They know how to kiss—"

"Khin!" Dad interrupted her urgently. "The kids are here."

"Was she going to say a--?" Sunny asked Willie, making her giggle. So much for stealth.

"I'll enlist Tevez," Dr. Warbles offered.

Sunny spent much time with the scientists in the following days, learning the true meaning of *kissing the sky:* taking a multidimensional image of his celestial surroundings. How could Sunny, or anyone for that matter, do that? Well, not just anyone could do that. But Sunny could because of his temporal allele.

This gene proved so complex that his dad started to call it the multidimensional temporal gene, or multi-temp., for short. The adults also called it many other names, but Sunny wasn't allowed to say those aloud (the f-- gene, the b-- gene, the other b-- gene, etc.). All the adults in Sunny's life became obsessed with it. They did nothing else but spend their time analyzing Sunny, teaching Sunny, tormenting Sunny. Well, not all the time. But almost.

He knew for a fact that Dad also spent a good part of his time with Uncles Triex and Fatie, planning Asimia's rescue. They had planned something but kept it tight to their chest. Sunny guessed it was because his dad didn't want him blinking about before the scientists pronounced him ready, or at least better. So Sunny put all his effort into learning to master his genes. Thankfully, the scientists allowed Willie to tag along.

There was a basic issue with his multi-dim training from the git-go. Dad called the problem fundamental and another word, *intrinsic.* Put simply, it was this: teaching Sunny in the three spatial dimensions was easy for the physicists. But the fourth, the temporal, was impossible because Sunny was the only one in this world who could muster and/or exist in another extratemporal time. So, how could anyone else teach him?

That stomped Dr. Khin initially, but not for long—only a day or two. Unfortunately for Sunny, she came up with the concept of *adjacent time.* "Come, my boy," she'd tell him, "fix the time coordinate of now in your brain. Can you do that?"

"Can't anyone?"

"Was that a yes?"

"Yes."

"Ok. Now. Memorize that." Then, half an hour later, "Can you recall the time you've memorized half an hour ago?"

Cakewalk. Unfortunately, there was more. "Go there."

"Half an hour in the past?"

"Yes."

"But I was already there."

"So? The me of half an hour ago will record if there were two Sunnys."

"Huh? Wouldn't we have known that—know that now?"

"No, since we haven't done it yet. We're doing it now."

They tried that. Did it work? Dr. Khin insisted that it did. Her notes indicated that there were two Sunnys whenever they pulled the stint. However, Sunny could only remember one of himself, and his memory was blurred. Dr. Khin brought the doctor to examine him. His conclusion: being in the same space/time more than once was inadvisable. It caused a dilution of consciousness.

The fancy words meant Sunny became dizzy, puked, and had difficulty speaking and recalling. Despite Sunny's discomfort, they practiced the method until Sunny was able to retain past coordinates for a few days at first, then a week, two, and finally a month. Sunny could blink to the past coordinates he had stored in his mind at will.

Victory? Success? Well, one could claim yes, but only up to a month. How could Sunny find time coordinates from two hundred years in the past? Well, here came Dr. Tevez, the astronomer and celestial cartographer, and the concept of *sliding the kiss:* creating coordinates from adjacent ones.

So far, Sunny had learned to kiss the sky—to fix coordinates in his memory. He had also learned to retain coordinates and repeat them. Dr. Tevez now taught him how to create coordinates from adjacent ones. This was much harder than the other two techniques because he needed to learn the stars to accomplish it.

Why? Because stars moved. The entire universe moved, together as a whole and individually in quanta, in all sorts of strange ways: expanding, shrinking, bursting, imploding, rotating, orbiting other celestial bodies, and more. Because the stars' locations changed with time, it was possible to extract the time coordinate from each individual *kiss* (slice of sky) and *sliding down that kiss* from the stars' known spatial relationships as a function of time.

Wow! It would easily take him years to learn the stars! Luckily, there was Willie. Yep, *his* Willie. She had a photographic memory. Where Sunny struggled to memorize a single slice of the night sky, she would recall it after glimpsing it once! Then, she would place it in Sunny's brain through their bond.

Was it that simple? Well, no. Of course not. Willie struggled with the temporal aspect. So Sunny had to form a composite of Willie's star maps in an endless sequence of adjacent times while sliding the kisses. Give them a few millennia…

Meanwhile, many other events went on in parallel. Dad worked on Sunny's multi-temp gene, trying to create a splice to augment what seemed missing or damaged. Sunny accompanied him to his lab often, delighting to see all the instruments in action—and discover what the café served for lunch that day. He'd always bring a box back to share with Willie.

But Dad needed more input for the splice—some of the Pathfinders' DNA would be the most advantageous. But how to find that? The last time Wolfpack was on Phe'lak was… four years ago when Silvia unlocked! Did he leave anything Dad could use? A hairbrush, a discarded piece of clothing?

There was another way—Asimia's blood. Dad had made a temporal splice for her before the Grand Migration, so could he not use her blood to extract some of that splice for Sunny? But Dad had only enough of Asimia's blood left to make another dose of the anti-null worldmaker splice they lost in the fight with the K'tul at the Halfway Inn. So he hoarded those last precious drops.

The plan to rescue Asimia went through many iterations. Despite trying to hide it from Sunny, he and Willie were expert eavesdroppers and bonded to all the adults. So they knew of the

three failed attempts at the K'jen lair, emm, temple, under
Snakeman's nose. At least His Premier Glory didn't catch them.

Another month passed. It was all Uncle Triex could do to
delay Asimia's transfer to Hellbound. The greyk'tul unit who
descended from the spaceship in the courier all but occupied the
K'jen lair, making it impossible for Ops Rescue to proceed. Then a
second unit joined them from the Crater, Mn'ianka's, with his
twisted mage K'nista, sealing the Ops' doom. Uncle Triex barely
managed not to get caught.

Dad became distraught, then despondent. His moods turned
darker, and he spoke little. He often sat at his desk at night, unable
to sleep. Sunny tried to console him with words, hugs, and soft
kisses, but it was in vain. He tried hard to think of a way to enable
his dad to at least see his beloved one more time. It didn't come to
him… He fought with Willie about it, but when his dad turned to
drink, Sunny made up his mind to try harder… maybe if he…

Meanwhile, the scientists had an incredible breakthrough!
Led by Dr. Tevez and his infinite star maps, and utilizing the
methods they taught Sunny—kissing stars, sliding them, etc.—they
cracked the code: They extracted the time coordinates from Sunny's
slips to the peculiar planet!

All the celestial times of Sunny's blinks were two hundred
years in the past, the time of the Grand Yandar Migration! And they
were so close together that they fell within the margin of error.
While they couldn't pinpoint them exactly, they felt sure of the
following sequence:

Sunny rescued Wolfpack, Snowfox, and Mouse from the
K'tul courier's cannons. At a nearly identical time, Sunny and
Willie witnessed the K'tul courier blasting the planet—and went
inside it. About ten years later, they met the princesses on the
peculiar planet's beach.

This last was highly significant as it meant Yandar folks
existed on the planet after the K'tul blasted it—they survived the
attack. But was it consistent with the migration's success? They had
no way to know that. And could Sunny go there? Well, no, not
exactly, but also yes! He could go to the approximate time vicinity
and slide his way to some adjacent time, perhaps even the exact.

Dad forbade it.

Sunny and Da in Dad's Lab

Future Time: At the cordon in Paria, continuing from Chapter 14. Sunny's POV.

15. Rescue Ops.

*D*espite Uncle Triex's many plans and four failed attempts, the greyk'tul prevailed. After many escalating threats from his brother, Wolf, Snakeman agreed to surrender Asimia to Hellbound. Sunny didn't even get a chance to hatch his plan of getting his dad near her.

The dreaded day of Asimia's transfer approached five months after Sunny began training with the physicists. It was a marvel Uncle Triex managed to delay this inevitable event by half a year! It was a testament to his immense influence over Snakeman.

Asimia's imminent transfer to Hellbound precipitated plans for a fifth attempt. Since they failed four times at the K'jen temple, his Uncles decided to try the Crater. They set their aim for the day of the transfer. They would snatch her when the K'tul got her out of the K'jen stasis pod to place her into one from Hellbound. It didn't do to mix pods! Uncle Triex got Snakeman up in arms about that detail.

Uncle squeezed the last month's delay from this demand. Wolf had to decide if he should pick this fight with his brother when Snakeman was at least as potent a mage as Wolf himself. At least that was how the K'jen told it. Wolf must have thought so, too, because Hellbound sent a pod in the end. A third Courier arrived with the second still at the Crater, berthed and staffed with the unit that prevailed on Asimia's disposition.

The day before Asimia's transfer, the Blue House received special visitors. It was early enough in the morning that Sunny hadn't started his daily training with the physicists. He was still eating his breakfast with Willie and his dad.

The doorbell rang, making Sunny jump from his seat at the table, dislodging his betrothed. Ever since Dad asked him if he knew the age of majority, it crystallized in Sunny's head that he had betrothed Willie to eventually marry her. Not that it changed his behavior toward her. It gave him another way to think of her.

He ran to the door with the strongest sense of anticipation. It was two Tjourhien, a man and a teen girl. But when they came inside and flipped their hoods back… it was Lady Emmiat and her husband, Phe'laki Captain Russel!

Aunt Nara offered them breakfast, but they declined. Auntie ordered coffee, but again the two refused, saying they needed to return to the Sea Urchin before anyone missed them. They insisted they could talk in the kitchen while "you feed your children."

The children are Willie and me, Sunny realized. *How embarrassing.* After Uncles Fatie and Triex joined them, Dad shooed all the kitchen staffers out and looked at Sunny expectantly. He obliged his dad with a quiet spell.

"We hear you're brewing something," the Phe'laki captain began out loud, facing his wife. He put a hand up to deny any objections or denials. "Hold, please. My wife has something important to tell you."

Sunny remembered that Lady Emmiat couldn't speak out loud on account of Mn'ianka cutting her throat. She used guard sign. "Don't worry about any leaks. We only learned of the plans from Yanus in private, in guard sign, when he came to deliver the fish. Impossible for K'tul to overhear," she signed.

"Good," Uncle Triex signed back. "But what is it, my lady?"

Out of the blue, Sunny became aware of an affinity between his uncle and this brave young noblewoman. They would make a good match. He was a High Prince of Yenda. He had been king and viceroy of that moon. She was a Princess of Orange, King Lucent's bio niece. Would Uncle have picked her instead of Willie's mom if the lady Emmiat's husband had not returned from the dead?

"Don't think it!" Willie's mindvoice rebuked him in his private frequency. *"He picked my mom before the woman's husband returned from the dead. Not only that, he fathered Tommy four years ago while my own bio dad still lived. He really wants my mom."*

"Oh," Sunny replied, chagrined and scandalized.

Lady Emmiat's information was very significant. "I'm sure you remember, my lords Fatie, Triex, when Pete sent us the worldmaker elixir at the Halfway Inn with Sunny. And that we lost Her Majesty before we administered the second dose." The Uncles confirmed that they remembered. Dad nodded, too.

Sunny also remembered that event vividly. It was when Dr. Pietro—before he was his dad—dispatched him from the Crags with this errand the moment he developed the anti-null serum. Sunny delivered the cure in two gigantic syringes, then lingered in stealth to watch.

They administered the first dose to Asimia, but when the time came for the second one six hours later, she had so faded that they couldn't find a solid enough spot on her body for the jab. Snowfox sent her off on Snowwind in the horse's other dimension to distance her from the null and prolong her life. That didn't work out too good; the K'tul found them, etc., but that wasn't the point here.

The point was that Lady Emmiat kept the second syringe with the elixir still in it. When the K'tul attacked the Halfway Inn, she hid it under a stone by the hearth.

"What?" Dad cried. "Could it still be there?"

"Oh!" Uncles Fatie and Triex exclaimed at the same time. Then Uncle Fatie, a bit deflated, added, "But we searched the inn."

"We searched the hearth but didn't remove any stones," Uncle Triex corrected him. "There's still a small chance, I would say!" Then, turning to Lady Emmiat, "Would you have those coordinates, my lady?"

"Can you get them from my mind if I think up the image?"

The image she conjured was very vivid. Sunny fixed the coordinates into his mind, and before any further ado from anyone, he blinked. Willie grabbed his sleeve and came along.

They found themselves in a ruined room at the Halfway Inn. Sunny twirled around to get his bearings. No K'tul were about, unlike the last time he and Willie were here. He remembered this room. The bar had been there… and the hearth… he looked at one corner of the ruins where the fireplace should be. Indeed, a structure that could have been a hearth remained there, crumbled and blackened, scorched.

He took Willie's hand and navigated the rubble. *"Careful,"* she cautioned in his private frequency. *"There's broken glass and sharp pieces of wood, like spears."*

Infinitesimally more cautious for his betrothed's benefit, Sunny made a bee-line to a small protrusion at the far wall by the hearth's ruins. He peeled off loosely held chunks, but others had fused. "Move," he commanded, waving his arm in an inclusive motion that allowed his open palm to point at the rubble. It moved.

"Who are you?" Willie mouthed. "Should I fear you?"

"Why should you fear me?"

Oops, he blew it. He should have said, "Yes, you should," and maybe made a scary face for emphasis. But he didn't. And not only that, but he also felt compelled to add, "I'm only your Sunny." What the heck was wrong with him?

"There!" she whispered, pointing at something and ending Sunny's misgivings. "Is that…?"

They brushed rubble and dirt off a mangled object. Willie extricated it the last few millimeters and held it in her hands reverently. Sunny took a hold of her elbow and blinked them back to the Blue House's kitchen. They had gone for about half an hour in *relative time,* but he used his adjacent time learnings to bring them back to a few heartbeats after they left.

"Sun—" Dad shouted, but they arrived before he had the time to finish. Aunt Nara wrestled Willie away from Sunny and into her arms.

"What happened?" she demanded. "You blinked for a few breaths."

Lady Emmiat brought both hands to her mouth as if to stifle exclamations, even though nothing would come forth from her vocal cords. But she signed. "A temporal! Like Silvia!"

Dad, who had pulled Sunny into his arms, caught the meaning on the lady's fingers. "Silvia is a temporal? Are you sure, my lady?"

"Sure as anyone could be with an infant temporal. But straight wormholing alone couldn't explain her comings and goings and the times between them. But my lord helped her to lock that."

"She locked on her own? As an infant?"

"Yes," the lady signed.

"Oh, my!" Dad exclaimed with an intense gaze at Sunny. "Why didn't *I* know that?"

No one had an answer. "We best be going," Captain Russel reminded his wife. She nodded. But Sunny wanted to show the lady the syringe. He nudged Willie, and she produced it from her pocket.

"Look, my lady," he said, "we found it where you hid it."

"Oh, my!" Lady Emmiat exclaimed with her fingers. "You found it! When? Oh, just now, your temporal blink! But is it destroyed? Does it still work, Pete?

"I'll be!" Dad exclaimed, reaching for the syringe. Sunny happily passed it to him. Dad turned it every way, up, down, sideways, and pronounced there was still liquid inside. "I have to go to my lab," he mumbled. He turned to go, but Sunny took his hand.

"I'll take you," he offered. Captain Russel and his wife departed, bidding best luck recovering the splice. Sunny waited for Dad to incline his head and blinked the two of them to the lab.

A few hours later, Dad determined that the syringe contained enough liquid and it was good. He transferred it to a new syringe with the needle separated to avoid mangling it again or inadvertently jabbing someone and wasting the precious stuff. Then he brought Sunny to the cafeteria and bought him two deluxe lunch boxes. They returned to Dad's office, from where Sunny blinked them home.

The adults spent the rest of the day and well into the evening planning. The Blue House should get a revolving door. People came and went, prominently the archers—captain Chimeran's original team and many new volunteers, whom she trained as part of their *exercise program.* She had a full squad.

Uncle Triex distributed a few red K'jen uniforms to them. Yanus handed out homemades—Molotov cocktails, oil, and aerosol bombs. The archers applied explosives to their arrows and filled double and triple quivers.

Aunt Nara called it a night shortly after midnight and demanded that her husband send everyone away. Uncle Triex did, but it was another hour before the house emptied.

Sunny eavesdropped as much as he could. He used a new spell he learned, and listened even after Aunt Nara forced him and Willie to go to bed. Aunt didn't allow him to sleep in Willie's bed anymore—and he no longer blinked in his sleep thanks to the pills the doctor fed him. So he overheard many more details than Willie.

The next day found the house ominously quiet. It was a dark day, cloudy with a threat of rain or worse—they got hail lately. Even the heavens objected to this cruel treatment of their Queen. Dad's mood was equally dark. He forbade Sunny from taking part in the rescue.

But it made no sense. After half a year of training, Sunny may not have been ready yet for precise excursions hundreds of years in the past, but he could blink to places in Paria where he had coordinates, fixing the temporal to the present time.

He had amassed a goodly bundle of those: the K'jen temple, the docks, anywhere in the cordon, including the hospital and the college, his dad's lab and office there, the Crags, and more. The Crater was among them. Could he blink the entire resistance team there? Hmm. He had never blinked more than himself with a few others. But he could ferry the team a few at a time.

And he could use his mage skills. He'd practiced many combat spells. Uncle Triex, although not a mage himself, brought him scrolls from Snake on how to gather energy for blasts and fire. Sunny found the K'jen methods unnatural but learned them anyway. He could blast and flame violently. But Dad wouldn't hear of it.

So, entirely without Sunny's blinks and mage help, Uncles Triex and Fatie assembled the Cordonite Resistance Fighters—Chimeran's team—at the Crater. They went *on foot!*

Captain Chimeran and her archers were eager for such an opportunity for action against their oppressors. They thirsted for revenge. Uncle worried they would give in to heroics. He gave them a last lecture before they departed the Blue House. Sunny heard with his listening spell from his bed, pretending to be asleep.

"Keep your positions at the Crater's perimeter and wait for my mark. No heroics. I don't want to lose a single one of you. And no flying! We're to pass for K'jen if they spot us. Be sure your cloaks cover your wings."

They were well armed with their "practice" bows, explosive arrows, and homemades, but had no swords—a huge disadvantage in hand-to-hand. So this Ops was a hit-and-run. Rather, a hit, *grab,* and run. A *precision* grab: They needed to snatch Asimia when she was out of the first stasis pod and before going into the next.

Uncle Triex had planned the transfer from the K'tul perspective in his role as Snakeman's First. He appointed himself as the Snake's envoy and would personally supervise the transfer. He and Uncle Fatie practiced saying Snake's real name to sound more official. *S'tihsa* and *His Glory S'tihsa*. It annoyed Auntie and Dad.

The plan went like this: When Uncle Triex's real K'jen underlings opened Asimia's stasis pod, Uncle would lift her in his arms to supposedly place her into the pod from Hellbound. Uncle Fatie would be present to assist in case things went sideways. Snakeman had allowed both to carry their swords.

Just before he placed Asimia into the second pod, Uncle Triex would give the signal to the cordonite resistance in their specific group-chat frequency. They would cause havoc at the Crater's perimeter with the oils and aerosols, making it look like a K'jen mage attack. This would allow Uncle to escape with Asimia.

And this is where Sunny marveled the most! First of all, *how* would Uncle escape with Asimia? Would he slink away through a throng of K'tul? They'd see him! They'd kill him the moment he started to run with Simi in his arms. They'd cut him to pieces with their scimitars. The mages would blast him!

Second, Sunny could easily blink Asimia and the Uncles out at that point if only they allowed him to come along.

But Uncle Triex had sided with Sunny's dad, with more misgivings of his own. He doubted Sunny's blink accuracy, especially under a load of adrenaline. He didn't want to lose Asimia in some uncharted space, and who knew when. Plus he worried that the mages would trace Sunny's blink and implicate the ghetto! And that would be the end of all Yandar and Yendal life on Phe'lak.

Sunny countered that he could bring Asimia elsewhere, say, to the Crags. But Uncle insisted that a mage of K'nista's caliber could trace him anywhere. And there were *two* greyk'tul mages at the Crater. The second one had arrived with the third courier.

Uncle also wanted to pin Asimia's theft on the K'jen. If he, S'tihsa's Envoy, snatched her in plain view, the grey would think that the red reneged on the deal. After that, all the cordonites had to do was sit back and watch the two K'tul factions destroy each other.

Fine. Sunny stopped arguing but resolved to follow the group in stealth. He would blink in and snatch Asimia and the Uncles at the exact time the resistance swung into action. It would still look like the K'jen reneged. Sunny could pass as a K'jen witch.

He guarded those thoughts even from Willie, knowing it would be dangerous, and he didn't want to risk her. And this was another marvel. He'd normally beg her to come along. Now he'd leave her behind? *Not to risk her?* What was wrong with him?

Then there was Dad… there was no keeping *him* behind. The Uncles lost many shouting matches. Dad insisted he had to be there to jab Asimia with the elixir the moment they had her out of stasis. The Uncles thought it could wait until they brought her back to the cordon. But Sunny understood Dad's logic. They may fail to rescue Asimia, but she would no longer be nulled if they jabbed her anyway! Although… wouldn't that jabbing action get Dad killed?

When Dad threatened to trail them, the Uncles relented. They preferred having him with the team where they could watch and protect him rather than following after them alone.

Great, Sunny thought. *They need me* more *now, to protect my dad.* He waited in bed pretending to be asleep until they all left the Blue House. He was about to get up to follow them, but he opened his eyes… and the doctor was kneeling by his bedside. Before Sunny could react, Doc jabbed him with a potent sedative.

"No! Oh, no!" he yelled. "What have you done?" But it was no use. He slept through the entire Ops. No. Only the beginning.

He awoke suddenly in fright as Willie shook him vigorously, and the doc pulled a giant syringe from his arm. "Sunny!" Willie screamed. "They got our dads! Wake up! We need to save them!"

"Are you awake, my boy?" asked Doc. That was the understatement of the century! He'd pumped enough adrenaline into Sunny to wake the dead.

Aunt Nara burst into the room. She wore the Yandar Flyer uniform, with her "practice" bow clipped to one thigh, a quiver to the other, and a chest belt overflowing with home-mades. "Come, son," she cried. "Is he awake, doc?"

"You can't go dressed like that, Auntie," Sunny mumbled. Then he found his voice, "It'll give us out," he shouted. "You need a redk'tul uniform. Does Uncle have spares? Wait. My dad has."

"We're wasting time! Come!" yelled Auntie.

"I'll adjacent us," Sunny yelled back, diving into the wardrobe he shared with his dad. He rummaged through Dad's clothes, flipping many over his head and creating a pile on the floor. He found a red uniform. "Here, Auntie."

"What do you mean you'll adj—what's this?" She took the uniform from Sunny's hand and started stripping.

"Ah, no! Here you go again!" Sunny cried, whirling around. He found another uniform and donned it over his PJs.

"You can't shoot your arrows either, Aunt. Here, have some shuriken." He retrieved Dad's chest belt from the closet. It was studded with darts of K'tul design. "Take these, they're K'jen," he told Aunt Nara.

She threw the belt over a shoulder. "Let's go!" she shouted, unclipping her bow and quiver and dropping them where she stood. "I'd kill for a sword." She stared at Sunny. "Won't they expect a mage from the K'jen and not a handful of darts?"

"They'll get a mage. Come." He grabbed his aunt's hand.

"I need a uniform!" Willie wailed, diving into the wardrobe.

"You'll give us away, Willie. You're too small!" he shouted.

"Am not! So are you!"

"But I can levitate, and you can't!" His K'jen cloak hung from his shoulders, revealing his PJs, and dragged on the ground behind him. He waved his hand before his face, and his countenance changed. He became taller; his skin turned purple, and he grew horns. He did the same to Willie, who'd scrambled into Dad's red leather shirt because she couldn't find another K'jen garb.

"You two are too skinny," Auntie exclaimed in dismay. Then, "Hurry, that's good enough."

Sunny blinked them to the Crater's coordinates that Willie put in his head, but slid them back to the time when Willie shook him on his bed. *Slide the kiss.*

They popped out of Sunny's blink into open air at the Crater's vast docking field in the midst of chaos. The two couriers from Hellbound berthed behind them, and to their right was a transport with the red snake logo on its side.

You'd think the world had filled with greyk'tul. It normally made weeks of gossip to see a couple of them together, now a dozen meleed around a few yards from the transport, with many blackk'tul swelling their numbers! Like they needed reinforcements when they sported two grey witches, one of them K'nista!

The K'jen were yet more numerous! Uncle emptied Snake's lair for this Ops. Could some of them be the Resistance in disguise? They were supposed to stay at the base's rim!

Although fewer, the greyk'tul had the advantage over the K'jen. They surrounded them, keeping them pinned with spells and crossbows. They had forced the three K'jen leaders to their knees with black scimitars about their necks. Sunny immediately realized the scene was more complex than it looked. Many active spells buzzed around the captives: disorientation, hold, psychic block.

But the three on the ground didn't have K'tul complexions. Why, one was an even! "My dad!" Sunny mumbled in dismay. He pulled Willie and Aunt Nara behind Snakeman's transport. He had to use a spell and all his strength to hold Auntie back. She had dropped shuriken in both hands, ready to throw. "No!" he whispered forcefully, unable to mindspeak her. He had to use another spell to keep the darts from flying. "Please, Auntie, don't exhaust me.

"We'll save them, you'll see! And use guard sign," he signed to his aunt and Willie. "We need stealth; they can feel my spells."

"Are your spells not K'jen?" Auntie's fingers asked.

"Yes. But that doesn't save us from the greyk'tul. They hate the K'jen." That was the result of two years of Uncles' cultivation.

As they watched, Snakeman's transport opened a hatch, and out of it came a band of blackk'tul carrying a red box that looked like a coffin—Asimia's stasis pod! But why didn't the grey witches spell it from the transport to one of their couriers? He concentrated on it and felt many K'jen spells binding it. Snakeman had spelled it against magical transport—another one of Uncle's ploys!

Two greyk'tul met them at the bottom of the transport's steps and turned to escort them toward the courier. But hadn't they planned to transfer Asimia into Wolf's pod? Sunny counted on that. His mark to strike was when she was out of the red coffin.

He watched eagerly. When the K'tul cleared enough space from the transport to deposit the pod on the ground, another pod popped beside it. This one was black with Wolf insignia. A third(!) grey witch accompanied it. Sunny had never seen this mage before. But Hellbound sent two witches!? And K'nista made three! Against a lone boy with mangled genes!

Too late to change his plan, Sunny watched breathlessly as the greymage ordered the K'jen to position the red pod beside the black. He waved his hands and shouted words in K'tul. Oh, was that how they opened those things? Sunny thought they needed DNA. But maybe some didn't. Sure enough, the pod opened with a loud woosh, letting copious cold fog escape.

The mage reached into the pod and pulled the motionless body of a woman out of it. Frozen and pale beyond the normal complexion of a silverblood, the woman was stunning to behold! Beautiful beyond measure, even in this deathly predicament!

Asimia! My sister! The thought popped into Sunny's brain on its own. No! *You can't have her, monster!*

Sunny stepped from his cover and blasted the mage with a barrage of spells. A ruckus of explosions followed from the perimeter—the cordonites joining in with their home-mades. Sunny hadn't been far from the K'tul mage. The concussion from his blast cocktail shook the ground under his, Willie's, and Aunt Nara's feet, throwing them to the ground.

Willie screamed, but Auntie stepped from cover and loosed her shuriken. She jumped her nearest blackk'tul and wrestled his scimitar from his grip. She whipped around, cutting and slashing, purple streaks streaming from the arcs of her blade.

Sunny hurdled another violent blast: fire and booms, concussion. The blackk'tul fell back in disarray, but the grey witch fired back, catching Sunny square on his chest and hurdling him backward. It left Auntie alone among the K'tul. They swarmed her.

Willie broke cover, screaming. She charged the blackk'tul with fists and wing talons, flinging them off her mom. As Sunny crashed to the ground yards back, the devils hacked at Auntie and his betrothed! Cold rage enveloped his body and sank into his soul. He twisted, turned, whirled, compelled, and launched himself to land before Willie amidst the backrobes.

"Behind me," he ordered aloud while blazing the K'tul with targeted lightning, avoiding Willie and Aunt Nara. Where did he learn to do that? It was a K'jen spell.

Willie and Aunt fell behind him. Aunt bled from a hundred cuts. Oh no! Her red blood would betray them!

The grey demon scrambled to stuff Asimia into the black pod, chanting frantically. His chants crescendoed. Many yards in the other direction, Mn'ianka threw the captives to the ground. They had been on their knees, and the violent blows crashed their heads to the pavement. K'tul feet stepped on their necks to hold them down.

Sunny turned frantically from Simi to Da and back. Who to save? "Forget her!" Aunt Nara yelled at the top of her lungs. "They won't kill her. "Saved *them!*"

"Simi! Unfreeze! Get behind me!" Sunny boomed a command spell to Asimia as he whirled toward his dad and uncles. His spell broke through the K'tul psychic block. Asimia heard him!

"Sunstorm?" she replied. *"Is that you, my darling? Have you come to save us?"* Her mindvoice sounded hopeful, but abruptly turned to horror: *"Pete?!"* she cried. *"My love! Be gone from here! They'll kill you!"*

But even as her mind thawed enough to mindspeak those words, her body remained frozen. She could not obey Sunny's command to get behind him. Spells from the most powerful K'tul mages held her—Snakeman, K'nista, and these two other grey devils who came from Hellbound. She couldn't struggle. The K'tul witch pulled her, frozen and stiff, toward the black pod.

"Simi! Behind me!" Sunny repeated his command. But she fell to her knees through the witch's claws. The witch bent after her.

"Leave off!" Dad's mind cry tore Sunny's brain. *"You're hurting her! Son! The dueling spells will tear her apart."*

Sunny felt for the K'tul witch's spell on Asimia. He tried to bring it to his own body—succeeded—it threw him to the pavement and crushed him with unspeakable evil. It was a *bind* spell, of body and soul. It would kill him… her…He dropped his own spell.

Victorious, the devil mage took full control of Asimia and shoved her into the black pod. Shaking from rage, Sunny turned his tear-streaked face to Dad and Uncles. Mn'ianka lifted his scimitar execution-style over their heads. He had paused as if he wanted Sunny to witness the atrocity.

Sunny boomed a summons into his dad's and uncles' brains, *"Behind me. Run!"* and blasted another barrage of targeted spells in their direction. Mn'ianka, the greyk'tul who held the prisoners to the ground, and those who backed them up flew violently upward, backward, and finally downward, crashing hard, meters away. Except for…

K'nista, who, to that point, had stood by Mn'ianka admiring his First's handiwork. Unaffected by Sunny's attack, he waved his hands and blasted back, throwing Sunny in the air, holding him in magelock, and savaging him with fire, lightning, and concussion.

But Sunny didn't burn. Neither was he injured in any other way. He countered with a negate spell and a shield. He dove from the air, expanding his shield to envelop his dad and uncles. He retreated, with the men scrambling to find their feet. The four ran together like the hounds of hell pursued them. They reached the transport where Willie and Aunt Nara had retreated.

"Fall back. Retreat." Uncle Fatie sent to the resistance fighters who continued to raise hell at the perimeter. Sunny threw a retreating shield after the cordonites that would follow them to the cordon. He then blinked his group to the Blue House in Dad's room.

They spilled from Sunny's blink onto the floor. There was enough blood to soak the carpet! Sunny felt squeamish but controlled his stomach. *"Doctor!"* one of the Uncles mindyelled.

"Give me the syringe!" Sunny yelled at his dad. "There's still time!"

He must have looked wild with adrenaline because Dad flinched to look at him. "No, Sunny," he yelled. "Stand down!"

"There's still time, Da." He dove on his dad, fishing in his red cloak's pockets. *"Simi!"* he mindyelled. *"Coordinates."* Then to Dad, "She's in the courier, in stasis, but I can still feel her."

"Me, too," Dad yelled back.

"Coordinates! Please!" Sunny mindyelled again as he pulled the syringe from Dad's cloak. Improbably, a set of coordinates materialled in his head. But it wasn't Asimia. It was…

"Silvia? That you? Hold on, I'm coming!" But Dad grabbed his sleeve and pulled him down.

"Stay!" he ordered. "They'll kill you, too!" He turned to the room, to the Uncles, "Help me hold him."

But Sunny blinked to Silvia's coordinates. Dad, attached to his sleeve, came along. They landed on the bridge of a K'tul spaceship—Hellbound. It looked like the courier's bridge he and Willie had been in by the peculiar planet. Only this one was vast. From its window, Sunny saw a smaller ship approaching. *The courier from the Crater, bringing Asimia.*

Facing away from Sunny and his dad, an immensely horned, purple K'tul demon strangled two little girls. *Wolf.* He whirled about, bringing the girls into full view. It was Silvia! The other was

K'tul! They wore rags for clothes and bled from many wounds.
Their arms bore welts, burns, and bites!

"Blink us, Sunny! Now!" Dad whispered, in echoes of his
commanding voice.

"No, Da, we have to rescue them!"

"I thought you'd say that. Are these your princesses?"

"No! That's Silvia, Da! Can't you tell?"

Wolf dropped the girls, extended his arm, palm facing
upward, and clenched his fingers violently a few times. As the rest
of the K'tul on the bridge scrambled about, Asimia's pod
materialized before Wolf.

"Asimia!" Dad exclaimed loudly.

"This you want? You brought your serum?" Another clench
of his fingers, and the syringe flew from Sunny's hand towards
Wolf. Sunny dove after it and caught it in the air. He crash-landed
hard on his wing within arm's reach of the monster. He scooted
frantically backward to get away, Wolf's maniacal laughter
following him.

Dad struggled to open the pod while greyk'tul grabbed and
pulled him savagely. "What do you want to do with this one, Boss?"
one of them asked in K'tul.

"Hold him, idiot!" Wolf spat, also in K'tul. "Well, well,
now! Two little red K'jen riding hoods paying me a visit? Haha. I
don't think so. The cloak does not make the blood. Shall we see?"

With a wave of his hand, he flung the red cloaks off Dad and
Sunny. "What have we here? Wings?!!" He spat the last in Yandar.

Sunny reached the girls. "Come," he yelled. "Get behind me;
I'll blink us away."

"No!" Silvia cried. "Leave us. He won't kill us. He wants us
alive. Ma, too. But he'll kill you! And your Da."

Sunny turned to his dad, reached out his arm, palms upward,
and clenched his fingers, executing an extraction spell. Where did he
learn that? From Wolf, just now, when he extracted Asimia's pod
from the courier. Dad hurtled from many K'tul grasping hands to
roll on the floor beside Sunny. Sunny threw a haphazard shield
dome around them. It wouldn't last long. Wolf already beat on it.

"Blink!" Sunny commanded. But there was a counter, and
his blink sputtered. He scrutinized Wolf. Did K'tul learn to blink?

"Blink!" he ordered again, but another counter interfered.

"Leave us!" Silvia boomed in his head. *"We must stay here. We divert him, or he'll destroy the world."*

"Please, Silvi," Sunny begged, *"let me take you to safety. I can't hold the shield much longer against him."*

"It will work out, Uncle. In a few more years—ten in total after my capture—help will come. Don't interfere, please!"

"What help? How do you know?"

"My gramma from Yand. And the Pathfinder! I know because I will bring them."

"Huh? How do you know what hasn't happened yet?"

"Because I already did it. Go!" and she did the strangest thing: She spat on his face.

"Whew! What did you do that for!" He started to wipe it off with the heel of his free hand—he still held the syringe in the other—but Silvia stopped him.

"Leave it, your dad needs it now that—"

She didn't get to finish. Sunny's shield sputtered and dissipated. Wolf hurtled him and Dad away from the girls. A barrage of spells followed. The Demon advanced on them. Sunny returned the fire, but he was no match to Wolf. He lost ground. "Blink!" Dad ordered forcefully, aloud.

Against his will, Sunny blinked. They spilled back into their room. An army of medics meleed about. They'd emptied the hospital and turned Dad's room into an Emergency Center. Darryl was also there. "A slide," Dad yelled at his tech, and Darryl produced a sealed slide and handed it to Dad, who had to fight the attention of a med woman. A nurse? Ah, she was a new doctor. The green double-headed snake featured on her sleeve.

Dad carefully scraped Silvia's spittle from Sunny's cheek onto the slide, then took another one and sealed it over the first. He handed it to Darryl, crying, "DNA pronto. Top priority in all haste. Full analysis. Report as you go. I'll come to the lab as soon as they let me." With that, he yielded to the medical ministrations.

On Hellbound, Wolf Against Sunny and Da

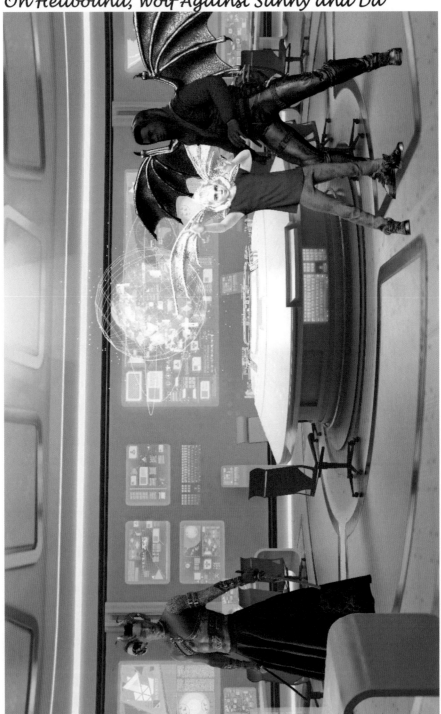

Past Time: On Yand, continuing from Chapter 12. Snowfox's POV.

16. The Stars, Darkly

Snowfox woke up early the following morning, intending to fly over to the training field to supervise the preparations. They had settled their departure time to the day after next to give Asimia two full days to recover from the null. They also decided not to tax the wormhole masters, so all exploration of the anomalous space ceased.

"Asimia," he murmured, patting the bed beside him. He found only Snowdrift and Hunter and remembered that it was Lucent's night. She answered, nonetheless, although he had spoken aloud, not in mindspeak. *"I'm here, love, in Moms' garden. RC is here. She wanted to speak with me in private."*

"Oh?" Snowfox nearly lost his composure. And there he thought they had settled the matter. But why would he believe that? Like his indiscretion wasn't enough, unintended though it might be, they added a baby on top. Asimia was right. He needed to own the whole thing. *"Should I come?"* he asked his wife sheepishly. Then he thought better of it and amended, *"Can I please come?"*

"No, love. She'd think I called you, and the presence of both of us may spook her. She said she wanted to speak to me alone. But I think you need to have your own discussion with RC. It's not right to leave it like this. Grab some coffee and breakfast. We just got here and haven't yet delved into it. I think she's trying to figure out how to lie to me."

"That's not good, love. Tell her to be straight out. I don't remember what happened at all. But it probably happened."

"I know you, Fox. I can't imagine you'd sleep next to a woman this gorgeous and... emm... just sleep."

"Ah, this is humiliating! You really think that of me?"

"Get your coffee."

He dressed hastily and made his way to the kitchen. Lucent was already there, just getting his breakfast. Snowfox ordered food for himself and his foxes and a pot of coffee and joined Luc.

"The gift that keeps on giving?" Luc asked. "She took Asimia from our bed."

"I know."

"Shouldn't *you* be talking with her?"

"I wanted to, but someone advised me to stay away from her and always account for my whereabouts until Asimia was ready for the next step."

"Wolfpack?"

"Yes."

"How old is he? He's like a sage."

"He's done something big but won't tell me what. I saw how severely injured he was. He healed older. Like he grew up years in the space of hours."

"His temporal ability, you think?"

"Probably. But something else, too. His injuries looked like war wounds. Like something or someone blasted him, burned him."

"And what's the next step?"

"What next step?"

"RC."

"Ah, I don't know. It depends on what *she* wants to do."

"She, RC, or she, our wife."

"Both. Asimia first."

"So what the heck happened? I took you for a virgin, not a womanizer."

"I was, man. I don't remember what all happened with RC. But I did wake up in her bed."

"You mean RC clipped your wings? What a nasty fate! You couldn't wait for your wedding night to give it to your wife?"

"What? No! Asimia clipped my wings, not RC."

Luc stared, and after many silent moments, Snowfox decided to come clean. "Asimia sent me to bring her betrothal papers to another man—"

"Oh, how cruel! So you brought the papers to Pete?"

"Yes. You knew about Pete? Of course. And it doesn't bother you?"

"You're an idiot, Fox. She fell in love with Pete when you were her brother. I couldn't win her attention over him, although I tried. He's so dashing and... adult. Yes, it bothers me that she chose him instead of me. But it bothers me more to leave him behind.

Distance makes the heart and mind do strange things. He will become a god. Can you compete with a god?"

"Look, man, I tried. The queen, and now the king, won't allow him to migrate with us because he's singular."

"Fine. We'll send Wolfpack to fetch him. So this drove you to RC's bed?"

"No. Of course not. I went to the field and got drunk with the archers. Chimera thought it wise to send me to RC with the army mage. I don't remember any of it."

"Oh," Luc exclaimed. "Is she coming? We should cut her."

"Who, RC?"

"No, Chimé."

Mercifully, this turned the discussion to logistics for the migration. About an hour later, Asimia joined them. They pulled a seat for her between them. She kissed them in turn, Luc first. She ordered breakfast for herself and Alex and remained silent while Snowfox died to ask her: What did RC say? How did she take it? Did they agree on anything? And so much more.

Luc was anxious to settle the final preparations. His Orange household migrants were to assemble at the field that morning, and he wanted to ensure they understood the pertinent logistics. But the most challenging task he had to carry out that morning was to announce who would go on the expedition and who wouldn't. All the greens would, and a few oranges. The others needed to await a second pass.

"And have we decided when this second pass will be?" asked Asimia.

"No," Lucent replied. I will dismiss the unlucky ones. They can reassemble later when we come back for them.

"What of the Yendai?"

"Them, too. If they don't wish to return to the moon, Hawk offered to house them on Yand until we settle them permanently." He kissed Simi, gave Fox a "be good," and went to find a teleporter.

Asimia finished her breakfast. Snowfox bent to steal a peck on her cheek, but she turned and leaned into it. "I'm sorry, love," she told him when they came up for air. "This mess is all my fault."

"Ah, no," Snowfox objected. "All mine. I shouldn't have gotten drunk that night. I'm such an idiot."

"Yes, you are," she agreed.

"Well?" Snowfox encouraged her.

"Well, she tried to convince me that the child is her husband's. After much discussion, I understood that she wants it that way. She feels very remorseful for taking advantage of you when you were obviously very drunk."

Snowfox winced. Again, he felt humiliated. "There's no excuse for my behavior. I know RC. She's very honorable. She wouldn't have... consented had she known I had not."

"A moment of weakness, I think," Asimia countered, "even if she knew. No, not if. I'm sure she did know you don't love her like a mate. But she's crushed on you—"

"No, I don't think—" Snowfox attempted to dispute that.

"It's that Chimeran I'd like to..." Simi let that drop. But it got her started. "'A few of us would like to oblige you!' What the hell! What does she take you for? One to service them all?"

"What?"

"Isn't that what she said to you that night before she bundled you up and shipped you to RC?"

Snowfox didn't remember that conversation. Only that Chimeran sent him to RC with a mage. "You heard that?"

"I did. I'm bonded to you. I can hear you from another star system. I heard it all!" She shouted the last sentence. So loudly in fact, that the staff emptied the kitchen and gave them the space. Simi was blazing mad. Alex took to hissing and growling.

Snowfox had no idea what to say. She remembered his night of indiscretion when he did not! "Geld me," he offered. "Take my head. Whatever you want. Just don't send me away from you."

"Oh, I would!" she cried. "But if I did all that to you, I'd leave our child without her father!"

Again Snowfox stared dumbfounded. "Our child?" he murmured when he found a bit of voice. "You don't mean RC's child... you mean..."

Asimia took his hand and placed it over her stomach. "No. Not RC's. I mean this child you put in my belly."

"Simi, my love!" Sudden joy overwhelmed him. For a moment, the new complexity this brought vanished. They signed papers for a chaste marriage because Asimia's life was at risk should she carry a worldmaker girl. They amended those vows, changing *chaste* to *childless*. Asimia got birth control. Yet she was pregnant.

He pulled his wife into his arms and held her tenderly. How he loved her! "Please, love," he murmured. "Can you ever forgive me? Trust me again?"

"There's nothing to forgive, my love. But trust… that'll come on its own. And I do want you to have that discussion with RC. Assure her that if she allows us to adopt her child, we will dote on her and love her as our own parents loved you. They never called you adopted. They called you their firstborn, and I swear Mom Yanara loves you the best of all of us."

"I'll try, my love, but we don't steal children, no? It's up to her. She may not wish her husband to think the child may be mine."

"It matters not to me who fathered her. She'll be my joy should RC allow us to have her."

Suddenly, it occurred to Snowfox that there were too many *hers.* "What do you mean by calling the babies *her?* Are they—"

"Both girls," Asimia finished for him. To his horrified stare, she elaborated, patting her belly, "If she is born with wings, Wolfpack will bring her back to Yand, and Hawk will raise her."

Yandar children grew their wings in childhood, but Worldmaker girls developed them in the womb. The doctor delivered them early via c-section, or else they would fly from their mother's belly, killing her.

"But," he objected, "we take this journey to separate you from Mom, and now we'll bring another worldmaker back to Yand? How does this make sense? Plus, don't you want our daughter?"

"Of course I do. Look, let's leave it open—fly with it (play it by ear)."

Asimia accompanied Snowfox to the training field, where he found RC and sat her down for that discussion. It lasted a long time because he wanted to make sure she understood that both he and Simi were sincere in their offer and not out of duty. He even offered to marry her! She turned both offers down. That her daughter would gain the status of High Princess meant nothing to RC.

That night in their bed, Fox loved his wife so passionately that he thought his heart would burst. Finally, when he left no doubt in her mind about his feelings for her, he pulled her on top of him and embraced her with arms and wings. They lay exhausted like that until the brink of sleep, when he uttered the words Asimia most wanted to hear. "You clipped my wings that night."

"And you mine, my love. Get some sleep. We'll need your strength in the morning."

The next morning, Snowfox awoke to find Asimia gone from their bed. *"Kitchen,"* she put in his head. *"Coffee."*

"Coming," he replied, hopping in the shower. *"My foxes?"*

"Stuffing their faces with Alex. Try that new citrussy stuff I brought from Riverqueen. It'll wake you up if nothing else."

He joined his wife for coffee and breakfast. Lucent was absent—back to the field and Orange. This was the day before. They expected Wolfpack any minute now. Sure enough, a loud pop announced his arrival with Mouse, sans wolves. A few minutes later, Uncle Yildiz and Grandma Stardust joined them.

"Everything ready?" Grandma asked, with a special look at Asimia. "How's Lorena? Working out?"

"Yes, thank you, Grandma," Asimia replied, then turned to Fox. "Count one more in our group."

Their group was the third wormhole. Wolfpack would take the lead, bringing the scientists, engineers, medics, craftmasters, builders, agros, and fishers—the personnel needed to make a new colony work. And also the principality of Orange, Lucent's household. Luc's mother and sister counted among them, as did the agro expertise. Fishing expertise came from the Keys. Wolfpack helmed the wormhole, and Lucent led Group 1.

Uncle Yildiz helmed Group 2, with Grandma Stardust leading it. They brought Grandma's palace personnel and household with their families. They all followed their queen. Hawk had to re-staff the palace and offices.

Simi helmed the third group, with himself leading it—and the expedition overall. They brought their household and most military units that accompanied the migration. And Yandar and Yendai mingled where they fit best.

Back to Grandma's question, "I don't know if we'll ever be ready," Fox said, "but Luc announced the First Transfer."

"First Transfer?" asked Mouse. "Is that an official name?"

"Yes. He came up with it to pacify those staying behind. We're only taking the greens and a couple of oranges. A total of six hundred, give or take a few."

"But we're coming back for the rest, no?" Grandma asked.

"Yes," Wolfpack jumped in. "Let us clear the first pass, and we'll see about the time of the Second Transfer. It may be soon, or will have to wait a while."

"But you expect to—" Grandma persisted.

"Yes."

"Ok, then."

"The Second Transfer has about two hundred or so," Snowfox interjected in that exchange. *Two* hundred so that Wolfpack could bring them on his own. "We left the bulk for the Third Transfer, which doesn't look likely to happen at this point."

"But we counted two thousand!" Grandma objected.

"We'll do our best," Wolfpack tried to assure her. "Let's see how we fair with the anomaly. And Simi—"

"Will do my best," Asimia cut him off. "I may be able to bring more in one haul."

"Stick to the plan, please, love," Snowfox objected. There was something that bothered him, and he wasn't sure what. Plus, the way Stardust and Wolfpack behaved... The way they looked at Asimia, how they talked to her...they knew!

Uncle Yildiz interrupted his thoughts. "Lunch with the dragon?" he asked Asimia.

"Wouldn't miss it, Uncle. Our last on this world." Her eyes misted as she said that.

"Do you want some company?" Snowfox offered. He, too, felt the weight of leaving their grandad, the dragon, behind.

"Sure, love," Asimia told him, squeezing his hand.

They dispersed for their morning chores. Snowfox found Lucent at the field and convinced him not to cut Chimeran and her Archer unit. It took a lot to change Luc's mind. He had to tell him of Asimia's pregnancy to emphasize their need for military protection.

It didn't go too well. They nearly came to blows. Getting two women pregnant was scandalous enough, but... Fox didn't even wait for his wedding night with Asimia!? After all the fuss he made amending their vows, declaring not to take another wife, not father a baby, and on and on...all true.

But as guilty and humiliated as Snowfox fell, there was not a thing he could do at that point to change the circumstances. Simi's safety was all that mattered—and her precious baby, regardless of who fathered her. It was hard enough that they would have to negotiate a potential null between them.

"Look, Lucent," he said, "I don't know whose baby Asimia carries. Does she look very pregnant to you? Either one of us could have fathered the baby."

"But I only…" Lucent objected, then paused and did the math. "Could she be only in her first month?"

"And does it matter? Could you turn your heart off to a baby you didn't father on her?"

Lucent stared at him. "No," he declared after a while. "I haven't thought of it that way before. Any baby she carries is my child, and I love them regardless. But you refer to this baby as her. Is it a girl, then?"

"It is."

A slight grin dawned on Luc's face that broadened into a smile. "A little girl? In truth? A daughter? Oh, how splendid!"

So Luc allowed the errant Archer Captain Chimé and her unit to join the migration. They allocated a part of the military contingent to the first two groups but kept most of the archers with Asimia in Group 3.

When he got a breather from all the expedition chaos, Snowfox sat by himself and his foxes and did the math. Simi took her birth control months ago. But his first few nights with her were before that. He had been careful, but… it had to have happened then. Asimia was… seven months pregnant! No! Impossible. RC was only about six and had a huge bump.

He tried to remember his mom Yanara's pregnancy with his brother Sunstorm. She was six months pregnant when Fox and his brothers found her on Tuncay after she fled Yand to free Simi from the null. He recalled vividly. Mom's belly was flat at six months! And at seven! Another worldmaker trait?

And Grandma knew! The new attendant she assigned to Simi was a doctor! Fox had heard someone call her Dr. Lorena. The Dr. was for the medical discipline, not the science as he had assumed. And all this secrecy! Asimia didn't want anyone to know, including their household doctor! She had the man going in Group 1.

After much self-torment, Snowfox decided not to cause further drama and to just fly with it. He'd be right beside Simi every step of the way. Wolfpack would intervene in case of a null and bring the baby back to Yand. And, despite all this fear, the baby could be born locked, like Asimia. They could have a few precious years with their daughter. Could he hope?

At lunchtime, Snowfox found Asimia and Uncle Yildiz on the field, and Simi teleported them to the dragon's lair. They brought an overflowing basket from the canteen and two bottles of Grandad's favorite wine from their own cellar. It was a tearful affair. They cried and vowed to bring Grandad to Phe'lak to stay with them all the time he wanted. They needed to clear the way first.

"Am I not singular?" he teased them while petting Alex.

"I have way too many singular men in my life," Asimia chuckled.

"Not me," Snowfox replied, flying with Simi's playful mood. He did much of this kind of flying lately. But he could feel vividly Asimia's anguish for the men she was leaving behind: Her beloved Grandad, both Blaze and Dragon, and another, Pete, the singular geneticist. This last gave Fox knots in his heart.

Everyone was jittery that night. The three of them sat down to dinner with Uncle Yildiz and Grandma Stardust, with a skeleton crew serving them. Everyone else had gone to the field, eager to transfer. These few remaining staffers had also moved their allowed belongings to the field. Their families already awaited them there.

Snowfox had much difficulty sleeping that night but decided against drinking. Look what it got him the last time. He tossed and turned forever until Asimia spoke in his head: *"We all need to sleep, my love. Come to my room."*

"But Lucent—"

"Him, too."

"Come, man," Lucent confirmed his presence. *"We need to rest tonight. Otherwise we'll end up who knows where tomorrow."*

"Should I teleport you?" threatened Simi.

"No, nah. Coming."

He went in his boxers to find Simi and Luc bundled up in her bed and joined them. His foxes jumped up and quickly curled up by his feet, ignoring Alex's hisses. The rascal calmed down soon enough and started to lick Snowdrift.

$\mathbf{T}$he fated day dawned. Wolfpack's mindvoice summoned them to breakfast. *"Come, sleepyheads. Hawk is here, too."* They found them with Uncle Yildiz and Grandma Stardust, already started on coffee. A row of platters awaited them on the bar counter on heater plates. An unfamiliar crew served the food.

"From the palace," Hawk told them, with a huge hug for his twin. "I sent the remainder of your household to the field. I didn't want them to be late," he added with a wink.

"Ah, thank you," Snowfox replied, "so thoughtful." But seeing the strange crew in the kitchen…

"Don't fret, my brother. I plan to fully staff the residence and maintain it. I'm trying to entice Mom to return and be my worldmaker, but that's a different story that isn't going too well."

"You'll keep the residence going?" asked Asimia, obviously affected. "I didn't dare ask."

"That's because you're silly," Hawk replied, tapping her nose like he used to when they were kids.

Lucent was anxious to inspect the assembly and ensure his household from Orange had taken their place in the first group. So everyone ate their breakfast without lingering and said goodbye to the kitchen that had been the center of the world for their tightly-knit family the first twenty years of their lives. They had to console Simi, and Snowfox didn't fare much better. But at least the household was coming with them.

The last handful of them had gathered in the courtyard before the stables. The only remaining groom brought Snowwind and Lightning, Simi and his unicorns. Neither could bear the thought of leaving them behind, even to bring them with a later transfer. Flyer was also there, surprising Snowfox.

"Are you gifting us Flyer?" he asked, making Hawk chuckle.

"You wish!" he replied. "Nah, no. He makes me look more the part of a king."

They had reverted the Unicorn Project's pastureland to the king. Hawk vowed to make the care and nurture of the Yandar herd a top priority for the Crown. He allowed Flyer his run of the mares.

He would be the only mature stallion in this small herd when Snow and Lightning left Yand.

There was also a gorgeous yearling colt. Lucent had bonded to him but decided to leave him behind, so the small herd had a second stallion. It broke Luc's heart. "I'll send for Luc's stallion in a few years," Fox told his brother. "But only if you have another colt."

"We may have a mare or two for you, too, then," he replied.

Asimia teleported them to the field. Oh, my! The green-tokened folks had already assembled in three orderly groups. The orange-tokened stood slightly apart, hoping and praying. The reds, forlorn, meleed around at a distance. It was a spectacular sight. Fox had not seen the field groan this much with people except when the military amassed to defend the city against the K'tul invasion.

Chimeran saw them and hopped-flew to meet them. She gave a military salute. "At your service, Your Majesty, Commanders, Wormhole Masters!"

"Impressive array. Did *you* arrange them?" Snowfox asked her, with a reevaluation of the woman's abilities.

"I led the arrangement, yes," replied Chimeran. "But everyone was so eager, and they had so well-rehearsed their part thanks to my lord Lucent." She inclined her head to Luc. He returned the gesture and then flew off to inspect Group 1.

Chimé continued, "We allowed everyone only one backpack and assured them we'll return for the rest of their belongings. They labeled everything and placed them there." She pointed at a huge tent that bore the writing: your belongings here. "We're also bringing provisions and tents so we can pitch a proper camp."

"You've done very well, Chimé," Asimia told her.

"And the cavalry?" Snowfox asked. "Surely their horses—"

"Of course." Chimeran pointed to the group furthest to the right, Group 1. Indeed, their single Cavalry unit had assembled there in military formation. Luc was among them now. His family had brought his warhorse from Orange.

"We're good," Lucent confirmed. *"Check out the other two groups, then let's go before everyone takes to bawling. You know how it goes when one starts crying."*

"They all follow," said Asimia. She had Alex in her pocket.

"Everything ready?" asked Wolfpack.

"I need a minute," Asimia replied. She brought her hand over her eyes and scanned the distance. Fox felt her heart flutter when she found Pete among the folks. His own heart clenched. But the sadness he felt in Asimia's… it wasn't right. He followed her gaze, and there, far away, Pete gazed back, unmoving, without a hint of a mindword.

"We'll send for him, my love," Snowfox felt compelled to say. She flinched and turned toward him. Tears ran from her eyes.

"And here I had resolved not to cry!" she murmured. "Now they will all follow suit. I'm sorry, my love, I thought I had settled this, but now… on the brink of leaving… of…"

"Not seeing him for who knows how long," he finished for her, "not having his aura beside you, his mindspeak in your ears. Go to him." What was he doing? He certainly lost his mind! But he couldn't bear the thought of bringing her like that, taking her so abruptly from this man she so obviously loved.

She couldn't believe her ears. "What?" she asked.

"I will not have you depressed and pining on this journey, my love. Go. Claim him. Tell him to hurry up and train his successor, and the Pathfinder will bring him. Tell him on my word."

She let go of his hand, kissing it first, and launched herself for low flight. Pete hadn't expected that at all. Snowfox felt the man's surprise through his bond to Asimia. He heard their words.

Pete looked bewildered as Simi approached him. She gave him a hug, then pulled back and spoke the ritual words. "I claim you, Pete, as my third husband after Snowfox and Lucent. I will take no other for this millennium and the next."

Pete kissed her hands wordlessly. "Claim me!" she urged him. But apparently he'd lost his voice.

"Claim her, man, or we'll miss our departure." Snowfox encouraged him, and watched him flinch, wince, and shake his head.

"How is this possible?" He asked. *"How am I bonded to you, Fox?"*

"I'm a telepath, and I think so are you."

"Indeed. But…"

"Claim me, Pete, please!" Asimia pleaded.

Pete straightened to his full height—he was a tall man.

"I claim you," he spoke the words, "Asimia, heart of my heart, as my one and only wife. I will take no other for this millennium and the next."

"Welcome to my family," Snowfox told him.

"It's my honor, my lord," Pete replied.

Finally everything was ready. Snowfox's foxes climbed into their backpack, and he gave the signal to Wolfpack.

"Here we go," Wolfpack broadcasted officially. *"First Transfer, First Group at the ready. Once my wormhole opens, step inside as we rehearsed. Ready?"*

"Ready!" Every person in Group 1 thundered. The rest of the field cheered! **"Group 1, Group 1,"** the chant went up so loudly that the cavalry had to steady their horses. Lucent trotted his to the front, beside Wolfpack, who led on foot.

He had explained to the other two wormhole masters that they should be ready to take flight at any moment—in case such need arose. So Asimia had not mounted Snowwind but stood beside Snowfox, squeezing his hand.

A loud pop startled everyone, although they had expected it. Wolfpack's wormhole opened, enormous! He stood before it, his twin infinite string contraptions in his hands, the straight and the Alice, spun like tops, radiating intense blue. He called to his sword, Ice the Pathfinder, on his back, and it gave a blast that blinded all that beheld it.

"Remember," he told the other expedition leaders, *"I will transfer my group to Altais directly. Asimia, Uncle Yildiz. Ready your groups, but wait for my return and my mark. I will escort you in case we encounter temporal difficulties around Baten. Clear?"*

Asimia and Uncle affirmed. Snowfox watched as the folks and cavalry in Group 1 filed into his brother's wormhole. It took minutes for all to pass! Wow! This was the kid who couldn't unlock on his own a few months back and needed his mom to show him.

When the last person went through, just like that, Wolfpack closed with another loud pop and vanished. Two hundred souls vanished with him.

Asimia and RC in the Worldmaker's Garden

Future Time: At the cordon in Paria, continuing from Chapter 15. Sunny's POV.

17. Volume One

*T*he woman doctor, Lorena, descended on Dad with two medics. "My son first," Dad begged, "I'm good, but he's hurt. See to him, please!" He turned and bellowed, "Sunny!"

Sunny stood right behind him. "I'm here, Da," he replied, scanning the room for Willie. "Willie!" he called. She burst through the door and jumped into his arms—onto him, in truth. They fell backward onto Sunny's injured wing, making him cry out in pain.

Dad shoved off the medics and scooped Sunny into his arms from underneath Willie. "Don't argue, Doc!" he yelled while Willie scrambled to regain her composure. "Fix my son. He broke his wing, saving us all."

That wasn't precisely true, but close enough. Wolf broke bones in Sunny's wing when he hurtled him across the bridge of Hellbound. But they were all injured. Dad had a mangled arm that the Renegades crushed at the Crater during Asimia's failed rescue. Aunt Nara had many cuts from K'tul scimitars... but Willie had scrapes on her arms! That was the worst!

He fussed over her while she glued herself to his side. She held his hand and even gave him a quick peck on his cheek. Wow!

It took an hour for the medical profession to finish with them and depart. They left instructions for the various pills, powders, salves, poultices, slings, and splints. The last two were in high demand, as the group had suffered many broken limbs. They had gone against top K'tul brass. No one had expected to come out unscathed. If only they managed to save Asimia...

The new doctor lingered behind. *Another one smitten with my dad,* Sunny thought. She tried to pull Dad aside, but he ignored her. He was utterly unavailable, and this was not the best of times.

A few hours later, while Sunny and his dad were in their room, Darryl reported the first result from Silvia's DNA.

"This makes no sense, Sir, but I'm sure we didn't contaminate the sample."

"Oh? What is it? Go ahead."

"Princess Silvia's age, Sir. She's sixteen."

"What?" Dad and Sunny exclaimed at once.

"No!" Dad countered. *"We saw her clearly. She was close enough to spit on my son's face. She was a little girl, seven or eight years old, which is as it should be. She was four when the K'tul invaded us."*

"Right, Sir. We know. We ran it twice. Should we rerun it?"

"No. Save the sample. I need her genes and…" he hesitated, looking at Sunny. *"Leave it, but store it properly. I'll come as soon as I can and run the rest myself."*

Darryl affirmed. Dad continued to stare at Sunny. "Time to work on a few revelations, right champ? Let's find out who you really are? Silvia knew you much more than an orphan from the palace or the boy who brought the meds to reset her mom's worldmaker gene. She called you Uncle. How could that be now? I have an idea about it; shall we test it?"

Sunny shrunk back in fear. "No, don't be afraid, my boy. It matters not to me what we find, but I suspect it's important. Some folks may have missed you or are missing you now… or then…" He let that trail. "My head is spinning from all this temporal sh--."

Sunny's lower lip trembled. "Some people may be missing me?" he asked in his tiny voice. "Will they come to take me away?"

"Ah… Sunny…" Dad started but paused, thinking as he spoke. "Some very important people may come for you, my boy, but I'll be damned if I let anyone take you from me. Come, there's much to do before we get to… *if* we get to that point. Mysteries to unravel. Temporal genes to splice. Buy a couple of lunch boxes from the best cafeteria in the entire ghetto."

That got a giggle from Sunny. The college had the only cafeteria in the ghetto. "And tonight we get drunk," Dad concluded. "Hmm, but how do we go to my lab? I can't carry you on account of my broken arm and the couple of ribs, and your broken wing. Shall we get the horse?"

"I can blink us," Sunny offered.

"Straight shot? Not sideways? Not two hundred years ago?"

Another giggle from Sunny. "Straight shot, Da."

"Should we bring Willie?"

"I think we better."

Sunny went to his dad's lab often, but Willie did not. So, while Dad busied himself with his various instruments—cursing under his breath for doing the work with only one hand—Sunny took Willie on a merry tour of the lab, the wing, the office, and some of the college's grounds. They ended up at the cafeteria. The coin his dad gave him was enough for a generous lunch with sweetments and two brimming lunchboxes to take home.

It was dark when Dad finished his work for the day. He left instructions with his techs, whose eyes bulged to see so many injuries on Sir and Sunny. Then Sunny blinked the three of them back to the Blue House.

They called them to dinner, so Dad had to wait another hour to get drunk. No one said much at the dinner table, but Aunt Nara stared at Sunny. She finally blurted, "I want them engaged."

What? No! Sunny was not yet eleven! But Willie… she approached twelve… A glance at her revealed such an anxious look that Sunny decided to hold his many objections.

"And they'll remain chaste until they marry." Auntie glared at Dad accusingly, but Sunny couldn't guess what for.

"What's this about, Nara?" Dad retorted, looking more flabbergasted than Sunny felt. Since when do we engage kids—"

"Are they kids? Is your son a kid?" and before Dad could say he's just eleven, Auntie stormed from the room. Uncle Triex followed her. Willie burst into sobs and chased after them. Sunny got up to follow Willie, but Dad pushed him back into his seat.

"Fatie?" he asked Uncle.

"A disturbing order from Snakeman," Uncle replied. "Part of his deal with the Renegades to delay Asimia's transfer. Triex only accepted it because he wanted to get Simi back."

He looked up defiantly. "Not only for you, Pete, or because she's our sister and we love her. Everything is at stake. If we recovered her… and your elixir worked… she could have vanquished the K'tul! But that K'nista betrayed us. You saw how treacherous—"

"What order, man?!" Dad bellowed. "I have a good bottle of whisky waiting for me."

"He wants to bring more women to his brothel."

"What?" Dad erupted. You agreed to **that?!!"**

"No, not straight! Triex put parameters—"

"**Parameters?!** Are you insane? What parameters?".

"That Snake would leave alone all girls below eighteen and every married woman."

Dad gave him an indignant, rageful stare, ready to bellow again. But his glare morphed into wonderment. "Isn't that all our women?" he asked. "All over eighteen are married, right? Is that why we had so many weddings lately?"

Uncle nodded. "Yes. They're all married now except for Dr. Lorena. Would you be availa—"

"No!" Dad cut him off. "But are you not?"

"No," Uncle replied. "I took an oath never to marry again when the K'tul butchered my wife on Yenda."

Dad stared at him. "Why? And wasn't that more than two hundred years ago? How old are you?"

"Same as you."

Sunny thought that '*same as you*' had two meanings: The obvious, that Uncle Fatie and Dad were of the same age. And also that Uncle had gone two hundred years without… emm… a wife, and Dad had also done the same.

"Well," Dad went on, "make an exception with the doc because I won't. But Nara now. Did she learn of Snakeman's demand and freaked out?"

Uncle nodded again.

"But Willie's twelve, man! We have six more years."

"Tell that to her mother."

Dad turned to Sunny. "Do you mind getting engaged to Willie? I mean now, in a few days?"

Sunny didn't know the correct answer. "The K'tul will get her if I don't?" he croaked. Dad nodded. Sunny nodded, too.

"Yes, you mind, or yes, you don't?" Dad asked.

"Don't," Sunny squeaked. In truth, he was terrified. He stared at his dad with eyes wider than saucers.

"Oh, my!" Dad exclaimed. "They're too young, Fatie. Look how you scared my boy. Come, son, don't fear. I'll talk to Nara. We can hold the engagement and wedding at the same time, the day before Willie's eighteenth birthday."

"But I'll be only sixteen," Sunny protested.

"You'll have my dispensation."

Dad got really drunk that night. Sunny pretended to sleep in his bed, which they had moved to Dad's room when Aunt kicked him off Willie's. Dad's thoughts were jumbled chaos, but Sunny deciphered that he missed his betrothal papers to Asimia. He joined him at the desk, where he still drank.

"Da, I know where your papers are."

"You do? Where?"

"I'll get them, but don't turn to look."

"Why not? Ah. It's ok, my boy; I know you keep a box of treasures under your bed."

Shock and awe. "You do?"

"Yep, bring it here; let's see what you've squirreled away."

Sunny crawled under his bed, retrieved his treasure box, and brought it to the desk. He opened it with a wave of his hand.

"I'll be!" Dad muttered. "Sealed with magic!"

Sunny handed him the scroll, and Dad unrolled it eagerly, wiping his eyes. "You had it all this time? Why did you take it?"

"I don't know," Sunny replied with his tiniest, squeakiest voice. Should he blink?

"No, don't blink!" Dad exclaimed, grabbing Sunny's hand. I'm not mad at you—just happy to have it back."

Sunny's curiosity took over his fear. "Why didn't you, Da?"

"Didn't what? You read this, right? Of course you did! I was supposed to claim her whenever I trained my successor, and I was no longer singular. King Hawklord released me twenty years ago. But when I came to Phe'lak, I saw how happy she was with Snowfox that I didn't—"

"And Lucent," Sunny interrupted.

"What Lucent? Ah, yes, and Lucent. But I was saying, she'd just had a child, and I didn't want to... didn't know how to intrude."

"But you wouldn't intrude. She still loved you."

"How do you know that?"

"She called you, *'Pete, my love,'* at the Crater."

"She did, didn't she?" But something in the box diverted Dad's attention. "What's that?" he asked.

Sunny thought Dad meant the other two papers he had stashed in his box. One was his betrothal to Willie, the other, thick as a book, *The Chronicles of Phe'lak: The Grand Yandar Migration,*

Volume One. It was the first tome of the Chronicles Prince Philip wrote to memorialize events and people of the new Yandar world. Sunny had lifted it from the palace while they fled.

But Dad passed on that and pointed at Willie's colorful ribbons. "Are those the ones Willie wore in her hair on her eleventh birthday when you called her *'porcupine hair?'"*

"No. These are the ones the princesses gave her."

"What??" Dad jumped from his chair, dislodging Sunny, who had climbed onto his lap. Although he was eleven now, Sunny was still small enough to do that. It gave him so much comfort.

"What princesses?" asked Dad. "Surely you don't mean Silvia and the K'tul girl."

Sunny cringed and cowered back. "No, don't be scared, my boy!" He sat back down and pulled Sunny onto his knees again. "I only need to understand. You mean the girls on the peculiar planet?"

Sunny nodded.

"Hmm, I wonder if they left DNA on these," Dad mused.

"The girls kissed them in Willie's hair before we blinked away. And Da… one of the girls' name was Ritchie."

Dad jumped again. He was almost out the door before Sunny grabbed him by the sleeve. "Please, Da, I can't blink in the dark," he lied. "Let's sleep now. We'll go in the morning."

"To my lab," Dad confirmed. Sunny nodded, and Dad acceded. He hit the bed and started to snore immediately. Sunny curled up beside him and went to sleep, too.

The following morning, Sunny awoke to find his dad at his desk, pouring over Volume One. "Dad?"

"Ah, Sunny, come, son. See what marvels Philip recorded."

Sunny climbed onto Dad's lap, and they poured over the book together.

"Dad, I was wondering why Philip wrote this," he asked.

"How do you mean?"

"I mean why Philip and not a historian? Wasn't Philip born in the plague? Twenty years *after* the migration?"

"Indeed. I was here when Phil was born. They brought me from Yand to help with that pandemic. It nearly wiped out the entire new colony!"

"But you found a cure?" Sunny knew the history of the pandemic and his dad's prominent role in ending it. But he loved to hear his dad tell the tale.

"Indeed. From our dear friends the Yendai. The disease didn't affect them. I developed a splice and a vaccine from their DNA. The same splice allows some mixed couples to have kids."

"Like Aunt Nara and Uncle Triex?"

"Precisely."

"But Tommy is…" He didn't know how to say it.

"Struggling," his dad finished for him. "Indeed, some do better than others. The Pathfinders' kids thrive while Tommy ails. But don't fret, my boy. I make a serum for him that he takes once a year. There's hope for him. I believe he'll thrive in the end.

"But the Chronicles. I think the plague was precisely why the migrants decided to document their journey. Philip was eleven— your age—when he wrote Volume One. His mom died from the disease, birthing him. I think Philip wanted to record his history."

Sunny shook his head. Philip's story affected him. "Simi adopted him?" he asked.

"Yes, Asimia and her husbands adopted him. They doted on him. He was their only child for two hundred years."

Sunny nodded again. He knew that Philip perished in the siege, fighting against the K'tul. He became Warleader when his father, King Snowfox, led the last of the civilians—Sunny and Dad among them—from the palace to the relative safety of the Crags.

Philip didn't last long on the walls. He led a sortie that claimed his life and made Hrysa the Warleader. She had been barely older than Willie. Sunny visited her on the walls, trying to blink her to safety. That reminded him of something.

"Dad," he asked, "when Silvia spoke to me on Hellbound, what did you hear? Did she say help will come ten years after her capture? Is that seven or eight years from now?"

"Ah, not so sure. This temporal discombobulation may have affected time as we reckon it. She did say to leave things be, and help would come from Yand because she summoned it. What of it, son? Come, look over here." He pointed at something in Volume

One. "It's about your Willie and her ancestor, who, I believe, was one of your princesses."

"You mean Ritchie?" asked Sunny.

"Yes," Dad replied. "She wouldn't leave my head since you mentioned her last night. I wanted to see if there was any mention of her in the Chronicles, and look!"

Sunny focused where Dad pointed. It said that Ritchie did not arrive on Phe'lak with the main transfer, but ten years later. She spent ten years on the peculiar planet! Philip did not write *peculiar* but called the planet Chi-Draconis 5. But Sunny understood it to be the red planet with the auroras.

"Dad," he said, "she looked happy on the red beach. She wasn't alone. I mean, beside the other princess, there were more people there. People who loved her."

"I wish Philip wrote who brought her ten years later and why," added Dad. "It seems important, but I can't fathom it."

"But she's *our* Ritchie, right? Willie's gramma?"

"I don't know any other Ritchie, son. Do you?"

Sunny shook his head. "Ok," Dad concluded. "Enough for now. Will you blink me to my lab? Do you and Willie wish to tag along? It will be another boring day, but—"

"Breakfast?" Sunny squeaked, interrupting his dad. He meant, could he please have his breakfast first?

"You know they serve breakfast at the café? I was about to say you ought to try their pancakes."

Sunny's eyes went wide. *"Willie!"* he mindyelled. *"Come! Breakfast at the café. They have pancakes!"*

Dad took a few days to exhaust his samples and complete all the tests. When finished, he called a conference with the Uncles, Aunt Nara, the physicists, and the doctor. Not the woman, Lorena. The regular guy. Dad avoided Dr. Lorena.

The Uncles and Aunt assembled in the Hearth Room, and the doctor joined them shortly. But not the physicists. "They'll join us soon," Dad explained. "I wanted to go over this first part without them, in case you want to keep this information private."

To the stares toward the doctor, he added, "The doctor already knows, I believe, right Doc?"

"I know many things," he replied. "Which do you mean?"

"Nara's parentage."

"Ah, indeed. I ran a paternity test on her mom at Fox's request. But that was centuries ago, before the plague." Yandar doctors could do simple paternity tests but not full DNA analysis.

"And have you shared your results with anyone, Doc?" asked Dad.

"Indeed I did. With the parents. No, only her dad and Fox and Asimia. Her mother remained on Batentaban's planet."

"What?" cried Aunt Nara. "I thought my grandmother died on that forsaken planet. You say she remained there? She lives?"

"Where did you hear that she died?" asked the doctor, surprised. "She was well, last I heard. Ritchie arrived on Phe'lak ten years after the rest of us. We learned RC wished to stay on Baten."

"Who learned that?" asked Dad. "Who brought Ritchie?"

"Why, myself, Asimia, and Snowfox. And I don't know."

Aunt flinched. "Wait," she said. "Should the kids hear this?"

"Why not?" Dad replied. "They'll eavesdrop anyway. Best to hear from us so they can understand it properly. Anymore, Doc?"

"The results of the paternity test—"

"Which I already ran and have right here." Dad padded a wad of papers.

"Look, Pete," the doctor said defensively. "Snowfox made me swear to secrecy. Ritchie did not come to us alone. Her father, Harry, accompanied her, and he didn't wish—"

"What?" Aunt Nara exclaimed again. "I didn't know my grandfather—"

"He perished in the plague, my dear," the doctor interrupted her. "But not Ritchie. "Asimia gave her wards—"

"The same as the royal family received from their mother Worldmaker Yanara," Dad finished for the doctor. "But why didn't Asimia weave wards for Lucent? He nearly died from the disease."

"The wards only work for children," Sunny told his dad.

"And how would you know that?" Dad asked.

Sunny shrugged his shoulders. He didn't know.

"But Asimia warded *you,* Nara," Dad continued, "when you were born. And your Willie and Tommy, at their birth." He added, "Same as she did Hrysa and Silvia. Am I right?"

"Yes, indeed, me and Willie, but not Tommy. She was already nulled when my boy was born." She peered at her husband, Uncle Triex, as she said that. Uncle pulled her against him on the sofa and put an arm around her.

Willie looked at that longingly, but Sunny held onto her. *"Please, stay here,"* he begged in her private frequency. *"This news scares me."*

"Me, too, Sunny."

"And you," Dad turned to the Uncles. "When did *you* learn of Ritchie's paternity?"

The Uncles exchanged glances. Uncle Fatie spoke first. "We suspected. RC was pregnant at the time of the migration, and there were only two possible fathers. Her husband or—"

"And—" Uncle Triex interrupted, but Dad cut him off.

"Snowfox asked you to protect them, right?"

Uncle Triex looked at his wife, who winced at Dad's words.

"Is that why you married me?" she asked Uncle Triex, her voice filled with dismay.

"No! Please don't start that again, Nara!" Uncle rebuked her. "Go on, Pete," he told Dad. "Enough suspense. The results, please."

"Ritchie's biological father is Snowfox," Dad pronounced. "He came to me before the migration when he learned of RC's pregnancy. He begged for a paternity test, but RC refused. Consent is mandatory for such matters, so we didn't chase after her fetal DNA. She had married her beau and wanted to allow him to believe that he was the child's biological father.

"And I think she didn't want to cause more trouble in Snowfox and Asimia's marriage. She knew Fox didn't love her like a mate, although he offered to marry her when he learned she was pregnant."

Aunt Nara burst into tears to hear Snowfox didn't love her grandmother. This also made Sunny wonder: *How could someone father a child with a woman he didn't love?*

"I'll explain it to you later," Dad told him privately, making him flinch. Dad heard everything(!) He had rabbit mind ears.

"Please don't cry, sweetheart," Uncle Triex murmured, pulling Aunt Nara tighter.

But the meaning of this news began to sink into Sunny's head. Ritchie was Snowfox's biological daughter! Sunny remembered vividly the night of Ritchie's execution—when the archdevil Snakeman took her wings… it was too much! He burst into sobs. Willie followed suit. Aunt was already balling, squirming in her husband's arms and beating her fists onto her chest.

"That night when they took her wings…" she moaned, her speech broken by sobs, "he hugged us and sobbed with us as if he hadn't lost a warrior but a child! A daughter! He's my grandfather!"

Willie broke from Sunny and hopped to embrace her mom. Sunny followed her. The three crowded on Uncle Triex and bawled as the rest wiped their eyes. "He loved you, my love," Uncle whispered, caressing Auntie's hair. "Truly, he did. When we lost Ritchie, he dragooned me to watch after you and the kids. And no, that's not the reason I married you. I could watch you fine without the bond."

Aunt Nara nodded among her sobs.

"Sunny," Dad called him. "Come here, my boy." He offered his embrace, but Willie... "You, too, Willie," Dad amended. Sunny took Willie's hand and pulled her from her mom. He climbed onto his dad's knees, and Willie crowded beside him. Dad hugged them both. "On to the next bit, I think," he said. "The physicists are due any minute."

"Yeah, sure, man," Uncle Fatie told him. "This went so well; why not hit us with the next?"

"Fine. But before I go on," Dad amended with a fierce look at Fatie, "let me conclude with the significance of this first result. Nara, or I should say, Lady Nara, you are a High Princess of Highwings on account of being King Snowfox's bio granddaughter.

"The title to pass to your kids in perpetuity. You, my dear Willie, are also a High Princess. My dear Nara, you are Fourth in line to the throne of Highwings. I'd get up to take a knee, but…" he indicated Sunny and Willie.

Everyone stared at Dad. "Fourth?" Uncle Fatie broke the silence. "Isn't she first?"

"Asimia is first," Dad countered.

"No, She's the Queen. Nara is first."

249

"Ah, yes. Third then. Silvia is still on Hellbound."

"And how would that come to pass when Snowfox didn't have the decency to claim my mom?" Aunt Nara interrupted the friendly banter. "You argue for nothing."

"Why do you think that, Nara," Dad rebuked her. Snowfox was a better man than most. Certainly better than me. Not only did he claim your mother as his bio child, he offered to adopt her."

"And how do you know this?"

"He told me before he parted from the Crags—which, by the way, he did to draw attention away from all of us refugees and onto himself and his family!" Dad replied severely.

"Anyway," he continued, that night, he gave me a letter he had personally drafted and signed many years ago. The letter says he claimed Ritchie to be his biological daughter and granted her the rights of First High Princess of Highwings should she ever wish it. Asimia also signed that paper, making it indisputable. I know their sigs. They're authentic."

"And how did Snowfox know his paternity since you refused to run the test... oh, right, *you* ran it, Doctor!" Aunt Nara concluded.

"I did, as I explained, with her father Harry's consent. But they demurred from the honor of High Princess. They wanted a normal, peaceful life. They accepted Snowfox's letter because it passed the titles to her offspring in perpetuity. Right, Pete?"

"Indeed," Dad confirmed. "Ritchie and Harry signed it below Asimia's signature. Right here." He produced the letter from his pocket and handed it to the doctor, who took it to Nara. She poured over it, marveling the more she read.

"Oh!" she cried, bursting into new sobs.

"That's all good, Pete, but why did you say Nara is third to the throne?" Uncle Fatie persisted. "Isn't she second after Silvia? A granddaughter after a daughter?"

"Ah, no," Dad enlightened him. "My son, Sunny, is the second in line to the throne of Highwings. This rascal right here."

Everyone erupted with, '*what? How could it be, etc..*' Sunny flinched and tried to disappear, but Dad held him fast.

"But if we were to find the Sword of Highwings," Dad continued, all this would be moot. "It would choose. And my money is still on Sunny."

"Why?" all the adults asked simultaneously.

"Because, my dears, when Lord Frost forged the Sword of Kings, I lent him Asimia's genes in an infusion combining her most prominent attributes: worldmaker, wormhole master, shifter, dragoon. She didn't have the temporal allele then, but Wolfpack the Pathfinder did. I added that to the draft, as well as the pathfinder allele, also from Wolfpack.

"Is anyone else we know here in our now closer to that brew besides Sunny and Silvia? With Silvia on Hellbound, the sword would pick Sunny from all others."

"So any unrelated pathfinder, worldmaker, shifter, blinker, blah, blah, could trigger the sword and gain our throne?" asked Uncle Fatie, visibly scandalized.

"And how many of those do you know?" Dad retorted. "No, of course not. On top of all those traits, this person must be biologically related to Asimia. Like a bio child, bio parent, or sib."

"Oh, I see!" Uncle Fatie exclaimed. "Silvia is Asimia's biological daughter…but you also meant… a biological sibling? A brother?" He turned a sharp, accusing glare at Sunny. "Sunny… Sunstorm?"

"What?" Uncle Triex erupted, also glaring at Sunny. Sunny burst into wails, and Willie followed.

"Now, now, my boy," his dad comforted him, caressing his hair and pulling him tighter into his arms. Willie squeezed closer. "It's not so bad to be Lord Sunstorm, is it? You are the Fourth High Prince of Yand and your brother King Hawklord's Heir to Yand's throne. I was present when he installed you.

"You're also the First High Prince of Tuncay and the Second of Highwings, emm, the First now that we lost Philip. You can be king of three worlds. You can eat all the chocolate ice cream you wish. Isn't that grand?"

"And some for Willie?" Sunny asked, consoled a little.

"Indeed," Dad agreed.

"We saved our lunch boxes. Can we eat them now?"

"In a bit. The physicists will arrive any minute."

"Ok," Sunny said aloud, and in private mindspeak, *"But I only want to be Sunny, Da. Please don't let them take me away."*

"I will never!" his dad vowed. *"I told you a hundred times. It matters not who you are, were, or will be. You are always my son! My Sunny! Ok, Champ?"*

"Yes," Sunny replied before Dad turned to the Uncles. "What do you two remember of Sunstorm?" he asked them. Uncles looked at each other. "Not much," said Uncle Triex. "That he existed," Uncle Fatie confirmed.

"Same here," Dad agreed. "A few grand events early on, like when Hawk installed him as his heir when the boy was five, but nothing after that. Isn't that strange? Doc? How about you?"

"He was a baby, maybe one year old, when we migrated. He later visited us as an adult. I think he married at some point."

Willie tensed. "Married?" Dad hurried to ask before Willie started crying again. "Have you met his wife? What was her name?"

Doc looked at Willie and then at Nara. "I'm sorry," he told them. "It wasn't Willie. It started with Mi… like Mira or Mila—"

"Mina?" Aunt interrupted him. "But that *is* my Willie. It's short for Willemina, my daughter's proper name." She returned everyone's amazed stares. "What? You thought it was Willow?"

"It could also be Aramina, Amina, or…" Uncle Triex began but dropped it under Auntie's fierce glare and Uncle Fatie's elbow.

"Don't you find it strange that we don't remember Sunstorm?" Dad asked the Uncles. "I lived on Yand the past two centuries, and the two of you on Tuncay, in the Worldmaker's household. The boy should have grown up and lived with you since you are family. Are you not Lady Yanara's honorary adoptees?"

"We are indeed." Uncle Fatie affirmed. "And we did live in her household on Tuncay for two hundred years. We should know Sunstorm intimately. At the very least, we should remember important events such as his wedding. Do you think Yanara—"

"Erased our memories of him?" Dad finished the sentence. Uncle Fatie nodded. "Indeed, I do think that. But why?"

"Maybe he has a vital part to play in this weird dance with the peculiar planet and the success of the migration," Uncle Triex offered. "But if they know that, why haven't they claimed the boy?"

Sunny squeezed tighter into his dad's arms if that was possible. He was ready to bawl again. Dad patted his shoulder gently, easing his anxiety a little. "Because it hasn't happened yet to this point in time," he said. "Aghh, this temporal thing! It's so unsettling. They're waiting for that event, whatever it is, to happen."

"Does that mean they're still coming?" Sunny squeaked.

"Not necessarily," his dad told him.

Saved by the physicists! There came a knock at the door, and Drs. KhinMarMar, Warbles, and Tevez entered the Hearth Room, ending the unsettling discussion.

The meeting with the physicists had nothing to do with DNA or family relations. It was about the twisting of time. The subject was Sunny's training—Dad wanted to accelerate it. It was boring for the others, so they retired to allow Sunny, his dad, and the three physicists to carry out their discussions in private. Sunny fidgeted so much that Dad summoned Willie back.

The following months passed quickly but tediously, with Drs Khin, Warbles, and Tevez teaching Sunny, tormenting him with more and more daring feats of temporal maneuverings, and analyzing his mistakes. By the year's end, Sunny thought that if he hadn't mastered the art yet, he never would.

Meanwhile, Dad sacrificed the scraps of Asimia's DNA he had been hoarding to prepare a splice for Sunny. He theorized the Pathfinder's temporal allele he had spliced on Asimia's wormhole gene would transfer to Sunny—at least to some measure.

One lovely afternoon after being dismissed from their classes, Sunny blinked Willie to the Crags to share their lunchbox Dad sent home with Darryl. They sat at the Runway cleft, dangling their feet off the cliff's edge. They finished every scrumptious morsel and licked the containers and wrappings.

Willie got sticky, sweet goo all over her mouth and chin and a little on her nose. Sunny found that comical. He pointed at the smudges and called Willie *'sticky face.'*

Willie giggled at first but took offense when Sunny didn't let up. "Why, Sunny, that's quite enough now! Cut it out, or I'll tell your dad."

"Ah, there you go with your threats again!" Sunny objected. He jumped to his feet, turned his back to her, and peered down the cliff. There was still enough light to let him see the waves crashing on the rocks below.

"Come," he said. "I'm bored. I'll blink us home." But when he turned around, Willie had vanished.

Sunny and Dad at the Desk with Volume One

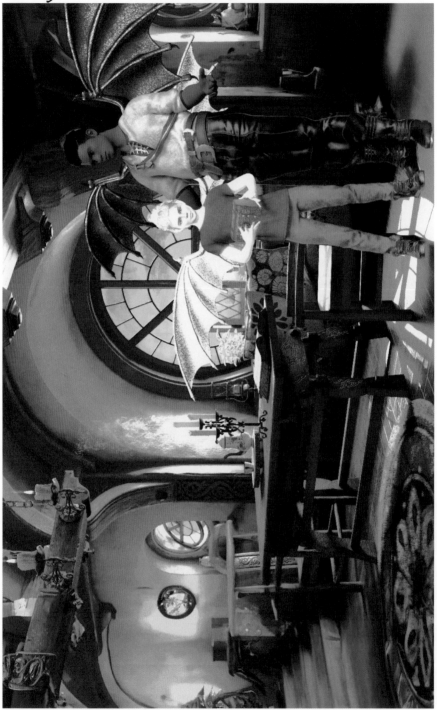

Future Time: At the cordon in Paria, continuing from Chapter 17. Sunny's POV.

18. *Without You*

"**W**illie?" Sunny called. "Where did you go? I'm bored. Can we go home?" When she didn't answer, he thought she had run inside the caves. He was annoyed with her. She made him search and search. First their family's cave, then the larger caverns, the warm pools, the scientist's and engineers' domains, the infirmary. She was nowhere.

Maybe she dove from the cliff to the water? To tweak and scare him? He ran out of the maze to the Mouth, hopped a few good ones on the Runway, and launched himself, yelling, "Willieee!" out loud. But nothing. There was no sign of a smallish flyer or a silly diver. Nothing of the sort. Nor did she answer his mindcalls. She blocked him utterly.

He dove into the ocean a few times in case she ran into trouble underneath the waves—still nothing. Soaking, exhausted, and scared out of his wits, he reasoned she must have gotten so mad at him for calling her *'sticky face'* that she flew home.

How long had he been searching? Could she have made it home already? He cringed to think of all the dangerous spots she had to fly by or through to get to the cordon. Aghhh! Women!

"Dad!" he mindyelled his dad. *"Where are you?"*

"Still at the lab, champ. What's up? You sound… excited? No! You're scared! Why are you scared, son? Are you in danger?"

Sunny blinked to the Blue House. He ran around like a mad boy, calling his betrothed's name at the top of his lungs and mind: "Willie! *Willie!*" But there was no answer.

"Aunt Nara! Where are you? Have you seen my Willie?"

Aunt Nara didn't answer him either, throwing him into total panic. Household staffers rushed to his aid, but none knew where Willie or her mom were. They said soft words, trying to calm him, but he would have none of that.

"Where's my Willie?" he yelled and yelled.

They called the housemaster. The woman bustled to the kitchen where Sunny had ended up in his rampage. "Calm, my boy," she told him. "But who's Willie? Has someone hurt you? Was it this Willie person?"

Sunny's brain was on hyperdrive and couldn't comprehend the meaning of the woman's words. "What do you mean?" he shouted. "*My* Willie! What other Willie is there? My betrothed!"

"We don't know this—"

But Sunny didn't hear her—did not wish to hear more of this. Staffers around him looked perplexed, bewildered. He cupped his ears with his hands, blocking their words, and ran to Willie's room. Her bed was neatly made, and not a single thing was out of place, nothing like the accustomed chaos of Willie's stuff thrown about haphazardly. Her presence was poignantly missing altogether.

"Willie!" he wailed and blinked.

He found himself at the peculiar planet, in its atmosphere, the K'tul courier blasting the world below with its celestial cannons. The planet burned. Sunny blinked to an adjacent time to avoid the bombardment and landed on the planet at the red beach. "Willieee!!" he cried. The K'tul attack continued in this new time. How long had they been blasting this poor world? Explosions rocked the earth around him and under his feet.

At the edge of his vision, he spied Yandar people. Were they the same ones? The princesses' people? They ran in panic as an Archer formation launched into the sky after the courier! It was madness! The courier blasted them all, archers in the sky and people on the beach. One by one, the flyers dropped from the heavens. One by one, the runners on the beach faltered and fell.

"No!" Sunny screamed. Was Willie among the people? Did the K'tul blast her to oblivion? Was that how she disappeared?

"Willieee!!" But no. She wasn't there. He blinked again. He found himself inside the courier ship, K'tul scrambling their firing sequence. As Sunny landed, a startled K'tul whirled his way. It was Snakeman! Snake raised his arms, aimed his fingers, and… Sunny blinked away. Willie had not been there, either.

On to the moon—the stables a few different times. Nothing. To the Crags. Nope. The Blue House—

Dad grabbed him. "Stop blinking, son!" he shouted. "Come, tell me what happened to cause you this anguish."

"My Willie, Da. She's gone, and I can't find her."

"Who?"

That was too much. Sunny burst into wails. Dad squeezed him tighter in his arms and rocked him. Sunny bawled wordlessly forever. He had to make his dad understand. How? Ah! Sunny took Dad's hand and placed it over his heart.

"Feel this, Da. Look. See my Willie." He poured image after image, scene after scene, the two of them crowding in the fish cart's false bottom, dangling from Mn'ianka's hands, running around in the streets of the cordon and the training field, sitting together at the Crags or in the kitchen or dad's office eating their lunch boxes. Her birthday, pulling her hair, Aunt Nara yelling at him and chasing him from Willie's bed... and so much more.

It all gushed out while Sunny sobbed, whimpering out her name. "Williee... I called her *'sticky face,'* Da. Now she's gone! I made my Willie disappear, and you don't even remember her."

"Oh, my!" Dad exclaimed. "It happened! As Khin predicted." He pulled Sunny slightly back and stared into his eyes. "Stop crying, my boy. I believe you." Then he bellowed, ***"Khin, Elliot, Tevez! Blue House, now!"***

A minute passed without a response. "Ah, no! Rats!" Dad cursed. "Not them, too. Ah, but I remember them. ***Sometime this century! Preferably now!"*** He mindyelled again.

"What in the name of—"

"Now, Khin!"

"Coming," replied Dr. Warbles, *"Tevez and I."*

They arrived before Dr. Khin, but she wasn't far behind. Dad ushered them to the kitchen, threw the staff out, and had Sunny lock and soundproof the room.

"What burned your breeches?" asked Dr. Khin.

"It's happening!" Dad practically yelled. "Like you predicted, Khin. We lost two."

"What are you talking about?" Dr. Khin shouted back.

"You're not making any sense, Pete," added Dr. Warbles. "Please slow down and explain."

"Any of you remember these two?" Dad replied, projecting an image of Willie and her mom, Aunt Nara, into their brains. Drs. Tevez and Warbles shook their head no.

"No," Dr. Khin spoke for the three. "Who are they?"

"Khin, do you remember when you hypothesized that we needed to intervene in the Grand Migration or people may start disappearing?"

"Yeah. You mean it started happening? These two?"

"Yes. My son's betrothed, Willie, and her mother, Nara."

"But they're both too young to have come with the migration. The girl for sure. The mom, too, I dare say."

"Indeed. I don't think Nara is more than fifty. But some event had to have happened that prevented their existence."

"Of course," and "right," the scientists exclaimed. They became excited, waved their arms, and spoke all at once. Sunny burst into new wails.

Dad patted his back gently. "Now, now, please don't cry, my boy. We'll figure it out. You'll see." Then he scrunched his face, thinking. *"Doctor!"* he mind-bellowed, *"Blue House! Now!"*

"Pete? What now? Some disaster befell us?"

"Just come, Doc."

"Coming. I'm bringing Lorena. She wants to talk to you."

"I can't deal with that now, Doc. We have an emergency."

"Trust me. You want to hear this. Lorena was in Group 3 during the transfer."

"Why didn't you say so? Bring her. Hurry!"

They kicked a few more things around while waiting for the doctors to arrive. Since Nara had to have been born on Phe'lak because of her young age, it had to be an ancestor of hers that didn't fare well in the migration. Either stayed behind on Yand or, more likely, the K'tul courier killed her. Or him. This merited much discussion, whether it could be a *him* or had to have been a *her*. *Her* was more likely, they all thought.

Sunny cut through that discussion to tell them that when he blinked to the peculiar planet just now, the courier had attacked the planet and killed many people, maybe all *hims* and *hers* both.

"Oh, this means we should expect more disappearances!" Dr. Khin uttered in dismay.

"Focus, Khin," Dad told her. "Who was Nara's ancestor on the expedition? Do you remember one person, Ritchie, that Darryl mentioned? Didn't he say she was ten when someone brought her to Phe'lak after the rest of the migrants?"

"Da, Ritchie was Willie's gramma!" Sunny told his dad.

"Ah, should we bring Darryl?" Khin exclaimed.

"No, leave him. I got him analyzing Willie's second ribbon, the one that belonged to Sunny's second princess. I resisted thus far because… Oh, my! I did say **Willie's** ribbons. But I had started to think of them as Sunny's ribbons. It must have been when Willie disappeared."

"What ribbons?"

"The princesses on Peculiar gave them to Sunny."

"To Willie, Da," Sunny corrected him. "Willie gave them to me after."

"Back to Nara's ancestor. Maybe Ritchie didn't make it to Phe'lak?"

"Maybe Ritchie's mom didn't join the expedition?"

"Maybe…"

The doctors arrived. Sunny lowered his block for them to pass into the kitchen. "Lorena has a story to tell," said Doc. "Please, my dear."

"Is this why you—" Dad began, but she interrupted him.

"Tried to corner you to have a private discussion? Yes. Precisely. Oh, you thought—"

"No! Of course not. Well, because of Snakeman's rule—"

"About our unmarried women?" Dad nodded. "No worries, Pete. I need no husband when they come knocking. I won't be a woman then." Stares. "I'm fluid. I'll transition to a man."

The doctor was *fluid?* Sunny had heard such tales of a few folks switching genders but never met a real one.

"Can you let her tell her story, Pete?" Dr. Khin chastised Dad. "We're dying here!"

Dr. Lorena told her tale. She migrated in the third, Queen Asimia's group. A few months back, Queen Emerita Stardust had assigned Dr. Lorena the task of caring for her pregnant daughter—"

She didn't get another word out. "Wo, hold, wait!" Dad cried. "You mean Stardust's *granddaughter*…Asimia? Asimia was pregnant!??" The doctor inclined her head.

"No. This couldn't be! I made birth control for her. She…" he paused, rose, deposited Sunny on his chair, and paced the room. Slowly at first, but then maniacally. Sunny whimpered, objecting to the separation, but Dad ignored him. *"How?"* he exclaimed. "No, it's impossible. Unless…"

"She was pregnant, Pete," Dr. Lorena interrupted. "As to the *how,* well, even as a doctor, I know only one way to get a woman pregnant. So, either your birth control didn't work, or somebody got to her before she took it."

Dad turned ashen. "I have no knowledge that Asimia had a baby two centuries ago. Any of you?" he asked the adults in the room. They hadn't either, except for Dr. Lorena.

"She had the baby on the peculiar planet while K'tul assaulted us from a courier."

"So the baby perished?" asked Dad, utterly discombobulated.

"No!" Sunny and Dr. Lorena exclaimed together.

"She's my princess, Da. Ritchie's friend on the planet."

"I don't know about Sunny's princess," the doctor continued. "But Asimia's little princess did not die."

"How do you mean that?" shouted Dad.

"She was born with wings, a tiny, beautiful worldmaker girl. I cut her from Her Majesty's womb before she could fly out and kill her mom. Not that she had the strength. She was weak, nulled." The doctor paused her narration and wiped her eye. "Mother and daughter had to separate, or the little one would die."

"Oh my!" Dad cried. "Like idiots, we had all assumed the baby would be the stronger and null-kill Asimia because Asimia was not as strong as her mother. But it was the other way around!"

"Oh. Why would you assume that?" Dr. Khin asked. "Asimia's mother, Lady Yanara, is an exceptionally strong worldmaker. Stronger than *her* mother, Yira, or her grandmother, Yolinda. Exceedingly so, I might add. Your assumption about Asimia's strength—weakness—was unfounded."

"Obviously," Dad agreed. "But what happened then, Doc."

"That's just it." Dr. Lorena continued. "I don't remember the rest. It's like a fog blanketed my brain, beginning a few hours ago, and wiped my memories. *Blurred* is a better word to describe it than *blanketed."*

"And you were going to tell me the other day, but I didn't pay attention! And now you lost the memory!" Dad berated himself.

"Wait, Pete," Dr. Khin told Dad. "I think we can glean more." She turned to Dr. Lorena, "Tell, my dear, when the K'tul attacked you, what did Snowfox do?"

"He rallied the archers and mounted a defense."

"Do you remember who those archers were?"

The doctor searched her memory. "Like I said, it's blurred. I can't see their faces. I don't recognize them."

"Ok. But then, presumably, you left the planet because you are here. Who came with you? Did Ritchie?" asked Dad.

"Who's Ritchie?"

"Da!" Sunny cried out. "Our book! It would say, no?"

Dad gave him a blank look, then tore for their bedroom like a madman, Sunny on his heels. Da reached Sunny's bed first, flipped it, and Sunny dove for his treasure box. They fished Volume One from it and scrambled the pages, leafing furiously.

Everyone else scampered into their bedroom. "What's this," "What are you doing?" etc..

Dad brought the book to the desk, and Sunny climbed onto the chair. With everyone peering over their shoulders, Sunny found the page.

"No!" Sunny yelled. "It should be right there, Da!"

"I'll be!" Dad exclaimed. Any mention of Ritchie had gone.

"What?" bellowed Dr. Warbles. "Do you care to share?"

"The mention of Ritchie is completely wiped out from the Chronicles," Dad marveled. "Does that mean whatever we do is futile?"

"No!" Sunny cried. "We must find her, Da, and save her! Without her, my Willie will never be!"

"I'm not exactly sure what all this is," Dr. Khin attempted to add a measure of reason, "but I'm assuming that Ritchie was mentioned in this history book and is missing now? Use your brains, man. If it disappeared, it could also reappear—when we fix whatever mess caused the disappearance. And I say I know how!"

"How?" everyone erupted together.

"Sheesh, not all together now! Obviously we have to warn the migrants of the K'tul trap."

"And how will we do that?" Dad demanded.

The others barraged Dr. Khin with questions. Dr. Khin took Sunny's hand and walked out of the room. "First I need some coffee, then more alcohol, and immediately now, to sit. Where do you want us, Pete? Kitchen or hearth room? Let's make a plan."

"Kitchen if you want coffee."

Everyone followed her.

Such a plan seemed simple at first, but the devil was in the details, as Dad put it. And there were plenty of those. All they had to do was blink back to two centuries ago at the time of the Grand Migration or slightly earlier and warn them of the K'tul courier lurking about the peculiar planet around Baten. But who to tell? The expedition military leader, King Snowfox? Or Queen Asimia? The Pathfinder made more sense to everyone.

The precise *when* caused many problems and arguments. Not that the exact *where* was much easier. Dad, Dr. Khin, and Dr. Warbles remembered a meeting place or two: Dad's office in Dragonslair, the capital city of Yand, or the kitchen in the Worldmaker Palace, also in Dragonslair. But they couldn't decide on either one.

Their most daunting factor was Sunny himself. He, with his mangled temporal allele, had to make a precise two-hundred-year jump back in time, with perfect spatial accuracy, into an office or a kitchen. Otherwise they could materialize in something unnatural, like in one of Dad's experiments or an oven in Asimia's kitchen. Or among their older incarnations and startle themselves out of existence.

Sunny was a nervous wreck to hear such plan, let alone do it. But do it, he must! It was the only way to get back his Willie! Everyone else was equally eager to dive into it immediately, arguing it didn't matter which location; the time was clear, so just do it.

But Dr. Khin held them back. She said it didn't matter when they embarked on this Ops. only when they got there. Dad had many misgivings about that. Every moment that passed, he argued, they should expect more people to vanish. Dr. Khin countered that this was most likely a single event. If anyone else were to disappear, they would have already. They left it at that.

Sunny was very confused. The days passed with him thinking only one thing: get his Willie back. He couldn't sleep and blinked randomly, so Dad begged the doctor for more pills and kept him sedated pretty much always. But this didn't keep his heart from breaking. Willie's absence hurt him physically, too. He couldn't breathe. He hyperventilated. He might as well die. Dad never left him alone.

But the reason for the delay proved worthwhile. Dad brewed a temporal splice for Sunny, exhausting Asimia's DNA to the last drop. It came in two doses, like most of Dad's concoctions. Sunny tolerated the first infusion, but the second knocked him out.

Wow! The fuss the adults made over him! You'd think he was dying. Was he? Nah. It was because they had plenty of time by then to think of many additional horrendous possibilities to freak themselves out. *Of course* there could be another event. Or two, or three, etc. Why would the misery end at only one?

And sure enough, about two weeks later, Dad noticed the class he taught at the U. looked rather bare. And didn't they have a larger household? Who heard of a viceroy (Dad) and two high princes (Uncles Fatie and Triex) only having a staff of three?

Both doctors attended to Sunny around the clock while he fried. On the second night of his fever, Sunny overheard Dad's mindspeak coming from the direction of his desk. It was in private and guarded, but Sunny comprehended the conversation! It was with Dad's tech, Darryl. Despite feeling out of sorts, he trained his eavesdropping ear.

"Darryl!" Dad bellowed. *"What do you mean mixed DNA? How can this be? How did you mess up this sample?"*

There were very few mixed DNA folks among the Yandar population. It meant that more than the standard two DNA donors created the baby. The only such person Sunny knew was Captain Chimeran. She evened but had golden wings and silver-white hair like his own. So this turn in the discussion merited his undivided attention. He forgot his various aches for a few moments.

"Three distinct DNAs, Sir. We have no doubt whatsoever. Could two people have left DNA on the ribbon?"

"I suppose that's possible. Go on. Maternal gene."

"Her Majesty, Queen Asimia."

"Paternal?"

"His Majesty, my lord Snowfox. And..."

"And? Sometime this century, Darryl!"

"You, Sir. The second paternal donor is you."

That knocked Dad into silence—and sobs. He cupped his face in his hands and cried for what seemed like forever. It went on until Darryl's mindvoice came again, inquiring, *"Sir, are you there? We've also analyzed the meta characteristics. We found many such alleles. Do you want to know?"*

"Shoot, man. Might as well know."

"Worldmaker, wormhole master, mage, shifter, temporal—"

"Temporal?"

"Yes, Sir. Much stronger than your son's, Sir. Nearly on par with the Pathfinder."

"You don't say! Oh, my! I wonder..." Dad let that trail off until Darryl had to interject again.

"Is there something more, Sir? We were wondering if we could take the afternoon off today?"

"Yes, yes, go, enjoy your evening."

"Thank you, Sir. Out."

Seeing his dad in so much anguish made Sunny crawl from the bed. But his feet didn't touch the floor when the door burst open, and Dr Lorena flew in. "Where are you going, young man? Back to bed with you. Is it time for your injection?"

"No! I... my dad!"

"Let the boy breathe for a moment, Doc. Come here, my Sunny. Seriously, Doc, leave us be for a few."

"Fine. I'm just outside."

Dad scooped Sunny onto his lap, and Sunny melted into his embrace. "Dad," he asked, "was that the princess's DNA? Is she your daughter? And my niece?"

"Yes to both, it so seems."

"Will you not want me now that you have her?"

"You are such a silly boy!" Dad exclaimed. "Wild horse wouldn't drag me away from you. No." He tapped Sunny's nose, making him giggle. "Not even that. Wild unicorns. No. Dragons. Dragoons?"

Sunny burst into full giggles that lasted a few moments. Dad always knew how to cheer him even in the most depressing predicaments. "We have to save them, Dad," he finally said. "Both of them. All of them. I want my Willie back."

"How are you feeling? You're still hot," Dad pronounced after pressing his hand on Sunny's forehead.

"Only a little. I feel much better." He tested the truth of that pronouncement. Hmm. He did feel somewhat better. "Do you think the second splice made me sick because it was stronger? Or because I fought it, and it failed?"

"Hard to know, champ. I think it may be because it caused changes to your DNA code. I'm hoping it was the designed changes working on your temporal allele, making it stronger. Does it feel any different?"

Sunny shrugged his shoulders. "How would I know?"

"Hmm. Good question. Let's try this. I'll fix a *kiss* in my head, and you try to read it and project it back to me. Ready?"

Sunny nodded. With *'kiss,'* Dad meant a set of coordinates. He fixed a temporal kiss from two days ago. Cakewalk. Not a challenge at all. He went further back in time. How about last month? A year ago. Sunny got those, too, although they had altered from his memory due to Willie's absence. They slid back years this way. He reproduced the time of Dad's migration to Phe'lak twenty years ago. Finally Dad gave him a doozy.

"How about this." *This* kiss was different. It was a different set of stars. A different constellation. Not Draco. It was the Bear—Ursa Minor. The star was white, the planet stark, volcanic. Ah, it spun to its other hemisphere and lit up Sunny's world! It was Yand. Half inhospitable, half panoramic—stunning.

"Is it Yand, Dad?"

"It is. You can see it? Can you go there? No! Don't blink!"

Too late. Sunny was sitting on Dad's lap, so they went together. They found themselves at the place and time of the coordinates Dad had sent to Sunny's mind. It was a vast field in a huge city. It brimmed with people. Another incarnation of Dad was there, too, a younger one.

His current dad doubled over in pain and started to vomit. "Back!" he groaned. Sunny grabbed a handful of Dad's sleeve and blinked them back. Dad ran to the bathroom and puked his guts out. Sunny, weary at catching hell, inched slowly behind him.

"Da? Are you ok?" he asked in his small voice.

"Oh, you sweet, little temporal blinker boy, extraordinaire!" Dad shouted. "You did it, son! I'd give you a hug, but I'll probably puke all over you! Doc!" he bellowed "Antiemetics, pronto. In the bathroom." And in mindspeak, *"Khin, Warbles, Blue House now. Sunny did it!"*

Sunny ran to fetch the meds and collided with Dr. Lorena. "Did somebody ask for an antiem?" she asked. She held a humongous syringe with an enormous needle.

"Not me!" Sunny yelled and shrunk back quickly in case the doctor mistook him for the patient. "My da, in the bathroom." Then, "Da! She's got a gigantic syringe!"

"Lorena?" Dad called the doctor. "Call the physicists, please, while I…"

"Which one?"

"All of them!"

"My boss, too?"

"Who's your boss?"

"Doctor Drew."

"Who?"

"The doc."

"Sure. Ouch! Sheesh! Who trained you?" Sunny guessed that was when that gargantuan syringe plunged into Dad's arm.

The physicists assembled in the kitchen again—all of them. It seemed that only Sunny could tell when someone went missing. So they had taken to the habit of asking him at the beginning of each conference. "Everyone here?"

"Yeap." Uncles Fatie and Triex had arrived a bit earlier. They were in the kitchen already, where they had assembled a good assortment of alcohols and goblets—another new habit since Uncle Triex was single again.

"How you doing, scamp?" Dr. Khin asked him. That couldn't be good. Sunny shrunk behind his dad, who shielded him protectively. At least Dad or the Uncles wouldn't vanish, Sunny kept telling himself. They came later.

Dad recounted Sunny's incredible feat to the group. He blinked two hundred years back to Yand to exact coordinates! Wo. The immensity of that hadn't hit Sunny yet. In his mind, he was simply able to control his aim. Plus Dad gave good coordinates.

They spent hours arguing and trying to decide how to put Sunny's newly realized triumph to good use. Dr. Warbles made the point that since Sunny blinked to the training field at the time the migrants had assembled—that was where Dad's coordinates had led—they should simply repeat it. Get there and tell Snowfox. Such and such, blah, blah, and abort.

Hmm. What about the fact that all of them were present at that gathering? Dad recounted his complete incapacity in the presence of his earlier incarnation. Dr. Warbles still argued that *Sunny* could warn them since he hadn't been there that original time. He could mindspeak the expedition leaders. Who better than their own brother?

But Sunstorm was a babe of one year at that time. How could the present Sunny convince them he was *that* Sunstorm and bearing such dire news? They would probably take him for a deranged boy. Plus, Dr. Khin worried that by being in the same time twice, besides the obvious stomach emergency, they risked creating a paradox that could have catastrophic results for any future outcome.

In the end, they agreed to nix this possibility and move on to the next. But what next?

"Didn't you all in the first group make it straight to Altais?" Dr. Lorena asked. "Wasn't the Pathfinder able to pass the anomaly without being pulled down to the peculiar planet?"

"Right!" exclaimed the others together.

"What of it?" asked Dr. Warbles.

"Why, Elliot, my dear," Dr. Khin told her colleague. "I believe the doc meant that since the Pathfinder brought us, he will be there at that precise time of transfer. We can go back and warn him! That's it! That's the perfect opportunity! When do we go!"

Everybody erupted in exclamations and questions that turned into arguments. They all wanted to go. They forgot the stomach problem when meeting their old selves or the utter-destruction paradox. They had a million arguments: Dr. Tevez could best help with the coordinates. Yes, but Dr. Khin could help with the temporal kissing and sliding the sky, etc.

Finally, Uncle Triex bellowed: "Now, enough! You've already forgotten that you were all there the first time? It should be me, my brother, or Pete who should—"

"*I* will," Uncle Fatie exclaimed. "I'm the strongest telepath."

"No, you're not," Uncle Triex objected.

"Neither of you have the coordinates," Dr. Warbles told them. "Telepathy will not get you there."

Sunny mind whispered in Dad's specific frequency, *"Da, are you a strong telepath?"*

"Strong enough. But I'm not sure if I can match those two."

"Can you mindspeak someone from across the planet?"

"I think so. But why across the planet? Won't we go near the Pathfinder?"

"In case I miss."

"What?"

"Dr. Tevez," Sunny asked his astronomy professor, *"can I please have the kiss? And a few adjacents in case I need to slide?"*

Dr Tevez gave him a set of sequential temporal slices of the sky around Altais at the time the Pathfinder transferred his group. He marked the one of his migrant group's arrival as principal. He also provided a range of spatial coordinates about the principal on the planet they landed on. He marked a perimeter. People didn't venture beyond that, he said. Outside that rim were rocks and brush where a boy and his teacher could land safely and unseen.

Dr Tevez gave vivid coordinates. Although all that had transpired in their private mind frequencies, Sunny had opened his end for his dad to hear all this.

"Da," he said, *"not a boy and his teacher. A boy and his **dad**, I think. You?"* Dad inclined his head slightly. Sunny took his dad's hand and blinked them to Altais.

They exited his blink into darkness, scaring Sunny—

"Open your eyes, silly!" his dad whispered.

Oh. Sunny opened his eyes. A new world was all around them. They stood behind large boulders covered with shrubs. More greenery extended beyond the rocky area. But there were no people there, no migrants, and no Pathfinder.

"Have I missed, Da?" Sunny asked, disappointed.

"Let's wait a minute." A minute later, still nothing. A few more minutes, and Sunny readied to blink, but Dad held his arm fast. "Hold," he whispered. "Something comes. Can't you feel the vibrations in the air?"

Before Sunny could examine vibrations or air about them, a loud pop scared him half back to Phe'lak. An enormous wormhole opened, and people dashed out of it, some bounding, others hopping or running—but orderly somehow. The last to emerge was the Pathfinder. He blazed from head to toe in blue lightning that resolved into a humongous sword, a brow gem, and two sets of tops spinning in his hands.

Sunny hadn't considered what the Pathfinder looked like. He was supposed to be his brother, but the last time they met, Sunny was his Sunstorm incarnation and remembered nothing from his brief seven-year life on Tuncay. Wolfpack would be in his early twenties when Sunstorm blinked to Phe'lak two centuries ahead.

If somebody asked Sunny to describe the Pathfinder after so many stories had turned him into a mythical creature, Sunny would say one of great stature and immeasurable aura, like a god from the heavens. But when the lightning subsided, what was left to see was an even teen, maybe sixteen or seventeen years old. A rather smallish one at that, although exceedingly beautiful.

He has Ma's eyes! Sunny thought without knowing why.

"Wolfpack!" Dad mindcalled the Pathfinder in guarded.

"Pete?" The Pathfinder replied, looking around him to locate the mind source. *"Is there danger?"*

"Here. Follow my guide. Come alone. It's very important and urgent. Yes, danger. K'tul!"

Wolfpack helped the last stragglers out of his wormhole—that had remained open all this time! He issued a few orders, closed his blink, then made his way to their rocks. "Pete!" he exclaimed. "And who is this? Ah, don't tell me; I'm not supposed to know."

"Sun—" Sunny began.

"Storm." The Pathfinder finished. He gave him a warm hug, then one for Dad. "I just left you on the field," he told Dad. "You're from the future. I know you fought a K'tul war on Phe'lak. Help is coming. Hang on a while longer."

"Indeed, Silvia informed us. But the K'tul are here now! They're after you and the migration. Hear me out. You must intervene." And Dad told the Pathfinder the entire story of what Sunny saw.

"Wait here," the Pathfinder said. He blinked out, then back in the same breath—temporal. Wow, it was so strong! Astounding! Would Sunny ever master that time dimension like that?

"I saw the courier behind one of Peculiar's moons," Wolfpack said. He looked shaken. "I must stop the other two groups. If they can't transfer past the anomaly on their own, the K'tul will have a shot at them." He scrutinized Sunny. "It was you!"

Uh, oh! Sunny got caught. "What?" he squeaked. "Did I cause the temporal?"

"You may have added a small part to it, but no. I don't think you caused it. I meant to say it was *you* who saved us."

"Ah," Dad exclaimed. "So it was true, as I surmised? It was you in that wormhole my son saved? With the man and woman… Snowfox and Mouse?"

"Indeed. But your *son?*" Wolfpack stared at Sunny.

"I adopted him," Dad confirmed. "It's a long story."

"Give me your thoughts."

Dad projected the entire history of the past few years into the Pathfinder's brain: the siege, Highwing's fall, Silvia and Asimia's predicament. When he finished, Wolfpack nodded and said, "There are many actions you don't know that had gone on—will go on— later in your timeline. I will tell you only what you need to know, then I have to run.

"I will bring help from Yand eight years from your now to free you of the K'tul scourge. But some of you were not—will not— be there when I came—come."

"Oh, you've already done it?"

"Indeed. It's the reason I speak with so much certainty. I will tell you who will not be there when I intervene so you can act accordingly to protect them. Triex will not have a second wife on Phe'lak—only a Yendal one on the moon. And you two, and your Willie, will not be present. But Fatie and Triex will feature prominently in the event. And Russel and Emmiat will operate the inn at the docks, the Sea Urchin.

"So we perished—will perish?" asked Dad.

"My Willie?" Sunny whimpered.

"No! Of course not. You need not perish, Pete. You only need to be elsewhere." With that, another hug, and a kiss on the top of Sunny's head, he set his tops, sword, and brow gem to buzz and blinked away.

Sunny and Pete Warn the Pathfinder at Altais

Altais, Delta Draconis, dawning at left; the Chi Draconis Binary in the heavens.

Past time: In the Altais system, continuing from Chapter 18. Sunny's POV.

19. Aurora

Sunny looked at his dad. "What do we do now?" he asked.

"Hmm. Not sure. I think maybe we should go back home and see if Wolfpack's rescue worked."

"But doesn't he need time?"

"He'll have two centuries, son. Can you take us back? Should I project the coordinates to you?"

Sunny nodded, and Dad filled his mind with the spatial and temporal coordinates of home. They matched Sunny's. He blinked them. They found themselves in their room in the Blue House. Sunny tore off screaming at the top of his lungs: "Willieee!"

But Willie didn't answer him. His calls turned to wails until he burst into loud sobs. His heart broke into a million pieces. His dad grabbed him as he ran, embraced him tightly, and rocked him like a baby. But it didn't help. He might as well die. He might as well go back to the peculiar planet and die with Willie's gramma.

Dad let him cry himself out, then gave him a double dose of his sedative, the kind that prevented him from blinking in his sleep, and tucked him into bed. He kissed Sunny's forehead and whispered, "Get your rest, and we'll try something different when you wake up. I'm thinking on it."

With that, he walked out of their room. Before sleep took Sunny, he heard his dad's voice asking Dr. Lorena to stay with Sunny until he returned. Where was Dad going?

Past Time: On Yand, continuing from Chapter 16. Snowfox's POV.

At Dragonslair's training field, where the migrants had assembled, Snowfox stood at the helm of Group 3 with his wife and watched in awe as his baby brother Wolfpack directed the migrants of Group 1 into his enormous wormhole. This kid had come a long way from the uncertain youth their mom had to unlock. What happened to him to have caused such a transformation? It was like he had undergone experiences of centuries in a scant few months.

"I will transfer my group to Altais directly," he told Asimia and Uncle Yildiz in mindspeak that Snowfox could hear. *"Ready your groups and wait for my return and my mark. I will escort you in case we encounter temporal difficulties around Baten. Clear?"*

It was very clear. Snowfox put an arm around Asimia's waist, and the two of them watched Group 1 vanish into the wormhole. Lucent and his Orange household went with them, as did the unit of Cavalry. The Archers remained with Groups 2 and 3.

Then they waited. Minutes passed. Snowfox could feel Asimia getting anxious beside him. "It's alright, love," he whispered. "Trust our brother. Give him another moment."

The moment passed, and many more after that, but still no Wolfpack. *"Let's get our wormholes ready, Uncle,"* Asimia mindspoke Uncle Yildiz. He agreed. Two loud pops followed. The two wormhole masters guided their groups into the cavernous open mows of the paths.

Snowfox ushered his archers and waited for Asimia. She'd enter the wormhole last, and close it. She had her two sets of infinite cosmic strings in her hands and set them to spinning.

Suddenly a wormhole opened above them—Wolfpack.

"Go!" Uncle Yildiz mindcalled. Simultaneously, Asimia and Uncle stepped into their wormholes.

Wolfpack spilled from his. **"Abort, Abort!"** he boomed aloud and in mindspeak. **"K'tul! It's a trap!"**

Snowfox grabbed Asimia and spun her around. She fought her wormhole, with him lending his strength, although for not. They kept it open for a few heartbeats. "Out!" Snowfox yelled as Simi burned her hands from the violence of her spinning tops. "Chimé, RC, Harry, the civilians, quick, guide them out!"

Sheer panic and screams erupted behind him. Folks scrambled, maddened by fear, throwing themselves to reach the front and exit the wormhole. But inch by inch, it collapsed; it closed around them.

"Fox!" Asimia yelled. "Restore order, or we'll all die here."

"Back, everyone stay inside," Snowfox yelled, shoving people back and calling his archers to help. "We'll transfer now!"

"And the Pathfinder will find us," he hastened to add.

To Asimia, **"Go, my love!"**

With a herculean effort, he and his archers pushed the people back into the belly of the worm—the safest, most comfortable location in a wormhole. "We need to ride it!" he shouted. His archers amplified his command. "Everyone stay calm. Go, Asimia."

Asimia let the wormhole close behind her. She had set her exit coordinates to Altais. But the temporal anomaly around Baten grabbed them, and she couldn't pass. The infinite strings in her hands buzzed and blazed as she spun them furiously. Her hands bloodied from the effort. And yet, she could not steer them out of the temporal goo. Nor could she keep her wormhole open!

It sputtered. It stopped spinning. It lost its chirality. Asimia collapsed. Two hundred folks held their collective breaths, then filled the void with screams as the worm ruptured, spewing them out. Fox grabbed Asimia, lifted the tops from her hands, and spun them. "Simi!" he yelled. "Come to, or we lose all our people!"

Another voice joined him, *"Asimia!"* it commanded. *"Spin your tops. Now!"* It was Wolfpack, bringing a huge wormhole that expanded, opened its mouth and surrounded, swallowed the flailing people. Was it all of them? Fox could not tell.

Asimia regained strength and reclaimed control of her tops. She joined Wolfpack, and the two of them blazed their way through the temporal space and guided the wormhole to new coordinates at the Pathfinder's command. They landed on what had to be the peculiar planet. Asimia dropped to her knees, gasping.

Yildiz and his Group 2 were already there, looking as frazzled as Group 3. "I brought them first," Wolfpack shouted. "They collapsed faster than you."

"What now?" Snowfox asked his brother as he patted his wife's back. "Did you say K'tul? Where? Here or Altais?"

"Here."

"How many? How close? How urgent the danger?"

"A courier. Behind a moon. I'd say imminent. They're scoping this planet. They have cannons. I'm sorry Fox."

"Why this planet? You think the anomaly grabbed them as it did us? And what are you sorry for? You saved us all."

"I should have timed it more."

"We may have jumped your mark," said Snowfox, glancing at Simi. She was ashen, unable to speak.

Alex jumped from her pocket, size shifted and growled, spreading his fur. "Oh, pipe down," Wolfpack told him, and miraculously, Alex obeyed. Then, "Are you OK Simi?"

But Asimia was not. She vomited her guts. Lorena elbowed Snowfox out of her way. "You must have figured out I'm a doctor? And that your wife is pregnant?" She spoke in a low voice but severely, as if she accused him of the crime of making his wife pregnant. "Seven months," she went on. "Way before your wedding or her birth control."

What could he say to that? "Yes." He looked for RC, wondering how she fared. It occurred to him there may be other women carrying. "Doctor—"

"Please call me Lorena, my lord. I'm sorry I snapped at you. We're all discombobulated here."

"Any injuries?" he asked.

"Not sure yet. Her Majesty first."

That made Fox wince. He wished they brought more doctors. Their household doc had gone with the Pathfinder in Group 1 to ensure that at least one physician transferred safely. "Is your group at Altais? Safe?" he asked Wolfpack.

"Yes. I don't think the K'tul know about Altais."

"Good."

A glance at Group 2 showed Grandma Stardust ministering to Uncle Yildiz. *"How have you fared?"* he asked. *"Your group?"*

"We have injured," Grandma replied. *"And Yildiz is out of sorts. His hands are shreds. I don't think we're going anywhere unless Wolfpack passes all of us to Altais. But that would risk the K'tul following us. We need to regroup. How's Asimia?"*

"Rattled. Pregnant. I'm sure you know."

"I do. Seven months. Like an idiot, you couldn't wait for your wedding or, better yet, until we came through this trek. Lorena, you got this?"

"I do," Dr. Lorena replied. "Go, my lords. Her Majesty needs a few minutes to settle her stomach, but she took no injury besides her hands. I'll bind and pad them so she can spin those tops of hers to save us all."

Snowfox and Wolfpack started toward their grandmother.

"Your daughter's fine, too, although weak. She should be flattering her wings by now," Lorena yelled to their backs.

Snowfox missed a step. *"Go, love,"* Asimia said in his mind. *"We're both fine. I'll join you once I swallow the pills."*

"No you won't!" Lorena told her emphatically. "You'll lay here until I say otherwise."

"The world is burning, Lorena!" Asimia objected.

"No. It's just some K'tul. Didn't we beat them before?"

"My mom bent our sun!"

"Exactly. You do the same to these devils once I fix you."

Wolfpack grabbed Snowfox's arm. "Come, Simi is fine. Let's go figure our way out of this jam."

"Bring your commanders," said Grandma. "I called mine."

"How about only Chimeran? RC is pregnant."

"Yes, I know. But do you think she'll stay away from this?" Snowfox shook his head no. "Can she even fly?" Grandma persisted with an accusing stare. "She looks like a whale."

"Ah, can we leave it, please? The K'tul?" Snowfox snapped.

They left all the captains and lieutenants off. Wolfpack relayed that after transferring his group to Altais, he scouted the vicinity for potential dangers. That's when he saw the K'tul courier behind one of Peculiar's moons. He couldn't see how it could have traced his wormhole to Altais. It looked to have its attention trained on Peculiar as if it hunted something specific.

"Asimia!" Snowfox exclaimed. "They want to abduct her again! But how did they know—"

"Suppose that the temporal space ensnared them as it did us," Wolfpack interrupted him. "What if they were behind that moon back when we had our—"

"Mishap!" Snowfox finished. "They could have seen Simi when you two landed on this planet with Mouse and me frozen."

"Exactly," Wolfpack finished. "I'm not sure if they're stuck here or they lay a trap for Simi. But they may have seen us already."

"Right," added Snowfox. Couriers have powerful scopes."

"And celestial cannons," Grandma added.

Everyone winced. "We must protect Simi. Wolfpack, can you transfer her to Altais immediately?" Snowfox asked his brother.

"Indeed," said Grandma, gazing beyond his shoulder. "But I think she'll need to protect *us* first." Asimia had approached stealthily. She tapped Fox's arm, and he made space for her to sit. Alex and the foxes growled and yelped, clearly agitated.

"I heard all this," said Asimia. "I think I better shield this planet until we figure out what to do. You can't send me to Altais and have the K'tul follow me. They'll find our folks of Group 1! We must take care of the K'tul threat *here.*"

"How, love?" asked Snowfox.

"I was nulled when they abducted me the first time," Asimia replied. "I'm not nulled now. I do not fear them."

"Can you destroy them?"

"No, not easily. But we can find another way."

"I have something," said Wolfpack. While he searched the heavens around Peculiar for K'tul, he spied another star! Baten had a smaller companion. Chi Draconis was a binary.

"Do you remember at first we thought this planet was rogue? Then we discovered its orbit was highly elliptical and thought Altais pulled it? It's Baten's companion that pulls it. Peculiar orbits both stars of this binary! Baten didn't capture it as it meandered through Draco. It originated from the companion star, and something corrupted its orbit."

"Ah! If we move this planet back to its original orbit, will that end the temporal anomaly?" asked Asimia. "I mean, *move*—not end—the anomaly from Baten to its companion? It would afford us a clean, direct route between Yand and Phe'lak."

"Precisely!" Wolfpack exclaimed. "That's what I was about to propose. Can you do that, Simi? Can you move the planet?"

"I think so," Asimia replied.

"I'll help with the temporal wormhole," Wolfpack offered.

"And that's so great in the grand scheme of things, but how does it help our present predicament?" asked Grandma, bringing them back to the immediate K'tul threat.

"Well," said Wolfpack, "Simi moves the planet and everything orbiting it toward the companion star so it can recapture it. And seal it all there. How about if the K'tul courier is included in the bundle that Simi moves?"

That alerted Fox. "You mean like Mom tethered the K'tul armada behind the moon Calypso when they first attacked us on Yand? How did *that* work out?" The tether held for about a century, but broke at the war's end because of the null, leading to disaster.

"It worked out just fine," Wolfpack countered. "It took a major null to break mom's tether from those spaceships."

"Right. A mother-daughter null!" Snowfox exclaimed, gazing at Simi and his worldmaker daughter in her belly.

"She'll be fine," Wolfpack assured him. "It's too early. The baby hasn't found her wings yet. We'll be far away from here then."

"I…" Asimia interrupted. "That's a tall order, little brother, even without the null. I'm not sure I can do all that from Altais."

"You can bend from this system," Wolfpack replied. "Baten has a few stable planets. We'll find one. I'll transfer everyone to Altais first and come back to help you manage the anomaly. Once you move the planet and tether the courier, I'll transfer us to Altais, and we can resume our way to Phe'lak imm…"

Was he going to say immediately? He finished with, "As soon as we catch our breath."

Asimia scrunched her face in deep thought, sending Snowfox's meta senses to near-explosion. "We can try," she said.

"Good," Wolfpack surmised.

Stardust shook her head. "We need Yanara."

They all winced, but no one contradicted her.

The devil is in the details. The migrants couldn't be on the planet while Asimia moved it. But if Wolfpack transferred them to Altais, the K'tul might trace his wormhole. They needed to divert the K'tul somehow while Wolfpack transferred the folks. But how?

They argued forever. When it became clear that the solution would not come readily, they decided to shield the planet first and then figure out how to divert the K'tul. It had been their initial intent, anyway. But the temporal anomaly had gotten thicker. Asimia could not wormhole herself into the planet's atmosphere to weave the shield spells. Wolfpack had to help.

He needed to remain in the atmosphere to hold the wormhole open, or it would collapse and kill her. And the shield spells required time. They brought a nimbus of air with them, but it only lasted long enough to spell a slight arc. It would take years to shield the entire planet like that.

Snowfox was pleasantly surprised—and scandalized—when Chimé brought him a pair of air packs. They had decided not to bring those. "For Her Majesty and the little lord," she told him, meaning Asimia and Wolfpack. "We each brought one, so there are a few more hours of air if they need." He was too grateful to object.

He gave them to his wife and brother, and they made them last, using them to supplement their air bubble rather than relying solely on them. They made more progress. But alas! Halfway through the task, they attracted the attention of the courier!

"So what does it mean to have a half-shielded planet?" Fox yelled at Simi and Wolfpack as they landed, breathless.

"We're under the shielded part," Simi yelled back. "They have to come from the other side to get us."

"So, no celestial cannons?"

"I hope not. I think they'll land on the far side and launch transports. Those have no celestials but can cut us with fire beams."

Those "lesser" K'tul weapons were laser-beam types that fired in continuous sweeps.

Simi issued orders in mindspeak, *"Uncle, Gramma, convene. You, too, Fox. Summon Chimé and RC."*

"And Harry," he added. "On it."

So, their situation progressed from stealth to full-out defense under active attack. Sure enough, the courier landed. They knew that because Wolfpack had taken watch at the far hemisphere and reported it. But why did Simi think they would launch transports? No sooner than it touched the ground, it lifted again. It came at them in its entire glory, bringing its celestial cannons.

They had maybe an hour before it reached them on propulsion. Once again, their situation progressed: from active defense to mad scramble. Wolfpack materialized at the makeshift conference and took charge. Even Grandma deferred to him. He was their lifeline out of this mess, and everyone knew it.

"We needed to distract them so we could transfer to Altais without them tracing us," he said. "We succeeded, using ourselves as bait. They won't look to Altais while destroying us here." He took a breath and issued orders. "Uncle, assemble Group 2 for transfer. Scramble."

Uncle Yildiz jumped to his feet and scrambled his folks, aided by his wife, the most experienced taskmaster. It took them a few minutes, no more. Asimia offered to help, but Wolfpack wanted her to save her strength. She needed to be ready in case something delayed him, and the K'tul arrived before he returned. Asimia understood his meaning well, judging by the look on her face.

Snowfox cringed at their odds. They had two units of Archers, and one was going to Altais with Group 2. They thought of holding them back, but that would leave Groups 1 and 2 without aerial defense. Cavalry did nothing against attacks from the sky.

Grandma hugged Asimia, dragooned Lorena to watch over her, and bade Snowfox to defend her with his last breath. Fox and the doc vowed. Group 2 departed on Wolfpack and Uncle Yildiz's combined wormhole—it took both of them to clear the anomaly.

Group 3 assembled quickly to await the Pathfinder's return. The folks were scared. They didn't know all the details, but enough had leaked. '*K'tul,*' they murmured. The ones with small children and pregnant women neared panic.

That made Snowfox look at Asimia. He couldn't believe his eyes! Did she look flashed? How had he missed that? "Love?" he inquired, rushing to her side. Dr. Lorena shooed him off. "Stay away and hush," she told him, bending to Simi's belly. To his horror, his wife's stomach moved! Not from Asimia flinching at the doctor's ministrations. It moved on its own. The baby stretched her wings!

No! he thought. *This is the wrong time.*

"She overexerted herself," Dr. Lorena put in his brain. *"We must not alarm the folks? Can you keep it together, my lord? I won't let anything happen to them."*

Right. *Them!* With their string of misfortune, the baby would be born unlocked and null Simi from her first breath. If the K'tul attacked before Wolfpack returned for them... and Simi was nulled... He vividly remembered a couple of days ago when Mom came to say her goodbyes. Simi was so weak from that null that he had to help her dress. And carry her in his arms because she couldn't walk on her own.

My Simi, he thought. Oh, how he wanted to envelop her in his arms, protect her, take her away from all this danger. But how could he take her away from their infant in her womb? Not that he had that luxury. No one else was left to take charge here, to save these good folks from the K'tul.

He rallied his archers. They broke ranks from the Group 3 formation and surrounded him. He had been their commander in the war that claimed the lives of so many colleagues. These were the survivors. They lived only because of his leadership—because he kept it together against impossible odds. They would follow him to the ends of the universe.

He explained simply that the K'tul courier may reach them before the Pathfinder returned to transfer the civilians to Altais. They would have to fight it. "We've done it before," he reminded them. "Get ready. On my mark, scramble and launch for tornadoes." Those were aerial combat maneuvers executed at neck-breaking speed. "Two passes. Chimé take the first—"

"I'll take the second," RC volunteered before he could finish.

"*I'll* take the second," he corrected her. "Harry, integrate your troops into the two groups. RC, sit this one out."

"Like hell, boss."

Snowfox sent an imploring glance at Harry, but he shook his head. There was nothing he could do to stop his wife.

Everyone obeyed his command, while RC disobeyed.

Can she even fly? Fox wondered, echoing his grandma's concern. A glance toward his wife told him she was in a dire mess. He could see the baby's wings fluttering in her belly even from this distance. Still, Simi resisted the doctor's attempts to sedate her and deliver the new little worldmaker.

Another one disobeying. My type of woman, I guess.

Suddenly, a shadow from above blanketed the sky and threw them into darkness. The nightmare materialized: the K'tul courier arrived before Wolfpack returned.

"To me! Launch!" Snowfox ordered his flyers, then boomed to the assembled Group 3 folks' minds, *"To cover. Now! Doc take my wife. Snowdrift, Hunter, go to Alex. Protect Simi!"*

He didn't wait for the results. He launched himself into the sky, trusting his archers would follow him. They did. They spread out in the heavens in twin formations, one below the other. He led the first, the higher one. Good thing they came equipped.

"Hover. No! Higher!" The courier flew low. Too low for celestial cannons? Was there such a thing? Fox thought it meant to make a single pass and rake them with its fire beams. He took advantage of that. He led his archers above the ship while Chimé approached from below. *"Unclip your bows, hover. Use your explosives. Fire at will."*

The archers above and below the courier unclipped their bows. They loaded their explosive arrows, drawing their strings behind their ears, aiming, ready to loose… But not a single arrow flew. Asimia struck the earth. And Wolfpack appeared in the sky.

The concussion from Asimia's strike hurdled the courier to the heavens. It also blew the archers violently from their positions, ruining their formations and maybe their lives. They fell haphazardly at incredible speed, much faster than a diving falcon. They backwinged frantically, but it was no use. They would crash momentarily… now…

Asimia struck the earth again. This time, a blanket of air rose from below the falling archers, enveloped them, and broke their deadly trajectory. Mad scrambles all around him; Fox beat his wings and righted himself. The flyers about him did the same. All but one.

As the unit regained control of their wings, a single flyer still fell. RC! Unable to account for her heaviness and the awkwardness of her pregnant body, she beat her wings wildly, labored in vain… she wasn't going to make it.

Fox dove mindlessly after the crashing woman. He reached her a few feet off the ground and wildly grabbed whatever he could—arms, legs, clothing, furiously beating his wings—tearing them. They struck the ground together, he below her.

"Nooo!" Who screamed? Asimia?

"Simi…" That guttural scream came from him. He feared his wife had dove after him. He pulled his arm from the wreckage, bringing it out bloody. Harry descended on him and RC from the heavens before Asimia did, extricated his wife from the jumble, and lifted her in his arms. Rivers of blood gushed on Snowfox.

"Doctor!" he yelled. He opened his eyes and saw the doc hovering over him. "Not me! See to RC!"

"She's pregnant," he added like the world didn't know.

The doctor gave Asimia a look, and Simi shooed her off after Harry and RC. Simi and Wolfpack crowded about Fox. "Love," Simi murmured, caressing his brow. Why was her palm bloody?

"Where did you send them, Simi?" he asked his wife, meaning the K'tul.

"Not far. Just past the atmosphere. I didn't dare risk a bigger bend and place them on top of Altais with our people there. They may be stuck in the anomaly, but we shouldn't count on it. Their engines are different than our wormholes. They provide orders of magnitude more propulsion. They'll undoubtedly give us another go. We have no time to spare."

She turned to Wolfpack. "Transfer them all to Altais. I'll divert the K'tul."

"No!" Snowfox cried. "You'll do no such thing. *"I'll* divert the K'tul with the archers. Wolfpack—"

"Fine." Asimia agreed.

Good. He turned and boomed orders to the migrants and his archers' brains. *"Scramble. Transfer formation. Now! The Pathfinder will bring us to Altais before the K'tul return."*

To his archers, he added, *"All military personnel to me! We'll divert the K'tul to buy our folks safe passage."*

"They're too high, boss," cried Chimé.

"We'll wait for them to make another pass. Wolfpack, you go on my mark." The idea was that Wolfpack would make his transfer when Fox engaged the K'tul so that the K'tul wouldn't trace Wolfpack's wormhole.

But something felt wrong. Asimia had agreed too easily to go with Wolfpack. *She only pretended. She meant to stay behind and fight the K'tul!* Snowfox whirled in her direction, but he was only in time to see her rocket herself to the sky. Booms followed. Fire. Explosions. *Bends!*

She'd attracted the courier's attention. It veered and gave pursuit. ***"Now Wolfpack!"*** she mindyelled into their brother's head. Wolfpack spun his tops, blazed his sword, shoved all the folks inside his wormhole, and transferred. But he didn't get far. A beam of fire streaked the sky from the K'tul ship, blasting the Pathfinder's wormhole apart. Sonic booms followed. The cannons!

As Snowfox watched in horror, the concussion blew his brother to the heavens, where he suspended and drifted lifeless. The migrants of Group 3 spilled from his collapsed wormhole, scattered about the sky, some beating their wings wildly, some only falling.

"Launch!" Snowfox boomed to his archers, launching himself to the sky. ***"Save them!"***

As he and the scant number of rescuers turned to salvage whatever they could from this disaster, he glimpsed the doctor at a distance, tending to RC. *"I lost her,"* she mindsent.

Future Time: On Phe'lak, the Parian ghetto. Sunny's POV.

In the cordon in Paria, Sunny struggled to wake from his nightmare. He needed to blink. His dream showed it clearly: A catastrophe befell the migrants while crossing the temporal space around the peculiar planet. The K'tul courier discovered them, attacked them, and killed RC. Not exactly. RC fell from the sky, and his brother Snowfox didn't get to her in time.

Sunny's sister, Asimia, attempted to divert the K'tul while Wolfpack blinked the migrants of Group 3 away. But that didn't work either. Fire beams and sonic booms from the courier struck Wolfpack and his wormhole before it closed completely. The migrants spilled from it as the Pathfinder was hurdled to hover lifeless in space!

"Blink!" Sunny yelled in his sleep. But nothing happened. *"Dad!"* he frantically reached for his dad. *"Where did you go?"*

"I'm right here, son. I went after some alcohol. What's the matter? You need to blink? No! don't blink!" To Sunny's horror, he called the doctor. "Doc, more sedative! Now, before he blinks to gods know where."

"No, Da!" Sunny cried. "Adrenaline! Wake me! I must blink to them, or they'll all perish! They're spilling from Wolfpack's wormhole and causing our people to disappear here at the cordon."

But the doctor approached him as he slept. He was completely powerless to stop her and her gargantuan needle.

"No! It's all over!" he screamed. Did that come out loud?

The doctor plunged the needle into his arm.

"Ah! What have you done, doctor?" he yelled aloud.

"It occurred to me," she replied, "that I don't remember every detail of my group's transfer because some of it has not been written yet. *You* will write it, my lord, Sunstorm. Go! Save them!"

"Coordinates! Wolfpack!" Sunny mindyelled. Nothing.

Dad grabbed the doctor's wrist and yanked it back violently, "What have you done, Doc?" he yelled.

"What I had to," she replied. "Adrenaline, to save us all."

"Brother!" Sunny mindyelled again. *"Coordinates."* A stray thought crossed his mind. Wolfpack was dying. His air had gone. Not a smidgeon of conscious speech of any kind came from him.

"The sky kiss!" Sunny sent his brother across the time-space distance between them. *"Fix the kiss in your brain, Wolfpack!"*

And there it was. With his last dying action, Wolfpack kissed the sky that surrounded him. Sunny took that last kiss from his brother's brain and slid it backward in time as much as he could. It was only a few heartbeats back. Was that enough? He blinked.

He found himself hovering above the peculiar planet, and Wolfpack... not suspended lifeless beside him.

Fire, booms, and violent eddies all around, as Wolfpack fought to keep his wormhole from falling apart. He blazed brightly, all his contraptions pulsating, beaming. He almost had it, the gaping mouth was closing, it would transfer... No! A fire beam clipped its end. Wolfpack dangled by a wing talon. All the migrants of Group 3 scrambled to hold on to whatever structure the wormhole still held.

Another concussion hurtled Wolfpack violently into space, savaging him as he fought to dive, to right himself. He saw his brother. ***"Sunstorm!"*** he boomed into Sunny's brain as he dove. *"Help me hold it together!"*

Sunny grabbed Wolfpack's extended hand as he tumbled by him and rocketed the two of them into the collapsing wormhole. They combined. *Dad said I have the dragoon gene,* Sunny thought. *What would Drace, a real Dragoon, do?* He channeled his brother Drace. He set himself to spinning so hard that he might as well be a beam of light and lightning. He encircled the space around him with both arms, clenching his fists and striking the air.

He weaved a summon spell. Or was it reconstitute? The wormhole axis shifted inward and resumed its spin. Was it the correct chirality? **No!**

"I'm reversing it," Wolfpack mindyelled.

The Pathfinder spun his marble thingies and blazed his sword. His brow sapphire burst into blue pulsating waves. The wormhole held—was it enough? The migrant group moved... transferred/blinked through twin interwoven wormholes, one from Wolfpack, the other from Sunny.

They popped out on Altais amidst the other two groups. Sunny still glowed wildly, and so did his brother, the Pathfinder. "Did it trace us?" Wolfpack yelled.

Sunny didn't know, nor could he stay there. None of these people will know him in the future, so he shouldn't let them see him now. Wolfpack knew this. *"Help Fox. Go here,"* he told Sunny.

Sunny blinked to the coordinates his brother put in his head and found RC falling from the sky and Snowfox diving to catch her. They ran out of space. They would crash onto the earth. Sunny threw a blanket of air under them, and when they did crash, it cushioned their impact. They spilled not a drop of their blood.

Satisfied that RC and Snowfox survived the catastrophe, Sunny blinked back to his own time, in his room at the Blue House, and yelled at the top of his lungs, "Willie!" But Willie had not returned!

Past Time: On the peculiar planet. Snowfox's POV.

Snowfox crashed to the ground with RC on top of him. "You ok, boss?" she yelled.

"Yes. You?"

"I'm good. But don't do crazy things like this again! You should've left me fall."

"Sure. I'll remember next time."

"Nice of Her Majesty, your wife, to blanket us like that. Or we'd both be goners for sure."

"Right," agreed Snowfox. Where was his wife? A quick glance about showed him that Wolfpack had transferred Group 3. Good. At least that much succeeded. Now Asimia… and the K'tul.

Another strike on the earth, this one much stronger. It boomed to the heavens and sent the archers flying, not on their wings—on the concussion. He ran to his wife. She was on her knees, panting. "Where did you send them, love?" he asked her. He meant the K'tul.

"Far, far from here. I've had it with them," she cried. Then she did something strange. She summoned the doctor. In horror, Snowfox watched his wife's belly rock violently. Their daughter was eager to exit her mom's womb.

Wolfpack returned from Altais, confirming that the K'tul had vanished from Draco. He was just in time to watch his niece's birth.

Snowfox helped the doctor with the procedure. She used a spinal block so that Asimia could also witness the birth of their little one. She was the most beautiful tiny girl Snowfox had ever seen. Doc placed her in his arms, and he knelt beside his wife—his one and only beloved wife—and showed her their infant.

"Fox," Wolfpack told him. "Simi can't stay here. She nulls the baby."

The doctor confirmed. "She won't live long, my lord. Her Majesty must go."

Oh, how they cried! Asimia was inconsolable, and he was not much better. How could they leave their newborn behind? Who could watch and sustain her? She needed a wet nurse.

"I have a little milk for her," RC whispered behind him. "I will stay." She looked at her husband, Harry, who nodded.

"We'll love her like our own," he said.

The remaining archers gathered around them. They vowed to stay behind, too. They figured they had enough provisions to start; then they had no doubt this beautiful planet could provide.

"Come, Simi, Fox," Wolfpack urged them. "Altais awaits. Then on to Phe'lak. I'll return for these folks and see if they wish to join you. If they do, I'll take my niece back to Yand. Hawk can raise her. Do you have a name for her?"

Snowfox looked at Asimia, but she deferred to him. "You have the best names for babies," she told him. "Did you not name Sunstorm?"

"Well?" Wolfpack prompted him.

"Aurora," Snowfox whispered. Then, overtaken by the emotion of the moment, he lifted his newborn daughter to the sky.

"Aurora!" he boomed. **"This world's Avatar!"**

This world, Aurora's world, echoed and amplified the baby girl's name: **Aurora, Aurora...**

Wolfpack Suspended Above the Peculiar Planet

20. Borealis

Wolfpack brought Snowfox to Altais, with Simi bundled up in Fox's arms. Thunderous cheers went up when they popped from the wormhole. Snowfox had not expected this reception. At a glance, he saw the Group 3 folks dazed from their rough transfer from the peculiar planet. But the first two groups had arrayed themselves in transfer order.

They expect to depart for Phe'lak immediately, he realized. *Well we should, before the K'tul return.*

Lucent, Grandma, and Uncle Yildiz broke ranks from their groups when they saw what fell from Wolfpack's latest wormhole. Luc ran out first, yelling, "What happened?" He wrested Asimia from Snowfox's arms as the others arrived on his heels and wings.

"What the hell! She bleeds? Lorena?" Grandma bellowed.

"The baby—" Snowfox began, looking around for a spot to accommodate Asimia.

"I'm busy!" the doctor yelled back at Grandma. "Find us a quiet spot. And hold your questions. We had the baby."

"Sweetheart…" Luc exclaimed, looking around to find such a quiet spot.

"This way," Grandma ordered, grabbing Luc's sleeve and dragging him behind her. She led to a tree behind a boulder. Snowfox laid his jacket on the ground, and Luc deposited Asimia on it. But he didn't leave her side. When Doctor Lorena elbowed him, he moved a few millimeters. She erupted.

"Listen good, everyone, I'll say it only once. She's not in danger but needs medical attention. Snowfox. Bring Drew and his bag. I've used all the goodies from mine. Then leave. All of you."

"Doctor Drew!" Fox mindyelled. *"Please come quick!"* Dr. Drew had assisted in Asimia's birth, which had also been via c-section. The doctor scrambled from the ranks, followed by two others. It was Luc's mom and sister.

"Yildiz, strike the assembly. We're not going anywhere for a few days," Grandma ordered Uncle Yildiz. "Pitch a tent camp. Start with one over here. Summon all the medical professionals we brought with us and their bags! Now, love!"

Uncle didn't know what to do first. "The medics and a tent for Simi," Grandma told him. "All of you, give the doctor room."

Everyone stepped a few paces back, but not far.

"The baby?" asked Luc. His mom and sister crowded him anxiously. "Where is she? Is she—"

"Fine," Snowfox told him. He recounted the events as simply and briefly as he could. "We left the baby with RC," he concluded. "The Doc is going back. You can, too. I will in a bit."

But Luc got stuck on RC. "Why?" he cried. "Why did you leave our daughter with RC? What the hell?" He raged on. His mom had to hold him back.

"She was born nulled, man!" Snowfox shouted back. Wolfpack put a hand on his shoulder. "We had to bring Simi away, or Aurora would die!" His foxes started barking, punctuating his words. Alex, who had ridden in the backpack with them, growled and swiped at Luc. Luc barely withdrew his arm to avoid the gashes.

"You all shut it!" Doctor Lorena spat. "The baby was fine when we left, but needs my attention. Wolfpack? Will you oblige me? Drew got Simi."

"Coming, Luc?" Wolfpack offered. "You want to see your daughter?" Luc, his mom and sister, and Dr. Lorena scrambled. She had a fresh med bag.

"Asimia nulled the baby?" Luc's amazed question was the last thing Snowfox heard before Wolfpack's wormhole closed.

"Sheesh!" exclaimed Grandma. "We're exhausting the Pathfinder. You remember he's our lifeline, right?"

Wolfpack popped back. "Baby's fine, and Luc is over the moon," he said. "He's calmed some. We need to bring a wet nurse and helpers. RC is not going to manage two babies on her own."

But Wolfpack was bleeding. Grandma was right. "You need a rest, man," Fox told his brother. "You didn't fare too good in that last transfer."

"A fire beam got us before I closed completely. But—"

"You saved it!" Snowfox exclaimed. "How impressive!"

Wolfpack accepted the respite gratefully. Grandma called for water rations and made sure Wolfpack had his fill. His hands were bloody, and he had many welts and bruises on his arms. Snowfox realized they needed to allow Wolfpack and Asimia a few days to recover before they transferred to Phe'lak. He also wanted to ensure the K'tul had gone for good. But that was more work for Wolfpack.

First he made sure Asimia was fine. Then, with Grandma's help, he gathered up the new princess's due in attendants, medical supplies, and a wet nurse. He dragooned the good woman to also help RC with *her* precious baby.

He accompanied the group to Peculiar and spent time with his daughter. Dr Lorena and her medical team decided to stay. Many archers also volunteered. They thought this was their calling. And numerous folks followed suit.

In fact, a large contingent from Queen Emerita's household in ladies in waiting, attendants, a stable hand, two war horses— nearly the entire Group 2—turned in their petitions to stay. Why? Not because they learned of the baby. Snowfox kept that strictly on need-to-know. But their queen, Stardust, announced she would remain on Peculiar. She and Uncle Yildiz decided to adopt Aurora, and colonize the planet!

Snowfox's relief at this news was tainted by sadness and guilt. Grandma and Uncle would give his daughter a loving, lovely home to grow in, but would forego their dream. They 'd never reach the promised land. It was his uncle who first proposed the migration; his dream of the celestial dragon had started it all. The two had been so excited about making their fresh start on Phe'lak.

He accompanied them to Peculiar and witnessed their first meeting of the baby. Oh, how they rejoiced! They cradled her in their arms and called her daughter! By the time Wolfpack returned him to Altais, Fox's heart was more at ease. He shared the images with Simi and held her tightly as she cried.

"Oh, my precious daughter, my Aurora!" she wailed as sobs racked her body. "Oh, how I wanted this baby! Now I know how Mom felt to leave me and flee to the stars."

So much anguish poured from her! Snowfox heard it all. Felt it all. It combined with his own, tearing his heart, emptying his chest of breath. He mourned more for her, his beloved Simi. For she, a mother, was doomed never to see her infant girl again, never to hold her tenderly in her arms and sing her lullabies. Or watch her grow…

Asimia cried for days. Her physical wound healed enough, and time came for their final transfer to Phe'lak. The folks were subdued, missing their Queen Emerita and sensing that something had gravely wounded their new queen. It wouldn't do to bring a dispirited bunch like this to the promised land when they set out exuberant, with stars in their eyes, all but a few days ago.

He called a brief council with Simi and Wolfpack—Luc was on Peculiar with their daughter. "I have an idea," he told them. Such and such, and so and so. It surprised both of them, but they agreed it was worth to try it. Wolfpack departed for Peculiar to execute the plan while Fox and Simi assembled the three groups.

The folks were anxious and fidgety. How could they transfer with only one Wormhole Master and Groups 1 and 2 leaderless? But when the susurrus reached a fever pitch, a wormhole boomed open above their heads, and out of it flew Wolfpack and Lucent, and… Grandma Stardust and Uncle Yildiz!!

Snowfox had held his breath for this part. The arrangements he offered Grandma and Uncle were to complete the journey they had begun together, help them settle in their new home, and, most of all, bring hope back to these dispirited migrants. Then the Pathfinder would bring them back to the exact point in time he took them from. They would not miss a heartbeat with Aurora.

Wolfpack had assured Fox that he could do that. And here Grandma and Uncle were in the flesh! Asimia jumped into his arms, elated, and they joined the thunderous cheers and whoops of the migrants!

"Strike the camp!" Snowfox shouted. "Assemble for transfer! To the stars!"

"To the stars!" the entire assembly thundered.

"To Phe'lak!"

"Phe'lak! Phe'lak!" went up the chant to fill the world.

Snowfox and Asimia took their positions helming Group 3, Grandma and Uncle Group 2, she on her warhorse, and Lucent and Wolfpack Group 1.

"Wormhole Masters," the Pathfinder boomed into their brains loud enough for everyone to hear. *"Take your coordinates directly from me. Ready your infinite strings. On my mark."*

With that, he blazed his own contraptions. *"Mark."*

Three giant wormholes opened, and all the migrants filed in by their groups. There were no anomalies or K'tul from there to Phe'lak—only one short, sweet hop.

Future time: On Phe'lak, in the Cordon in Paria. Sunny's POV.

Sunny saved RC and blinked back to his own time, breathless and bleeding from many cuts. With his heart in his mouth, he ran like a crazy boy, yelling his betrothed's name at the top of his lungs, "Willie!" But Willie had not returned! His screams of anguish filled the Blue House and spilled into the streets of the ghetto.

He made to blink to the Crags, thinking she may have returned there since that was the place he had seen her last. His dad hustled from their room and grabbed him. "Don't blink! Tell me what you did, and I think I know how to bring your Willie back."

"How, Dad? And how do you know that I did something... and it worked..."

"Look," Dad pointed around them. "How many household staffers do we have?"

Sunny lifted his tear-streaked face and looked at his dad in amazement. "All of them!" he cried. "They're back!"

"Right. You saved their ancestors, right? And RC?"

Sunny nodded, still amazed and perplexed. "But Willie..."

"Remember what our book, Volume One, said? Willie's grandmother, Ritchie, migrated ten years after the others. Willie isn't here because that event hasn't happened yet. Who do you think brought Ritchie to Phe'lak?"

"Me!" shouted Sunny. "It was me!"

"Not *was*. *Will*. I had surmised the Pathfinder brought her, but then your Willie would be here now, wouldn't she? Come, my boy; we must go bring Ritchie to Phe'lak."

Sunny took his dad's offered hand and blinked them to the one kiss of sky tattooed in his brain—when he and Willie met the princesses on the peculiar planet's red beach. He slid it forward by several minutes so he wouldn't be there twice.

He didn't err in his aim. They popped out precisely where he meant to. Dad stared at the spectacular auroras in the far distance.

The people were still there, playing in the shallows. They caught Dad's attention. But only one of the girls was with them. She hung behind the adults. "That's Ritchie," Sunny told his dad. "I don't know where Aurora went to."

Dad jumped to hear that name. "Aurora? Her name?"

Sunny nodded.

"I heard that name before… from Snowfox or Asimia… or was it you? Is she your other princess?" Sunny nodded again. "Come, my boy, Let's take care of our business."

The people welcomed them. Aurora's parents had taken her home ahead of the others, and nobody made much of it. They remarked that the boy—they meant Sunny—had just left, then there he was again. But what happened to his friend? —they meant Willie. Sunny made to answer, but Dad squeezed his elbow.

Dad told the people that Willie was the reason they returned. He took Ritchie's mom, RC, to the side and they spoke together. After much discussion, deliberation, begging, and even an argument, RC would not relent. She and her husband, Harry, were happy with their daughter in this beautiful world. Why ruin it?

Desperation welled at the back of Sunny's throat. He started to speak, but the words wouldn't come. *Channel Drace,* he told himself. *Like you did when you broke her fall and again when you rescued Wolfpack's wormhole.* Oh, did that come out loud?

"It was you!" cried RC. I knew it. It didn't make sense. I couldn't fathom how Her Majesty fought the K'tul and still managed to throw that cushion under us."

"She could've done it," Dad murmured, but Sunny elbowed him and he subsided.

"It *was* me," he told RC. "Please, my lady, if your Ritchie doesn't go to Phe'lak, my Willie will never exist." It was too much. His lower lip trembled, a prelude to tears. Sure enough…

"Now, my boy," RC told him. "And who might you be, again? The geneticist's son doesn't exactly tell of your origins."

Dad answered faster than Sunny. "He's Snowfox and Asimia's brother, Lady Yanara and Lord Frost's bio son, Sunstorm. His mother bent Yildun with him in her stomach. It mangled his genes, or he might as well be…" he let that trail, and Sunny didn't want to know how he would have finished it.

"Look," Dad continued, with an arm around Sunny. "It's not a good idea to tell you of your daughter's future. But I promise you she will be glorious. Brave beyond measure. A nation's hero. They sing songs of her deeds. But most of all, she had a family who loved her, one of them my son's betrothed. Feel how the boy's heart breaks without her. He can hardly breathe."

Sunny burst into sobs. "Williiee," he whimpered.

It affected RC, but her husband more so. "Give us a little time," he asked Dad; he took his wife by the arm and guided her to the side. Much time later, they returned, RC stifling sobs. Harry spoke. "RC wishes to stay, but I will accompany Ritchie to Phe'lak so she is not alone. She's only ten."

And this was precisely how Philip had noted it in Volume One! Ritchie was ten when she transferred to Phe'lak with her dad.

After a glance at Sunny, Dad told Harry, "Enter the palace and ask for Snowfox or Asimia. They'll know what to do."

Sunny blinked them to Phe'lak in straight time. It was ten years after the original migrants set foot. They found the young colony thriving. The migrants had already established the twin cities of Karia and Paria, which bustled with industry. Also a fishing community by Paria that would blossom into the Parian Keys.

Sunny and Dad left Harry and Ritchie on the palace steps, and Sunny blinked the two of them back home, the Blue House in the Parian ghetto, two centuries in the future. "Williiee!" Sunny cried, breaking from his dad's arms and tearing through the house.

"Sunny?" came Willie's perplexed voice from somewhere inside the house. "Where have you been?"

Sunny fell to his knees and wept. His Willie burst through the door and hopped onto him, causing them to fall backward. "I love you, my Willie!" he cried. "I will never again call you *'sticky face'* or *'porcupine hair.'* I don't even hate your porcupine hair. It's only those ugly braids."

"Ooh, Sunny, you had to go and ruin it! I'm telling your dad!" But she didn't move an inch from his arms. "I love you, too, my Sunny," she whispered after a very long while.

That night, Dad and Uncles Triex and Fatie brought the family to the Sea Urchin for a quiet but celebratory dinner. Willie and Aunt Nara had no idea what they celebrated, and they didn't tell them the truth. Instead, Uncle Triex told Aunt Nara it was to show his appreciation for their marriage, although it was not their anniversary. She accepted it with much happiness all the same.

The proprietors, Captain Russel and Lady Emmiat, served them in a private dining room normally reserved for Snakeman. Uncle Triex had the seals to merit it. He and Dad had requested special treats for Sunny and Willie, and they had them ready: all their favorite finger foods and sweetments. The adults allowed them to indulge.

They followed the feast with a private walk at the docks. Willie was exceedingly happy. It was so sweet, Sunny didn't know what to do with himself. He pulled Willie's hair, but not hard, more like a caress than a pull. She didn't seem to mind a single bit.

Sunny and Willie on the Bridge at the Parian Pier

They met Wolfpack one more time. He popped up in Sunny and Da's room late one night while Sunny was reading Volume One at the desk in his jammies.

"Wolfpack?"

"Sunstorm?"

"You look different." He summoned Dad, "Da, come quick!"

Dad ran in, panting. "What? Something happened?" Then he saw Wolfpack. "Wolfpack?"

"Pete?"

"Are you the same Wolfpack we met on Altais' planet?"

"I am. Only a few days older. You know Sunstorm saved me and the two hundred souls I was transferring in my wormhole."

"Oh, so it did happen like that? I thought he was fibbing."

Wolfpack glanced at Sunny. "Does he do that a lot?"

"Hmm... occasionally."

"Please call the Yendai and Lady Nara."

"The Yendai? Fatie and Triex?"

Wolfpack nodded. Everyone assembled in the room. Willie sat beside Sunny on his bed and whispered, "Is this the Pathfinder? I thought you fibbed again." After a moment, "I thought he'd be bigger. You said he's like a god." All adult eyes trained on them. Sunny turned bright pink.

The reunion was a little awkward. Wolfpack had been close to Sunny's uncles and dad, but he was two centuries out of synch from their current incarnations. So they stuck to business. They had many questions, and he answered what he could without breaking the proper timeline, as he put it. Sunny understood that meant he couldn't tell them things that risked changing essential events.

He told them it would turn out alright, as Silvia said. Significant events had unfolded in his recent past. "A teen Silvia slipped two centuries back in time to seek aid from Mom Yanara to save her mom and dad and her world from the K'tul. Wolf held her prisoner on Hellbound for ten years in her—and your—timeline. She brought Hrysa and George with her to my time. She plucked them from a different point in that timeline—my distant future and your recent past."

Everyone nodded agreement. "Yes, it must be when they disappeared from the Crags," said Dad. "Hrysa left us notes, but she and George vanished. None of us could sense her. And we've the strongest telepaths amongst us," he indicated the Uncles. "But you said a *teen* Silvia brought Hrysa and George to you. When they disappeared, Silvia should have been only six. Ah! Is that why you said *'from a different point in her timeline?'*"

"Indeed."

"So where are they now? Are they safe?" asked Uncle Triex.

"Now? Let's see. *Now* they're safe on Tuncay two centuries ago, as is Asimia, although she's in stasis to avoid the null with Mom Yanara and Silvia—who don't null each other."

Dad breathed a massive sigh of relief to hear that Asimia was safe. Sunny thought he also felt gratified that his theories about the worldmaker gene proved true: worldmakers didn't null each other randomly. Only when the on/off locations on their gene were different. Asimia's were different from Mom's and Silvia's. He had concocted that serum to switch her gene and avoid the null.

"So, you rescued Asimia from Hellbound?" asked Dad. "We tried to nap her before they brought her there, but... it didn't go too well. Has the rescue already happened in our timeline?"

"Indeed." Wolfpack continued. "That event has already happened in your time, and also Snowfox's rescue. We found him in the courier that transported Silvia to Hellbound the day after her capture. That was two years in your past. He was in pieces—"

Everyone erupted with questions. "So that's what happened to him," said Uncle Fatie. "We knew he got on the courier that transported Silvia. He spoke to us from there. But we couldn't reach him after that. None of us."

"He was gravely wounded," added Uncle Triex. "Is he..."

"Indeed he was. His wings were in shreds... But he recovered with much care, as has Asimia." He wiped his eyes. "It's just so sad that she's in stasis. We placed her pod in the Cave of Stars—it draws energy from the star matter in that cave. The younger Asimia has migrated for Phe'lak only just, in my time. But you know that."

Everyone nodded. "We will release the older Simi from stasis as soon as you, Pete—I mean the younger you who is on Yand in my time—comes up with the splice to reset her gene."

"Oh, he won't," Dad interrupted him. "He was on the wrong track. But—"

"No, Da!" Sunny warned his dad in his private frequency. *"Keep your serum, please."* To Dad's surprised stare, he added, *"Trust me, you'll see."*

"So where is Snowfox now?" asked Uncle Fatie. "Is he coming back?"

"He is. He's a few years ahead from now at the Sea Urchin."

Everyone erupted again, but Wolfpack halted them and continued. "We also found Lucent on the moon."

This elicited a few smiles. Sunny and Willie giggled.

"But why is Fox at the Sea Urchin?" asked Uncle Fatie.

Wolfpack explained that eight years from this time, he will lead an ex-temporal rescue from Yand with Mom Yanara and Silvia, two exceedingly strong worldmakers. They will defeat the K'tul and form an unexpected alliance that will precipitate a favorable K'tul regime change. The K'tul will leave Phe'lak as part of that treaty[*].

"You must do nothing that would change the outcome," he concluded. "That's why I'm here. You must preserve the proper state of affairs."

"Which is?" asked Uncle Triex.

"You stay alive," Wolfpack replied. "Don't bring Lucent back from the moon. Fatie and Triex, you'll play a part in the—"

"The Ops?" Uncle Triex finished for him.

"Exactly. On the other hand, you four," he indicated Sunny, his dad, Willie, and Aunt Nara, "you cannot be here."

They had heard it before, so it didn't surprise them. "I'll blink us away, but when?" asked Sunny.

"Wait for Fatie's mark. He'll give it when he sees me again eight years from now," Wolfpack replied, looking at Fatie.

"And the peculiar planet?" Dad asked. "Can you pass the temporal anomaly now?"

"After we arrived safely on Phe'lak and Asimia fully recovered her strength, I brought her to the vicinity of the peculiar planet. She bent it toward Baten's companion star, and it recaptured it. The temporal anomaly still surrounds it, but it no longer affects the wormholes between Yand and Phe'lak."

The adults had many more questions, but Wolfpack wouldn't say more. With a few awkward hugs, he left them.

Time passed. Now that they had the Pathfinder's assurances about the future, Sunny and his family relaxed and lived their lives

---

[*] Find these events in *Worldmaker of Yand-Eltanin*, Book 3 in the Worldmaker™ series.

in a more orderly way. Uncle Triex enhanced that by extracting more concessions from Snakeman for the cordon. The community thrived to the extent possible under the K'tul occupation.

Sunny married Wille six years later, on the day before she turned eighteen. Dad officiated the simple ceremony. Willie made a stunning bride! Sunny blinked them to a special place for their honeymoon: the peculiar planet in its new location! They had a fantastic time! They returned buzzing with excitement, but they wouldn't tell any tales.

As time approached Intervention Ops—or Inter Ops for short—the name Sunny had given the ex-temporal rescue from Yand, Aunt Nara became anxious about where to go. Dad kept his cool, although Sunny knew otherwise. Willie was in on his plan.

So where to go? Dad and Auntie argued. The moon was not an option, as Pathfinder had forbidden it. That left Yand or Tuncay. Tuncay made more sense since Sunny came from there. But what time? If they went to the present, they risked disturbing the events of Inter Ops, jeopardizing its success. The past was no better. At the time of the migration, Sunny was a babe on Tuncay, and Da lived on Yand. One of them would be at the same place twice.

When the anticipated day dawned, and Uncle Fatie gave the mark, even Dad revealed his anxiousness. They gathered in Dad's room—Sunny had moved back into Willie's—and deliberated. "Do you trust me?" Sunny asked. "I know the perfect place to take us."

"Our honeymoon place!" Willie exclaimed, unable to contain the surprise any longer.

Dad and Aunt Nara agreed. They gathered their travel gear in Dad's room in secret and hoped the staff and cordonites would forgive them for leaving. Sunny blinked them. They landed on a red beach with spectacular auroras blazing on the horizon.

Dad and Aunt Nara looked around them wildly. A group of people played in the shallows in the distance. *"Gramma!"* Willie yelled. She jumped up and down, waved, and got their attention.

"It's us, Gramma, Granda," Sunny joined his wife. *"We've come to stay if you would have us."*

"Coming," came the happy reply from Gramma. She and a few folks launched toward the time-traveling group—Sunny brought his family back in time to ten years after the Grand Yandar

Migration and a month after he and Dad brought Ritchie to Phe'lak. It was one week after he and Willie spent their honeymoon here.

Dad shielded his eyes with his hand, trying to identify the flyers. "I'll be," he shouted as they approached. "Where have you brought us, son? I thought this was the peculiar planet for a moment, but that's... isn't that Queen Emerita Stardust?"

"Queen again, Da."

"Your Majesty!" Dad exclaimed when the flyers landed to indeed reveal Gramma Stardust and Granda Yildiz. "I thought you transferred to Phe'lak with the Grand Migration. I met you there during the plague, did I not? Ah, wait! When is this time?"

Gramma chuckled. "Indeed we did. And you remember correctly. We stayed on Phe'lak until the plague and through much of it when we decided to split the population to ensure the survival of at least some. Surely you remember that part?"

"I do," Dad confirmed. "But I was swamped developing the vaccine and then administering it and quarantining myself for six months. I thought you did the same, then took a non-infected group to colonize another planet. The word spread that you went incommunicado."

"That was my idea," chimed in Granda.

"The deal we struck with Fox and Wolfpack," Gramma explained," was to bring us back in time to when our granddaughter was born. We adopted her; she is precious to us beyond all the stars in the heavens. We wouldn't miss a day with her. This time is ten years after the Grand Migration and ten before the plague on Phe'lak. None here were infected, so no need to worry."

"We're all immunized," said Dad, sounding a little dazed, as if his brain spun ahead of his tongue. What he must think! "Your granddaughter..." he continued haltingly.

"Daughter," Gramma corrected him. "A few days ago, when Sunny and Willie spent their honeymoon here with us, we invited them to bring you all to pass the interregnum."

"The what?"

Gramma laughed. "Interregnum," she repeated, "as my grandson named it: the two centuries awaiting regime change."

"Ah, it's not a fitting name!" Dad complained. There is no interregnum in this timeframe. Only Asimia's reign. Regime change will come after the success of Inter Ops. And it's **K'tul** regime change." He stifled chuckles. "You exceeded yourself, Sunny!"

"I'll try harder next time," Sunny replied, smiling.

"But your grand—I mean, daughter," Dad brought the subject back. "Is she... of course she is... Asimia's daughter?"

"She is that, and more. Would you like to meet her?"

"I would. Oh, yes, how I would!"

Sunny's grandparents parted, and a young girl stepped shyly forward. Sunny nearly ran to the girl, his niece, eager to give her a big hug, but Willie held him back. *"Let your da first,"* she told him.

As the sun's rays caressed his niece's skin, her complexion ran through a ripple of colors, like a rainbow or the auroras of this beautiful world. It settled on even, only translucent, ethereal.

Dad dropped to his knees, cupped his face in his hands, and wept. Not only in tears. In giant sobs from the depths of his heart. He cried with all the sorrow and anguish he suffered alone all those years without his loves: the girl standing before him and her mother.

"That was so beautiful, Sunny," Willie told him, having heard his thoughts. "You ought to be a poet. But he was not alone *'all those years.'* He had *you*. He loves you at least as much as her."

Sunny embraced his wife as his niece gently touched his dad's brow. "I'm Aurora," she said. "Are you my bio dad?"

"I am," Dad replied, wiping his eyes. "One of them."

"The other is Snowfox," said Aurora. "I met him many times. My bio mom brings him, but she doesn't stay."

"You know you have two bio fathers?" asked Dad. "How?"

She shrugged her shoulders. "I'm this planet's avatar. I know things. Can I hug you?"

And she did! Dad hugged her back, kissed the top of her head, and told her how much he loved her.

The other woman who came to meet them was RC. "Are you my Ritchie's daughter?" she asked Aunt Nara in a rich contralto.

Emotion flooded Auntie's face. "Are you my—"

"Gramma, RC. I met your Willie on her honeymoon with that bratty prince over there."

"Ah, sheesh, not you, too, Auntie!"

"Gramma to you, young man. But come, we have much to catch up on. Willie told me some about my Ritchie, but you must know more." With a look at Gramma and Granda, she guided Aunt Nara in the direction they had come from.

"Where are our manners," said Grandad. "Let's go to the residence to settle our guests."

"Actually," Sunny began, "me and Willie have one more thing to do first."

"It doesn't involve blinking centuries away, does it? Or staying away for centuries?" Dad scolded him in a menacing tone. "Oh, what am I saying? Just don't come back centuries older! I want my teen son with me to grow beside me. You got that?"

"Yes," Sunny squeaked like a ten-year-old. Willie giggled.

"Swear to me!"

"Pinky swear, Da! Sheesh!"

"Both hands visible—no crossing fingers behind your back."

Sunny looked to the heavens, kissed the sky, and fixed that kiss in his brain. He took Willie's hand and blinked them away.

They popped out inside a cave so magically beautiful that it made Willie catch her breath. Many colored flowers and fragments of stars blanketed the walls, stirring in spectacular rainbow waves.

"Sunny, what is this place?" she asked. "It's so pretty but also… creepy. Do you feel that?" A ripple went through her body.

"This is the Cave of Stars on Tuncay," he told her. "My granda—uncle—Yildiz hid his heart inside these walls when the K'tul took him so they couldn't torture Yand's location from him. His heart remained here until my mom Yanara found it."

Willie listened intently for the first part, but then something diverted her attention. It was a stasis pod, the reason Sunny brought them here. Someone was inside it: Asimia, their beloved sister and queen. She looked utterly frozen, forgotten, and forlorn.

"How can they keep her here, love?" she asked in dismay.

"They don't mean to keep her here forever. Remember what the Pathfinder told us a couple of years ago?" Sunny paused for a second and shook his head. "Relative time," he added. "When he visited us in the Blue House two centuries ahead from now?"

"I remember, Sunny. He said they will release her as soon as your da… oh, I see what you mean! It's so confusing with the time jumps! Your dad of the past time finds the remedy to reverse her worldmaker gene. But we already had the serum in the future. Why did you stop your future dad from giving it to the Pathfinder? They would have had her out of this awful dark box by now rather than keep her in here for how long? Two centuries?"

"No! I brought us back to one week after the Pathfinder rescued her from Hellbound. Wolfpack leads Inter Ops on Phe'lak now as we speak. I mean in the future."

"What? Ooh, Sunny, you confused me again!"

"Hey, you married Pathfinder number two. You could have refused me," he teased her, stealing a quick peck on her cheek.

"Kissing the sky? Not always a Pathfinder as I remember it," she retorted, smiling. "What are we doing here, my love?"

"My dad of this time isn't going to find the remedy to reverse Asimia's null-inducing gene. She'll stay in this pod for two centuries because, without the remedy, my mom Yanara and Silvia will null her and cause her to die. But we can intervene."

"Silvia is here, too?"

"And Hrysa and General George. But they're on Phe'lak now with the Pathfinder for—"

"Inter Ops," Willie finished for him, catching on. "We're to take Asimia with us, aren't we? A third wedding for her perhaps? Your dad's first?"

"I can only do my best."

"And if your best is not enough, you must try harder," she teased. "But won't Aurora null Asimia? Ah, you have the serum!"

"Indeed." He produced the elixir in its syringe.

"You lifted it?"

"From Dad's desk drawer. I had it in my box for days. But I think he knows."

"You mean he knows your entire plan or about the syringe."

"Both, I think. Otherwise he would have asked me if I lifted it. And it's the other way around."

"What is?"

"Asimia would null Aurora. My niece is an avatar. Asimia, a worldmaker, trumps her."

All the while, Sunny worked the pod's lock, unlocking it as the Pathfinder taught him with K'tul DNA—Mn'ianka's, the monster who menaced him and his wife when they were children.

Willie helped him guide a limp and slumbering Asimia to the warm pool nearby. They immersed her, clothes and all. While Willie rubbed Asimia's arms to warm and revive her, Sunny jabbed two injections into his sister's arm: one the precious anti-null serum, the other adrenaline.

It took a while, but slowly, Asimia rediscovered her senses. They found blankets in a makeshift camp in the cave's depths, got her out of her wet clothes, and bundled her tightly. Sunny conjured up a small warming fire, and they sat together and talked.

They introduced themselves—they had been children the last time Asimia saw them at the Crags shortly after Karia's fall. She had been Her Majesty to them at the time. Sunny revealed his true identity: her brother Sunstorm.

Asimia knew most events since her rescue from Hellbound and that her family was safe. But what about Snowwind and Pete? Her last memory of Snow was of the K'tul capturing them in the Burning Woods. And of Pete at the failed rescue attempt at the K'tul base. She was ecstatic to learn that Snow had recovered and was on the moon with Lucent in the future. But what of Pete?

Sunny evaded that question. He revealed that he helped the migrants escape the K'tul and the anomaly at the peculiar planet. And that **now** was a few months **before** the Grant Migration departed from Yand.

"Another Pathfinder!" Asimia whispered with a hoarse throat. "I had strange perceptions during my rescue from Hellbound. Silvia was a teen, and she and Wolfpack were out of time. All true?"

Sunny nodded. They conversed for a long while, allowing Asimia to recover from stasis, the drug to take effect, and her to digest all this crazy sideways temporal info they hurled at her.

After a few hours, Sunny thought it was time. "You and we," he indicated himself and Willie, "have to pass two centuries until we catch up with when Inter Ops plays out. We have a place to go—"

"—and would like very much to take you with us, Your Majesty," Willie finished for him, anticipating his words.

"Please, call me Asimia. You're my sister now—and my husband's great-granddaughter, am I right? You're Nara's girl?

Ritchie's?" She stifled a sob to say Ritchie's name. "You know I wanted her."

"I do, Your—I mean, ah, Lady Asimia."

"But what is this place you wish to take me?" Asimia asked.

"I've come to give you a choice, my dear beloved sister," Sunny replied. "You can stay in stasis for two hundred years or spend that time with us... and people who love you."

"And people who love me? Not only you, but also others?"

"The two injections I gave you were not both adrenaline. One was a gene splice that a singular geneticist prepared especially for you from whatever scraps of your DNA he had preserved for years. It will reverse the orientation of your worldmaker allele so that you and your mother and daughters don't null each other."

It was too much. Asimia crumbled and burst into sobs. "Singular," she whispered as she cried, "Pete!" Then, "My Aurora!? Could you possibly mean them? If not, this is exceedingly cruel. Of all the torments I have endured... the cruelest yet."

Sunny took his sister's hand and placed it over his heart. He projected the kiss he stole from the peculiar planet's sky: **The planet Aurora**, at its red beach, with his dad, Pete, and niece, Aurora, the planet's namesake, hugging each other under the bright rays of the smaller star in the Chi Draconis Binary—

The Star Borealis.

"I can take you there. To them."

Asimia nodded imperceptibly. Sunny took his wife's hand in one of his and his sister's in the other and blinked to that red beach ten years ahead. As spectacular auroras danced on the horizon, two long-lost loves awaited Asimia with open arms.

Sunny and Willie at the Docks in Paria

Illustrations

Appendix A - Geographicals

ALTAIS The Delta Draconis star in the Draco constellation.

BLADED HILLS The hills that extended from Paria to Karia and beyond. They hugged the coastline on their east side and were forested on their west side. They eventually merged with the Phe'laki Mountains. They were very steep and sharp, resembling blades of swords, hence their names.

BATENTABAN Also **Baten.** The star Chi Draconis.

BOREALIS A star in Draco.

CHANSHAL PASS 1) A high-mountain pass on Yand, in the West
2) A mining settlement on Tuncay.

CHI DRACONIS The star Batentaban in Draco.

THE CORDON Also **Parian Ghetto**. A green zoned area in Paria housing Yandar and Yendal war refugees.

THE CRAGS The largest cave complex of the Shrouded Caves, high in elevation, bordering the ocean to the east and the woods to the west.

DELTA DRACONIS The star Altais in Draco.

DRACO The constellation home of the stars Eltanin and Rastaban, and the planet Phe'lak and its moon Sentinel 1.

DRAGONSLAIR Capital city of Yand.

ELTANIN A star in Draco, one of the Eyes of the Dragon.

THE FOOT A cave in the woods behind the palace, beginning the Shrouded Caves.

FROZEN MOON Turunc's sixth moon.

THE GHETTO Also **Parian Cordon**. A green zoned area in Paria housing Yandar and Yendal war refugees.

HALFWAY INN A famous inn at the Parian Keys.

THE HEEL Another cave in the woods behind the palace, also part of the Shrouded Caves, higher in elevation than the Foot cave and closer to the Crags.

HIGHWINGS 1) The Yandar valley and city on the moon Tuncay.
2) (**New**) The Yandar Kingdom on the planet Phe'lak.
3) The palace in the city of Karia.

IOS 1) The third moon of the planet Yand
2) Another name for the planet Phe'lak.

KARIA Capital of the Yandar Kingdom of Highwings on Phe'lak.

THE KEYS 1) **Comi Keys**-A fishing province on Yand.

2) **New Comi Keys**-A fishing community of Tuncay.

3) **Parian Keys**-A fishing community on Phe'lak.

THE MOUTH The entry cave of the Crags on top of a steep cliff overlooking the ocean.

ORANGE 1) A city on Yand.

2) A Yandar city on Phe'lak, in the eponymous province.

OYTPOST IOS A military base on Yand's third moon, Ios.

PARIA A Yandar city on Phe'lak. The capital Karia's port.

PHE'LAK Phe'laki's home planet; orbits the star Eltanin in Draco.

PHE'LAKI HEIGHTS The highest mountain range on Phe'lak, home to the Phe'laki tribes.

POLARIS A tertiary star system on the tip of Ursa Minor's tail. Polaris B, the smallest star in the tertiary, is Tuncay's sun.

RASTABAN A binary star in Draco, one of the Eyes of the Dragon.

RIVERQUEEN 1) The second largest city on Yand.

2) A city of the Yandar Kingdom on Phe'lak.

THE RUNWAY The long, narrow cleft fronting the Mouth. The Yandar refugees used it to launch themselves for flight.

SENTINEL 1 First moon of the planet Phe'lak.

TURUNC Pronounced Tourounch. A planet orbiting Polaris B.

TUNCAY Pronounced Tounjae. Turunc's moon.

URSA MINOR The constellation where the Yildun and Polaris star systems are located.

YAND Yandar's home planet; orbits the star Yildun in Ursa Minor.

YENDA Yand's first moon. Origination world of the Yendai.

YILDUN A star on the tail of Ursa Minor, below Polaris. The Yandar's sun.

Appendix B - People

Yandar (singular and plural). Winged, empathic humanoids, originating on the planet Yand. Their lifespan counts in centuries, at times millennia. Average height 5'8" to 6'2".

Three races:

Silverbloods: silver-white complexions, hair, and wings; dark blue eyes in predominantly sapphire hues.

Evenbloods: dark complexions, hair, and wings; primarily dark green eyes, rarely blue.

Goldenbloods: goldish-turning complexions and wings, that darken with age. Blond to red hair; amber to brown to black eyes.

ALEX Asimia's and then Silvia's shibal cat. Can size shift.

ASIMIA Also **Simi.** A silverblood Worldmaker and Wormhole Master. Yanara and Frost's bio daughter. Sapphire blue eyes, height 5'11". Her shibal is Alex.

AVALEE A Yandar woman in the Parian cordon.

AURORA A little girl.

BLAZE The Yandar form of the Dragon of Yand. Yanara's bio dad, A goldenblood with a huge wingspan. Height 6'2".

DRAGONLORD Also **Drace.** Yanara's third son. A Dragoon. A blue-eyed evenblood, height 5'11. His dragon is Lavender.

CHIMERAN Also **Chimé.** A female flyer of mixed DNA.

DARRYL Sr. Dr. Pietro's genetics technician on Yand.

DARRYL Jr. Dr. Pietro's genetics technician on Phe'lak.

Dr. DREW The Chief Physician of the cordon's hospital.

EAGLEWING The Sword of Highwings—it picks the Monarch.

Dr. ELLIOT Also **Warbles.** Quantum Mechanics expert professor.

EMMIAT (pronounced **Emma**) Also **Emmy.** Silvia's nanny. A goldenblood with amber eyes, height 5'11".

ENAMELIA Also **Ena.** A Yandar woman. Sunstorm's nanny.

FROST Yanara's husband. A military commander during the K'tul Wars on Yand. A famous smith and archer. Asimia and Sunstorm's bio dad. A silverblood. Sapphire-blue eyes. 6'2".

HAWKLORD Also **Hawk.** Yanara's second son. Mandolen's bio son. A green-eyed evenblood. Height 6'2".

HRYSANTHIA Also **Hrysa.** Asimia and Lucent's bio daughter. A goldenblood with greenish-amber eyes. A teen of 5'9".

HUNTER Snowfox's fox. A small white snowfox.

Dr. KHIN A Professor Emerita with Wormhole speciality.

LAVENDER Dragonlord's lightning dragon. Purplish hide.

Dr. LORENA a woman physician.

LUCENT Also **Luc.** Prince of Orange. Asimia's second husband. Hrysanthia's bio father. A goldenblood. Amber eyes, 6'1".

MANDOLEN Yanara's wife and bio mother of their three evenblood sons. The Warleader of Yand during the K'tul Wars. An evenblood with emerald-green eyes. Height 6'0".

NARA A Yandar evenblood woman. Willie and Tommy's mother.

OPHIRAN The Dragon of Yand's name

DR. PIETRO Also **Pete.** Renowned geneticist and university professor. An evenblood of bluish-green eyes. 6'1".

RC A Western Archer woman who joined the Yandar migration.

RITCHIE A warrior woman. Nara's mom and Willie's grandmom.

SILVESTREAM A unicorn mare.

SILVIA Asimia and Snowfox's bio daughter. An eight-year-old Worldmaker in Borealis. Silverblood with turquoise eyes.

SNOWDRIFT Snowfox's fox. A small white snowfox.

SNOWFOX Yanara's first son (adopted). Asimia's first husband. Silvia's bio father. He has two snowfoxes, Snowdrift and Hunter. A silverblood. Turquoise blue eyes, height 6'2".

SNOWWIND Asimia's unicorn. White as snow. A shifter, can shift into another dimension.

STARDUST Queen of Yand. Yanara's adoptive mother. A striking goldenblood of more than a millennium of age. Height 6'0'".

SUNSTORM Yanara and Frost's bio son. A sapphire-blue eyed silverblood.

SUNNY A silverblood boy.

TOMMY Willie's brother. A three-year old boy.

WARBLES See **Dr. Elliot.**

Willie An evenblood girl.

WOLFPACK The Pathfinder. A temporal Wormhole Master. Yanara's fourth son. Green-eyed evenblood. Height 5'8".

YANARA The Worldmaker of Yand. Frost and Mandolen's wife. Asimia and Sunstorm's bio mother. Mother of Snowfox, Hawklord, Dragonlord, and Wolfpack. Flame-red hair, amber eyes, and gold wings. Height 5'10".

YANUS An evenblood Elder of the Parian cordon.

YILDIZ A goldenblood wormhole master. The Dragon of Yand's son and Yanara's bio brother; Height 6'2".

Yendai (plural; singular is Yendal).Telepathic humanoids, originating on Yand's first moon Yenda, with centuries-long lifespan. Average height 5'2" to 5'8".

FATIE Fatiador, the Magnificent. King of Yenda during the K'tul Wars in the Yildar system. He abdicated his throne to follow Yanara and her family to the moon Tuncay. He later migrated to Phe'lak. Blue-eyed blond, 5'9". His sword, Bluetip, flames blue. Fatie is not fat.

MOUSE A Dragoon. Fatie's adopted daughter. A 5'2" blue-eyed blond.

SQUIRREL A Dragoon. Fatie's adopted son. A 5'4" light green-eyed blond.

TIGER The king of Phe'lak's first moon, Sentinel I.

TRIEX Triexador, the Wise. Fatie's older brother by a year. He was King of Yenda at sixteen for one year, then abdicated his throne to his brother Fatie. He migrated first to Tuncay, then to Phe'lak with Fatie. Blue-eyed blond, 5'9". His sword, Flame, flames red. He has a fighting knife, Stiletto.

Phe'laki (singular and plural). Non-psychic, large humanoids, indigenous to Phe'lak, of centuries-long lifespan and many skin complexions and eye colors. 6'3" to 6'7". A Clanswoman leads their Thirteen Tribes.

GEORGE A general of the Palace Phe'laki Guard. Philip's bio-grandfather. Hrysanthia and Silvia's grandfather by rights. Height 6'6".

MARKA George's mother. Leader of the Phe'laki Clans. 6'5".

RUSSEL George's brother. Leader of Silvia's personal guard. 6'5".

Tjourhien (plural, pronounced Tourien; singular is Tjourhian, pronounced Tourian). The Phe'lakir's fourteenth tribe. They rebelled and joined the K'tul against their own people because of the ambitions of their Clan Leader.

K'tul (singular and plural). Empathic and/or telepathic humanoids. Savage and Chaotic. They breed prolifically, which drives them to expand and brutally colonize other planets with disregard of destruction and genocide. Centuries lifespan. High elites are horned, blue or purple-skinned. Common K'tul are grey and non-horned. 5'6" to 6'0".

Three races:
Grey: most common, non-horned.
Blue: very rare elites, horned.
Purple (Maroon): also very rare, horned.

Military Ranks:
Excellency (Admiral): Commander of Space Fleets.
Elite Council of Mages: The admiral's council of ten top mages.
Greyk'tul: Also the highest rank, highly skilled and trained. Organized in Elite Units of five, with a Mage (the Fifth officer with a title of Glory) and a Captain (the First Officer).
Blackk'tul: Also **Blackrobes.** One rank below the grey.
K'jen: Also **Redhoods** or **Redrobes.** A religious order that wears red and has the most mages among their ranks, some very potent.
Renegade Greyk'tul: Greyk'tul Elite Unit 1 went renegade, i.e. rebelled, seeking to depose the Excellency *(Eltanin).*

K'NISTA. A very powerful Mage. Resurrected Wolf whom Frost killed in the battle of Outpost Ios (*Yildun*). Kidnapped Asimia and traded her for a princely group of pups, Mn'ianka among them (*Polaris*). Abducted Silvia (*Queen of Highwings*) Purple-skinned and horned. 5'9".

MN'ESYA Wolf's wife and Mn'ianka's twin sister. Blue-skinned and horned. A child in Borealis. Adult height, 5'10".

MN'IANKA. The Renegades' leader, referred to as First (for First Officer). Wolf's nephew, the K'tul Emperor's cousin. Blue-skinned and horned. 5'11".

S'TIHSA Also **Snake or Snakeman,** code name **Foureyes.** Wolf's brother. A powerful mage and the leader of the K'jen religious sect. Horned.

WOLF The K'tul Excellency (Grand Admiral). Commander of the K'tul Space Fleet, the spaceship Hellbound, and the Mages' Elite Council (a type of Privy Council of ten Elite mages). Purpled-skinned and horned. 5'9".

314

Appendix C - Familials

Yandar, Yendai:
The practice of more than one spouse is allowed. Spouses can be any gender without prejudice. Families with more than three spouses are rare.

Marriages are governed by rules written in contracts, always between two spouses, and can vary. One person can marry two people with two different sets of rules. Depending on the contract, her spouses may or may not marry another spouse (or more).

Exclusive monogamous marriages between two spouses of any gender are common.

Children are cherished. Marriage contracts always include the disposition of children.

Phe'laki:
Plagued by a genetic disease that kills their female children, they struggle to maintain the species.

Women marry many husbands, but men take only one wife as there are few women.

Matriarchs head families with many men (husbands and sons) and only one or two women.

Women share husbands who fathered female babies.

K'tul:
Born in litters of eleven to thirteen pups by gender.

Important males (blues and purples) buy wives from other important males by the litter.

The commoners, the greys, do not. They normally marry one woman and father only one to two litters. However, the greys so outnumber the blues and purples that their majority is clear.

In addition, blue and purple elite sires practice infanticide and child murder, especially of male children, to control threats to their power.

BROTHER/SISTER Born in the same litter.
COUSIN FROM MOTHER Born to the same father and mother but in different litters.
COUSIN FROM FATHER Born to any wife or litter of two brothers.
TWINS A boy and a girl, born in the same birth sack.

Worldmaker™ Series

Yildun: Yanara's power is her planet's last defense against a savage invader. But her daughter's unlocking her inherited trait threatens to null Yanara at the worst possible time. Will their world survive the assault?

Polaris: Escaping the aftermath of a bloody interstellar invasion by the savage K'tul, Yanara brings her family to a new moon. Will the family finally find peace there, or will the vengeful K'tul discover them again?

Eltanin: Yanara brought her family to a faraway moon to eke a peaceful existence. Until a stranger arrived seeking aid, hurtling them back into war with the ancient enemy.

Queen of Highwings: Somewhere in Draco, Hrysa battles the invaders to free her planet and to come into her own—to become Queen of Highwings.

Worldmaker Stories: Nine short stories in the Worldmaker Universe, including Fluid and Unlocked.

About the Author

The author is an award-winning poet, novelist, and Ph.D. Scientist. She immigrated to the US as a teenager, due to war in her native country and is a naturalized US citizen. Her scientific work yielded many patented inventions of new composite materials aimed at light-weighting vehicles. Her passion is writing sci-fi/fantasy. She has penned 9 short stories and five novels in the Worldmaker of Yand Universe. She lives in Florida, on the ocean, with her son and their four cats, and continues to write.

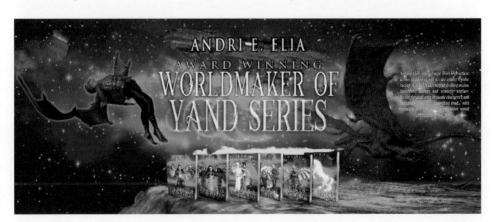

Printed in Poland
by Amazon Fulfillment
Poland Sp. z o.o., Wrocław

32906557R00179